Two Rooms to Let

1901-1952

By Marion Weatherby

To the late Ethel and Joseph
A loving mother and father

Copyright © Marion Darby 2008

ISBN 978-1-4092-0121-2

Book 1 – Marguerite 1901-1927

1. A time of change
2. The unexpected
3. Across the water
4. In enemy territory
5. On safe ground
6. Home at last
7. A pinch of snuff

Book 2 – Albert 1901-1928

8. A breath of sea air
9. The long trek
10. To sail away
11. A rude awakening
12. To walk the streets

Book 3 - Marguerite and Bertie 1929-1934

13. Spring in the air
14. The decision
15. Two Rooms to Let
16. A new life
17. Repercussions

Book 4 – Richard 1934-52

18. A second chance
19. Decisions
20. The evacuees
21. Real War
22. A double tragedy
23. Near misses
24. A new house
25. To wave goodbye
26. Memories
27. Another woman
28. To shake hands
29. Out into the world

Book 1

Marguerite

1901-1927

BOOK 1

CHAPTER 1

A TIME OF CHANGE

A waxen moustache and a face with character was the reflection in the mirror of the gentleman, because that is what he was, a gentleman, sitting at a desk well-covered in books, but an orderly desk. A desk laid out with conformity.

A dull day with hardly enough light creeping in through the window to enable the occupants of this office to see the work that was to hand. Frederick Sinclair wiped his brow with tiredness and begrudgingly accepted the fact that although it was only 11 am the gaslight must be lit. Yes, a man of character in his mid-thirties who watched every penny that was spent, but a man who could be quite thoughtful and generous to his employees. A very discerning solicitor in a City office.

A kindly man much thought of by John Mullen, his articled clerk, a short thick set young man with a mop of curly hair. Not a good-looking man but a good worker. Frederick had shown great kindness to John since his first days in the busy office; perhaps the memory of his harsh junior days not being so far behind him.

There was a noise outside in the busy street which could just about be heard above the clicking of the horses' hooves and the screech of wheels as the carriers brought their horses to a standstill. What was that shouting? What was that noise? John went to the window. At the end of the street he could just see a crowd of people gathering.

"What is it, John?"

"I am not sure, sir, I can't quite see." Hesitating and with difficulty he lifted up the heavy sash window. "Ah, yes, sir, people are rushing for the papers."

"Rushing for the papers, John? Go down and see if you can get me one, for some reason they were sold out this morning."

Frederick rubbed his hands, as the cold draught from the opening of the door hit him, and then pressed on with his latest case. It was necessary to make haste with the work as he had a more important family matter to deal with tomorrow. The family meant a lot to this solicitor of the Victorian era.

After a short while John returned with the morning edition of The Times. "Bad news, sir. Grave news at midnight from Osborne House. Let me see, where was it? Oh yes, sir." John pointed out a piece for Frederick to read.

Frederick shook his head, and turned to John: "The worst may be expected at any moment. It will be a sad City, John, on the passing of her Majesty. Yes, a sad City."

Frederick Sinclair and John Mullen busied themselves with the matters in hand, and the day quickly passed.

As daylight began to fade Frederick crossed to the window, as was his usual practice at this time of day, and watched the lamplighter at the first lamp in the street. He cherished this moment of time and was very aware that the lamplighters' days were numbered, as the lamps were soon to be replaced by electricity.

Some time later, glancing at the grandfather clock, which stood elegantly in the corner of this crowded room, Frederick noticed that it was already 6 o'clock. "You make haste home now, John. I still have work to do. I will be at the office as soon as I can tomorrow. You have plenty to carry on with?"

"Yes, sir." Replied, a somewhat weary John. John gathered his things together and soon bid his senior good night. On going to the door he hesitated and turned and said to Frederick, "I hope tomorrow your own news is not too bad, sir."

Frederick standing up and going over to John patted his arm in appreciation for his thoughtfulness and replied, "Thank you, John, for your thoughts, thank you. Goodnight."

With the office now to himself Frederick busied himself with his work. Another hour soon passed before he extinguished the lights in the office and with care made his way down the stairs to the street. He hailed a hansom cab and stood well back whilst the horse drew up to the curb. Frederick was a rather fastidious man who hated to be splashed or have his clothes soiled. The cab made its way from the City, gathering speed on the straight run after leaving busy Holborn, and Frederick Sinclair began to relax. On reaching the turn-off for Bloomsbury Street a crowd of people were once more gathered around the newsvendor awaiting news of her Majesty. The cab man called for a way to be made, and the horse expanded his nostrils and snorted with frustration and excitement, before finally entering Bedford Square. A square of very elegant houses built in the late 1770's and planned on the lines of the Kings Circus in Bath. The cab soon arrived at the home of the Sinclair's. Steps, edged in coade stone, led up to the front door. Above on the first floor was a welcoming balcony with railings to match those protecting the area steps. Overall it made a very good impression to visitors to this prestigious square.

The cab door was soon opened by George, Frederick's footman-cum-butler. George, a man of fine physique well-liked by the Sinclair family, had been watching for the return of his master and spotted the cab as soon as it turned into the square. Soon Frederick was up the steps, his black bowler and gloves taken by George who laid them on the hall stand.

"The mistress is at home, George?" asked Frederick of his well-versed servant.

"Yes sir, she is awaiting you in the drawing room." George turned and opened the polished oak door on the right of the oak-panelled hall. All visitors arriving at the Sinclair's residence were immediately impressed by this beautiful hall with red carpeted staircase leading to a galleried landing above. A magnificent chandelier was the centre piece.

Through the door could be seen a well-dressed woman, sitting beside a large marble fireplace in front of a huge log fire. Emily was a petite woman in her early thirties, whose well-contained figure made her look even younger. She had long dark hair taken up into a bun which emphasised her fine features. She was a self-assured young woman.

The heavy rich velvet curtains were tightly drawn to keep out the winter's cold. At one end of the room stood the piano with music opened as if someone had recently been playing. Emily had spent a pleasant afternoon playing bridge with friends on their estate in rural Harrow. On returning she had spent a while playing the piano and had then gone to the nursery and read to the children, giving Nanny a break, but now, as usual, she sat awaiting the return of Frederick, her fine needlepoint on her lap. Whatever time Frederick arrived home his dearest wife would be waiting.

Standing aside for his master to enter George announced, "The master has returned, Ma'am."

"Thank you, George," replied a smiling Emily.

George shut the door as he knew that after a busy day these moments were precious to husband and wife. Frederick was soon down on his knees grasping Emily's hands to his lips. "And how is my precious this evening? Still as beautiful as ever!"

"Oh, come, come, Frederick dear," answered Emily with some warmth. "You are late tonight, Frederick. You must be tired. You must let John take on more of the work." Emily said with concern.

"Yes, my dearest, I will, but I had to leave everything in order, as tomorrow will be a short day in the office," replied Frederick, at the same time taking some snuff from his small valuable gold box on the mantelshelf above the fireplace.

Frederick and Emily were now well-settled in married life, having met fourteen years previously in 1887 at a Hunt Ball. Frederick had courted his Emily Baldwin for two years and felt himself a very lucky man to have attained the hand of his beautiful wife. Their first born, conceived soon after their first anniversary, was a lovely daughter, Rachel. Alas the time would soon come for her to leave her well-loved governess, Miss Hannah, to attend the Ladies Academy.

Frederick and Emily had enjoyed their only daughter and lavished love upon her, although they dearly hoped for a son it was not to be. When little Rachel was five years old they were blessed with another daughter, Marguerite, who had been difficult to rear, and had it not been for the wealth spent and care given to this small daughter, she would not have reached the age of five years. Many a time they thought they had lost her, therefore she was very precious to Frederick and Emily, and especially to Frederick. Emily's attention had been taken up with their third daughter, Sarah, born when Marguerite was two years old. Sarah was as beautiful as her elder sister, Rachel, and poor Marguerite was very much the middle child. She was not so small, in fact, unusually plump, for a child of five years.

It was not long before Frederick felt hunger pains "Come, Emily, we must eat. Cook will be impatient to serve." Frederick led the way to the dining room and pulled the bell rope to let Amy know that they were ready for their meal. The table was already laid and the cutlery shone on the beautiful starched linen table cloth. The mahogany sideboard, with finely carved pheasants on each side door, stood out in the reflection of the gas light.

Down in the kitchen everything was steaming on the range and Amy in her maid's uniform, making her look younger than her years, on hearing the bell jumped up from the table and left the room. Cook, a buxom woman in her late thirties, made for the stove calling Mary, the kitchen maid, to help. Mary, not much more than a child, hurried to obey.

Amy was soon serving the meal fetching it from the dumb-waiter, which Mary was loading from below. A piping hot tureen of soup, followed by roast duck in orange sauce, and to finish, apple tart, the apples specially picked and delivered the previous autumn from the Kent orchards.

After the meal Frederick retired to his study for a glass of port and to smoke his favourite brand of cigar, which helped him to recover from the traumas of the day; later joining Emily once more in the drawing room. This was the time of day when they were able to catch up on any news, interrupted only occasionally by Frederick pulling on the bell-rope, summoning the servants for more logs or to bring their evening hot drink; or Frederick reaching up once more for his gold snuff box.

"The news of her Majesty is grave today, Emily. Did the servants bring the latest news to you?" asked Frederick.

"Oh, no, tell me, Frederick."

Frederick moved over to Emily pointing out the headlines on the newspaper and reading out to his wife, "The worst may be expected at any time." They both stayed silent for a few moments, gazing into the embers of the now fading fire, with their own thoughts.

"It is indeed a sad night," said Emily, breaking the silence and looking up at her husband, "Let us hope tomorrow brings better news."

Frederick pulled up his chair, and sat beside his wife, and taking her hand replied, "Yes, and for us too, Emily." Letting go of his wife's hand, and with a change of voice, Frederick asked, "How have my little trio been today?"

"Well, Miss Hannah says that Rachel is working hard and should do well at the Miss Beaumont's Acadamy, bless her. Nanny says Marguerite has been a little tiresome, but no more than usual. Who knows, she may be worried about tomorrow. Sarah, of course, has been as sprightly as ever;" and so, as usual, Emily brought her husband up to-date with the comings and goings of the day.

They sat for some time talking of their family, and then Frederick rose, and placing an arm around Emily's shoulder, looked down at her. "We can only hope tomorrow for better news my dearest."

Emily looked up at her dear husband and nodded and whispered, "Yes, I do hope so Frederick dear for both our sakes." For a while they both sat quietly,

Emily once more having returned to her needlepoint, and Frederick, as was his habit at this time of day, having a quiet read.

After a while Frederick was aroused from his reading by the striking of the clock in the hall. He suddenly realised that it had struck eleven, and closing his book he rose wearily from his chair. "Come, my dearest I think it is time we retired and got a good night's sleep."

"Very well, Frederick, but the evenings together seem so short." Emily laid her needlepoint to one side and rose from her chair, and followed Frederick from the room.

On leaving the drawing room Frederick stopped to talk to George, and after bidding him goodnight hesitated at the turn of the stairs to glance at his Father's portrait. Yes, he thought, you were my age when you sat for this fine study, and that reminds me, after the worries of tomorrow I must put the matter in hand.

*

The dawn of a day when many things would change! A dull day, but being January perhaps this was better than rain or snow.

The servants were up and about early in the Sinclair household, as there were the coals to fill and the stoves to light. Then there were the large kettles to be filled and heaved up on to the black-leaded stove, the black- leading of which had been the young kitchen maid Mary's first job. This was a job she did not mind doing first thing in the morning as it helped to warm those cold limbs.

Before long the kitchen, now warm from all the activities, was a welcoming winter sojourn. Soon Nanny appeared to take a few minutes respite before continuing her nursery duties. Nanny a small woman with a kindly face, who kept her age to herself, dressed in a large white apron which covered a long navy woollen dress, liked to join the servants at this time of day for warm oats and milk.

"Morning Nanny," called Cook from duties at the stove.

"Morning to you," called back a somewhat weary, or shall we say, a not quite yet woken Nanny. She had had a restless night with a disturbed mind.

"Well, I wonder what news today will bring forth," remarked Cook.

"I just don't know," was Nanny's tearful reply.

"Oh Nanny don't take on. I am sure everything will be alright." Cook, realising she had been a little hasty in passing comment, left the stove and endeavoured to comfort Nanny. They sat round the well-scrubbed kitchen table chatting. After a while, and feeling the benefit of the warm oats, Nanny bade farewell to the kitchen staff and returned once more to the nursery quarters.

Whilst Nanny had been partaking of breakfast Mary had been and lit a fire in the nursery, being sure to place the large fireguard edged with brass carefully around the fire before the children woke. Nanny found the nursery welcoming after the chill of the stairs and landing.

It was not long before Mary once more appeared at the nursery door with the jugs of hot water. What a weight to carry up those stairs, but Mary enjoyed her visits to the nursery. And so Nanny woke the children. It was 7 o'clock and the first job Rachel had to do on rising, and sitting on the edge of her bed, was to brush her long dark curls sixty times. This she used to find a bore but since having started to learn French with Miss Hannah she enjoyed practicing her numbers each morning, une, deux, trois.... Little Sarah listened in astonishment as the words came out. "What are you saying Rache?" she regularly asked.

Rachel was becoming quite tall for a ten-year-old and was very much a Sinclair in looks and like her Father, but she had her Mother's assured manner. She was becoming very good at her lessons and was very attentive and keen. Nanny often looked at her these days and wondered what well-to-do family this eldest daughter of her well-beloved Sinclair family would marry into. Mind you she was becoming a little cheeky and had no patience with Marguerite and was really ready to go to the Ladies Academy.

Marguerite was now five-years-old, but oh so difficult to wake up in the mornings. It would be, "Now wake up Marguerite," so many times from Nanny, and Rachel would call impatiently, "Oh, come along Maggie." This would annoy Marguerite, as this was a name she did not like, and she would ease herself out of bed pouting and saying crossly, "You know I don't like that Rache." Poor Marguerite had been ill so many times and was becoming so plump that it was not surprising she took so long to wake up. Marguerite's hair was fairer than her sisters and very fine and Nanny would gently brush it and put a large bow at one side, which Rachel thought looked silly. Marguerite had not the confidence of her elder sister, but at five-years- old appeared to have a warm nature, especially with her small three-year- old sister, Sarah.

Sarah was often out of bed before the hot water arrived and Nanny had to watch that she did not get in Mary's way. Sarah was a lovely small child and was very much like Mama in looks with petite fine features and long dark hair like Rachel. She loved to cuddle up to Marguerite and the two were very attached to each other.

On the first floor of the elegant house in Bedford Square, Frederick and Emily were woken by Amy, who had been a very loyal maid since their early married days. "Tea ma'am, tea sir!" carefully placing a silver tray, containing a delicate early morning tea set, beside the bed. She then opened the heavy red velvet curtains slightly, showing the small balcony and letting in a little daylight.

As Amy turned to leave the room, Emily, by now awake, raised herself, "Tell Cook I will be down to the kitchen to discuss the meals at about 8.30 am."

"Yes ma'am," replied Amy. As she went to go out of the door she turned, saying, "Oh ma'am, should breakfast be served at eight o'clock or will you visit the nursery first?"

Without any hesitation Emily replied, "Breakfast at eight o'clock!, please Amy. Nanny has her instructions."

By now all was a hustle in the Sinclair household. Mary's next task was to take the hot water jugs and place them outside Frederick and Emily's bedroom door. She was glad she did not have to take them in as at home she had been used to Mother, Father and the seven children all sleeping in one room. She could not get used to all of these individual bedrooms, and, as a thirteen-year-old she was still very shy of her elders.

Breakfast had been laid in the dining room the night before and on arriving at table Frederick summoned Amy to serve. Frederick and Emily always partook of quite a large breakfast, but, this morning they were slow to eat. Before long Nanny ushered in the three small girls, who ran to kiss good morning to their Mama and Papa. Emily usually had a chat with the girls in the nursery later so she left it to Frederick to talk with them. The children by this time had had their breakfast in the nursery and were all eager to talk at the same time. Frederick, wiping his mouth with the stiff starched white serviette, which looked very large to the children's eyes, soon had them under control. "Now Rachel, you will attend your lessons as usual this morning with Miss Hannah."

"Yes," answered an eager ten-year-old, "I will be taking a French lesson this morning, Papa."

"Good," answered a proud father. "Work hard at it, remember it will soon be time for you to compete with other girls at the Ladies Academy and we wish you to do well."

"Yes, Papa," replied Rachel.

Frederick reached out his hand to bring Marguerite a little closer, "Now my little Podge," this was a nickname of his for Marguerite which she did not mind as she adored her Papa, "this morning you are coming out with Mama and Papa."

"Me too," called out a hopeful Sarah.

"No, my dear you will go for a walk with Nanny in the park." Sarah showed signs of a slight pout, but, nevertheless, she enjoyed her visit to the park with Nanny. The children chatted away to Papa whilst Nanny discussed a few things with Mama, but soon it was time to leave and return to the nursery.

"Thank you, Nanny, we will collect Marguerite from the nursery when we are ready. Now run along children," and this was about all Mama said to the children this morning. The morning ritual over, off they ran.

George the butler's first job in the morning was to clean the shoes, which he had collected from outside the bedroom doors the night before. This he did in a small ante-room off the kitchen, where the vegetables and fruit were stored. The cleanliness of this room was the kitchen-maid, Mary's, responsibility, and woe-betide if Cook found it untidy. On completing this job he once more returned them to outside the bedroom doors. He had to make sure he was waiting outside the dining room for his orders of the day; having first checked from Cook as to what time breakfast was being served. Frederick expected to see him there on leaving the dining room after breakfast.

Soon the dining room door opened. "Good morning, George. Now, as I will be late to the office today, would you mind fetching me a Times to read before I leave the house. I would like to see what news there is from Osborne House. Will you also have a cab waiting here by ten o'clock for the three of us."

At this time in the morning Frederick was quite quick with his orders and many a time George had to be quick-witted. "Yes, sir, certainly sir," answered the loyal servant.

Frederick and Emily returned to their bedroom to prepare themselves for the task ahead. The bed had been freshly made and, by the smell of polish, you could tell the brass knobs at each corner had just been cleaned. The room had been tidied whilst they had been at breakfast. Before long George brought the Times up to them. Frederick hastily found the news he wished to read. "Ah, Emily, here it is," reading out loud to Emily, 'the Queen has slightly rallied since midnight. The slight improvement of this morning is maintained.' Of course, we must remember, my dearest, that this was yesterday's news from the Isle of Wight, but nevertheless, our dear Queen is still fighting."

The time soon came to collect Marguerite from the nursery. Emily made for the hall whilst Frederick went to fetch his dear Marguerite. On arriving at the nursery it was small Sarah who ran up to her Papa hopefully holding out her outstretched hand. "No, my poppet, not today!" Looking over to where Marguerite, dressed ready for going out, was still sitting cosily on her bed, Papa said, "Well my little Podge off we go, the cabby's horse is waiting." The mention of the horse soon got Marguerite up from her bed and she crossed the room quite eagerly to join her Papa, giving a big hug and kiss to Nanny and little sister on the way before leaving the warmth of the nursery. They joined Mama in the hall and it was not long before George was holding open the door of the cab, but first Marguerite knew that Papa had something in his pocket. "No Marguerite I haven't forgotten." Papa usually had a lump of sugar taken from the breakfast table especially for his little Podge to give to the well-deserving cabby's horse. This was a ritual that Marguerite loved and she did not mind how much the horse licked her open hand.

As the cab left the house Nanny and little Sarah waved from the nursery window. On returning their wave Papa was sure he saw Nanny wipe a tear from her eyes. He glanced to see whether his wife and small daughter had noticed but hopefully they had not seen. Papa glanced once more up at Nanny and thought, poor Nanny, it may not be as bad as you think!

*

Emily's confinement with Marguerite, as with her other two daughters, had been at home. She was attended by a private midwife, helped by a maternity nurse who was due to stay for six weeks. After a few days baby Marguerite showed signs of slipping away, and she was rushed to the London Children's Hospital, where she was kept for many weeks. During the next three years she was in an out of this hospital many times. Even when she was not actually staying in hospital she visited often to see the Doctors, and this entailed endless waiting around with Mama. As she grew older these visits upset and worried Marguerite and it all became a most frightening experience for her, as each time she went to the hospital, in her small child's mind, she thought she was in a for a long stay with no visits from Mama and Papa. At that time no visitors were allowed in the Children's Hospital.

After much thought, and being a family of not meagre means, Emily and Frederick decided to refer Marguerite to a Harley Street Paediatrician. Since the 1840's Harley Street had become the street for Doctors specialising in all sorts of ailments, and it was always the hope of Mama and Papa that their small daughter would grow out of all her medical problems.

Marguerite these days quite cherished the outings with Mama and Papa and had become quite used to the unpleasantness that she sometimes had to endure. Being the middle child it was one opportunity to have all their attention. It was also great fun sitting squashed between Mama and Papa in the cab, wrapped in the musty smelling rug, and feeling quite safe, watching the scenes of London pass by.

Soon the horse was keen to be off and the cab left Bedford Square and turned into Tottenham Court Road. Marguerite chatted away to Mama and Papa. She became quite excited listening to the Cries of London but was quite horrified at the way small boys, bucket and spade in hand, seemed to dash between the horses hoofs collecting the horses droppings. She was really thrilled when Papa stopped the cab and bought some violets. What a kind lady and quite fat like me, thought Marguerite. "Papa, will I sell violets when I am a big girl?" asked a fascinated Marguerite.

Papa gave a laugh, "Oh no, my little Podge, I would hope not."

"Why not, Papa?" asked Marguerite, and so the questions went on, keeping Mama and Papa really amused. Yes their little Podge was good company.

Soon the cabby was calling to the horse to stop and, pulling on the reins, they drew up outside a house similar in style to the house in Bedford Square, which made it easier for Marguerite to accept. Mama and Papa were soon out of the cab helping their small daughter down the high step. Her legs were still very short and clumsy.

Visiting this Specialist did not mean a long wait as at the hospital, and the kindly receptionist was soon handing the Sinclair's over to Nurse Watson to be shown into the Doctor, Marguerite still clutching her bunch of violets in her warm hand. Nurse Watson's nurse's cap, which reached to her shoulders, reminded Marguerite of the picture she once saw of children in the Roman Church, as Mama called it.

The Doctor, a tall good looking gentleman, had not long been in his own practice, but was already proving to be a very good paediatrician with a very kindly approach. He was already much loved by his small patients. "This morning Marguerite I would like you to stay with nurse to be weighed, whilst I talk with your Mummy and Daddy."

Marguerite looked upon this as a different place to a hospital and having always been used to Doctors and nurses she was not at all perturbed and went off happily. As she left, Mama and Papa could hear her offering the sweet-smelling violets to Nurse Watson; this was typical of Marguerite's generous nature.

Dr. Spencer's consulting room had a warm atmosphere with comfortable chairs and fresh light curtains at the windows. He had dispensed with the dark green or brown screening, dividing off the cubicles, as at the hospital. It was a very tidy room. Frederick could not help but compare it with his office, where, although he was very fastidious, being a busy City Solicitor he had piles of reference books and files that had been around for years gathering dust round his very old rolled-top desk and in every nook and cranny. What a difference to this consulting room.

"Do sit down. Marguerite is in good hands with Nurse Watson". In an endeavour to make these worried parents feel more at ease, he went on to say,

"The weather is not too bad for the time of year?" Dr. Spencer had a very relaxing manner and soon the Sinclair's were ready for the consultation. The Doctor sat for a while studying his notes and getting his facts right before looking up and speaking. "The results of the tests carried out last month on Marguerite are now to hand, but I am afraid there is some reason for disquiet."

"In what way, Doctor?" asked a worried Papa.

"Well they have shown that Marguerite has a rare disease of the kidneys, which is one of the reasons for her obesity and the reason for her battle during her short life to survive," the Doctor replied showing concern for these parents.

"Yes, but Doctor can nothing be done about this?" asked Mama with some urgency.

"At present no, Mrs Sinclair. Of course, research is being carried out all the time on kidney diseases, but at the moment I am afraid nothing can be done." The Doctor tried to sound comforting. Mama and Papa looked at each other with great concern and tears in their eyes.

Frederick went on to ask, "Dr. Spencer will you please tell my wife and I what the outcome will be? This will enable us to be prepared for the worst."

Dr. Spencer hesitated a moment before speaking. "The obesity will inevitably cause strain to the heart muscles, and, of course, a weakening of the heart itself." Dr. Spencer had no need to say more, Frederick and Emily knew what he was trying to tell them. "Of course I will continue to keep a close check on Marguerite, and, in the meantime, I will watch the research field very closely." Dr. Spencer tried to reassure these parents of this small child.

"My wife and I appreciate that you will do your best for our small daughter, Dr. Spencer, and we thank you for being frank with us." Frederick felt that this was all he could say in his distress. For some time Emily and Frederick sat talking to this young Doctor and they really felt that whatever the outcome Marguerite was certainly in the hands of a good paediatrician. Before finally shaking hands, Frederick asked, "Do you wish to see Marguerite today, Doctor?"

"No I do not think this is necessary, but I will just say goodbye to our little patient," and beforeMarguerite arrived the Doctor expressed his sorrow that the news was no better.

On being summoned Nurse Watson brought Marguerite in to say goodbye, and, with heavy hearts, the family left the building to once more hail a cab for home.

Nanny had returned from her walk in the park with Sarah and was watching anxiously for the return of the cab. The kitchen staff also sat anxiously around their table, hardly speaking a word, just drinking tea. They knew from Nanny that at last the Sinclair's would know the result of important tests. George stood in the porch glancing towards the entrance to the Square. By the time the cab arrived he was on the pavement ready to open the cab door. The family got out and the sugar lump was as usual given to the cabby's horse and a sad Emily and Frederick slowly stepped indoors.

Marguerite returned to the nursery to join Nanny and Sarah whilst Frederick sent George with a message to John at the office that he would not be into work that day. It was to be some hours before Emily and Frederick felt they could face telling the news to Nanny

*

The next morning Nanny did not appear in the kitchen for her usual warm oats. Mary took these up to her in the nursery before lugging up the jugs of hot water. Before meeting up with her friends in the kitchen Nanny had to come to terms with what might be the ultimate outcome of her small charge Marguerite's illness. Although not unforeseen, nevertheless, it was a bitter blow to Nanny, as she looked upon these Sinclair children as her own and shared Mama and Papa's anxieties.

This was to be a day no different for small five-year-old Marguerite, except perhaps a wishful hope for another cab ride. One slight variation, Nanny did not seem to be hurrying her to get her out of bed this morning, so she lay quietly and watched Sarah who was endeavouring with such care and concentration to dress herself.

With heavy heart Frederick was back to normal routine. Soon a cab was at the door and George was wishing his master a good day in the office. George had not been able to enlighten John yesterday with any news.

On reaching the City Frederick was soon to learn, from the morning papers, of the passing of her Majesty. What a sad headline 'Death of the Queen. Her Majesty passed away in peace' followed by a message from the King. "Yes John, this is indeed a sad day," was Frederick's greeting. They sat for sometime mulling over Frederick's sad news. This was indeed a day when Frederick and Emily had to come to terms with the illness of their own small child, and what was thought to be the inevitable outcome, and the passing of a well-loved Queen. A day the Sinclair's would remember for a long time.

Later that morning, when taking her daily orders to the kitchen, Emily made time to sit with the kitchen staff and to enlighten them as to the severity of Marguerite's illness, and it was with heavy hearts that they continued their duties. Yes, the Sinclair's were a thoughtful family to their below-stair staff.

Life for the Sinclair family soon returned to normal. A close watch was kept on Marguerite, but not so as to cause undue concern to the child. Later Marguerite was forced to forego a number of childhood pleasures, in case she should tire herself, but one event she was allowed to attend stayed in her memory for ever.

*

After some months Frederick began to plan a surprise for his family. London had not seen a coronation for sixty-five years, and in June 1902 Frederick planned to make sure his family were to enjoy the sight of this memorable event. Unfortunately, this was to prove a costly business, as, owing to the future Edward VII having to undergo surgery for the removal of his appendix, the coronation was postponed for six weeks, necessitating a further transaction for seats, but to this affluent London family it was not of too much concern.

Marguerite's illness caused trouble in many ways. It caused discourse between husband and wife, which they had never experienced in their married life together. Emily was adamant that Marguerite should stay at home and not view the coronation.

Frederick thought otherwise. "Now come, come Emily it will be a memorable occasion for the child," said a very determined Frederick.

"But just think of all those germs she will be exposed to in all those crowds." Emily was by now becoming really annoyed.

"My dear, we shall have seats in one of the stands. We will not be with the milling crowds." Frederick hit back with determination. They argued on this point for well over a week. He wanted this day to be a special day for the Sinclair family as a whole. If Marguerite did not attend Nanny would also miss the event, as she would have to stay at home and look after her charge.

Emily finally reluctantly relented, but added, "Frederick, if anything should happen to our small daughter, because of your obstinacy, I shall never forgive you!" Frederick looked at his wife with apprehension, but, nevertheless was still determined to have his way.

The coronation was to be one of the highlights of the young Sinclair girls' childhood. Plans were soon put in hand for a dressmaker to attend to make the girls' dresses. The dressmaker came in and out of the house for what seemed to these excited children hundreds of times. The dresses were of white tulle edged in embroidery- anglais and threaded with pink ribbon. No young lady was properly dressed unless her outfit was offset by a hat; the large rim, surrounded by pink handmade flowers, protected the girls' small faces. This was thought by their Mama to be a necessity against the August heat.

Soon all was ready and the hansom cabs, previously booked by Papa, arrived. Rachel, being the eldest, had the privilege of travelling with Mama and Papa. Marguerite was slightly annoyed, nevertheless, she was to travel with Nanny and Sarah. She felt very hot indeed, as Mama had made sure that under her refinery she was warmly clad. Thankfully the weather was fine and as it was rather cloudy not too hot. The streets were crowded with people and the decorations were fantastic. Slow progress was made by the cabs and Marguerite thought she had never seen so many people. They passed many street urchins, taking the chance to cash-in on the event, by selling small Union Jacks and other red, white and blue souvenirs. Fortunately the two cabs had by luck been able to follow each other and arrived in Trafalgar Square together. It was not too far for Marguerite to walk to the Mall. Before finding their stand Papa stopped and bought each small daughter a Union Jack from one of the boys shouting their wares. Marguerite thought what dirty hands and face the boy had, and did she see him picking his nose, nice children didn't do such things!

Mama was not at all in favour of Papa purchasing these flags. As she said to Nanny, "You do not know where they have been made. Some back street hovel I should guess." She really was quite annoyed with Frederick, and warned each child they were not going to keep the flags.   Frederick foresaw trouble in this respect.

Finally they reached their stand and Marguerite had difficulty in negotiating the steps to their seats. After what seemed a long time the processions appeared in the distance and the crowds began to cheer. The children had never seen so many horses. Their manes were plaited beautifully and their heads were held high. What a sight. The girls clapped and clapped until Marguerite could clap no more. To Mama's horror Sarah not being able to clap her small hands and wave her flag at the same time put the small wooden stick in her mouth. Nanny was soon instructed to hold it for her. Mama dreaded what the outcome might be!   The cheering and clapping became greater as the fifty nine-year-old King passed by. It really was deafening to a small child's ears. As a six-year-old Marguerite was to remember the splash of gold of Queen Alexander's gown as she passed by with the King in their magnificent coach. And so the processions came to an end. After all that excitement Marguerite began to wane and she cuddled up to Nanny and went fast asleep. Suddenly she was awoken by the cheering and clapping as the King and Queen passed by once more on their return to Buckingham Palace.

Now came the part that Emily was dreading the finding of cabs to take them home. She did not like the thought of jostling with all these crowds. Papa helped Marguerite to climb down from the stand, whilst Nanny looked after small Sarah. Papa then led them back through the crowds through Admiralty Arch and so into Trafalgar Square.

Frederick whispered something to his wife and Emily's immediate answer was, "Oh no, Frederick, enough is enough!" Rachel glanced at her Mama and Papa and thought 'oh not again', they were always cross with each other these days.

Marguerite and Sarah, by now two tired little girls, stood patiently with Nanny oblivious of the discord between their parents. Suddenly Marguerite spotted a lady selling violets, she recognized her as the same fat lady whom Papa had bought violets from before. She broke away from Nanny and Mama, and Papa's disagreement was soon forgotten as Papa felt a tug at his sleeve. "Papa, Papa," exclaimed an excited Marguerite, "Papa my violet lady."

The observant London Cries lady had spotted the small girl's excitement, "Violets, sir, lovely violets."   Much to Mama's disgust Papa was soon buying each daughter a bunch of violets. The tired, but excited children stood in the pushing crowds clutching their violets whilst Papa endeavoured to hail cabs. The children were frightened as Papa got so near to the horses in his endeavour to attract the cabbies attention. Eventually he was successful and the children, and no doubt Nanny by this time, were glad once more to be tucked up in a cab.

Papa ordered the cabbies to take them first of all to see the beautiful arch set astride Whitehall, erected by the Canadians in the style of Temple Bar in honour of the new King. The entire arch was made of straw and grain grown on Canadian farms. A sight Marguerite was never to forget. They then rode along the Embankment, which was beautifully decorated, as also were the boats on the river alongside. This was not the way home! Where were they going?

No they were not going straight home. Rachel in Mama and Papa's cab waved in excitement to her little sisters following in their cab. Emily was not amused and cast looks of scorn at Frederick. Soon they were leaving the river behind and Nanny was pointing out to the small girls the enormous building of St. Paul's. This seemed huge towering above the cab.

It was not long before they were pulling up at Papa's office in the City. To complete the exciting day Papa had another surprise for them. For many weeks he had been planning this. John greeted them with much politeness, and to the girls delight Papa had arranged for them to participate of a lovely tea; after which John was very honoured when small Marguerite presented her violets to him. What a generous and sweet little girl, he thought. After the tea-things were cleared away, Papa told them all to shut their eyes and not to open them until they were told.

For many weeks Frederick had been sitting for a well-known artist and he was today going to present his portrait to his well-beloved family. He quickly hung it above the marble fireplace near his desk; quite up to expectations his family were thrilled.

Frederick's apologetic wife turned to him with admiration showing in her eyes. "My dearest, it is so good and you look just like your dear Father in his portrait. I am so sorry I did not appreciate the surprise you had in store for us." Frederick had no need to speak, all was forgiven.

Marguerite stood beneath her Papa's portrait and was enthralled to see her dear Papa looking so grand. What an end to a perfect day. It was indeed three very tired young ladies that later that evening returned to the shelter of their home.

The following week, and for a long time after, the girls were to depict the coronation in their drawings. Nanny was kept busy mixing up the paints and this kept them happy for hours. In fact, Rachel was becoming very keen on art and, in this respect, was proving to have quite a talent.

The Sinclair family regularly attended their Parish Church and their new dresses were to be worn many times as Sunday best. The three girls were much admired and thought very much of by their neighbours and friends and by their fellow parishioners. Emily and Frederick were certainly very proud indeed of their three delightful daughters. Rachel was not so keen to be seen dressed the same as her small sisters, and many an argument occurred, on a Sunday morning, with Nanny.

Emily would have liked Frederick to have brought his portrait home from the office and to have it hung next to his Father's, but Frederick was opposed to this. Although he had fond memories of his Father he had always felt that he could never compete and rise in the field of Law to the heights that his Father had reached. The late William Sinclair had been called to the Bar in the Inner Temple, and Frederick felt that an ordinary Solicitor in a City office was a comedown. No, he did not wish to be reminded of this every time he walked his staircase at home. In his office the portrait would remain.

One Sunday, some time later, Marguerite was very slow to prepare herself for the Sunday service, and appeared to be very listless. Nanny sought Mama and Papa's advice. It was agreed she should be allowed to stay at home with Nanny caring for her. During the morning Marguerite showed signs of a temperature and was very flushed indeed. It was with great relief that Nanny heard the family arrive home. By tea-time it was felt necessary to send George for Dr. Spencer, and Marguerite's small bed was moved into the visitors' room.

As soon as Dr. Spencer arrived he examined Marguerite thoroughly but said it was too early to diagnose exactly what was causing her distress. He warned Emily and Frederick that since the coronation there had appeared outbreaks of diphtheria in some areas, especially amongst the poorer population of London. Emily thought of that wooden stick in Sarah's mouth and went cold with fright. Oh no, where would this epidemic spread?

Frederick, in his mind, could hear Emily saying, 'If anything should happen to our small daughter, I shall never forgive you.' Also his immediate thoughts turned to his other two daughters. What if they should also develop it?

Dr. Spencer went on to say that, of course, he trusted they realised that if the diphtheria should strike, all confirmed cases would have to be moved to the Isolation Infirmary, and all contacts would be confined to the house.

That evening the atmosphere in the Sinclair's household was, to say the least, very tense indeed. Papa offered to sit with Marguerite and he prayed by her bedside as he had never prayed before. In the night she became delirious and George was awoken and sent once more to fetch Dr. Spencer. The Doctor stayed until morning and was on hand when Sarah began to show signs of illness. He examined and administered to this other small child and once more said time would tell as to whether it was diphtheria. By this time he, himself, began to fear the worse. Fortunately Rachel and the rest of the family still seemed quite well.

A number of days went by. Dr. Spencer pointed out that this could be the incubation period. Little Sarah's condition seemed to remain static but Marguerite was gradually deteriorating. Slowly a few more days were to pass and Sarah seemed to gradually recover, which raised hopes that it was not going to be the dreaded disease. Once Sarah made an improvement she certainly seemed to bounce back very quickly.

With Sarah's recovery, all attention was on Marguerite who seemed to get weaker and weaker. After some days Dr. Spencer was able to confirm that it was not diphtheria but a rare infection, which with Marguerite's diseased kidneys had taken its toll. Although all concerned were very relieved the seriousness of the situation did not decrease. During the day Nanny took it in turns with Emily to sit with Marguerite, and at night either Frederick or Emily slept on the chaise-longue beside the bed. Neither of them were able to sleep.

Marguerite had been ill for about three weeks when the crisis came. Dr. Spencer remained with the family all night. It was not thought Marguerite would last the night. Dr. Spencer stood at the end of the bed and took out his pocket watch and looking at it remarked, "The critical hours are between 3 o'clock and 4.30 am. It is now 2.45 am. It is now in God's hands."

As Marguerite seemed to get weaker Frederick glanced across the bed at his dearest Emily, her face was so taut, and Frederick could hear her once more saying 'I shall never forgive you'.

BOOK 1

CHAPTER 2

THE UNEXPECTED

I shall never forgive you! I shall never forgive you! Frederick suddenly realized that he had dozed with exhaustion and was dreaming. He sat up with a start and saw Emily, with her finger raised, telling him to be quiet. Dr Spencer beckoned from the bottom of the bed for him to join him outside the bedroom. Frederick wearily got up, and after a quick glance at his very still small daughter, left the room.

Frederick looked with concern at the Doctor. "Mr Sinclair relax I have to tell you that I think we are over the crisis. Your little daughter is now in a relaxed sleep. I think the worst is over." Frederick was shaking with relief. The Doctor hesitated for a moment in thought, and then said "It is now 6 o'clock, I will stay with you until 8 o'clock. If all is well then I must make for my surgery."

Frederick shook the Doctor's hand, "How can I thank you enough. Have you spoken to Emily, Doctor?"

"Yes," replied the Doctor, "May I suggest that you persuade her to have a rest. It has been such a long traumatic night."

"Indeed yes Doctor. Now you have given us the good news. I will fetch Nanny to take our place at the bedside. Thank you Doctor. We shall never be able to repay you." With that, a much relieved Frederick, went to take the good news to Nanny.

With both the younger Sinclair's being so ill life in the schoolroom, with Miss Hannah, had ceased. When Marguerite improved the decision was taken by Emily and Frederick to make arrangements for Rachel to attend the Ladies Academy from the New Year. Preparing Rachel for her entrance at least gave Miss Hannah something to concentrate on and relieved Nanny of a more and more difficult Rachel.

New Year 1903 came not too quickly for an excited Rachel. Marguerite was still in the spare bedroom, but before leaving for the Academy on her first morning a very grown up and proud Rachel went to say goodbye to her sister. She was really looking forward to a proper school. There were now about forty of these Public Day Schools in and around London and competition between them was great. Rachel looked forward to adding German and Latin to her languages.

Marguerite was now sitting up in bed and was pleased to see her sister and longed to have a peep in her school bag, which looked so heavy. Even at seven years of age Marguerite was looking forward to when her time would come to go to the Academy.

As winter was left behind and the first signs of spring appeared it was considered that Marguerite was well enough to join her sisters once more in the nursery. The spare bedroom was to be prepared for twelve-year-old Rachel. It was now considered that as Miss Rachel was at the Academy she was too old for the nursery. Marguerite felt not a little jealous at parting with the bedroom she had been accustomed to for so many months.

*

The next three years saw Marguerite build up her strength, but the obesity for her age was even worse. As a ten-year-old no mention was made of preparing her for the Ladies Academy in two years time; although Miss Hannah found her very competent in her lessons, especially in French, considering her numerous absences from lessons. Marguerite asked Miss Hannah to have a talk with Papa, but events were to postpone such a talk.

One cold February morning, although suffering from a heavy cold, young Mary was carrying out her usual duties of taking the hot water to the bedrooms. On her way to the nursery, her eyes being hardly open, she missed a step and Mary and hot water fell to the bottom of the stairs. Her screams were heard all over the house. Having just handed the water to Mary, and realizing what had happened, Cook was first on the scene, followed closely by Papa. Marguerite and Sarah rushed passed Nanny to Mary, but were soon told to return to the nursery. They sadly did as they were told, as Papa lifted Mary and carried her to one of the best bedrooms. Papa immediately sent George post-haste to fetch Dr. Spencer. Rachel went to the Academy as usual, but the two sad small girls sat at the nursery window looking out at the dismal day. Miss Hannah knew it was pointless trying to distract them. They saw Mary's Mother and Father arrive. The girls thought they looked a kindly, although worried, couple. The parents were devoted to their eldest daughter, who had had to leave home at such a young age. A bedroom was put at their disposal.

The next few days saw a very silent house as Mary lay near to death's door. Dr. Spencer called in many times, and gradually over the next few weeks Mary showed signs of improvement and her parents were able to return home to their other children. The Sinclair's sent them off carrying a large box of food.

After this tragic accident, Frederick decided that his home should be fitted with the latest plumbing, and had bathrooms installed. Not many months passed before this work was put in hand and no more hot water was to be carried up and down the stairs.

*

As in all Edwardian families it was the custom to have musical afternoons or evenings round the piano. Marguerite enjoyed these occasions and was very proud when she was allowed to sing.

As Frederick returned from the office one evening the Doctor was just leaving. "Good evening, Vincent. How is the patient?" The Sinclair's and the Doctor were now on Christian name terms.

"I am pleased to say coming on well," replied the Doctor.

"My wife and I appreciate all you have done, Vincent, and we would be honoured if you would dine with us one evening."

"I would be delighted to," replied the Doctor.

"Shall we say Saturday then, and do bring your good lady."

"Thank you Frederick, until Saturday then, goodbye." Vincent and Frederick shook hands warmly.

As soon as Mary began to recover the girls were allowed to pay short visits to her. On this particular Saturday it was Marguerite's turn. "Mary, would you like me to read to you, or," hesitating, "perhaps you would care for me to sing to you?"

"I should love to hear you sing, Marguerite." Mary had often heard sweet voices coming from the drawing room and it was difficult to say whose voices were which. She longed to know what Marguerite's voice would be like. Marguerite rose from the bedside, and although fat for her age, stood as elegantly as she could, hands clasped in front of her. She commenced by singing 'Won't you buy my pretty flowers'. Mary lay entranced by this sweet voice.

Down in the dining room Dr and Mrs Spencer dined with the Sinclair's, including fifteen-year-old Rachel, who now took meals with her parents. It so happened that the bedroom that Mary was being nursed in was above the dining room, and as Marguerite's voice reached them they sat enthralled.

*

Dr. Spencer was the first to speak. "Tell me Frederick, who has such a beautiful voice?" but before Frederick could answer they listened again whilst Marguerite sang 'Rock me to sleep'. They continued their meal whilst enjoying the singing. When the song was finished the Doctor asked once more "Frederick do tell me who has such a beautiful voice?"

"Why our little Podge, I mean Marguerite, your patient," answered a very proud Papa.

"My patient, Marguerite, how marvellous." The Doctor seemed so pleased that it was his young patient.

Up in Mary's bedroom Marguerite noticed that her final song had indeed rocked Mary into a relaxed sleep. Marguerite crept quietly from the room back to the nursery.

Back in the dining room they were waiting for Amy to serve their dessert. The Doctor asked Frederick, "May I, as your guest, be so bold as to ask if after our meal Marguerite may sing to us a selection of her songs?"

Frederick, showing signs of surprise, "But yes, Vincent, that is if my dear Emily would be so good as to accompany her on the piano."

The Doctor immediately turned to Emily." If you would be so kind, Emily, it would give us great pleasure."

"By all means," replied a very pleased Emily.

Miss Rachel listened with astonishment, her young sister was to sing to Mama and Papa's guests. This had never been known before.

Rachel suddenly realised that Papa was saying something. "Rachel, please go and tell Nanny to prepare Marguerite to sing in about an hour's time. Nanny and Sarah may come and listen."

An even more astounded Rachel stood up, "Yes, Papa, certainly Papa." She left the room in haste, jealousy welling up in her chest. Both young sisters were now to encroach on what she considered was her privilege these days to be with Mama and Papa when they entertained. I mean to say, she thought, neither of them were even at the Academy yet! Emily's eyes followed Rachel. Did she see an air in the way she left the room and a definite sign of defiance? Oh dear, thought Emily, maturing girls, and we have two more daughters to go through this off-handed phase yet! On her way to the nursery Rachel was thinking to herself, how silly our Podge to sing for guests, what a bore.

Rachel burst into the nursery and, not looking at Marguerite or Sarah, spoke to Nanny in a high-and-mighty voice, "Marguerite is to sing to Mama and Papa's guests and you and Sarah are to come and listen. You must be ready in an hour."

Nanny, taken by surprise, did not, at first, take in what Miss Rachel was saying, "I beg your pardon Miss Rachel. Do please talk normally and I might then be able to understand what you are saying," requested a puzzled Nanny.

"You are to prepare Maggie to sing to Mama and Papa's guests," and having delivered her message she flounced out of the room to return to the dining room before she missed her dessert.

Marguerite could not believe what she was hearing, "Do you think she was teasing," she asked Nanny.

Nanny had no time to reply, eight-year-old Sarah had not missed a word of what Rachel had said. "No don't be silly, Marguerite, you heard what Rache said, you are to sing to Mama and Papa's guests, and we are to come down too." By this time Sarah was jumping up and down with excitement.

It took a few moments for Nanny to gather her senses but soon she was getting the young girls organised. "Now girls we have an hour to get ready. Marguerite you take a bath whilst I prepare your best muslin dress and endeavour to find a bow for your hair. Sarah, please change into a clean dress, whilst I get myself ready." The girls did not need telling twice of the arrangements and off they rushed.

By the time Marguerite had had her bath Nanny had put on a clean starched apron, over her navy dress and was ready to cope with Marguerite's hair.

It was not long before a proud Nanny accompanied the girls to the still deserted drawing room, the family and guests still being at table. Marguerite looked through the music in the piano stall and placed, what she thought was suitable, in position for Mama. Surprisingly she was not nervous, just a little breathless from the excitement.

"Now relax, my little Podge, until the guests arrive." Fancy, thought a bemused Marguerite Nanny used Papa's nickname.

Soon Mama and Papa were showing the Doctor and his wife into the room. "Hello girls! How lovely to see you both. My wife and I are so looking forward very much to Marguerite singing to us. From what we have heard in the distance, you Marguerite have a most charming voice." "Thank you, sir", the Doctor certainly seemed appreciative.

"Thank you, Doctor, it is a pleasure," replied a quite confident Marguerite.

Mama took a few moments to discuss with Marguerite what she should sing, and it was finally decided to commence with Marguerite's favourite, which had so caught the Doctor's attention earlier, 'Won't you buy my pretty flowers' followed by 'Grandfather's clock' and finishing with 'Loves Old Sweet Song'. The Doctor and his wife sat and listened in wonderment at this child's sweet voice. When she had finished the guests clapped heartedly. Rachel not daring to show her jealousy clapped less enthusiastically. After bidding farewell to the guests a very tired, but satisfied, Marguerite returned with Nanny and Sarah to the nursery. That evening she was soon fast asleep.

Later, whilst enjoying his port with Frederick, the Doctor referred once more to Marguerite's singing. "My dear Frederick, your daughter really has an exceptional voice for such a young child. She should be trained in the art." At this the Doctor hesitated and Frederick began to wonder what he was going to say. "I was wondering, Frederick, would you permit me to introduce her to my dear friend Professor Muller? I am sure he would be enchanted with her voice and could possibly coach her further in this art."

"Why yes, of course," replied a surprised Frederick. "If you feel it would not be too much of a strain on her heart Vincent, as I believe the training is intense," asked Frederick with some concern.

The Doctor endeavoured to reassure Frederick on this point. "I have your daughter's welfare very much in mind as always, Frederick, but, if she is not to attend the Ladies Academy to further her education, as already discussed, then the enjoyment of singing well will be a great asset to her and I am sure this will keep her happy."

Frederick could not help but agree and shook the Doctor's hand and said he did not know how to thank Vincent for all these kindnesses to his family.

Arrangements were soon put in hand for Professor Muller to meet Marguerite, and for years to come Marguerite was to be for ever thankful to Dr. Spencer for this introduction. She was thrilled at the thought of meeting such a Professor and probably to be given the chance to train properly in the art of singing. She was a little disappointed to learn that she was not to attend the Ladies Academy, but her disappointment was soon overcome by the new turn of events.

Dr. Spencer called by one day to leave a message that Marguerite was requested to entertain after dinner at the Spencer's residence in front of Professor Muller. She was to be accompanied by Mama and Papa. The excitement that this caused Marguerite was to worry Mama and Nanny. Rachel could only show utter disgust at the arrangements.

The dressmaker was once more called in and Marguerite was measured for a beautiful velvet gown; the top to be smocked, in keeping with a child of her age.

Easter Saturday 1906 soon arrived and Nanny and Sarah waved from the balcony as a proud, and perhaps a slightly nervous, Marguerite left with Mama and Papa. Miss Rachel was nowhere to be seen.

*

Where was Miss Rachel? Why was she not on the balcony waving goodbye and good luck to her younger sister?

For the past few months Rachel had been asking to be allowed to go home from the Academy with her friend Bridget. Mama immediately became concerned, and asked, "Rachel, what is her surname?"

"O'Reilly, Mama. Why do you ask?" Rachel was by now getting a little impatient.

"Just as I thought," replied Mama, "Bridget O'Reilly, the answer is definitely no, you are not going to their home. We do not wish our daughter to mix with the Roman faith." As a fifteen-year-old Rachel argued and argued to no avail, she was forbidden to go home with Bridget.

At last the time had come. Rachel was determined to get her way. She waited patiently, as here was her opportunity. She knew that Mama and Papa's minds were taken up with Marguerite's forthcoming appointment, so she made her plans. On this Easter Saturday, whilst Mama and Papa prepared themselves and Nanny was busy with Marguerite she seized the opportunity. She very quietly went downstairs to the hall and gave instructions to George to hail a cab. He thought this strange, but it was not up to him to demand an explanation from Miss Rachel. She was growing up now and he supposed she knew what she was doing. A cab was hailed and off went Miss Rachel. In the hustle and bustle she was not missed. The family knew of Rachel's jealousy of Marguerite and did not think it amiss when she was not on the balcony to wave goodbye.

The evening went well for Marguerite, and, as prophesied, Professor Muller was enchanted by Marguerite's repertoire and offered to take her as a pupil. He suggested that she should add Italian and German to her studies and enquired as to whether she played an instrument. Owing to her poor health she had not commenced with piano lessons, but Mama and Papa agreed with Professor Muller that she should commence immediately, as this would be of great help with her singing and for pitching her voice in practice. From this moment Marguerite's life was to change and her future was mapped out before her.

Having had such a worrying time with Marguerite's health, Mama and Papa could not believe what was happening and could not thank Dr. Spencer enough for giving them this opportunity. They bid farewell to Dr Spencer and his wife, and Professor Muller, and it was a tired but still excited family that returned home.

Meanwhile, Rachel was having a thoroughly enjoyable time in Kensington at her friend Bridget's home and had met eighteen-year-old brother Declan, whom she thought was a delightful young man. Bridget's parents had gone to the theatre. The time seemed to fly, and, to her horror, it was already dark.

"Bridget," exclaimed a worried Rachel, "I cannot go home in a cab on my own now it is dark. Will you come home for the night with me?" Rachel hoped she would say yes. Surely if her friend was with her Mama and Papa would not be able to be too cross.

Bridget had other ideas. "Why don't you stay here, Rachel. Declan can go with a message." The suggestion was too tempting, all thought of what Mama and Papa would say went out of Rachel's mind. Off went Declan to say that Rachel was spending the night with a friend.

On arriving home the Sinclair's were met in the hall by a very concerned Nanny and an agitated George. Declan, whoever he might be had just left the message. Mama and Papa were furious and George was reprimanded in no uncertain terms. Never again was he to let any of the Sinclair daughters out of the house without an escort and either Emily or Frederick's permission. He was told, in no uncertain terms, that a young girl in these Edwardian days did not do such a thing.

The next morning Rachel had not returned. Over in Kensington Rachel had gone to Mass with the O'Reilly's, an experience she found puzzling, full of mystery and bewilderment. The Latin was too fast for her and the Irish accent of the priest quite incomprehensible. The service seemed so long and she just did not know how Bridget sat through this each week, no wonder the congregation seemed to fidget. She did not really enjoy her Sunday lunch with the O'Reilly's, as by now she was becoming worried at the thought of having to face Mama and Papa, and was by now feeling quite ashamed of her deceit.

On her return home that afternoon a rather annoyed George greeted Rachel and ushered her immediately into the drawing room. The lecture she was to endure was to be remembered for the rest of her life. She was then banished to her room. Marguerite and Sarah were then called down and were told in no uncertain terms by Mama and Papa of how they would be expected to behave as they grew older and never, never, were they to go into a Roman Catholic church or to ever dream of attending Mass. Many years later Marguerite was to recall this childhood episode in her mind with a wry smile.

Arrangements were soon put in hand for Rachel to have classes with the young curate at the Parish Church in preparation for confirmation. "Just in case," Mama said to Papa, "Rachel had got other ideas."

Papa was adamant though that Rachel should still be allowed to continue the friendship with Bridget. Papa was so much more accommodating than Mama.

*

The years were to pass. In 1909 Rachel was presented at Court and her name was added to Mama's visiting card. At about this time she also spent a number of hours playing tennis with the friends of the family in Harrow - the attraction being the young Edward Tremaine.

Rachel was not too sure whether she agreed to the plans being made for her to study art for two years in Paris, but Mama and Papa had their way and at the end of the season Rachel went off to Paris. Time soon passed in Paris for Rachel, but, nevertheless, although she had enjoyed her stay, and it had enabled her to advance in her art considerably, she looked forward to returning to England and Edward Tremaine. Edward had often visited her in Paris and their relationship had developed and they were to be married in 1912.

Before the marriage of the Sinclair's eldest daughter Great Britain was to face the shocking news of a tragedy at sea that was to shock the world. On a Spring-like day in April 1912, John was as usual to leave the office ahead of Frederick, but he did not get further than the newsvendor. He could not believe his eyes when he read the latest news 'Great Loss of Life, TheTitanic Sinks'. He purchased a paper and rushed back with this tragic news to Frederick. The family were greatly distressed as they learnt of the demise of a great friend of the family. This terrible news dampened their spirits as they prepared for the family's happy event.

Marguerite refused to be bridesmaid to her sister, as by now she was really quite ungainly plump and was very conscious of this fact. She had also already decided that she did not wish to be presented at Court.

The marriage of Rachel and Edward was a great occasion in the Sinclair household. The first of the three Sinclair daughters' to marry, and Rachel made a beautiful bride attended by Sarah and Bridget. Bridget had to obtain a dispensation from the Pope to attend the wedding. Much to Rachel's chagrin Professor Muller had persuaded Marguerite to sing 'The Lord's my Shepherd'. This young girl's voice filled the church.

The wedding of Rachel and Edward in June 1912 was indeed a memorable occasion for the Sinclair family. It was also the beginning of many changes for Marguerite.

*

Apart from a relapse in health, now and again, as Marguerite grew up her singing voice had matured and Professor Muller was still much impressed with his protege. Suggestions were being made that when she was seventeen she should study in Germany for two years. Mama and Papa were not too sure about this, the memories of the past being still very much in their minds, but Professor Muller decided the time had definitely come when he must talk once more with Emily and Frederick Sinclair.

On leaving the reception Professor Muller shook hands with Emily and Frederick. "It was so kind of you to invite me. I was so proud of young Marguerite; her rendering of the 23rd Psalm was superb. May I invite you both to dine with me next Thursday?" asked Professor Muller.

"It is very kind of you, Professor. Indeed we would be very honoured, thank you," replied Frederick.

"Of course, you will bring my young protege," requested a smiling Professor.

"You are so kind," replied Frederick.

The next few days passed rapidly, and it was a weary Marguerite that set off with Mama and Papa the following Thursday. It had been an exceptionally hot week and this had taken a toll on Marguerite. She dreaded the thought that she might have to sing at this dinner She was very uninterested in the journey to Golders Green, which was very unusual for Marguerite. Mama and Papa remembered her excitement on her previous outings. They were rather concerned and arrived at Professor Muller's grand house with some trepidation. They were immediately shown into Professor Muller by his butler. Drinks were served before a meal of unusual delicacies was partaken.

When the male members retired for port Professor Muller mentioned to Frederick the main reason for inviting them to be his guests that evening.

"My dear Sinclair I think it is time that we discussed your daughter's possible study time in Germany." Professor Muller being aware of the Sinclair's concern over their daughter's health wished to approach Frederick first on this matter, as he was not too sure how emotionally involved were Mother and daughter.

"Professor when were you thinking she should commence," asked a concerned Frederick.

"This we would have to discuss with Marguerite herself," replied the Professor. He intended to tread gently.

Frederick went on to point out that he thought that some time should elapse, enabling Marguerite to overcome the excitement of the previous week's wedding; also allowing time for the weather to cool. This heat was really too much for Marguerite.

After some discussion it was time to rejoin the ladies and the Professor and Frederick had agreed that the matter should be brought into the open. It had also been agreed that Professor Muller should be the first to refer to the matter.

"Marguerite you look a little tired tonight. It must be all that excitement last week." The Professor certainly had a way with the fairer sex.

"I think it is the heat, sir," replied Marguerite, still hoping she would not have to sing that night.

"Yes, I think it is a little too hot this evening. Too hot to sing, don't you think?" added the Professor questioningly.

"Yes sir," answered Marguerite shyly and much relieved.

"You know my dear you need a change of environment. Perhaps a short holiday before getting down to more studies," the Professor was certainly treading carefully thought Frederick, as he turned to see his wife Emily's reaction to this conversation.

"Would you now care for a coffee, my dear Mrs Sinclair?" Before Emily had a chance to reply the Professor had beckoned the butler to bring in coffee for the Sinclair's.

Oh you are an artful old devil thought a bemused Frederick. You are biding your time nicely. Frederick knew only too well the difficulties they were to face to persuade Emily to part with yet another daughter. The older she got the more possessive she had become with her daughters.

"Yes, a short holiday, in the autumn perhaps, in Heidelberg before commencing two year's studying at the University there," suggested the Professor.

Marguerite looked a little taken back. "Heidelberg, sir, but we do not know anyone there, sir."

Emily, very uncertain as to where this conversation was leading to and not intending to lose another daughter to the world so soon, quickly announced, "Heidelberg is a city quite unknown to any of our family, my dear Professor."

Hans appeared once more with the coffee, and after placing it on the low table, with a sharp click of the heels left the room. "Do sit down ladies," said a very hospitable Professor. "I will tell you about Heidelberg."

They made themselves comfortable and Marguerite began to feel much more relaxed as she listened enthralled as the Professor told them of this beautiful University city. He told them of how he had friends, by the name of Gerhart, living on the outskirts of the city in the hills. He also mentioned a son and daughter by the name of Emil and Erica.

The mention of a son and daughter made Emily feel much happier with the idea. The Professor certainly made it all sound so attractive. Emily could visualize, should Marguerite go, of perhaps Frederick taking her on a foreign holiday. Yes she began to quite like the idea. As the evening passed, and before the Sinclair's left for home, the Professor had certainly, it would seem, won them over to the idea, and it was more or less agreed that Marguerite should make her visit later that year.

In the cool of the late evening and on her journey home Marguerite felt very much better. She really felt the evening had been a tonic and a great success.

*

Young Sarah, now thirteen-years-old, had been at the Ladies Academy for sometime and was really working well. She was not good at languages like her sisters but enjoyed most of all domestic science. It was her ambition to win a scholarship to the National Training School of Cookery. At this stage she had no wish to study abroad.

Ever since Rachel had vacated her bedroom to go to Paris the two sisters had had their own bedrooms. At this time sadly Nanny left them to look after younger children. Marguerite and Sarah really missed their beloved Nanny, but appreciated that her time and energy was wasted with them now that the nursery was to be used no more.

This June evening Marguerite joined her sister and sat on the edge of the bed and enlightened young Sarah as to where Heidelberg was situated and all about what she had learnt that evening from the Professor. Young Sarah was horrified at the proposal that Marguerite should leave home and go abroad for two years. She had not been too worried when Rachel left for Paris, but she was so close to her sister Marguerite and was broken-hearted. "You cannot possibly leave me all on my own. Oh please don't go Marguerite," pleaded a now tearful Sarah.

"But my dear Sarah I cannot let this opportunity slip away just like that," announced a still excited and determined Marguerite.

"Oh do as you like Maggie," shouted a defiant Sarah, as Marguerite left the room.

BOOK 1

CHAPTER 3

ACROSS THE WATER

Do as you like, Maggie! Marguerite smiled to herself, at the same time she thought that sounds like Rachel not my little sister Sarah.

Plans were soon put in hand and it was agreed that Marguerite should leave for Heidelberg at the end of September. Professor Muller was to accompany Marguerite to his friends and would take a short holiday whilst Marguerite settled in. Once more the dressmaker was kept busy. As the time approached poor Sarah thought the days seemed to rush by. She was certainly not looking forward to being the only daughter under her Mama's eye.

A cold September day, more like late October, saw Marguerite very warmly clad for the long journey and boat crossing. She had seen Dr. Spencer the day before and he had instructed her as to how to care for herself and to take no risks with her health. This was the one thing that was worrying Emily and Frederick and the Doctor had endeavoured to reassure them. On her arrival in Heidelberg the Professor was to introduce Marguerite to a very good physician.

The family were all gathered in the hall; even Cook and Mary had been invited to say good-bye. George was on the pavement awaiting the arrival of the Professor. Was that a screech of wheels? The Professor had arrived in his new motor car to take them to the boat train!

It was now time to say goodbye. Marguerite could not believe what was happening. She hugged Cook, who was by now quite tearful. She turned to Mary, they had become quite close since the accident and occasionally Marguerite had accompanied her to her home. She had got to know Mary's family quite well and shown them many kindnesses.

When Rachel went to Paris, Papa had bought her a set of three brown leather cases with her initials on the lid in gold. Marguerite had thought how fine these cases looked with R.E.S. for Rachel Elizabeth Sinclair. It was now her turn and George was at that moment taking her three cases, bearing her initials M.V.S., Marguerite Victoria Sinclair, to the car. She would certainly treasure these cases for ever.

"Now," she realised that Papa was talking to her, "Now Marguerite, you have everything? Have you all your documents?"

"Yes Papa and thank you once again for my lovely cases," giving Papa a hug.

"Oh that's fine, must keep up the Sinclair name you know. Now look after yourself and don't lose your luggage whatever you do." Did Marguerite detect a break in his voice?

"Oh no Papa, I will take care," giving Papa a final hug. She then turned to Amy. "Good-bye Amy, take care of Mama and Papa for me."
Amy clutched her hands and said, "I will do my best."

It was now Mama's turn. "Marguerite you have left your rug on the chair. You will need that on the boat. Come along now pick it up." Mama with concern handed it to Marguerite. Marguerite had hoped to forget that, but it was not to be. She obediently took it, and then kissed goodbye to Mama.

Sara was admiring the car and would have liked to have travelled to Victoria Station with Marguerite, but thought it might not be wise. "Oh Marguerite, I shall miss you so. Do take care and stay not a moment longer than the two years. Are you listening Maggie?"

"Of course, Sarah, I promise you I will be back in the autumn in two year's time without fail." Marguerite hugged her sister.

"Promise Maggie," pleaded Sarah.

"Yes I promise Sarah," and hugged her sister even tighter.

Last, but not least, George. Shaking hands he wished Miss Marguerite all the very best until they meet again.

The Professor was now pressing Marguerite to hurry or they would miss their train. Everyone now gathered on the steps to wave a final goodbye as this latest new motor car drove out of Belgrave Square. It caused quite a stir in the whole square this second daughter of the Sinclair family leaving home.

They seemed to get to the station in no time at all and were soon making themselves comfortable in the train, the porter having put their cases on the rack above their heads. Between them they seemed to have an enormous amount of luggage. It was not long before the dirty smuts, and the smell of the soot from the engine, was coming in the window and getting in their eyes and making the white kerchief protecting their heads quite dirty. Marguerite got up and attempted to heave on the leather strap to close the window. The Professor came to her rescue and at last they managed to close the window and get the button into the hole. They then returned to their seats and relaxed and watched the passing countryside. Marguerite found the journey to the coast interesting especially passing the Kent orchards. How beautiful they must look in the Spring thought Marguerite.

Eventually the train pulled into Dover and a porter ushered them along and up the gangway to the boat. After their luggage had been deposited Marguerite and the Professor stood and watched as the many and varied passengers came on board.

The journey by boat, although very cold, Marguerite found rather invigorating. Professor Muller suggested it was better to sit up on deck and to take the fresh air. Perhaps Mama was right for once, the travelling rug did prove rather useful and Marguerite was very thankful that she had it with her to tuck round her legs on this long slow crossing of the channel.

The train journey from the French port seemed to go much quicker. The Professor had arranged for them to break their journey in Paris as he wished to introduce Marguerite to this city. She was to experience for the first time the night life of the French capital that she had heard so much about from her sister and she was soon able to put her French to good use. As she stood, that late evening, looking up at the Eiffel Tower she could still not believe that already she was so far from home. The hotel was fantastic and Marguerite felt quite like a Queen with this funny little man as her escort. How she would cope speaking German she didn't know; in her mind she was much better speaking Italian, but at the moment she was coping very well with her French and certainly enjoyed the night spent in this heart of France.

It was a rather tired Marguerite that woke up in Paris the next morning. She was thankful that a Continental breakfast was served, as she was far too tired to cope with eggs and bacon. In no time at all they were ready to leave for the station. Their train journeying was to end in Strasbourg, where they were to be met by Herr Gerhart. Marguerite enjoyed the journey. She found the flat countryside of France rather monotonous but even so enjoyed the various beautiful Chateaux that they passed. As they approached the German border the scenery suddenly changed and was simply perfect. She had never before seen so many vineyards, conifers and pine forests.

*

As arranged Herr Gerhart was at the station to meet them. The station was so clean with masses of geraniums displayed in boxes. Herr Gerhart greeted the Professor most heartedly and with a click of heels bent and kissed Marguerite's hand. She once more felt like Royalty, but where had she heard that click of heels before? Why yes, of course, Hans, the Professor's butler.

It took them about two hours to drive to the home of the Gerhart's. Even though Marguerite had not travelled in one of these motorised vehicles until yesterday she was certainly quite used to them by the end of the long slow drive to Heidelberg. They finally drove through some beautiful gates and up a long drive, and what appeared to Marguerite to be through a pine forest. Soon ahead of them was the most fantastic chateau. They were met at the door by Frau Gerhart, Emil and Erica. Emil appeared to be about the same age as fifteen-year-old Marguerite and Erica about two years younger. They were, in many ways, years older than Marguerite, as that very evening she was to find out.

The chateau was certainly a fantastic place. A magnificent staircase led up to a gallery, which on this first evening, appeared to Marguerite as a picture gallery; there were so many paintings of ancestors on the walls and cases containing all manner of antiques, as in a museum. Marguerite was shown to her room in one of the many turrets overlooking the beautiful pine forests. She had her own bathroom and was very thankful to laze in the bath and to change into some of her new finery.

After a meal of some very strange tasting sausage, which Marguerite covered in the potato and onions so as not to taste, Herr and Frau Gerhart retired with the

Professor, for an evening of recapping of old times, and this left the youngsters to get to know each other.

Young Erica asked Marguerite, 'Rauche sie, Marguerite?"

"Ich rauche nicht," replied a quick Marguerite. She hoped they were not going to speak German the whole evening to her! They were certainly not going to encourage her to smoke, that was one thing of which she was quite sure. Erica had already produced a very elegant cigarette holder and at thirteen-years-old smoked a cigarette with a great show of chauvinism. Whatever would Mama and Papa think?

*

Professor Muller was to make sure that Marguerite had a most interesting three week's holiday. He took her to Cologne, to visit the magnificent cathedral; to Frankfurt; Karlsruhe, an industrial town; and to Stuttgart, beautifully situated amidst the vineyards. He enrolled her at the Academy for Music Studies attached to the Heidelberg University and also introduced her to Professor Brunner. Heidelberg was set amongst wooded hills, the river Neckar running through, and the remains of the castle nestled amongst them. The narrow cobbled streets leading into cobbled squares. Yes, thought Marguerite, I shall enjoy this beautiful unspoilt German city.

As the Professor had promised Mama and Papa, he took her to meet Arzt Mullheim, who assured her he would care for her health whilst she was in Germany. He said she was never to be afraid to contact him at any time.

"I think you should also enter me for a German class," she suggested to the Professor.

"Nein, nein," exclaimed the Professor. "There is no need." Marguerite felt differently as after having been here for nearly three weeks she was becoming very tired of endeavouring to make people understand her. The Professor was adamant that she would cope. "You will learn, my dear, all you need to know for your singing purposes, whilst you are here. Please do not worry, Marguerite. You will be alright, I promise."

But worry Marguerite did. By the time Professor Muller was due to return home Marguerite was beginning to feel quite ill. Was this an inward want of Marguerite's to return home with the Professor. Yes, he thought, poor Marguerite is going to go through a bad spell of homesickness when I have gone. She will recover though. Hard work will soon take over.

*

Back in England letters began to arrive from across the Channel. The first letter told the family of the exciting journey and wonderful night in Paris. The second full of where she had visited with Professor Muller. Then there was a time without letters, but never mind their dear friend Professor Muller would soon be home once more with news. Sarah hated not having Marguerite at home, but she overcame her loneliness by joining Cook and Mary in the kitchen, putting into practice what she was learning in her domestic science lessons.

*

The first few weeks, after Professor Muller left Germany, Marguerite was very homesick indeed and could not put pen to paper. She used to lie awake at night recapping all of her past life and many a night she was to cry herself to sleep. Oh how she wished Sarah was with her. She wore herself out so crying that she had to succumb to paying a visit to Arzt Mullheim. He was a kindly Doctor and knew immediately what was wrong with Marguerite. He took the chance to examine her thoroughly and asked her to call again, by which time, as he only knew too well she would be more settled and much better.

Marguerite soon got into a routine, leaving for her music studies early in the day and enjoying the long lunchtime breaks with fellow students. Instead of returning home every evening, to the Gerhart's chateau, she would stay with her new friends joining in the many activities on offer in this busy University city.

In all good time, as the Professor had prophesied, work was to overcome her distress. She had many arias to learn and many practices had to be carried out at home. Emil sat, much to Marguerite's embarrassment, goggled eyed listening to her. She wished he would move away, but she did not know enough German to express her indignation. Her music lessons were far in advance to what she had covered with the Professor at home. Professor Brunner was very kind and patient. It had also become necessary for her to further her Italian studies, as so many of the musical scores were in this language, and later she was to be so thankful for these extra lessons.

She was introduced by the Gerhart's to many people and was to travel around Germany singing at many events, which was good for building up her confidence. First of all it was a great ordeal, but in time she got used to it. She thoroughly enjoyed the beer festivals on the banks of the Rhine. She was very shy indeed at the first few she went to, but in being approached to dance, by some of the rotund Germans, she could see the funny side of two fatties dancing together. What a sight we must make, thought a smiling Marguerite.

Mama and Papa planned to visit Germany for a holiday whilst she was there, but for business reasons were unable to go in 1913, but they planned to spend the last month of Marguerite's time with her. This she looked forward to as she had so much to show them.

These days, when her studies permitted, she endeavoured to write newsy letters home and time passed by very quickly. At the beginning of July 1914 she said a sad farewell to her fellow students and promised to keep in contact with many of them. During the following weeks she was kept busy with numerous appointments, and as the time for Mama and Papa's holiday approached she began to wonder, perhaps hopefully, whether Sarah would accompany them. She longed to see her younger sister again.

BOOK 1

CHAPTER 4

IN ENEMY TERRITORY

It was the 4th August 1914; by now Marguerite had convinced herself that her sister, Sarah, would accompany Mama and Papa at the end of the week for their long awaited visit. How she longed to see Sarah and to introduce her to the delights of Heidelburg. She was spending the day in Frankfurt, and had just come out of a restaurant and was on her way to a singing appointment when her eyes suddenly focused on a placard saying 'Great Britain declares war on Germany!'

Marguerite momentarily froze as it sunk in as to what she was reading. She had read the recent papers but in her young mind had not appreciated that it would come to war. Papa was to say later why was she not advised to leave before? Her instinct told her to run away and hide, like a hunted animal, but she did no such thing, she made tracks for the station and the train for Heidelberg, and what she now considered as home. She sat in the train very very conscious of the fact that she was a young English girl in an alien country.

On arriving at Heidelburg she quickly alighted, and, if her obesity had allowed her, would have run all the way home. When she arrived, by now feeling very hot, tired and sticky, she found Professor Brunner, Arzt Mullheim and Professor Braun, the University Lecturer of Geography, all gathered in the main hall talking quietly to Herr and Frau Gerhart. Frau Gerhart ran up to Marguerite, "Oh I am so pleased to see you, my dear Marguerite," she exclaimed in excited German. "Come and join us, we have many things to discuss!"

Marguerite was longing to have a bath and to change, but they all insisted that she should immediately sit with them. Marguerite looked with concern at all these people of distinction gathered here.

Kindly Professor Brunner explained to Marguerite that she must leave Germany immediately and that Professor Braun had come along to work out the best possible route for her to take. She had wondered why he was there! They felt that her German would let her down - just as Marguerite thought, hadn't she told Professor Muller that she should have extra German lessons, now this was proof! Nevertheless, she was quite heartened when they went on to say that as her Italian was excellent they had decided that she should travel as an Italian folk singer, making her way home by a devious route. She was to have her hair blackened, as her fair hair would give her away - oh why did she not have dark hair like her sisters', was Marguerite's immediate thoughts. As it was summer her travelling rug would act as a coat or something to sleep under at night - sleep under at night she questioned, she had never camped before, having been pampered since young. This travelling rug could also be adapted for use whilst performing. God bless, Mama, thought Marguerite, it was she who insisted that I brought the rug. Her mind travelled back to the scene in the hallway at home on her departure and Sarah's insistence that Marguerite should not stay a moment longer than two years. What a long time ago that seemed now. Much to her chagrin she was told that she should only travel with hand luggage and definitely not with any of her initialled luggage. Much to her horror they went on to say that this luggage would be disposed of immediately she had left, so as not to arouse suspicion should an inspection be carried out on the chateau.

It was planned that Arzt Mullheim would accompany her in his pony and trap for the first part of the journey. If they were stopped, being a Doctor, he would say he was visiting his patients, and hopefully they would not question Marguerite. It was instilled into her that she was to forget any German she knew and only speak in Italian and she was to take on the new name of Congettina Spirotti. Marguerite had great difficulty in keeping up with their plans, which were all discussed in German.

She finally managed to get a word in, and asked, "Will you please tell me when do we leave?"

"Why tonight, Marguerite!" they answered in one accord.

"Tonight?" exclaimed an astonished Marguerite. Herr Gerhart explained that it was best that she left immediately. She should not say a word to Herr Emil or Fraulein Erica about the plans, she was to just disappear. In fact an excuse was soon found to send Emil and Erica away for the evening.

After further discussion it was time for Marguerite to go with Frau Gerhart to prepare for this unknown journey.

*

In London Marguerite's last letter arrived saying how she was looking forward to Mama and Papa's holiday and how she hoped Sarah would accompany them. She said how she was so looking forward to returning home with them.

Frederick was becoming more and more concerned that with the present climate of news it would be too risky for them to take a holiday and that Marguerite should return home immediately. It was only the day before that he had agreed with John, in the office, to write to the Gerharts to this effect. It was, therefore, a very shocked Frederick that heard that Great Britain had gone to war with Germany. Just why had he not done something about the turn of events sooner? But as everyone was to say who would have expected England to go to war with Germany over a Servia and Austrio-Hungarian matter. These countries seemed so far away from England. Indeed the whole family and household were struck dumb by the news and they felt so helpless. Frederick tried immediately to

40

find ways of getting information through to Marguerite but to no avail. They had no idea as to what she was planning to do or even if she was still in Heidelberg?

*

Meanwhile, Marguerite up in her room at the chateau looked out at the pine forest for the last time, whilst awaiting the drying of her now black hair. She was deep in thought her mind going back to her arrival in this room and this chateau; suddenly she turned and looked across at her suitcases, still placed neatly in a pile; she went across and fingered the gold lettering and tears came to her eyes. It was like leaving behind part of the family; M.V.S., she shaped the letters with her fingers. Oh it was so unfair Rachel had her cases, as good as new, back in Harrow, and what a long way away that seemed at the present moment. Now she was to be Congettina Spirotti, and she wondered for how long? She must keep saying to herself 'Congettina Spirotti, Congettina Spirotti'.

She was to take as little as possible with her, only what she could carry comfortably. Fortunately it was summer, but a change of clothing was a must. She still felt the heat so, and still her weight was her main problem. She was to see Arzt Mullheim downstairs in Herr Gerhart's study once more before they left, and he was to advise her about caring for herself under whatever conditions she should meet. She had also to include in her bag Italian folk music, to make her new identity more realistic.

The next two hours passed so quickly and it seemed she had been back in her room hardly any time at all before she was once more called. Frau Gerhart checked her things and sent her back upstairs to collect a spare pair of shoes. She was to be so grateful for this reminder and her German hostess's foresight.

It was now quite dark. Arzt Mullheim had been back home and collected his medical bag, so that he would not be under suspicion if they should be stopped. He drew up in his trap. Once out into the open countryside and away from prying ears he would outline to Marguerite the route they would take and where and when he would be leaving her to her own devises. She shook hands with Professor Brunner and thanked him for his music teaching over the last two years. He said it had been an honour and she should be very proud of her voice. The other Professor had by now left. Lastly she said goodbye to Herr and Frau Gerhart, whose home she had shared and with whom she now felt so close. As she got into the trap she turned and took a last look at this beautiful chateau where she had at first been so homesick, but latterly so happy.

"Gute Nacht, Marguerite, and Auf Wiedersehen." Herr and Frau Gerhart stood and waved until the pony and trap was out of sight.

*

Marguerite could not believe what was happening to her. She found herself repeating in time to the beat of the pony's hooves 'Congettina Spirotti, Congettina Spirotti'. She suddenly realized that Arzt Mullheim was talking. "Now Fraulein

41

Marguerite I am able to stay with you until tomorrow midday, then I shall have to return to my patients, it will then be up to you. Remember Marguerite you are an Italian singer from Milan earning your keep, during the summer season, by singing at the beer festivals. You speak hardly any German. Now who are you Fraulein Marguerite?"

"Congettina Spirotti from Milan," answered a quick Marguerite.

"Correct, from now till we part you are Congettina to me, understand?"

"Ja, Arzt Mullheim," sighed a rather weary Marguerite.

"It has been agreed that, if questioned, Herr and Frau Gerhart will say that you left for home in July at the end of your studies, holidaying on the Rhine on your way." The Doctor certainly seemed to have it all planned for Marguerite.

"Is that where we are making for now?" questioned Marguerite.

"No Professor Braun thought that inadvisable and suggested that you keep away from that area and definitely away from large cities and towns. You are to travel through country keeping in the valleys of the mountains until reaching Holland. Professor Braun thinks it will then be safe for you to travel by train through to Rotterdam. It will then be up to you Congettina to get yourself to England." replied the Doctor, smiling with encouragement as he used her new name for the first time.

"So where are we going now?" asked Marguerite.

"I have a friend who runs a country club at the foot of the Vogelsberg. I will ask him to give you some practice there before handing you on to your first beer festival," announced the Doctor.

"Thank you." Marguerite thought that seemed very favourable.

"I believe you enjoyed visiting some of the beer festivals on the Rhine last summer, Congettina?" asked the Doctor.

"Yes, they were great fun," answered a thoughtful Marguerite. She smiled to herself, if only the Doctor realised how the thought of getting up and singing at one of these festivals simply horrified her, but if she was to get home she supposed she would have to overcome this fit of shyness.

They were now gathering up speed and the pony was trotting well and in no time at all Marguerite was sound asleep. Arzt Mullheim glanced down now and again at his sleeping charge and thought to himself I wonder if you realise Marguerite of the possible traumas you are going to have to face. I only hope your health will see you through! He knew only too well of the weakness of this young girl's heart. Suddenly Marguerite was aware of the screech of wheels as they came to a stop. In her half sleep she was conscious of a number of German voices.

The Doctor was saying, "Come, come I must get to my patient. I have shown you my papers!" They were then on the move again. Marguerite by now fully awake and very stiff, hot and sticky, realized that she had passed the hours of darkness asleep and dawn had now broken.

"What was that all about?" asked Marguerite.

"A chateau nearby has been broken into during the late evening and the police are stopping and questioning everyone. I showed them my papers. I said you were on your way to an engagement and they seemed quite satisfied," answered a quite confident Doctor.

Papers? Marguerite thought. What about my documents? She ventured to ask the Doctor "If I am questioned about documents, or asked to show them, what should I say?"

"Congettina, you apologise, in Italian remember, and say that you are a rather forgetful Italian and travelling around so much you unfortunately left them at your last assignment." The Doctor was certainly full of clever ideas, thought Marguerite.

"Tell me, Doctor, should I speak any German? I mean, how do I ask for lifts or as to my whereabouts?" Marguerite had many questions going through her mind.

"Be careful, Congettina, speak only broken German, remember at all times you are Italian," warned the Doctor.

After a while they pulled up at a small roadside cafe and partook of a good breakfast. Marguerite still hated the German sausage, but just the same was rather hungry and ate heartedly. On leaving the cafe Marguerite took a sugar lump out of her pocket and fed it to the pony, just like old times.

Soon they were on their way and passing a sign to Darmstadt, and before long Marguerite noticed that they were only a few miles from Frankfurt. She could hardly believe that it was only yesterday that she had stood in the centre of this beautiful German city and read 'Great Britain is at war with Germany'. It was not long before they could see the peaks of the Volgesberg range, possibly still quite a few miles away. On this warm summer's day the early morning heat haze time and time again obscured the fine view. Although by now Marguerite would be pleased to arrive at their destination, the thought of what tomorrow would bring, to say the least, was a little disturbing.

*

It was about mid-morning when they arrived at a country house, sheltered from the heat of the day by the mountain-side behind. A number of youngsters were strolling in the grounds. Franze and Olga Smidt met them at the door. "Well what a surprise, if it isn't our dear friend Fritz Mullheim. What brings you here?" Fritz and Franz shook hands warmly.

"Meet my friend Congettina Spirotti, a young Italian folk singer." Franz with the usual click of the heels welcomed Marguerite most warmly. Olga stood in the background, and Marguerite could not help but notice that she was not very welcoming. "Franz may I have a quiet word?" asked the Doctor in an urgent voice.

"Certainly, Fritz, come this way," turning to his wife he said, "Olga, take good care of our little Italian singer."

Olga quite coldly invited Marguerite to step this way. She showed her into a large drawing room where a number of people sat around. After showing her to a seat Olga seemed to disappear from sight. Marguerite looked around and noticed that at the one end of this spacious heavily panelled room was a small stage. She picked up a newspaper from the table in front of her, enabling her to study the folk around. Hiding behind the newspaper she felt less conspicious. Olga had certainly made her feel quite nervous. She realised that, although the people walking around the grounds appeared young, these people were definitely of a mixed age range.

It seemed quite a while before the Doctor and Franz Smidt appeared and during that time she did not set eyes on Olga, most strange. Franze Smidt apologised when he saw that Congettina was left alone. He beckoned a young girl, evidently a waitress, to fetch a cold buffet, and showed Congettina to a seat at a table where a number of people of her own age were gathered. Congettina found herself relaxing once more in the company of others and for a time enjoyed her meal, but before long her thoughts already turned to the fact that her friend the Doctor would soon be leaving her to her own resources. She must endeavour to speak with him alone to enquire as to whether he had enlightened his friend Franz Smidt as to her situation. Yes she must certainly do this at the next opportunity. What was that, what was the Doctor saying? 'Auf Wiedersehen?'

Marguerite realised that the Doctor was standing up and about to take his leave, he shook hands with Franz Smidt. "Thank you, Franz, and Auf Wiedersehen." Turning to Marguerite he smiled encouragingly and in very good Italian said, "Chow, Congettina. Sing well, and when you feel you are ready to leave here my dear friend Franz will give you a letter of introduction to friends on Lake Eder, near Frankenburg."

Before Marguerite realised what was happening she found herself saying, "Chow and thank you," and now it was her turn to stand at the door and wave goodbye as Arzt Fritz Mullheim started on his journey back to Heidelburg.

Her thoughts were far away when she suddenly realised Herr Smidt was speaking to her. "Hildergard will show you to your room. I have put you up in the attic, so if you wish to practice your singing you will not be disturbed." Marguerite followed Franz as he went to find Hildergard. They soon located her in the small ante-kitchen off the drawing room. Hildergard was the young girl who had prepared her lunch. She was only too willing to show Congettina to her room, this was up a winding staircase at the back of the house. Soon Marguerite was standing in a small very hot modest room, the small window hardly letting in any light or air.

At last Marguerite was on her own and she sat on the bed and suddenly wept both from exhaustion at climbing the steep staircase and also from a build-up of nerves from this sudden swift change to her life.

*

Fritz Mullheim had been at University in Hamburg with Franz Smidt. Franz as a student was a little wild. He enjoyed drinking and women. This was soon to prove to be his downfall, his fellow students went on to qualify in the medical profession but Franz soon fell by the wayside. Amongst the women he met was

Olga Munz the daughter of a General in the German Army. He felt he was on to a good thing, gave up his training, and was soon married. Franz built up quite a name for himself in the running of country clubs. He became well known in the nobility circles. Unbeknown to Fritz Mullheim, his friend's marriage was turning sour. Olga could not settle in the country and Franz still fancied women of all types. Olga longed for the days of her youth in Hamburg and would go away for long spells at a time, back to her old haunts. At this particular time she had just returned to a blazing row and had been standing cooling down, looking out of the window, when Fritz and Marguerite turned into the drive. It was sheer curiosity that took her to the door behind her estranged husband.

*

Marguerite immediately detected Olga's coldness, but not knowing the real reason for this she took an instant dislike to the woman and had already decided that she was not going to be happy in this house. A great wave of homesickness once more overcame her. She cried and cried until she realised that this was not going to do her health any good and to feel like this was not going to get her back to England. Fortunately no one disturbed her and after about two hours she managed to control herself and crept out of the room to find somewhere to wash. Perhaps she thought, looking around her as she washed herself down, it is better in these sparse conditions that it is mid-summer and not mid-winter. She changed into her one and only fresh attire and folded her travelling clothes carefully, as who was to know how long before they were to be needed. Her wash had certainly made her feel decidedly better and now she felt confident enough to venture back downstairs saying to herself as she went - remember Marguerite you are Italian.

Marguerite settled once more in the drawing room and was soon asked to join a group at an adjoining table. They took afternoon tea together. Marguerite became very weary from having to keep up a pretence of not understanding the German spoken, quite the opposite situation to what she had been accustomed to during the last few months when her confidence in her German had at last surfaced, and, of course, although she had slept sitting in the cart it had not been a restful sleep. After some time Herr Smidt appeared and beckoned to Marguerite to join him. Taking Marguerite's hand he said, "Congettina I would like you to entertain us with your folk songs later this evening!"

Marguerite was somewhat taken back as she had hoped to have had time to adjust herself to the situation. She also did not like the way his thumb was moving on her hand. Until this time Marguerite's experience with men had only been from the other side of the desk. She pretended to cough and pulled her hand away. "Later this evening Herr Smidt, so soon? Asked a tired and concerned Marguerite, at the same time making sure that he could not again reach her hand.

"We have visitors, Congettina, that need to be entertained," answered a cajoling Franz.

"Oh very well," answered a tired Congettina. "If you will excuse me, I must go and practice before dinner." She hurried from the room fearing that he would follow her. She had summed him up already. No she was definitely not going to be happy here. As she climbed the stairs she once more began to wonder as to the whereabouts of Olga.

On reaching her small room she folded and refolded her fringed travelling rug and draped it around herself endeavouring to make herself appear more like a folk singer. She flung it down, deciding to dispense with it on such a hot day. She got her music out and selected half a dozen songs which she began to practice. Fortunately her recent studies had covered the lighter side of music and the songs from different countries. Suddenly after a while there was a fierce knocking from below. What could that be, surely nothing to do with her. She went on singing. The knocking became louder. She ventured out on to the landing and to the top of the stairs, leant over the banisters and came face to face with a furious Olga.

Marguerite thought quickly - I am Congettina and do not understand. She went down a few steps and said in very quick and excitable Italian, "What is it you want Frau Smidt?" She knew very well what Olga was saying, she wanted her to stop singing, but if Olga could be unfriendly so could she. She shrugged her shoulders, as if not understanding, and went back up to her room and continued her practice.

After a while it was time to return downstairs to find the dining room, although her appetite was fast fading. She wondered for how long she would have to entertain this evening and what time this would commence. At the moment all she wanted to do was to relieve herself of her tight corsets and to have an early night.

On entering the dining room she felt she wanted to get lost in the crowd and she sincerely hoped that Herr Smidt would not spot her arrival. She certainly did not wish to join him at his table for a meal, she could not bear the thought of sharing the table with him or that terrible wife of his. She hurried to join the group she had had tea with and during the meal she began to relax. The food was not exceptional but she enjoyed the company of her new-found friends and for the time being forgot what lay ahead.

After dinner the men retired to the library for port whilst the ladies returned to the drawing room. Marguerite's attention was drawn to the quartet who were gathering on the small stage. They began to play quietly and Marguerite sat listening to the music, ignoring the chatter around her. Suddenly she felt a tap on her shoulder, Herr Smidt was inviting her to join him at his table. Marguerite had been so lost in the music that she had not realised that the gentlemen had rejoined the ladies. She reluctantly followed him to his table and Olga gave her a very cold greeting. Before long Herr Smidt was announcing to the guests how fortunate they were to have a young Italian folk singer to entertain them. As Marguerite approached the small dais she seemed to be in a dream, but soon the love of her music took over.

That first evening was to be the forerunner of a very exhausting three weeks for Marguerite, but her main worry during this time was keeping Herr Smidt in his place. This was a side of life that Marguerite had never experienced before in her sheltered life. In Edwardian England it was still very much the custom for young ladies to be chaperoned - Marguerite had certainly been flung in at the deep end. Many an evening was to end with Herr Smidt in a drunken stupor, and Marguerite was certainly very frightened of him and was quite sure that Fritz Mullheim could not have known that his friend had become a drunkard, as she was sure if he had known he would not have left her in his charge. She became very deft at returning to her room at the end of her performance. During this time Olga kept a very low profile and had not repeated the knocking episode.

The month of August was drawing to a close and Marguerite was beginning to think it was time she approached Herr Smidt, during one of his sober moods, for her introductory letter to the Beer Festival on Lake Eder. She would at least be moving nearer to hopefully getting out of Germany. She certainly did not seem to hear very much about the war in this quiet part of Germany. Marguerite was not sure when to broach the subject, but she made up her mind that she must seek him out the next day at lunch time. No sooner had she made that decision when she was thwarted.

That evening Marguerite left the stage and as usual made straight for the narrow back staircase. Oh no, whom should be blocking her way, lolling on the stairs in his usual drunken state, Herr Smidt "Congettina, my own little Italian. Come sit and console me." He had hardly uttered these words when he made a grab at Marguerite and pulled her down on to his lap and no matter how she struggled from his tight drunken grip he held her to him. He immediately began searching with his hands as this naive young English girl had never known before. She fought with all her might and at last managed to drag herself away and up the stairs to her room. She locked the door and collapsed in a heap on the floor.

After a while she recovered sufficiently to find the medication Arzt Mullheim had given her to take should she feel the necessity. She clawed the remaining clothes from her and vowed never to wear them again. She would wait until the house was in darkness and leave. She dared not yet leave the sanctity of her room to even wash. In her stark nakedness she collapsed on to the bed. Was it the medication or sheer exhaustion that caused Marguerite to fall into a deep sleep? She suddenly awoke shaking all over and to her horror found that dawn had already broken. She wrapped herself in her travelling rug, once more blessing Mama's foresight in making her take it with her to Germany. Gingerly she opened the door and made for the wash room. Oh, the bliss of feeling clean again and to be rid of that vile liquor smell, which she felt had enveloped her.

On returning to her room she quickly dressed into her travelling things and clutching her now nearly empty bag nervously crept down the stairs and made for the back door. Her hands being small but fat she had great difficulty in undoing the bolts on the heavy door, but at long last they gave way and she dragged it open, hoping that the heavy creaking would not disturb anyone. She hurried as quickly as she could across the grounds, praying that no-one would look out of their bedroom windows - perhaps they would think she was just going for an early morning walk, she hoped so!

*

Marguerite's immediate plan was to make for the lower mountainside of the Volgesburg range. She would endeavour to find one of the many cattle shelters that she knew were scattered on the mountainside, rest and gather her thoughts and allow herself time to plan her escape route. Whatever would Mama and Papa think of her wandering on her own out on the edge of a mountain? It was just not done for young ladies of this era to walk out alone, especially at this time of the morning.

In her exhaustion from the recent happenings the distant mountains seemed to get further away instead of nearer, but she plodded on and on, and was thankful that she was distancing herself from the memories of the night before. She was thankful for the coolness of the morning air, and after what seemed like hours, but fortunately for Marguerite before the heat of the midday sun, she finally reached an empty hut. She gathered what straw she could find to cover the damp floor, laid her rug down, sat down and was relieved to be able to unlace her shoes and rest. She was much relieved to think that Frau Gerhart had sent her back up to her room to fetch another pair of shoes, these certainly rested her feet for a while. She realised she was rather hungry, but, of course, until this moment had not thought of bringing food. She became hotter and hotter as she inwardly panicked as to what her next move should be, but at least she had found this shelter for her midday siesta.

After the heat of the day had past she decided to move further on to widen her distance from the dreaded Smidts. Her steps became slower and slower as she trudged on and on until the early evening making sure to keep to the lower mountain paths, her long heavy serge skirt getting dirtier and dirtier from the dust of the path and her hunger now beginning to tell. She told herself that she must not get lost in the late summer mist on this mountainside.

At long last another hut came into sight. Her hunger became intense. On looking around this quite spotless hut she noticed a milking pail and stool. Could she milk a cow? Yes, if hungry you can do anything Marguerite! The cows must have thought that is what she had come for as they pushed and pushed and shoved each other to get nearer to her. Where to start? Common sense prevailed. She left the hut with her milking stool and pail and found what looked like the gentlest cow and placed her stool in position and endeavoured to balance her fat self on it. Oh thought Marguerite if only I was not so fat and how much easier it would be to have a smock on instead of these most unsuitable clothes, but she certainly did weigh the small stool into position, and fortunately she had chosen a placid cow, which stood quite still. At first not much luck but with perseverance the milk flowed and Marguerite's hunger and thirst grew. The milk from one cow was quite sufficient for her needs, but she had great difficulty in getting the other cows to move away to enable her to carry the milk back safely to the hut. She shoved and shoved with all her might thankful that she had recovered some of her strength from her lunch time siesta; finally she made it back to the hut and closed the door quickly. Oh for the taste of that delicious milk, but first, whilst the milk cooled, she must make her bed. She was once more thankful for the summer weather, at least she could lie on her rug as her clothes would keep her warm; she was tempted to undress but hesitated, perhaps it would be best not to just in case anyone should pass by. At long last she was ready to drink; she tipped the pail up to her mouth spilling some of the milk down her front, she decided it was safer to place her cupped hands into the pail and she drank in this way, at least she would not waste any of the milk. She smiled to herself as she thought of how the milk should be good for the skin of her podgy hands. Milk straight from the cow, how delicious; never would she forget this experience. She wondered whatever she would have done if she had not found the pail and stool, she must be more careful in future to think of what she was to eat. She would certainly have to make for a village soon and buy some supplies. Fortunately Franz Smidt had paid her for her singing and she had a small amount of reichmarks. After a good sleep she must plan her route and her days with care. By now quite satisfied she lay down and, listening to the sound of the cows and their bells jingling in the night air, she was soon relaxed and fast asleep.

It was quite light and bright when she eventually awoke. She drank some more milk and was just tying the laces of her shoes when something drew her attention to the outside world. Was that her imagination or was that a voice? Marguerite sat up and glanced towards the door, that was most certainly a man's voice she had heard and gradually it was coming nearer. She froze with fright. She gathered the rug around her, at this moment, the memories of the past few days very close. A fair mop of hair appeared through the open top of the stable-like door.

"Guten morgan, Fraulein," said a deep voice.

Marguerite answered shyly, "Chow."

"You are not German?" questioned this fair young man.

"I am sorry, I do not understand." Marguerite was now careful to speak very poor German.

"Deutsch?" questioned the young man once more.

"Nein, Italienisch," replied Marguerite.

"You drink milk from my cows?" asked this young man, looking over at the now nearly empty pail.

"Sorry," nervously replied Marguerite, wondering what reason she was going to give him.

The young man opened the door and came in making Marguerite extremely nervous. "Fraulein, do not be afraid, tell me your name."

Marguerite hesitated, she was not at all sure how much to divulge, on the otherhand perhaps this would be her only means of finding her way through to Holland. "Congettina Spirotti, Herr...." at this point she hesitated.

"My name is Hans Peter," quickly answered this German, coming to attention with that hateful click of the heels that only Germans could do. "When I came last night to milk my cows you were fast asleep. I did not disturb you."

Marguerite pretended not to understand, but was slightly taken a back to think that he had visited her before without her knowing of his presence. How fortunate it was, she thought, that she had not undressed; she blushed at the thought. He thought she had not understood and now spoke in very slow precise

German. "My wife, Christa, says you come to our house. You would like?" questioned Hans Peter.

"Danke, Herr Hans Peter," replied Marguerite. She returned to tying her shoes and went to roll up her rug, meanwhile much to Marguerite's chagrin Hans Peter tipped away the rest of the milk. What a waste of good milk, thought Marguerite, I could have finished drinking that.

"You must wait awhile, I have my cows to milk," cautioned Hans Peter. Marguerite smiled at the mention of milking.

"I help?" she heard herself offering.

It was now Hans Peter's turn to say "Danke, Fraulein Congettina, that would be a great help." By this time the cows were becoming impatient and Hans Peter began to calm them, calling them each by name. She now knew who he was talking to when she heard his voice as he came on to the mountainside, he was calling to them.

Hans Peter soon had her organized and Marguerite could not believe how relaxed she felt as on this glorious summer morning she helped to slowly milk the cows. She thought what harm could she come to with someone who was so gentle with his animals, and had he not mentioned a wife? After some time they finished milking and Hans Peter was showing Marguerite how to carry two pails of milk held by a piece of wood across her shoulders; she was just thinking that she would never make it back to the farm without spilling the lot, when much to her relief she saw a young girl coming up the path, Hans Peter shouted a welcome to his wife.

He introduced Congettina to Christa and Marguerite took an immediate liking to this friendly young girl, who could not be much older than herself. As they went down the mountainside, Hans Peter and Christa carrying the milk with such agility, Marguerite in her mind was warning herself to remember she was Congettina Spirotti an Italian folk singer. It was at this moment that she remembered her music left behind on the piano in that dreaded house. That meant the end of the Italian folk singer.

Marguerite was far away with her thoughts when she realised she was being spoken to. "You are on holiday in Germany?" asked Christa.

"Holiday?" hesitantly repeated Marguerite once more intending to give the impression of knowing little German, but Christa took the answer to be yes on holiday.

"You are on a walking holiday, yes?" Christa went on to ask.

"I go to friends on the border with Holland." Marguerite found herself replying, once more using broken German.

"Where?" asked Hans Peter.

Marguerite hesitated. "Near Munster," Marguerite answered. It was the first place that came into her mind.

"That is where I come from," announced an excited Christa. "Near the border you say. Would it be Gronau, Ahaus, Bucholt?" she questioned.

"Right on the border," carefully answered Marguerite, at the same time thinking she might learn a great deal by this conversation.

"Ah, Gronau," replied Hans Peter.

"Yes, yes, that is it." Marguerite by this time was thinking I must remember Gronau! Gronau! She kept repeating the name to herself and was so intent in remembering the name that she hardly took in what Christa was saying.

"It is a long way from here Congettina," warned Christa.

"I know, but I am in no hurry," answered Marguerite, barely realising what she had said.

"But there is a war on, Congettina. Did you not know?" asked Hans Peter.

"A war?" asked Marguerite pretending to not quite understand.

"Yes," answered Hans Peter. "England has declared war against us," announced Hans Peter. From his tone Marguerite could not tell whether he was bitter about this or not. Marguerite showed surprise at this news.

By this time they had come down from the mountain and as they turned a corner there in front of them was a small stone cottage surrounded by broken down outhouses. Pointing Hans Peter announced, "Our small farm." Marguerite smiled with relief as she was not sure whether it was the hot summer weather or what, but she was now feeling very poorly and was much relieved when Hans Peter said 'our farm'.

*

Hans Peter and Christa had not long been married. They had managed to obtain this small derelict farm at quite a reasonable rent, but it certainly needed a lot of time and money spent on it. The announcement that Germany had gone to war with England was a great blow to this young couple starting out on married life together. Hans Peter knew that conscription had taken place at the end of July, but, by lying low at his farm, he hoped to delay the necessity for his departure into the German army, he did not wish to leave his dear young wife so far from her family in Munster and had he not his farm to look after?

Christa showed Marguerite into the cottage, whilst Hans Peter took care of the pails of milk, but hardly had Marguerite entered the small sitting room when she collapsed in pain. She was conscious of Christa calling out "Congettina, Congettina, what is the matter?" Christa rushed out and fetched Hans Peter and he carried her to the sofa. This sofa she was not to leave for a week or two. Of course she should have known better she had never been able to digest milk, owing to her medical condition, but in her desperation of thirst and hunger this fact had not entered her head, and she had drunk a pail full of milk straight from the cow. She was sick for days. How fortunate she was to have her own medication, prescribed by Arzt Mulheim; because she had these she was able to dissuade Hans Peter and Christa from calling a doctor.

Marguerite had a hard task explaining the reason for carrying so few personal effects. On explaining that she had lost her luggage with her documents - oh how she wished for her beautiful set of engraved cases - she pointed out that that was the reason for not remembering the address of her friends, Christa kindly went shopping for her and bought her a change of clothing, including a new skirt, a perky jacket and a hat. Marguerite was to often wonder whether they ever realised that she was an English girl on the run, but they never showed their suspicions.

*

At home in England the weeks were going by. It was now the middle of September and no matter how Frederick tried he could get no news through from Germany. Professor Muller, being of German extraction, had to keep a very low profile, so in no way could he help.

At this stage of the war, Frederick being over forty-five-years of age, did not feel the necessity to volunteer for war service, but after a few weeks the staff at Bedford Square became smaller. George decided that it was his duty to go and fight for his country. What could the Sinclair's say but to shake hands and wish him a safe return. Mary had already left to join her sisters working in a munition factory near their home, and her brothers, who were old enough, had already volunteered for service.

Sarah, still at the Academy, was so worried about Marguerite that she just could not get down to her studies for the College of Cookery. She decided instead to take first aid classes, so that she would be ready to help should the need arise. Although at present all they seemed to do at these classes was to roll bandages, but at least it kept her occupied. She endeavoured to reassure Mama and Papa of Marguerite's safe return. Had Marguerite not promised her that she would return without fail in the autumn of 1914. She tried to impress this on Mama and Papa, but really she was not so sure now that she herself could believe this.

With young Mary's departure Amy and Cook shared the work between them, and Mama, much to her anguish had to help with some of the housework. This was something she had not been used to. Oh, she so wished that Marguerite was home to take some of the burden off of her. On mentioning this to Frederick he was a little taken back, to say the least, had Emily really no idea of the trials and tribulations Marguerite was possibly encountering at this very moment. His wife was certainly very selfish. He dare not tell her of his fears for his second daughter.

Rachel was, at this time, expecting her first baby, and Edward was suffering agonies in trying to decide whether he should leave his young expectant wife at home, alone in Harrow, whilst he enlisted. He knew only too well that that is what it would come to in the end.

*

Three weeks were to pass and Marguerite began to feel stronger. Hans Peter had gone to market and Marguerite and Christa had spent an enjoyable day. They had made some fresh dainty curtains for the cottage. Marguerite encouraged Christa in this hand sewing. Marguerite begun to feel quite attached to this old derelict farm cottage. She had also taken the chance to wash and re-dye her hair as she still did not know how long she was to stay as an Italian and her hair began to show signs of returning to its normal colour.

On Hans Peter's return he did not call out as usual, and on hearing heavy footsteps Christa and Marguerite looked out of the window to see Hans Peter coming into the farmyard escorted on each side by what Marguerite presumed to be military police. They escorted Hans Peter to the front door, as Marguerite, realising that it was not very easy to make yourself scarce in a small cottage and that something was seriously wrong, made a discreet get away through the back door and up on to the near mountainside. By now the weather was much cooler and fortunately Marguerite was feeling much better. She gave Hans Peter and Christa about an hour on their own, hoping that the military police would have left, before cautiously returning to what she considered was her temporary home.

Marguerite was to learn that on going into town, on this market day, Hans Peter had been approached by some soldiers and asked for his Army papers; not being able to produce these he was asked for his reasons for not yet being in the Army, but not being able to reassure them he had been taken away for questioning. He had been roughly handled and brought home to collect his belongings. Christa was in tears as she told Marguerite that in her absence they had been discussing what to do and had regretfully decided to give up their farm, and Christa would return home to her family in Munster for the duration of the war. She could, therefore, give Marguerite a lift to Munster, if she so wished.

Of course Marguerite was very shocked to hear of Hans Peter's sudden departure and only thankful that she had made herself scarce, so as not to bring more trouble to this young couple. She was so sad to think of these newly weds having to give up their home after such a short time, but she was only too pleased to accept the lift to Munster. Hans Peter had had to leave it in Christa's hands to sell the animals and to dispose of any unnecessary items of furniture and to pack their belongings.

The next two weeks were really hectic. It was sad to see the new curtains taken down so soon, they had so transformed this small cottage. Christa folded them away carefully and promised Marguerite that they would be used in the years to come. Christa made several trips to market; Marguerite had made her excuses for not accompanying her, in her mind she felt it safer for both of them for her to lie low at the farm. Gradually all the animals were sold. The best farm cart was kept, together with the most reliable horse, for the journey to Munster. The day before departure was spent loading this to almost overflowing. It was planned that Christa and Marguerite would take it in turns to sit up front. A seat was made amongst the bedding, squashed in around the pieces of furniture and wedding presents. This made a comfortable, if somewhat lumpy seat. To be sure Christa and Marguerite would be very thankful when it was their turn to ride in the comfort of up front.

It was indeed two sad young girls that left this old farm cottage on a cold October day in 1914. A cottage that stood at the foothills of the Volgesburg. Marguerite was to often think of those memorable days spent with the young couple and to remember with appreciation the way they had nursed her back to health after her carelessness at looking after herself. They had certainly been an answer to silent prayer.

It was to be quite a long slow journey so an early start was made. Marguerite was adamant that Christa should be the first to sit up front as she left her first home in her short span of married life. The large hefty farm cart wheels seemed to grind through the long farm tracks shaking every core of Marguerite's body. It certainly seemed a long long way to the main road. Marguerite could feel every turn of the wheel and there seemed to be everything imaginable sticking into her plump body; for once she was thankful for her buxom figure, at least it gave her some protection. How slightly built Christa would cope in this position she dare not think, but Christa was a very uncomplaining young girl. After a couple of hours they stopped and took refreshments and then changed places. Although much more comfortable sitting upright, Marguerite found there was an art in balancing and she really was not at all sure which she preferred. Fortunately being Autumn there was not the heat of the midday sun to contend with, but, nevertheless, they stopped for the usual two hour siesta. Marguerite helped to put on the horse's nose bag. He was certainly ready for his lunch. As she assisted with the straps her mind went back to when she was a small child in London and her affection for the cabbies horses. During this siesta Marguerite endeavoured to plan in her mind as to what she should do on reaching Munster. In a town she would not have the sanctity of the mountain huts. She had still not decided what plan of action to take when Christa said they must be on their way again. Once more in the back of the cart she made herself as comfortable as possible - she was quite sure she would be black and blue all over by the time they reached Munster. To take their minds off the long journey they began to sing and Marguerite was only too happy to lead in this singing. The young German girl was astounded at her beautiful voice.

They had just passed a cross roads with a signpost showing Dortmund when, oh no, they were being stopped by the police. Marguerite immediately thought of documents, what was she going to say? She quickly reminded herself of Arzt Mullheim's advice, remember at all times you are Italian and you don't understand. She slid down amongst the bedding and remained quite still. Thinking about it afterwards, she was quite sure she held her breath. She listened whilst the three Polizists questioned Christa. Yes three Polizists not just one. On hearing that they were going back to families in Munster their husbands having enlisted in the German army they seemed quite satisfied and did not even walk round the cart. They signalled Christa to move on, as the horses were getting restless. Marguerite was to wonder once more if this young bauer's wife fully understood the situation she was in, or was it just a figure of speech to say 'we are going back to our families'?

Once on their way again Christa suggested that it would be best if Marguerite rode in the back of the cart for the rest of the journey. Marguerite suspected that Christa had possibly seen through her disguise. She suddenly made up her mind that the sooner she left this young German girl the better. She had been so kind to her and she did not want her to suffer on her behalf. Hesitantly she asked as to the distance from Munster to Gronau. "About 50 kilometres I would say," answered Christa. Marguerite was thinking to herself 50 kilometres, quite a way, as she bumped up and down in her now most uncomfortable seat.

It was now early evening and being the time of year nearly dusk. Fifty kilometres is a long way to go tonight thought Marguerite, but something told her that she must make haste. Speaking once more from her hide-out Marguerite announced, "I think perhaps I should try and make it to my friends this evening."

"This evening, Congettina?" questioned a worried Christa. "But it is already becoming dark."

"Perhaps I could get a charabanc from Munster?" asked Marguerite.

"I could drop you at the railway station," suggested Christa. "That is if you must go on tonight. I am sure my parents would be only too happy to give you a bed."

"That is very kind, but no, please drop me at the station," answered Marguerite. On and on they travelled and Marguerite soon made up her mind that on no account would she travel by train without papers. How would she get through the border? She did not know whether Germany was by now at war with Holland. Once away from Christa she would decide what to do.

Eventually they came to the outskirts of Munster and by this time Marguerite began to feel that she would never be able to walk again. She felt so stiff of limb from the continual jolting, but in no time at all Christa was assisting her down from the cart, laughing at their stiffness. Marguerite bid her friend a fond farewell and 'danke vielmals'. She waved until Christa was out of sight, when suddenly she realised that she had only known this family as Hans Peter and Christa. What was their surname? What a silly thing not to have asked. She turned, looked about her, with regret at the sudden parting, and a great loneliness swept over her. Where was she to go tonight? What was she to do?

*

October 1914 and a young English girl, not yet eighteen years of age, unchaperoned in a German city! Where was she to go? Feeling very dejected she picked up her quite heavy valise, kindly given to her by Christa for her belongings, and began to walk away from the railway station, which appeared to her a rather forbidding place.

It was now 8 o'clock in the evening, but the streets were still quite busy. The Germans enjoyed their evenings, even if it were only to stroll along looking at the shops or to sit outside the various cafes. Marguerite was suddenly conscious of walking along beside some iron railings and of people turning through a tall iron gate. She stopped and glanced towards the way they were going and noticed they were entering a church; without thinking she followed them. Not until she was inside did the smell of incense remind her that this was a Roman Catholic Church and people were attending confession in preparation for their Sunday Mass. Her mind went back to Rachel attending Mass with her friend Bridget, and of the distress this had caused Mama. She sat down in a pew and after looking around her realised that whilst waiting her turn she should be kneeling. She eased herself very painfully into a kneeling position - how every limb ached – and as she prayed for God's help she smiled to herself as she thought of how horrified dear Mama would be at her praying in a Roman Catholic church. Eventually it was Marguerite's turn to go in to the confessional box. She did not know what she was supposed to say but once more knelt down very gingerly trying not to show her distress. She looked at the priest through the iron grille. He had a kindly face. She hesitated and then in very slow German and showing some difficulty said, "Father, forgive me, I am stranded in this City with nowhere to sleep tonight!"

The priest looked questioningly at her. "Where are you on your way to, my child?"

"I am on my way to Gronau, but have left it too late to reach there tonight, Father." Marguerite felt it best to be honest to this priest.

The priest's lips were now moving silently. Whether he was praying for assistance or just abiding time Marguerite did not know, but his lips went on moving and then he said, "My child go and kneel in the church and say twenty Hail Mary's and five Our Fathers and I will see you later."

"Thank you, Father." Marguerite heard herself saying. She did as she was told and returned to a pew and eased herself once more gently on to her knees, but how to say the Hail Mary's she did not know. She looked around her and realised that in her panic she had not appreciated the beauty of this church. The vivid blues, reds and gold around the magnificent arches were indescribable. The whole beauty of the church was breathtaking and the whole place was so clean. For a while she sat entranced with it all. The Virgin Mary looking down gave serenity. As she knelt there she became very tired and that pain in her chest was returning. Oh no, she thought, do not let me fall ill just as I have found comfort. She quietly found her tablets and took one. Her head gradually fell forward onto her hands and she slept.

Marguerite was awoken suddenly by the priest tapping her on the shoulder. She sincerely hoped that he did not realise she had been sleeping - perhaps he would think she was being very devout. The priest bent down and said very quietly, "The confessionals are now over. I will take you to the Convent. The Mother Superior will be sure to find you a bed for the night." Marguerite still in a half sleep and wondering if she was dreaming looked up and once more thanked this kindly priest. Her limbs were now so set that he had to help her on to her feet. She slowly followed him from the church. She stood on the steps whilst he locked up the enormous door. She took some deep breaths and felt a good deal better. The iron railings continued round a corner and Marguerite realised that the convent was indeed next door to the church. They approached yet another heavy door and the priest knocked hard.

A young nun opened a grill at eye level and on seeing the priest unbolted the door. She crossed herself and said, "Good evening, Father. Do come in."

"Is Mother Marie Celeste free, Sister Philomena?" asked the priest.

"I will knock and see, Father," answered the young nun, once more crossing herself as she left them.

"That is our new novice, Sister Philomena. I am sure she will look after you well." On hearing that she was a new novice, Marguerite felt reassured.

The young Sister reappeared and making the sign of the cross said, "The Mother Superior will see you now, Father."

"Thank you, Sister," and he left Marguerite sitting in this cold but sparkling clean hall. Sister Philomena busied herself at a table preparing the places in the hymn books for compline.

It seemed only a few moments before the priest appeared again. "Well, that is all arranged with Mother Marie Celeste. I will leave you in the Sisters' good hands. Rest tomorrow and then on Monday, my child, I will take you to the border." Marguerite sat there quite stunned. Did she hear correctly he had said I will take you to the border? As the priest went to go out of the heavy doors he turned and said to Marguerite, "I will see you at Mass tomorrow at 5 o'clock then, good-night and God bless you."

I will take you to the border! How did he know? God was certainly caring for her. Well thought Marguerite I hope God will show me how to behave at Mass tomorrow?

Sister Philomena showed Marguerite to a small room. It just had the bare necessities, a clean bed, wash stand with jug and basin and a small altar. The hook on the door Marguerite presumed was all the novices needed for hanging up their habits. She wondered where they put their large beautifully starched and folded head pieces. They certainly looked like angel's wings and well cared for in such sparse surroundings. She remembered that she had read that they kept no other personal effects. Marguerite was only thankful tonight for these bare necessities. Sister Philomena said she would bring Marguerite a warm drink after compline.

How pleased was Marguerite to remove her travelling clothes, untie those boot laces, and then remove those cumbersome tight corsets. She washed herself down - how cold the water from the jug seemed, but better than burning yourself as that young Mary had those many years ago. She found her warm nightgown from her valise. Her hands were so tired she had difficulty in fastening the buttons at the wrist. She laid on the bed to rest and soon the most beautiful sound reached her as the nuns were singing at compline their voices blending together as one. She made up her mind to go to the compline service the next evening, if they would allow her into their privacy. Later when Sister Philomena brought the hot milk drink Marguerite was sound asleep and the Sister did not disturb her but left the warm drink beside the bed should she awake.

Early the next morning Marguerite was awoken by the tinkling of small bells waking the sisters for their early morning prayers. Marguerite lay listening to their footsteps and once more fell into a peaceful sleep. Some time later Sister Philomena appeared with a jug of coffee for Marguerite. Marguerite apologised for wasting the milk drink; she was only thankful she had not drunk it in hast the night before remembering too well her recent experience, she endeavoured to point out to this sister that she could not drink milk. Later she partook of breakfast in the refectory; the nuns had prepared hot bread rolls and there was the usual German sausage, but fortunately for Marguerite a jar of honey was also on the table. She then rested in her room until lunch pondering on what the priest had said the night before and wondering what tomorrow would bring.

A plain but wholesome lunch was served by the nuns but not a word was spoken, and Marguerite realised that this was a silent order. After lunch she took a walk outside through the cloisters until she came upon a small fountain where the nuns were having their free time when at least they were able to laugh and chat together whilst they fed the small birds; they seemed such a happy group of women of all ages.

As she prepared for Mass she was thankful for the skirt, jacket and hat that Christa had kindly bought for her. As at home, she could at least wear Sunday best to church. It was with some trepidation that she set off for evening Mass and made for the church next door. This time the church was full and Marguerite was quickly able to fall in with whatever the congregation did, but how her legs hurt as time and time again everyone seemed to genuflect nearly to the floor. She had recalled what Rachel had said about taking the holy bread by mouth and so remembered to keep her hands together in prayer. On leaving the church after the service the priest clasped her hands reassuringly in his, but said nothing.

Later that evening Marguerite attended compline sitting at the back of the small chapel; at first she did not join in with the singing, but the temptation was too great and as Marguerite's voice rose so some of the nuns glanced round. Mother Superior's voice soon brought their eyes round to the front again "Sisters, the dear Lord requires your attention, please." As Marguerite left the chapel Mother Marie Celeste hurried to her and taking her hands said "My child the good Lord has given you a most beautiful voice, use it to the Lord's advantage, and God bless you, my dear, and a safe journey." Marguerite could not help but smile to herself as she returned to her small room. Use it the Lord's advantage - if only he could have but seen her some weeks ago singing for that drunkard!

The next morning after early morning prayers Sister Philomena woke Marguerite and an early breakfast was served to her in her room. She was told that the priest would be collecting her at eight o'clock. As much as she would have liked to have worn her Sunday best she packed them away in her valise for who knew to what and where her travels would now take her. It seemed to be no time at all before Sister Philomena was helping Marguerite and her valise up into the small governess cart. The priest now warmly clad in his long black cape acknowledged her and they set off on their journey together.

Fortunately it was a cold but dry autumnal morning and in addition to the rug that the priest gave her to wrap around her legs she was glad of her own rug. She was certainly more comfortable in this small governess cart than the farm cart of her recent travels. The early morning mist gradually cleared and Marguerite could see how flat the terrain had now become. It was certainly very flat indeed. The occasional windmills made her feel that she was already in Holland. Yes Holland, she wondered once more if they were also at war with Germany and whether her difficulties of travel would be over on crossing the border. This was a point that was now beginning to worry her. She wondered how many miles there was to the border. This kindly priest did not seem to want to talk, perhaps it was too early in the morning for him to feel like conversing, and so she did not question him but dozed for a while. Suddenly she realised the priest was asking her a question. "You have been in Germany long?" he asked.

"Two years," answered a thoughtful Marguerite.

She wondered whether she should admit to being English, but her decision was soon made for her. She found herself telling him how she had been studying music in Heidelberg; then, much to Marguerite's surprise he went on to ask her in English. "How long have you been trying to get home?"

"Since the war broke out, Father," answered Marguerite. She did not know why but she did not question how he knew she was English.

The priest went on to tell her that on reaching Gronau he would make for a brother priest's presbytery on the edge of the river Dinkel. "I will leave you there in good hands. Father der Jong will see you across the river to the safety of neutral Holland."

Marguerite suddenly realised she had been given the answer to the question that had been worrying her and she now knew that Holland was still neutral. An answer to her silent prayer what a relief she felt as she realised that she would soon be safe.

*

Good progress was made but a governess cart does not cover ground very quickly and it was agreed that a break should be made for coffee. The farmhouse at which this respite was taken reminded Marguerite of Hans Peter and Christa's farmhouse. With sadness Marguerite thought of this young couple and of how their first home together had been cut so short. After this coffee break it did not seem long before the outskirts of Gronau were reached. Instead of going through Gronau a road to the right was taken and the river Dinkel was soon reached. After travelling along beside this pretty meandering river for a while they soon came upon a cluster of wooden chalets with a small wooden church amongst them. The priest told Marguerite to wait in the cart whilst he went into the small church. A number of people gathered around, which made Marguerite feel a little nervous and she was greatly relieved when she was joined once more by her companion.

The priest helped Marguerite down from the cart and on going through the church she realised that the presbytery was actually reached from the back of this small but delightful church. She was introduced to Father der Jong and his plump housekeeper. The presbytery was spotless. A lunch was taken together, after which once more Marguerite was bidding farewell to yet another German.

Father der Jong's housekeeper showed Marguerite to her room. Over lunch it had been agreed that Marguerite should wait until the next morning before crossing the border, remembering that this was a small community and suspicion could be aroused if a visitor left too quickly. Marguerite found herself once more attending compline, but quite different to the previous one she attended at the convent. Kneeling in this petite wooden church she could not help but think back to the beautiful singing voices of the nuns.

That night Marguerite retired early so as not to undo the welcome of this young priest. She was sure he had many matters with which to attend. She laid in bed mulling over her journey this far and wondering what tomorrow would bring. Knowing that she had arrived at the border she felt relaxed and slept well.

The next morning she was awoken by the closing of a door as the young priest slipped out to early morning Mass. Yes it was only 5.30am, Marguerite supposed this young man was used to rising early from his recent training into the priesthood.

Later, on arriving at table for breakfast, she was surprised to find Father der Jong already seated and dressed in casual clothes. He explained to her that they were to go fishing further down stream and he would casually drop her off at the far bank. Marguerite smiled to herself as she recalled to mind the different experiences she had encountered since leaving Heidelberg. She had certainly not thought of fishing. She hoped that her weight would not present too much of a hazard. On mentioning this Father der Jong smiled and reassured her. "Just sit in the middle of the seat Marguerite. I will do the fishing."

A good breakfast was partaken and it was not long before Marguerite was being helped from a small jetty into what seemed to Marguerite a rather small boat. Oh these long skirts, thought Marguerite, they are certainly not suitable for fishing trips. A young lad, wearing a black cap that Marguerite had noticed on arriving yesterday seemed to be part of the costume for the men in this community, was soon handing the fishing tackle to Marguerite; she gingerly lent forward to take these from him, trying not to show her inexperience of messing about in boats. As arranged they set off down stream, stopping now and then to fish, this certainly soon relaxed Marguerite. She was astounded at how many fish were in this river. Thankfully it was a dry morning weatherwise. God was certainly being kind to them.

After a while Father der Jong once more stopped the boat in mid-stream and told Marguerite he would now be making for the bank. He suggested they said goodbye now and recommended that she should make for the railway station at Enschede; it would be quite a walk but she should make it by midday. As they turned towards the bank Marguerite thanked this young priest for his help. He advised her not to wave to him but to just climb up the bank and walk away. Once more she would be thankful for Frau Gerhart's forethought in sending her back upstairs for those shoes. She would certainly need them as the small boat had become quite wet. At the young priest's instruction Marguerite caught hold of a branch of a tree leaning over the water and held on tight, whilst he fastened the boat, and then somehow she managed to step on shore and scramble up the bank and very discreetly Father der Jong was back in mid-stream once more fishing. Before losing sight of him Marguerite sat down and changed her shoes.

At long last thought Marguerite it would not matter if she asked passers-by for directions she could now put that Italian folk singer behind her. She could forget ever having learnt German and speak quite naturally in her native language, oh what a relief. Marguerite sat quietly and watched as Father der Jong went back upstream and eventually out of sight.

BOOK 1

CHAPTER 5

ON SAFE GROUND

Marguerite gathered her things together, tied her boots on to her bag, stood up and looked about her. The open fields seemed to go on for ever and ever. Marguerite was very thankful that the wind was not blowing too strongly, she could imagine how it could sweep across these plains. She could see a signpost, which from this distance, looked as if it was at a crossroads. She started walking, making for this point, stepping out and feeling quite refreshed from her good night's sleep. The air of the open fields of Holland certainly seemed to suit her and she swung along quite confidently and with renewed vigour.

On reaching the cross roads the sign bore no recognisable name to Marguerite, nor any indication as to which way she should turn for Enschede. The names shown did not mean a thing to her. She hesitated not knowing which way to go. On looking around she spotted, further on along the road, a windmill. Curiosity drew her towards it. She had never before stood under such a machine. The sails looked enormous groaning as they turned; they certainly made music of their own. She stood back in the narrow lane entranced by this object.

Suddenly a voice called to her and a man appeared. He was dressed in a fawn smock nearly reaching down to his wooden clogs. He appeared quite elderly. Of course Marguerite could not understand what he was saying to her. She crossed the lane to meet him. She asked in English the way to the railway station. He in turn could not understand her. Fortunately Father der Jong had written down the name of the railway station. She showed the note to this elderly Dutchman. He signalled to her to wait whilst he went inside the mill. He soon appeared with a young girl, who was dressed similarly to the miller, but she was wearing a white head-dress. This reminded Marguerite of the nuns' head-dresses, but a much smaller version. Much to Marguerite's relief this young girl could speak English. She invited Marguerite in to see the workings of the mill and to take a drink with her fellow workers. Marguerite found the mill really intriguing. She learnt that this Dutch girl's name was Giselle and that the elderly miller was her grandfather. She explained to Giselle of her necessity to get to Enschede. Once more Marguerite was fortunate, Giselle told her that a load of grain was being delivered to the station later that morning, and, as it would have entailed a walk of some distance,

Marguerite was only too glad to accept a lift. Whilst the miller's assistant loaded up the cart Marguerite made friends with the miller's horse. By the time she left, and although not speaking the language, she felt she knew the miller and his staff quite well. These Dutch folk were so friendly.

On arriving at the station Marguerite had to stop and think as to which port Arzt Mullheim had advised her to go. It was not until she looked at the large printed timetable on the wall of the station-house that she was drawn to the name of Rotterdam. Of course, how could she forget, but then a lot had happened since bidding farewell to Arzt Mullheim. She suddenly realised that she had no Dutch Guilders. She approached the ticket office with some trepidation. She asked for a ticket to Rotterdam and showed her purse. The assistant declined her German Reichmarks, but, after some hesitation, he agreed to accept the English currency. All this time the miller's assistant, having now unloaded his cart, stood by. He waited to see her on the train, which luckily for Marguerite was about due. She was certainly impressed at the cleanliness of the prettily laid out station. How she wished English stations looked so clean; they always appeared to be covered in black soot. Soon the small train arrived and this young man gallantly helped her up the quite high step into the train and saw her seated. The seats were of plain wood but once again quite clean. As the train took her away she waved goodbye to her newly found friend. It seemed some time since she had sat on a train. Yes it was the day war broke out, when she had hurriedly caught a train back to the Gerhart's home from Frankfurt. What a long time ago that now seemed.

Marguerite enjoyed her journey to Rotterdam. The train seemed to pass many fields being planted out with what she presumed to be bulbs. What a back aching job for the workers, but how colourful they looked in their different costumes. As the journey went on the train became quite crowded and noisy. The scenery was now becoming industrialised and she presumed they were coming to a large town. Marguerite's thoughts turned to what she should do on reaching Rotterdam. On pulling into Utrecht, the last busy station before Rotterdam, she had still not decided what her plan of action should be. After leaving Utrecht the train passed over the Rhine. Marguerite was so taken with the flat but interesting scenery that she soon forgot her worries of what lay ahead. Slowly the train pulled into Rotterdam. Marguerite gathered her things together and clasped her now well used travelling rug around her; by now she was quite used to this colourful makeshift coat. She carefully climbed down from the train and followed the crowd out of this busy station.

She had arrived in Munster as dusk fell but being mid-afternoon in Rotterdam she did not feel the immediate necessity to seek help. She wandered down to the docks to look at the large cranes and boats. Marguerite smiled to herself as she thought of what her dear Mama would think of her wandering in this lowly area unchaperoned. She was surprised at how relaxed she felt. It must be the feeling of freedom after having travelled for so long in an enemy country. After a while Marguerite turned back and left the dock area. She glanced in the various small shop windows that were now around her; some selling fishing tackle others just some small gifts and was tempted by the small wooden windmills. Yes she must get one as a souvenir of her early morning experience. She proffered her English currency to the shop assistant and this was accepted. She left the shop clutching her memento before being tempted by other gifts.

Marguerite was now becoming rather tired, and so she made her way to the more select area of Rotterdam where she came upon a wide road of elegant houses, a museum here and an art gallery there; suddenly she saw a gold plate on some railings at the bottom of some steps leading up to a front door; it reminded her of her own home that she had not seen for over two years. What did that say in brackets under the Dutch wording? 'Solicitor'? Was not her own father a Solicitor, and her grandfather, even though she could not remember him, a Barrister? Surely this Solicitor could help her. She turned up the steps and pulled on the iron bell pulley which made a loud clattering as the bell tolled within.

Whilst waiting for someone to answer the door Marguerite brushed herself down. She felt decidedly dishevelled after her fishing trip and train journey. She realised that no one was going to answer the door bell so she tried the handle and the door opened. She stepped inside, into a poorly lit hall. A voice called from an adjacent room. What was being said she could not tell but she followed the voice and noticed a plate on the door to the right, similar to the one on the railings, confirming that this was indeed the Solicitor's office. She peered around the door which stood slightly open. At a desk covered in papers sat a middle-aged man, a pucker little man in a dark suit and spotless white shirt. His appearance did not match his dusty office. Marguerite took this to be Dolf Endert, the Solicitor. Looking up from the work in hand he was surprised to see a young girl standing in the doorway.

"Excuse me, sir" she quickly said.

"Ah, you are an English maiden, yes?" asked this Solicitor, smiling at Marguerite. "I did wonder why no reply." He came forward to the door and shook hands. "Come in, sit down. How can I help you?" he asked.

She sat down shyly and faced this stranger across his desk. "My father is a Solicitor in London and my late grandfather was a Barrister," she said hurriedly.

Dolf Endert held up his hand "Slower, slower, if you please. Excuse me, I speak little English."

She smiled apologetically. Slowly and very carefully she told this Solicitor of her travels and how she wished to reach England.

"So your Papa is a Solicitor, yes? It is good?" questioned this friendly Dutchman. He stood up and took a heavy thick book from a shelf, blowing the dust from it. "We will find his name in this, yes."

Marguerite had no idea what book he had, but nevertheless replied "Yes, Frederick Sinclair is the name, sir."

He repeated the name "Frederick Sinclair, F. Sinclair," at the same time thumbing through the book "Ah, England, yes! Sinclair you say? Yes, yes!" going down the list of names. "It is Frederick Sinclair of the City of London, yes?"

"Yes, that is Papa, sir, my dear Papa!" Marguerite was now quite excited to think that her Father's name was listed in a book in Rotterdam.

"You wish to go to the City of London, yes?" he asked.

Marguerite was amused at the way this small Dutchman ended every question with yes. "My home is also in London, sir," answered Marguerite.

"We have many boats go to England, but there is a war and now not go London. They go to Hull," he informed Marguerite.

Miss Hannah had made the girls very conversant with the ports and towns of England, and immediately a picture of the Wash appeared in Marguerite's mind and further up that map of dear old England the Humber. Bearing in mind the journey she had just taken to reach Rotterdam, Hull did not seem at all far from London. "Hull would do quite well, sir, please." Marguerite tried not to sound too eager. She really did not mind where it was as long as it was the shores of England.

"Where you stay in Rotterdam?" asked Dolf Endert.

"I do not know, sir," answered Marguerite.

Dolf Endert looked at this young English girl and thought that if this was his own daughter, alone in a strange city, he would wish that someone would take care of her, and he found himself saying, "My wife will look after you, whilst I find you a berth," and then after waiting for her to take in what he was suggesting the kindly Solicitor asked, "You say yes?"

"Thank you, sir, that would be most kind of you." Marguerite was very relieved at how things were falling into place.

"You wait. I will close my work and take you to my house." Dolf Endert started to gather up the papers around him, very carefully placing them into the drawers of his desk and locking them away for the night. "You walk with me. I not like to ride after sitting in the office. Exercise is good, yes?" asked this spry little man. The door was dutifully locked and they set off together. Marguerite had great difficulty in keeping up with this small Dutchman. Although he had short legs he simply whipped along. Marguerite soon became short of breath. Dolf Endert looked at her and said, "I am so sorry! I hurry you, yes?"

"Yes," puffed Marguerite. Thankfully for her he slowed down and started to point out some of the interesting features of Rotterdam. Marguerite began to think that they would never reach his home, but after what seemed to her a long walk and after an extensive tour of the dock area, they skirted around the edge of a park and along beside one of the many waterways and eventually arrived at a typical Dutch homestead, with pointed roof and pretty garden. A young girl came running down the front path to meet them and Marguerite was introduced to Anna, Dolf Endert's eight-year-old daughter. She had a very pretty smocked apron over a plain red dress, and her fair hair hung in a thick pigtail down to her waist; she made an attractive picture and she shook hands very sweetly. Anna was very surprised to see her father with an unexpected visitor and ran back indoors to fetch her mother. A short plump woman appeared on the doorstep; she was dressed similarly to her small daughter but her pigtails were tied quite severely round her head. On being introduced by her husband she smiled warmly at Marguerite.

This Dutch family made their unexpected visitor so welcome, but Marguerite realised, whilst trying to make herself understood, how important it is to study languages. She wished sincerely she could speak in this family's tongue so that over the evening meal she could converse - she felt so inadequate. Perhaps one day she would learn the Dutch language, who knows? Nevertheless, Marguerite enjoyed her evening meal, but she could not eat the raw eel served as a starter - evidently it would appear by what was said that the Dutch treat this raw fish as a delicacy.

It was arranged that whilst this kind Solicitor endeavoured to find a berth for Marguerite on one of the vessels leaving Rotterdam for Hull, Marguerite would be shown the sights of Rotterdam by his wife, Olga. This Marguerite looked forward to very much. She had certainly taken a liking to this Dutch family.

Marguerite slept well that night, in her now safe haven, and was up early the next morning. After seeing Anna to school, Olga and Marguerite enjoyed their tour of Rotterdam and the surrounding area, and by the end of the day, with the help of sign language, they felt they knew each other well and had become good friends. That evening Dolf told Marguerite that he had been unable to attain a berth on a vessel leaving for Hull until the Friday, but this delay enabled Marguerite to spend Thursday resting and preparing herself for her sea voyage; she quite looked forward to this as she had enjoyed her crossing of the channel two years earlier. As the vessel was not due to sail until early Friday evening the whole family were able to see Marguerite off on what she hoped was her last stage of this epic adventure. She stood on deck on this cold and already foggy evening waving goodbye to her new-found friends.

On arriving on board this cargo vessel she had been distressed to learn that there was no personal berth for her, and she already had fears for what lay ahead. She was soon told that she was to fling a hammock at the corner of the crew's quarters - something she did not fancy at all. She made up her mind immediately on hearing where she was to sleep to stay dressed. There would be no night attire for her until hopefully reaching England and home, and she stayed on deck as long as she could watching the sights of this busy port pass by.

*

Once away from Rotterdam it seemed as though the fog sirens were sounding all the time, such a deafening noise. Marguerite began to cough with the choking smog and eventually decided there was nothing for it but down to the crew's quarters she must go; because of the war she knew that there was no telling how long the journey to Hull would take, a short sea trip could turn into days. A kindly seaman showed her how to sling her hammock; after doing this she climbed into it with great difficulty, wondering how she would ever get out of it again in a hurry. She was offered food but declined, she was already beginning to feel unsure where her stomach should be. As the vessel slowly reached the North Sea, and after what seemed like hours to Marguerite, the crew that were not on watch came to take up their sleeping quarters. Some were the worst for drink and the stench of the cramped living quarters had a decidedly worsening effect on Marguerite. The good Samaritan who had flung her hammock came to the rescue once more, just in time, as he approached with a white enamel bucket. To think, thought Marguerite, I was looking forward to this and I have I don't know how long cramped up like this - she would surely die!

Somehow or other she did survive that first night in those cramped conditions. How, she will never know. She literally crawled out on deck the next morning and felt slightly better for the fresh clean air, but she hoped this nightmare would soon be over. She reasonably enjoyed the day watching the seamen at their work, and during the daylight hours the fog seemed to clear and some progress was made, but as darkness fell once more the fog descended; through sheer exhaustion and from lack of sleep she finally returned to her hammock. She had not fancied any food all day and so with nothing inside her she felt decidedly weak, but whilst the quarters were reasonably empty she fell into a sick stupor for what must have been some hours. She was suddenly awoken, in what she thought was a nightmare of that incident back at the country club, but no, this was no nightmare, bending over her was a horribly drunk seaman, his leering face very close to hers, the smell of his breath absolutely distasteful to this girl of tender age. Before she could fling herself from her hammock, this drunken man was jumped on from behind, her good Samaritan once more came to her rescue; but enough was enough, whilst the seamen struggled on the floor, Marguerite quickly gathered her things together and rushed from her prison.

Marguerite did not stop to think where she should go - not far on board a vessel in fog at sea - but out of those quarters she must certainly get. This is where she nearly came to an untimely end; without thinking she rushed out on deck, a deck in pitch darkness, immediately the swaying of the vessel sent her from one side to the other, like a boxer in the boxing ring. Fortunately she managed to stay on her feet and the life raft, fixed to the edge of the deck, brought her to a sudden halt with a bump; she felt her heart pounding and pounding and knew that at any moment she was likely to pass out. Marguerite took some deep breaths, and whether it was the inhaling of the sea air or feeling the cold spray on her face, she slowly recovered her composure.

After Marguerite had gathered her thoughts she was very relieved to find that she was still grasping her belongings in her already very cold hands. She leant against the life raft shaking all over, not only with cold but with fright at her sudden ghastly awakening. As she gathered her courage she wondered what protection this small boat could give her. Would this life raft give her a shelter for the rest of the night? She endeavoured to climb up into it. Suddenly there was a shout in broken English. "I shouldn't do that. Please climb down you will fall." Marguerite did as she was told, warily looking about her. A young officer approached her and holding out his hand he said. "Come, come with me, I will look after you. I heard great noise and saw bad seaman. He will be controlled. I will see to that. Come I will see that you are safe" announced this young officer.

"Thank you, officer. Do not be too severe on him, he was worse for drink." And much to Marguerite's surprise she found herself defending that revolting man.

"Come with me. I go on watch. Please join me on the bridge." Marguerite thanked him and followed him carefully up the steps. The officer showed her into the small compartment, mainly full of instruments and the ship's wheel taking up most of the space. He informed her that it was now 2am and that they were due to arrive in Hull in one hour. Marguerite was very surprised to hear the time, she had slept longer than she had realised. Although a very confined space there appeared to be more air on the bridge. The officer handed Marguerite a seaman's heavy coat to cuddle down in, and he suggested that she should endeavour to sleep as there would be no need for her to vacate the vessel until morning. Surprisingly, after this latest escapade, Marguerite was soon sound asleep.

When Marguerite next awoke, feeling snug and warm, she found it was indeed daylight and the vessel had anchored and heavy cranes were lifting the cargo from the hold. She sat watching all the work going on around her, feeling safe in this small compartment. She was given a warm, rather tasteless, weak tea to drink. Yes, she thought, only the English know how to make a good mug of tea; nevertheless, she was very thankful for a warm drink, and sat quietly sipping it whilst watching the heavy cranes at work in the docks.

At 8 o'clock she thanked the officer, who was due to hand over his duties on watch, as he helped her to gather her belongings together and saw her down the gangway and on to English soil. What a relief to be back once more in her homeland.

BOOK 1

CHAPTER 6

HOME AT LAST

Standing on dry land once more, Marguerite stood looking around her wondering which way to go and at the same time thinking how dirty she felt and how she wished she could stop swaying. She wondered where she could find somewhere to have a wash and at last remove those clothes in which she had been so sea-sick. She wondered if there would be anywhere at this time of the morning? On this cold foggy October morning Marguerite wrapped her by now well worn and smelly travelling rug around her still shivering body and left the docks. After a while she noticed she was passing a hall, and she stopped and read the notice board; she smiled to herself when she saw an advert for the Band of Hope - how good to see everything in her own tongue. Band of Hope memories came flooding back of the time when she had asked Mama if she could go, with young Mary, to the Band of Hope. Mama was adamant that they could not go and she dare not argue with dear Mama; if Mama said no in those days it was no. Thinking about this she wondered how she would cope with her dear Mama after having been away for so long, she could foresee difficulties. Marguerite glanced towards the hall door and realised that it stood ajar, even at this time in the morning. On going in she was met by an elderly charlady with bucket and mop in hand - oh how that white enamel bucket reminded Marguerite of her recent dilemma.

"Can I help you, my dear?" enquired this elderly soul.

"Yes, please. I have just arrived at the docks having travelled for days. Have you perhaps a cloakroom where I could wash and change?" asked Marguerite.

"Of course, my dear. Now don't you make it mucky, I have just cleaned it; as much as my rheumatic knees will allow me," said the old dear shaking her finger at Marguerite as she spoke. She reminded Marguerite of the old cockney flower ladies. Oh how marvellous it was to be back in dear old England!

What a relief it was to Marguerite to have a good wash and to once more feel clean. She was relieved to find the outfit that Christa had bought her not too creased. How thankful she was that on running up on deck she had not lost all these clothes overboard. Once more she appeared in front of the dear old charlady who was now cleaning the step.

On seeing Marguerite the dear old soul with difficulty struggled to her feet. Clasping her hands together she said, "My, oh my, now you look a real lady."

Marguerite pressed some money into the old lady's hand thanking her from the depth of her heart for her kindness and at the same time asked the way to the railway station. Thankfully it was not too far to walk, and Marguerite took her time, taking in the scenery around her. Now she was in England it was such a relief not to have to rush or hide.

On finally reaching the station she was relieved to find that a London train was just about due. By the time it chugged its way into the platform and Marguerite climbed up into it she was once more feeling decidedly grubby from the black smuts emitted from a majestic engine standing at a nearby platform, but how good it was to see the young smiling face of the fireman as he shovelled in the coals in preparation for driving this engine out of the station. Marguerite settled herself into a corner seat, making sure she had her back to the engine, so as not to get an eyeful of smuts as the train travelled along. She must endeavour to shut the window should they come to a tunnel otherwise the smell would surely make her feel sick again. It was a Sunday morning and so the train was virtually empty, except for a few business people making their way to the big city. Marguerite relaxed and really enjoyed her journey; how good it was to look out of the dirty train window at dear old England passing by; it was a shame she thought that they were not as clean as the Dutch trains, but, on the other hand, they were more comfortable.

It was late afternoon when finally the train pulled into Kings Cross station. Marguerite could hardly believe that she was at last back in London. As she passed through the barrier she had to push her way through young soldiers queuing with their kitbags propped up beside them. She thought of Hans Peter back in Germany and wondered how he was surviving the inevitable interrogation for his failure to enlist. She hoped, for his young wife's sake, that the German army would not be too harsh with him.

*

The third Sunday in October was just another late autumnal Sunday in London. The Sinclair family returned from church where they had prayed sincerely for the safe return of their second daughter, Marguerite; this they had been doing for many Sundays as the weeks progressed into months. Many weeks seemed to have gone by since the outbreak of war and still there was no news from Heidelberg of Marguerite's whereabouts.

It was a long time since George had left for the front. They had received two letters from him whilst he was training somewhere in Wiltshire.

Sarah had joined her Mama and Papa once more for the typical English Sunday dinner of roast beef and Yorkshire pudding. After the meal, Mama, feeling the strain of waiting for news of Marguerite, had retired to her bedroom for a rest. Sarah was to join a friend's family for afternoon tea; she would rather have stayed at home, but, nevertheless, it would be a break from dear Mama. Papa had some work to attend to in preparation for a court case that following week and he too rested on the bed and attended to this. Amy had joined Cook in the kitchen for a quiet chat; she enjoyed these quiet Sunday afternoons sitting round the kitchen table with a cup of tea and homemade rich fruit cake.

*

Marguerite crossed the station forecourt, pushing her way between the soldiers, and hailed a cab, and, as if in a dream, she asked for Bedford Square. How would she announce herself to the family and what would her homecoming be like? All these thoughts went through her mind as she travelled though the quiet streets of the capital. Familiar streets that it seemed only yesterday she had travelled down and not two very long years.

On arriving at her home she glanced up at the windows; her Mama and Papa's room curtains were slightly drawn and no-one was looking out. Marguerite was glad, as she needed time to gather herself together after what had been such a long journey. She paid the cabby and turning she hesitated at the steps to the front door, and to her surprise instead of going up she found herself going down the area steps. What took Marguerite down the area steps she did not know, perhaps she needed a little respite before meeting the family, or perhaps it was unknown hunger that took her straight to the kitchen. She peeped in the window beside the door. Cook, who happened to be looking that way at the time, caught sight of the face at the window; her hand went to her mouth to stifle the scream that she was about to let out. Amy looked at her companion. "Why Cook, what is the matter? You look as though you have seen a ghost."

Before she could give an answer, Cook was up from her seat and hurried to open the door. "Miss Marguerite, Miss Marguerite, is it really you? Come in, come in." Cook ushered Marguerite into the warm kitchen. Amy stood up, she could not speak. She was really overcome.

Marguerite sat down at the well scrubbed kitchen table and tears of relief and excitement streamed down her cheeks. "Oh I am sorry, it is just," she was having difficulty in talking, "it is just that I am so relieved to be home. It has taken such a long time."

Cook and Amy both tried to speak at the same time there was so much to ask. After a cup of tea, which tasted so good, Marguerite slowly relived the past few weeks as she related to her dear friends of her experiences. She suddenly realised she had not enquired as to the whereabouts of the family, she had been so busy talking. "Are Mama and Papa at home?" enquired Marguerite.

"Yes, they are both having a Sunday afternoon nap and Sarah has gone to tea with friends," replied Amy. "She is expected to return early evening."

Marguerite pondered for a while and then turned to Cook asking, "Do you think I could have a wash and rest in your room, Cook?"

"Why yes, my dear, but what about your Mama and Papa?" asked Cook.

"I think I will wait until Sarah returns and meet them together." Marguerite having got over her seasickness suddenly realised she was quite hungry. "Cook, perhaps whilst I am resting would you not mind preparing me some sandwiches, please.

"Oh you poor dear, of course, you must be starving, how remiss of me not to think of doing so before.' Cook was quite worried at her thoughtlessness and rushed over to give Marguerite yet another hug. Cook's room seemed like luxury to Marguerite and she was glad that she was allowing herself time before meeting the family. She realised that some readjustment was necessary after the past traumas.

Meanwhile, Amy served tea to Emily and Frederick. After she had left the bedroom Frederick enquired of Emily, "Did I note a rather flustered Amy, Emily. I hope she is alright."

"All I noticed was that she was rather late with tea. I shall have to remind her that tea time is 4.15 pm and not 5.15 pm," answered an impatient Emily. Did it really matter, thought Frederick? Really Emily could be rather inconsiderate some times.

After a good rest Marguerite felt recovered and returned to the kitchen where the food had been laid out like a banquet, and Marguerite was soon sitting at the table and ate hungrily without any thought of manners; she felt she had not enjoyed a meal so much for a long time.

It was anticipated that Sarah would be home for supper and it was arranged that when all were gathered Amy would send a note down the dumb waiter. Amy rang the bell more vigorously than usual. On sitting at table Frederick enquired of Amy if she was feeling well.

"Why, yes sir! Why, yes!" answered an excited Amy.

"Then why have you laid an extra place, Amy?" asked a puzzled Frederick.

"Oh, have I?" queried Amy; she wished Marguerite would hurry.

Suddenly the door opened and there was a gasp from all three as Marguerite stood silhouetted in the doorway. Momentarily they sat frozen to their seats unable to believe what they saw and then Marguerite rushed to each one in turn. Not much supper was eaten that night as they listened to Marguerite's story of her escape. Later that night Sarah would hear even more as Marguerite did not wish to worry her Mama and Papa with some of the incidents.

The Sinclair family retired later than usual on that October evening. Sarah and her sister shared a room and talked until the early hours, and Marguerite wondered if she detected may be a little envy from her sister? At sixteen-years-old it all seemed rather thrilling to her ears, perhaps not quite realising the risks Marguerite had taken.

*

It was not easy for Marguerite to once more settle down to family life. She had arrived home just in time to celebrate her nineteenth birthday, but, in many respects, she felt a good deal older.

January 1915 saw Sarah at last take up her place at the College of Cookery and Marguerite took over her sister's duties at the first aid centre and the meticulously boring job of rolling bandages.   She was thinking of learning to drive one of the ambulances; on meeting up with Mary she had heard of this worthwhile job that so many women were doing.

Some Sunday evenings the Sinclair family entertained young officers passing through London.   Many of these officers would recall later those happy evenings gathered round the piano in Bedford Square.   Of the beautiful voice of the young rotund Marguerite.   More than one were mystified at her reserved manner, and they would have liked to have had more time in dear old blighty to have broken down that curtain.   Her young sister was different altogether and very easy to get to know and a delightful young woman, but on questioning Sarah about Marguerite all she would say was that she had been in some sort of drama.   Later in the stench of the trenches and thinking of home and those happy evenings in Bedford Square the memories of Marguerite were intriguing and more than one officer wished to return to the Square, when the fighting was over, to recapture lost time.

In the spring of 1915 Frederick and Emily became grandparents for the first time on the birth of William, a welcome son for Rachel and Edward Tremaine. Rachel was being well cared for at her lovely Harrow home.   A maternity nurse had been called in for six weeks and Edward was forever attentive; although he felt the pressures of a call soon to serve his country in the armed forces.   The months soon slipped by, and, in no time at all, Edward knew the time had come when he had to say farewell to Harrow and leave behind his young wife and baby son.

Edward had only just enlisted when a message was received by the Sinclair family that their loyal servant and butler George had been killed at the front. Rachel was in a frenzy as she feared her beloved Edward could be the next, although he was still in training on Salisbury Plain.   Frederick took the death of his friend and butler badly, but, nevertheless, he made it quite clear to young John Mullen, in the office, that he would not stand in his way if he should wish to enlist. John would often stand at the office window and ponder as he watched the young men marching off to war, but, no, he could not bring himself to go to the front to kill fellow men.   John was to bear numerous unpleasantness and abuse from those whom he had thought to be his friends but he was adamant.   Frederick would certainly have missed his young hardworking articled clerk; since the outbreak of war the pressures had grown with the legalities caused through the war, and the work load had become too much for one Solicitor on his own.

Since returning home Marguerite would often sit up quite late talking to her dear Papa.   They were to discuss many things and she endeavoured to comfort him over the loss of George.   Talking of John's decision she told her Father of her distress at the way Hans Peter had been marched off to fight and of her sympathy for the man in the street, whether they be English or German.   She talked of that young priest who was risking his life seeing people across the border.   She often wondered how they were all coping with the worsening effects of the war.   Yes she thought war was a terrible thing for the ordinary run of people.   A fact that was to be brought even closer home to her when early one morning there was an explosion at the munitions factory where Mary and her sisters worked. It was not Mary that was hurt this time, but her younger sister, Beth; although too young to be working in the factory she had gone to the toilet at the bottom of the garden when the explosion occurred at the nearby factory and she was sadly to lose a leg. Frederick was adamant that she should have the attention of the best doctors and nurses that could be found in these days of war, and when young Beth finally left hospital she moved with her mother into Bedford Square to convalesce at the Sinclair's home.

Marguerite was not to take up her ambition to drive, as on mentioning it to her forever attentive Dr. Spencer he advised her that with her past history it would be unwise. She supposed she should obey her faithful doctor, but when she considered the traumas of 1914, which she survived, she felt really fit. Nevertheless, her mind was diverted from her ambition with the caring for young Beth.

Gradually the war years were to pass, but life in London was never to be the same again; so many young men were not to return home and the promise of visits by these gallant young men would not materialise.

BOOK 1

CHAPTER 7

A PINCH OF SNUFF

The Sinclair family felt they were more fortunate than some when Edward returned from the war unscathed, but a man old for his years and weary.

Servants were impossible to get but Amy and Cook were two good old retainers. Sarah helped as much as she could in the kitchen and would certainly make a very good housewife one day.

As the twenties approached Marguerite and Sarah became very much young ladies of the era with short bobbed hair, and wore, as Mama would say, 'that ugly band' round their head; as for those shorter skirts, what could Mama say?

In 1924 Sarah was to leave home on her marriage to Robert Percival. His father owned a pharmaceutical factory and had taken his son Robert into partnership. Mama was well pleased as she felt both girls had done well. Marguerite rarely visited her sister Rachel at Harrow but escaped to Sarah's home at Wimbledon as often as she could.

By now life for Marguerite had become very tedious. At twenty-eight-years of age her weight had reached eighteen stone, and she felt tired both mentally and physically. Being the only daughter left at home she found herself very much at her dear Mama's beck and call; in fact her Mother at this stage had become unnecessarily demanding, possibly realising that she had only one daughter left at home whom she did not intend to let go. She became over-protective, which was very frustrating and difficult for Marguerite.

Many times Marguerite was to regret not having made a note of that young German couple's surname; if she had only known she could have corresponded and perhaps visited them. This would have certainly have given her a break from dear Mama, and she wondered if she was to ever know if Hans Peter had survived the war?

Gradually over the next two years Marguerite became adjusted to being the only daughter of the house. Amy and Cook were both becoming quite elderly and so she endeavoured to learn from them and to involve herself in household matters, even if it was only to escape from Mama's demands.

Frederick continued his usual routine of attending the office each day, but was beginning to hand over more of his affairs to the now middle-aged John, a bachelor well set in his ways.   Occasionally Marguerite would accompany her Father to the City and it was Papa's dear wish that perhaps a relationship would develop between John and Marguerite.   Marguerite showed no interest; in fact she was becoming used to the idea that she would remain a spinster, especially with the war having taken so many eligible young men of her age.   She enjoyed her singing and was still much in demand at social events, and it was a strange fact that as Marguerite's weight increased her voice became more powerful and had more depth.   She put in more practice and decided to once more to take singing lessons. This was all in preparation for a special family event - the celebration of her Father's sixtieth birthday, which was to be a memorable event with many notable friends attending.   She looked forward very much to her dear Papa's birthday.

During the morning of the early autumnal September day Rachel arrived with her husband Edward and ten-year-old son William, who was just about to go to Preparatory School in preparation for entering Harrow.   William was a young lad made much of by his doting parents.   Sarah arrived early afternoon with husband Robert, they were now in their second year of marriage and still very much newly weds.   Sarah was expecting her first child.   The three daughters were soon hard at work with Amy and Cook's help preparing the buffet for the evening.   Mama made it her responsibility to see to the flower arrangements, she was not used to kitchen matters, but life was certainly going to alter for dear Mama as this evening was also to see the retirement of Amy, leaving just Cook in service for the Sinclairs.

Whilst the three sisters were busy with their hands they were chatting and catching up with all the news.   Much to the amusement of Marguerite, Rachel and Sarah were discussing education. "I suppose, Sarah, you will be putting your child's name down at birth for a Public School?" asked Rachel.

"I think Robert and I will talk about that when the child is older, Rachel," answered a bemused Sarah.

"Oh you do not want to leave it too late," was Rachel's quick reply.   Really, Rachel was becoming so like Mama, thought Marguerite.   Oh well if she was to remain a spinster they would have no influence with her over such matters.

Soon Papa was arriving home and the party was under way.   Marguerite spent the evening, without appearing too rude, in endeavouring to avoid John Mullen; she was glad when the opportunity came for her to escape to her bedroom and prepare for her singing.   The guests certainly enjoyed Marguerite's fine voice that evening, and it was to be the first occasion when she was to sing so beautifully 'Oh for the wings of a dove'. Yes her voice was indeed in fine fettle.

It was then Amy's turn.   She was in tears when she found she was one of the celebrities of the evening, especially when Frederick presented her with a beautiful Wedgwood tea service.   Yes, she thought, this Sinclair family were indeed going to be hard to leave.

Dear Papa's sixtieth birthday was to be remembered for a long time.

*

Not many weeks were to pass before Marguerite's thirtieth birthday. She intended to take Mama and Papa to the theatre and to celebrate in a quiet manner, but Papa still loved to spring surprises. On the day of her birthday he arrived home early from the office and he slowly came up the steps to the house, perhaps, Marguerite thought, a little wearily for him. On opening the door Marguerite espied, peeping out of his coat, a small bright face; it was soon wriggling to escape; the sweetest King Charles spaniel. Frederick knew this was his beloved daughter's favourite breed and after the way she had sung at his party he wanted to show his appreciation with a special present. It was certainly the best present Marguerite had ever received and she was delighted. She told her Father, later that evening, that she had decided to call the small dog Snuff', for as far back as she could remember Papa had enjoyed his pinch of snuff - a habit given up during the war when it was difficult to obtain.

"In that case," announced Papa, standing up and reaching up to the drawing room mantelpiece, "you may have this extra small present," he handed Marguerite the small gold snuff box that he no longer needed. "This will be a small memento of your birthday and the day that Snuff came to keep you company." A small memento - little did Frederick realise the significance of this remark, as the next day he became ill.

The next evening on returning from the office, Frederick slowly walked into the drawing room and then suddenly without warning collapsed at Emily's feet. A frantic Emily shouted for Marguerite who rushed to her Papa's side, but she could do nothing but help her dear Mama to gently hold Frederick in her arms. Dr Spencer was immediately fetched, but it was too late, Papa had suffered a serious stroke from which he did not recover. The family were shattered. Papa had not been one to be ill and this was such a terrible shock to them all.

Marguerite, who was possibly the closest to her Father, felt as though life had finished. The funeral was so sad and the family were very worried for her in case the shock weakened her heart even more. Little Snuff was her saving grace, because all growing dogs need exercise and this necessitated a walk each day- a walk that took her further from home and enabled her to have an excuse to escape from dear Mama, but her interest in singing was forgotten, the memories of her last performance at her dear Papa's birthday still too close; in fact she was not to sing, or look at her music, for a number of years. It was, in fact, Emily Sinclair who after the funeral went to pieces, she missed her dear Frederick so much and most afternoons took to her bed.

*

Early in the New Year of 1927 Marguerite decided to approach Mama about turning out Papa's belongings, but Mama showed not the slightest indication to help in this matter. Marguerite did not intend approaching Rachel or Sarah, especially as Sarah's baby would soon be due, and so it was left to her.

Early one February day she set off for the City to sort out the office. This was to take a number of days, much to the pleasure of John Mullen who found her company to his liking. When the matter in hand had been dealt with and John knew that it was Marguerite's final visit he decided he must speak. "Marguerite may I be so bold as to say how I have enjoyed your company these last few days," stated a by now very nervous John.

Marguerite replied, perhaps a little warily, "I am so glad John and I thank you for being such a great help "

John was not used to handling women and wondered how to go on. "Uhm," giving a little cough and going over to Marguerite and taking her hand in his, he said, "I would indeed find it a privilege if you would find it in your heart to see me more often." He sighed with relief, now he had said it, why had he waited so long? Marguerite withdrew her hand in surprise and moved across to stand under Papa's portrait and turned and stared at this devout employee of her late Papa's and was quite lost for words. What could she say?

Book 2

Albert

1901-1928

BOOK 2

CHAPTER 8

A BREATH OF SEA AIR

The same year that saw the marriage of Frederick and Emily Sinclair another couple started out on married life, but a life quite different from the affluent couple in Bedford Square.

To Southend-on-Sea from Holloway Road, in north London, travelled the bride and groom, Albert and Mary Smythe. Albert at twenty-two-years of age was fortunate to have an apprenticeship to a baker, and was taking his young bride, twenty-year-old Mary, a petite young girl, to his one room near the bake-house, tucked away in a back street off the sea front, overshadowed by a gasometer. There they were to live for the short span of their married life.

Young Mary made the room quite comfortable. Their first year of married life was very happy. Albert commenced work at 3.15 am most days and sometimes worked all night, but in the afternoon or early evening the young lovers would often stroll along the promenade, perhaps sometimes stopping to buy some cockles and mussels. Mary would tease her young husband if he should so much as glance at the refined ladies with their colourful parasols.

This idyllic life was to soon end, as Mary was to bear children almost yearly. Thomas was to be their first born, arriving on their first wedding anniversary. He was a fine strapping baby. The next year it was Kate, followed in 1892 by young Albert junior, a puny baby, but to grow up in looks very much like his Father. Mary then had a year's respite, as her beloved Albert showed signs of sickness, but it was only one year's respite as Connie then followed; she was a really lovely baby and gave much joy to this devoted couple. Soon after the arrival of their last offspring, Eve, who from the very first was very much a Mummy's baby, Albert was to have a recurrence of the consumption and passed away, leaving young Mary with five small children.

This young mother, dressed in her widow's-weeds, was often to be seen pushing her heavy pram along the seafront at Southend. Gertie, the cockles and mussels stallholder, would smile at her with sympathy and would often have a quiet word. "Keep your pecker up, my dear, life will improve!" She ruffled young Thomas's hair, she had a soft spot for this little chap.

After one year Mary's life was not improving and she decided to return to London, where she had grown up and her Ma still lived. She had found it so difficult in the one room to keep control of her offspring. There was the washing to dry and the older children these days liked to run on the beach and this meant sometimes tar stains and the muddy sand marks to get off their clothes. She could stand it no longer!

Her Ma managed to obtain a flat for Mary to rent; it was a basement flat where Mary would be responsible to the landlord for the other tenants in the two storeys above. The flat consisted of a rather dark large front room, which Ma said could be used as a bedroom for all the family, and a smaller room at the back, which was, more or less, level with the garden and could be turned into a rather squashed kitchen and living room. Fortunately below all this was a cellar where on wet days the children would be able to play, if they could see between the washing! The front steps led up to the first floor, where a young couple lived, and above that were two more rooms, which were occupied by two elderly ladies. The only thing left to do was for Mary to decide how she was to get her family to London.

One day when she was feeling rather low in spirit she stood on the sea front, with her young bairns gathered around her, talking to Gertie. "I just don't know Gert how I am going to get this brood to London. I just don't know!" said a tearful Mary, shaking her head with worry. "I would just love to be back near my Ma now Albert's gone and left me on my own. There's this 'ere flat I would just love to take, but how, I ask, am I to get them all there?"

A cockney fellow happened to be standing nearby, and looking at this young mum in her widow's clothes with all those kids gathered round her, felt sorry for her. "I tells you what, Ma'am. I bet your cotton socks I could 'elp yer." He smiled at this young tearful girl, the children by now looking up at their Ma's tearful face. "Yeh! I knows I could 'elp yer," nodding his head as he thought what he could do. "What says you, if I lend you me 'orse and cart? Do you just fine that would. What says you?"

Mary looked at this young fellow, at last her eyes lighting up. "Would you be so good?" she questioned.

"Yeh, 'cause I could lend it to yer. What about next week, dearie? What says you?" patting Mary on the shoulder.

"Go on love, take it." Gertie insisted.

Mary let go of young Connie's hand and shook the young fellow's hand in agreement.

*

True to his promise, the young cockney fellow turned up with his horse and cart on the following Thursday, leaving instructions where Mary was to return it. Fortunately it was not far from where she was going to be living. To get the children out of the way, whilst she loaded on all their belongings, she sent Thomas off with them for a last look at the sea - for who knows, she thought, how many years it will be before they see the sea again or smell the fresh air.

Albert junior's memory, as a four-year-old, of that moving day, was all rather vague, but he recalled horse and cart loaded with all their personal possessions. Ma up front with baby Eve, who had just had her first birthday, and seven-year-old Thomas, a sturdy lad for his age, sitting next to her holding the reins; leaving in the back, tucked in amongst their belongings, six-year old Kate in charge of Albert and two-year-old Connie.   Albert recalled passing the cockles and mussels stall and all waving goodbye to Gertie, who shouted, "The best of luck to you all. Bless yer cotton socks."

And so it was goodbye to Southend-on-Sea.   Mary felt the tears streaming down her face as she recalled the happy days when she arrived as a young bride. Oh why could life be so cruel as to take her dear Albert away from her? She supposed she must be thankful for her little brood and she must put sadness behind her and start her life afresh; with those thoughts in mind they left the sea behind and turned out into the country for the long haul to London town.   Every now and then Ma's voice could be heard, "Now behave yerselfs, you two, or y'er get a clout. Just y'er do as Kate tells y'er. Do you 'ear me?"

Albert could recall small Connie kicking out with her fat legs, only because they had cramp, but young Albert was not to appreciate that, and gave her a hefty kick back.   With all the noise going on behind her Ma decided it was time to have a break and they turned off down a farm track.   The excited children jumped down and were soon scampering around in a field - the last time they were to do that for a long time.

In no time at all they were once more off on their journey.   It seemed a very, very long way and to go on for ever.   It became very cold and Albert and Connie huddled closer together and Connie was soon fast asleep and her weight felt like a sack of potatoes to the still small Albert.

Finally, on a cold February day in 1896, this young mother and her small brood arrived in Holloway Road, causing quite a sensation to the families standing at their doors.   As they had approached the outskirts of London the sudden noise had awoken Connie, and the children became quite excited.   Everywhere seemed cramped even to Mary who had grown up in London. Life looked so busy after the calm of Southend. Yes everything was going to be so different.

The basement flat seemed as cold and damp as the cart, but Ma soon found the bellows and got the fire going in the old black-leaded grate.   The children stood around tired and puzzled at their strange surroundings.   Soon there was a knock on the door.   The children stared towards it wide eyed - who could be knocking on their door? Ma knew that it would be their Gran Sparkes, but in their excitement the children had forgotten that Gran lived just down the road.

"Well open the door one of you,' instructed a tired but smiling Mary.

Thomas was the first to get up and on opening the door there stood Flo Sparkes, holding, in her arms, a steaming hot bowl of homemade lamb broth full of carrots and thickened with pearl barley.

*

Flo Sparkes had come down to the Holloway Road from Yorkshire before Mary was born, but like her daughter, as quite a young married woman she was left a widow. Flo was now sixty-years-old and lived above a shop. For years she had been an early morning office cleaner, but for all her bluntness she was well respected in the area.

It was Flo's cousin back in Yorkshire that had introduced her to young Albert, when he came down south and lodged temporarily with Mary and her mother. It broke Flo's heart when Mary left home, on marrying Albert, and went to live in Southend. On Albert's death she had been really concerned for Mary left with five kids. What was her only child doing with five kids? - Who would have thought it!

*

Flo had her hair covered with an old scarf, tied round and knotted in the front, it was her custom to keep her hair covered for her dusty office cleaning, and she had not thought, before leaving her flat, of taking it off. Her black woolly skirt nearly reached to the ground, and she was relieved to place the heavy bowl of broth onto the table before it spilt down her clean white apron. She had made herself spick-and-span this evening for these grandchildren, who had not seen Gran Sparkes very often. Turning to Kate she said, "Now Kate, make y'erself useful and find some dishes for this 'ere broth before it gets cold. They're all clean, I washed them yesterday meself." Kate was hesitant, she wasn't used to being dictated to - in her tiredness she wasn't so sure of this Gran they had come to live close by - but, nevertheless, the broth smelt good and she reluctantly got up and did as she was told.

Flo turned to four-year-old Albert, whom she was determined was not going to be called by his Father's name - her Mary would never get over her husband's death having another Albert around! No, from this moment, her young grandson was going to be 'Algie', and from that moment that is what he became to the whole family. "Algie, how did you enjoy y'er ride then?" she enquired of the puzzled small boy.

Albert looked up to see who his Gran was speaking to, and realising the question was being put to him he answered his Gran, at the same time asking himself what was that name she had called him; he didn't know whether he liked a funny name like that! "Allsright, I suppose!"

Ruffling his hair, Flo said, "I'm yer Gran you know, and 'Algie' you are going to be to yer old Gran from this day forward" and hesitating she added, "When speaking to yer Gran you says, allsright, thanks Gran, understand Algie?"

"Y'eh, thanks Gran." answered an unsure Algie. The family soon tucked into their broth, after which they began to be more favourably inclined to their old Gran, as the broth was really scrumptious.

Having always been used to one room, the basement and cellar seemed to be a mansion to the children; although they missed the sea at least they had a garden, which they got to know well, as the privy was at the bottom of the mud heap.

Algie was to later find this privy a good place to hide rather than go to the Board School, which was to be a new venture for him.

They had not been in London many weeks when it was Algie's fifth birthday and time for him to start school. He set off each day with big sister Kate and hurried along by Thomas who daren't be late otherwise he would feel the cane across his backside. Sometimes, when money was short, and there was none left for shoe repairs, they went barefooted. No, Algie's memories of school days were not happy. Cracked slates were condemned, and, as Algie had a paddy and was in the habit of coming down heavy with his fist onto his slate, it was always getting cracked. The headmaster's cane was forever being felt through Algie's thin trousers. Happier memories were of Sundays, when as a family, in their best clothes and all spick-and-span they set off for Mass, and then, in the afternoon, Sunday school.

Soon after Algie had commenced school, Ma took a walk one day with Eve in the perambulator and Connie toddling alongside. It turned out to be a rather long walk for three-year-old Connie, as Ma had an ulterior motive in this walk. She pushed the pram up Highgate Hill, as she had decided, now that she had got rid of the heap of mud and had a reasonable garden, she would take in washing - she had to do something to enable her at least to buy the kids' shoes. Gran Sparkes had suggested placing a card in a shop or two at The Archway and perhaps at The Tavern. This had brought results and now she was on her way to further the arrangements.

And so that is how it was that Thomas, and in later years Algie, would be found, before school, in the backyard turning the heavy mangle, whilst Ma fed the washing through. The sight of this giant monstrosity standing on its wrought iron legs at the back door was to be remembered by Algie for a long time. Algie patiently waited for Ma to tighten the tension screw on the top of the mangle before they could start rolling. He would look at this large wrought iron screw and long for the day when he could reach it. Often he would stand on tip toe and reach up, just in case he had grown in the night. If care was not taken when feeding the washing in, the mangle's heavy rollers bruised his small fingers badly. It always seemed a rushed job, especially when Algie became a server at early morning Mass. It was certainly a rush to fit both jobs in, but Ma was adamant that it was not a job for the girls, which Thomas thought very unfair. Mind you his interest in being a server soon waited and life became a little easier. Sometimes, if the washing had not turned up, Ma sent Algie the long trek up Highgate Hill to collect it. This took him longer than it should, as he hung over the garden walls day-dreaming of how one day he would have a garden just like them. He could feel his fingers itching with the thought of what he could do with his hands.

It was the custom for the children in the area to dart in and out of the horses hoofs shovelling up manure to sell to those posh houses up the hill. Ma dared any of her children do this and she kept a close watch on her buckets to make sure that none went missing, just in case they were tempted by the money. She was certainly not having them risk their lives or limbs.

As Algie got older he enjoyed going up to Chapel Street market, near the Angel. Ma was forever telling him off for going so far, she was frightened that he would get into bad company. By the time he was ten-years-old he had got to know some of the stallholders quite well, and he had a plan in mind to really make some money. He dreamt that he would be able to treat all the family, but first of all he had to have some money of his own! Where was he to get hold of such money?

BOOK 2

CHAPTER 9

THE LONG TREK

Algie went to see Granny Sparkes. "Gran can you lend me some dough?" asked Algie.

"Lend you some dough me lad? What for? And where's yer manners." admonished Gran.

"Sorry Gran, please Gran," pleaded young Algie.

"But what for, I asked yer?" Gran was not lending or giving this young Algie any money unless she knew what it was to be spent on.

"Well you sees Gran, there's this bloke down in the market that's selling Union Jacks and I thoughts as I would buy a whole lot and take them up the West End and sell them on Coronation Day," announced an excited Algie.

"And may I asks what you plan to do with the money when you sells them ere flags?" questioned Gran.

"I's give some to Ma and gives you your dough back," said Algie, and then hesitantly, hoping not to put Gran Sparkes off, "I'd keep the rest, Gran." He looked at his Gran expectantly. "What yer say, Gran? Please Gran."

"Whats yer Ma say abouts you traipsing off on your own, me young scallywag?" asked Gran.

"Well I's not told her yet, Gran." Algie was now looking rather sheepish.

"Well!, says Gran, "As yer going to hand some to yer Ma, which I am sure she can do with, with you young scarpers to bring up, I might sees me way clear to putting me hand in me pocket."

Algie rushed and hugged his Gran. "Thanks Gran, yer the best. Thanks a million."

When Algie broached the subject with Ma, she was not too keen. She said it was too far for him to go, but it was her Ma that persuaded her to give into Algie. Gran said "Let the young rascal go. It will be a memorable occasion for him." And so Ma relented.

So Algie was to buy his flags for that Coronation Day in August 1902 and in the early hours off set ten-year-old Algie, with his Ma's sacking bag over his shoulder, to walk to Trafalgar Square and Buckingham Palace. The bag was packed tight with rolled up small Union Jacks on wooden sticks; and as he plodded down Euston Road his bag got heavier and heavier, but he still had a long way to go and excitement egged him on. At long last he arrived and he took a swig of his Gran's homemade lemonade, before strolling slowly around Trafalgar Square and down The Mall to Buckingham Palace, all the time keeping up a continuous patter; "Buy yerself a flag. 'Ere yer are ladies and gents luverly flags for the nippers; buy yerself a flag. They aren't arf easy to wave. 'Ere you are. Where's yer dough. Luverly flags." He kept up this patter for what seemed like hours. He had never seen such pageantry in his life; and all those fine gentry with their young ones dressed as small replicas. He stood and stared at them up in the stands; and they certainly could see more of the event than he could, but who cares, he was doing really well. 'Yes, Algie boy,' he told himself, 'Yer done alright' He certainly had taken quite a bit of money, in fact, he had never handled so much before and on his long trek home his bag felt even heavier.

He went straight to Gran Sparkes with the money and they counted it together and split it, as arranged, three ways, and when he pocketed his share didn't he feel wealthy.

Later that evening when Algie eventually arrived home, Ma straight away got the tin bath off the hook in the backyard; she had already lit the gas under the boiler and the water was bubbling hot. The bath was placed in front of the black-leaded grate and she instructed her young son to "Get yer clothes off and into that ere water you get my young scallywag. Aren't I glad to see you back safe and sound." Algie wanted to tell Ma and his brothers and sisters of the excitement of the day, but she was adamant that that could wait until he was washed. The long trek had made him filthy - no doubt the dust from all those horses had covered him many many times.

After he had had a good soak - my his feet felt as though they certainly needed it - he had a good splash around and he nearly got a box round the ears for making the kitchen so wet and slippery, he quickly dressed into some clean clothes, and the family then gathered around the kitchen table to hear all about the Coronation. Thomas sat and listened to the story of his young brother's trek with envy and wondered why he had not thought of going himself. He had to admit his brother had his wits about him, although he was becoming rather a scraggy looking lad. Kate was not that interested about all the well-dressed gentry, she knew that the time would soon come when she had to go into service, and the tales brought back by some of the older girls were rather frightening and she was not really interested.

Now Connie was a different kettle of fish, she was really fascinated with the description of all that finery that Algie described. "Coo, Algie, I'm going to dress like that when I'm a lady. Just yer wait and see!" announced an excited Connie with the thought of what the future held.

Eve sat on her Ma's lap and just listened, as did her Ma who would have dearly loved to have seen all the pageantry. Eve was perhaps a little bored and was slightly annoyed that Algie had not saved one of those flags for her.

That evening Algie felt very proud that for the first time he had been able to hand his Ma some money. Yes very proud, but he was not to feel proud for long!

It had certainly been a memorable occasion, but my didn't Algie get into trouble when the next Sunday came and his best shoes were found to be worn to the ground, but it had been worth it - all those fine horses and the beautiful coach and four. Wouldn't he brag to his mates and wouldn't they be envious? But he was not to brag for long.

*

Some few weeks after the Coronation Algie became unwell. It was suspected that he had contracted something from the crowds. Ma was to say "I told you not to go trekking all that way. What did I say?" Soon Algie was to get worse and it was confirmed that indeed it was the dreaded diphtheria. A blanket, soaked in disinfectant, was placed at the door, and Algie was rushed to the isolation part of the Infirmary. He no longer felt a big lad, and, in fact, with this illness and feeling so very poorly he missed his Ma and Gran Sparkes.

Before Algie could return home eight-year-old Connie was to be received into the same ward. A very, very sick little girl, and it upset Algie to see her so ill and she was crying so much at having to leave her Ma, and in no time at all the nurses and doctors were rushing around with great urgency. As the days went by Connie got worse and worse and Ma was fetched and the curtains were drawn around her bed. Algie was to always remember his Ma's distraught face as she went behind the curtains to see Connie, and he knew only too well with his Ma appearing that things were not good as no visitors were allowed in the Infirmary. Algie prayed so hard "Dear God, please don't let my little sister die," but God must have been too busy or did not hear, because soon a trolley was brought and they took little Connie away with Ma following in tears, and she did not stop or look at young Algie. Algie began to panic - why didn't they tell him something? Algie called the nurse and asked "Where's me little sister gone to?"

The nurse ruffled his hair and gave a very non-committal answer, "She's gone away."

'Why don't they tell me?' thought Algie. 'I know she's gone and died. Why don't they tell me and why hadn't Ma said something to him?' As he lay in bed, getting further and further down into the bedclothes, he recalled that long journey from Southend when as a four-year-old he cuddled his small sister as she slept in his arms in that old cart; and it seemed only yesterday that she had said she was going to wear fine clothes when she was a lady. All these thoughts went through his mind and he began to sob and sob and still no one came to him; the nurses and doctors were all so busy and he was supposed to be on the mend. In his distressed state he began to blame himself for going to the Coronation and possibly having brought the dreaded disease into the house, and hadn't his Ma said, 'I told you so'. As he became tired from crying, and in his still sick state, he began to tell himself - 'I killed my little sister. That's it, which is why no-one is taking any notice of me - I killed my little sister. That is why they won't tell me she's dead. - I killed Connie.' He lay there getting more and more distressed as he convinced himself that her death was his fault! Eventually, through the exhaustion of sobbing and having been so ill, he was to fall into a deep but restless sleep.

*

The family were shattered to lose such a sweet eight-year-old. Gradually Ma was to be upheld in her grief by her strong Roman Catholic faith, and after this tragic death, she never missed attending Mass.   She was to say when kneeling in church she felt nearer to both her beloved Albert and little Connie and she consoled herself that at least her Albert was already in heaven to take care of his small daughter.

Gran Sparkes was conscious of the fact that it was her money that had enabled young Algie to go to the Coronation and she hoped her Mary, in her grief, would not take it out on the young lad.   It was indeed a very sad household that buried small Connie.

Back in the Infirmary Algie lay moping as he was not allowed home in time for his sister's funeral, and he felt forgotten and still blamed himself for her death. If only he had not gone to the Coronation! If only he had not gone!

Gran Sparkes was very conscious of the fact that poor Algie had been forgotten and was determined to make it up to him. She suggested that on leaving the Infirmary Algie should return to her flat, and Ma was only too thankful to agree to this arrangement.   When the day arrived to fetch Algie, Gran turned to her daughter and said "Look 'ere, Mary, whatever you do you mustn't take it out on Algie for Connie's passing. I was as much to blame." Mary looked at her Ma and sadly shook her head, but did not say a word. Algie looked at his Ma and Gran as they approached the ward sister's office, where he was waiting, and he shoved his belongings into their waiting hands and burst into tears.   It was his Gran who consoled him, and he was much relieved on being told that he was to return to his Gran Sparke's flat for a few weeks.

Young Algie enjoyed being pampered over the next few weeks, but Gran's neighbours did not appreciate seeing Algie arriving straight from the Isolation Infirmary with his Gran, and they let it be known that they were not happy with the situation; they shook their fists and shouted: "Shame on you, bringing a sick kid 'ere." - such was the fear of the dreaded diphtheria.

BOOK 2

CHAPTER 10

TO SAIL AWAY

Gran Sparkes did not often lose her temper, but she did with her neighbours on this occasion, especially when they started to call out again, "Shame on you bringing that sick lad 'ere'; send him back down the road where he belongs." She could stand it no longer and she went out to face them and in her Yorkshire bluntness she told them what she thought of them. She explained of her guilt at Algie's trek to the Coronation, where the family thought that he had contracted diphtheria, and of how she had encouraged him to go, thinking that to the extra money would help his Ma. Being true Cockneys they usually had soft hearts and it was only the dreaded diphtheria that on this occasion had frightened them. Their hearts soon softened and they turned and hugged dear old Flo Sparkes and all was forgiven, and from that day they always had a good word to say to young Algie.

Even with all the trouble that Gran Sparkes had to put up with it was definitely the right thing for Algie to have gone back with her; he was to find out that Gran felt as guilty as he did over the death of little Connie. Their chats together helped both of them to get over their sadness and the few weeks with Gran soon built up Algie's strength and he seemed to grow taller than ever. Soon it was time to return home to Ma and his brother and sisters, and not once did Ma refer to the Coronation.

*

Thomas was now twelve-years-old and he started work with a scrap merchant, and his meagre earnings were a great help to his Ma.

The following year Kate was old enough to leave school. For her it was the time she had been worried about for so long, time to leave home. Arrangements had been made for her to go into service with a notable family down in the country and Ma was to once more bless the day she had thought of going up Highbury Hill to get washing, as that is how the contact for Kate's job had been made. Ma was going to miss her eldest daughter so much, especially with the help of folding the washing; six-year-old Eve would now have to help with this task. An old leather suitcase was found, which had belonged to the children's Pa, dear Albert. Kate's belongings were soon placed in it, and the people from up the Hill arrived and it was a tearful Kate that said goodbye to her Ma and brothers and sister. Ma looked at her eldest daughter as she waved goodbye and thought, 'poor kid, you are not much more than a child. God take care of you.' It was then July 1903 and it was to be some time before Kate was to get a holiday, and it was too far away to pay a visit on Mothering Sunday.

*

It was at last Algie's turn to put school days behind him, and it could not come soon enough for him. He had always got on well with their neighbour, who had a stall in the Caledonian market, and that was where he went to work on that July day in 1904. He was to enjoy his days there, as he loved the cockney slang and bartering of market life. He soon learnt to sell all manner of goods, from pots and pans to garden forks and spades. It soon became his ambition to have a stall of his own.

*

At dinner table on a Sunday, four year's later, Thomas suddenly announced that he was going 'down under'. Ma looked puzzled, "You are going where?" she asked of her eldest son.

"Ma, I've got a job as a deckhand on a boat going to Australia," the seventeen-year-old announced to his astounded and horrified Ma.

"Oh, 'ave you me lad. We'll see about that, we will," answered a by now a very annoyed Ma. She was certainly not having this. Her eldest going off like that, oh no! But, no matter how she argued, Thomas was determined he was going and she was certainly not having this. Her eldest going off like that, oh no! No matter how she argued Thomas was determined he was going, and in no time at all the day arrived for Thomas to leave Holloway Road, London, England. The family gathered at Tilbury Docks to wave him goodbye. Kate had at last managed to get a short holiday to say goodbye to her brother. A quite grown up Kate, so different to the twelve-year-old that had left home; in fact Gran had hardly recognised her. The excitement of being in the docks, and seeing all the large ships and the heavy cranes loading on their wares took away some of the grief, especially to young Algie. He was really fascinated by all the commotion of the dock area, and he was also half inclined to wish that he was going on this adventure with his elder brother. As the ship sailed away to faraway shores, Ma, wiping her tears, thought of how Thomas had been a good son and brother, but why had he, at such a young age, to leave them? She wondered what he would have to face on this long voyage - she had heard such terrible tales. She had pleaded with him to write and she wondered at this moment if he would do so and how many years it would be before he was to step foot in England again?

*

Middle-aged Mary was now left at home with just two in the family. She was adamant that she was not going to lose these last two. No, she would never let these two go, and when the occasion arose Ma could certainly be a very determined woman. Even when it came to attending Mass, she endeavoured to enforce Algie and Eve to attend. Algie, having dropped out as a server some years before, would have none of this, but Eve dutifully accompanied her Ma each Sunday.

Algie was not strong and robust like his elder brother and the diphtheria had left him to grow up as a very tall lean lad, but whether it was because he was thin, he had bounding energy and could walk for miles. Sometimes, when he could take a morning off from the Caledonian Market, and unbeknown to Ma, although he had let Gran Sparkes into the secret, he and a pal would go down to Petticoat Lane with old junk and make quite a bit on the side.

At eighteen-years-old Algie was to meet the girl of his dreams and fall in love for the first time. After he had been walking out his Gladys for some weeks he decided it was time to bring her home to meet Ma, but what a disaster! He was quite sure that his Ma would approve of his choice, but Ma was to think otherwise. The following Friday he thought he would broach the subject, to give his Ma good warning. "Ma, I would like you to meet the girl I am walking out. She is called Gladys, and I would like to bring her home to tea on Sunday." requested a quite nervous Algie. He was not too sure of what Ma's reaction would be.

Eve gave a giggle, as all fourteen-year-old sisters are prone to do when an elder brother announces he's bringing a girl friend home for the first time. "Coo Ma, say yes," encouraged an excited Eve.

Ma was a little taken back by the sudden announcement of a girl friend. It must be serious if Algie wanted to bring her home to tea. Serious indeed, she thought, we shall see about that. 'And where, may I ask, does this Gladys, you call her, come from?" she asked.

"From Camden Town, Ma." answered Algie.

Camden Town, thought Ma, far enough away to not be too much on the doorstep. "Oh well, Algie, I suppose you might as well bring her home to tea, as long as it is not too often," and so Ma had given her permission.

Sunday came and Eve helped her Ma prepare the tea and the best table cloth was found. Eve took extra care with her appearance. Since Thomas had gone off to Australia and Kate hardly ever came home there was not much excitement these days, and she was really looking forward to meeting this Gladys. Tea was all ready when they heard the key in the door, and into the back room Algie ushered his Gladys. All went well, until suddenly during tea Ma turned to Gladys and asked "And why may I ask, do you want my Algie?" Gladys was quite startled by the question and hesitated to reply. Algie took Gladys's hand and squeezed it with encouragement at the same time trying to stop Ma asking any more silly questions, but Ma, without giving Gladys a chance to reply went on to say "All the more fool him!"

Algie was embarassed, and all Eve could say was "Oh Ma, you do say such silly things."

Gladys, without more ado got up from her seat and said "Algie, please take me home. I can see where I'm not welcome!" Algie tried to pacify his first love but without much success, and much to Ma's amusement and Eve's disappointment they left in quite a hurry.

Eve shouted at her Ma, "Really Ma, you have ruined the best Sunday for a long time," and went into the bedroom crying.

Ma shouted after her, "You keep out of this m'lady. I know when a girl's right for my Algie or not," and having said that Ma went down to the cellar to sort out her washing.

Algie endeavoured to resolve the disagreement with Gladys, but it was not to be and that was the end of what he felt could have developed into a good relationship, all because of Ma. This was to be the trend whenever Algie tried to introduce a girl friend to Ma, and so he decided that when Miss Right came along he would definitely not introduce her to his Ma until he was well and truly wedded.

*

The years were to go by, and just when Algie was making a way for himself in the market, England declared War on Germany. Algie, not wanting his Ma and Eve to be at the receiving end of bad feeling, decided it was his duty to enlist. Ma was heartbroken, but this time understood where her son's duties lie.

Kate was once more to visit home. As Eve was to say, she always seemed to put in an appearance when one of the family was about to leave home, but this time, for a change, she intended to stay a little longer. She arrived a couple of days before Algie was to enlist, and she flounced in and went straight up to Ma, saying, "Mrs Law, at your service."

"What's that?" shouted a bewildered Ma.

"I married my Cecil last week, before he went off to the front," announced a bemused Kate.

"You did what?" asked a by now cross Ma.

"I'm married Ma, and as I'm twenty-three, just in case you have forgotten, there is nowt you can do 'bout it," answered a defiant Kate. Ma did not care how old Kate was, she resented not being put into the picture before, and she gave her defiant daughter a piece of her mind.

Algie took his sister out for the evening to celebrate and to hear all about her Cecil, but it did not matter what Algie said to Ma and how much he tried to make his Ma see sense she would not accept the fact that her eldest daughter had married without her approval. A cloud was to hang over the household, and it was, therefore, a very subdued party that saw Algie off to enlist. Kate was to leave home for her country lodgings immediately afterwards.

Algie marched through the city, with some of his comrades from the market, feeling quite proud of the fact that he was off to fight for his country.

BOOK 2

CHAPTER 11

A RUDE AWAKENING

Algie enjoyed his time in training down in Wiltshire as the air of the Salisbury plain was to him like an unexpected holiday. Whilst there he took the opportunity, before being moved to a transit camp, to take twenty-four hours leave and visit his sister Kate in Dorchester. He found Dorchester much to his liking, as he had always been interested in history, and, the very short time he was there, he enjoyed the historic town. By chance his new brother-in-law, Cecil, was home, and this gave them a chance to get to know each other. Algie was pleased for this opportunity as Cecil was just about to be posted to France. They got on well and Algie was pleased for his sister Kate. Why did his Ma have to be so cussed over the marriage? Before Cecil went away, it was confirmed that Kate was expecting their first child, and Algie hoped that she was not going to be like his Ma and have one each year!

In no time at all Algie's days of training were over, and before going overseas he went home to the Holloway Road to say goodbye. The final evening of his leave he spent with Gran Sparkes, who was now showing her age. Algie was sorry that he would miss her eightieth birthday, as he had a soft spot for his dear Gran.

To a young man aged twenty-two years, from a poor background, the anticipation of time to be spent abroad caused some excitement; although he was to wonder what was to transpire after experiencing the cramped conditions of the troopship. It seemed that they no sooner stepped onto foreign shores than it was dig, dig, and yet more digging all the time. The weather seemed to immediately turn wet, and the trenches, which they had dug, soon filled up with water. His thoughts of an enjoyable time turned into a nightmare, as told in his letters home. He was certainly not to enjoy these next four years.

*

At home, with Algie having gone to war, Ma was already regretting her harsh words with Kate. She now had only Eve to keep her company, and, in no time at all, both of them were working alongside each other in a munitions factory, fortunately not far from home. At least she could still keep young Eve under her thumb.

Gran Sparkes missed the company of her grandchildren and was beginning to feel rather lonely. So many people were either away in the forces or at work in these new factories. She just didn't know what was happening in the world, but everything certainly seemed to have gone wild. Yes, life was very quiet these days for Gran, but she looked forward to her letters from Algie. At least he wrote, not like that Thomas whose letters had got fewer and fewer, as the years went by, and now appeared to have ceased. She wondered if he would turn up one day, having been posted back to England in the Australian army. If he did, she would give him a piece of her mind, never letting them know how he was getting on.

Did Ma and Gran detect a slight disappointment in Algie's first few letters home from France? They seemed to be full of the shocking weather. 'It arn't arf wet here, rain and rain all the time. The officers aren't too bad, in fact quite 'uman at times, if you keep on digging'. Keep on digging thought Gran. What are they doing? That doesn't sound like soldiering! The news that no-one could make broth like his Gran, pleased her. He always ended his Ma's letters with, 'please write to Kate and let me know when the kid arrives'. Algie was to wait and wait to hear news of Kate, as Ma would not write to her daughter, and neither of them would bend in their relationship. All Ma would say was that she never did like writing letters, and didn't she write to Algie every week, wasn't that good enough? Algie felt that he could not trouble his Gran. Algie was in fact entrenched, with his battalion, keeping the Germans back from Ypres. He thought this was hell, but was to fare much worse later in the war. He wrote home, 'Ma, as a kid when visiting the lav down the garden I saw the odd rat or two and was scared, but Ma, you get past being scared 'ere - they are as large as cats and hundreds of them. We need a Pied Piper like the nursery rhyme you used to read to us as kids!'

*

In the Spring of 1915, after the battle for 'Hill 60', Algie was sent home on leave and so missed the initial taste of the ghastly new German weapon of poison gas. Both Ma and Gran Sparkes were shocked to see how thin Algie had become and they did not like his sickly colour. After a few days, and much to Ma's annoyance, he went down to see Kate in Dorchester, and he was thrilled with his small niece Ruth. Cecil had been home on leave six months before and Kate was longing for his next leave. Algie quite envied his sister's close relationship with her Cecil, and he only hoped that this young husband would come through the war unscathed.

On returning to London his leave was to pass very quickly. He hated saying goodbye to Gran Sparkes as he had noticed how aged she had become, and as he hugged her goodbye he had a premonition that he would not see her again.

*

July 1916 saw the advance on the Somme; the fighting at the front was intense and sordid and the rat-infested trenches deplorable. The morale of the troops was indeed becoming low when in the September a new machine became available to the British Army; the tank was used for the first time. This machine proved to be a great boost to the troops.

At home Ma and Eve dreaded each knock at the door, in case it was bad news, so many families had lost loved ones.

Back in the trenches Algie swore that once this godforsaken war was over he would never step foot off England's green and pleasant land ever again. Nevertheless, considering his poor physique he was standing up to the trials and stresses of the war very well.

In the June of 1917 the first American troops joined in the fighting, and Algie wrote home to say that, 'things were hotting up, and perhaps, Ma, we will be 'ome soon'. In the August, 'Hill 70' was captured; this was followed in the October with the battle of the 'Passchendale Ridge'. Another Christmas, but a Christmas with a difference. Orders were given that there should be a temporary ceasefire over the festivities. The two opposing armies came together over the front line to play football, sing carols and joke together, and Algie was to think 'why is there a bloody war, they are only 'uman like us and just want to get on with their lives?' It just didn't make sense to this cockney lad. Algie took the chance, in this lull in the fighting, to write to his Gran.

*

Gran Sparkes was to receive two lettters on that winter's day. The one from Algie was really quite cheerful, he was full of socializing with the enemy. At last, thought Gran, a bit of sense amidst the carnage. She next opened her other letter, she did not recognise the handwriting, but as she read it she collapsed with a letter in each hand.

It was a bitter cold winter's day and both Ma and Eve were exhausted from their work at the munitions factory, they could not work quickly enough or turn out enough parts required for this seemingly never-ending war. As they passed Gran's flat, Eve suggested that they popped in to see if Gran had any broth on the boil.

"Why not," said Ma, "I could certainly do with a warmer." Gran Sparkes did not consider it necessary to lock herself in, she would say, 'everyone round 'ere knows the poor old soul'. Ma and Eve knocked and walked straight in, Eve called out, "Any broth today Gran, we're both starving and cold." She had no sooner said it than she saw her Gran collapsed in the old chair by the stove, a letter in each hand. Ma rushed up to her Mother, shaking her and saying "Come on Ma, yer don't usually fall asleep at this time of the evening! Ma! Ma!" but she knew only too well that it was too late. She shouted to Eve to run and get a Doctor. The Doctor soon confirmed, what Mary feared, her Ma had been dead for some hours. Dear old Gran Sparkes, who had never lost her Yorkshire bluntness and had hardly known a day's illness, at eighty-two-years of age had passed peacefully away sitting in her chair, with a letter from Algie in one hand, and, what was this other letter? Neither Ma nor Eve stopped to look, their concern only being for Gran.

Gran Sparkes was buried in the cemetery up the road. There was only a small gathering, Ma, Eve and some neighbours. They had not thought of contacting Kate. Algie they would write to, and, as to where Thomas was these days, who was to know? Later, sitting over a cup of tea, Eve suddenly remembered the other letter, and turning to her Ma, she said, "Ma, what did you do with the letters that were in Gran's hands?"

Ma, still feeling the shock of her Mother's passing had to think for a few moments. "I suppose I put 'em on the mantelpiece when I took them from yer Gran. I don't know, I was in such a state," answered a tearful Ma.

Eve gave her Ma a hug and said, "Never mind I'll look tomorrow." She only hoped she would find them!

The next day Eve was up early and went round to her Gran's flat. On finding the letters she was soon to find out the reason for her Gran's demise and sudden death. Gran had received a belated Christmas letter from her granddaughter, Kate:-

'My dearest Gran,
*   I am shattered, on the day I gave birth to my little Tommy I was to 'ear that me darling Cecil had been killed at the battle for the Passchendale Ridge. Ruth and Tommy will now never know a Daddy. Gran, please tell Ma - if she's interested, and please ask 'er to let Algie know. Cecil and he were good pals for such a short time.*
*   Hope y'er well Gran.*
*   Yer distressed granddaughter,*
*   Kate.'*

On having this letter read to her by Eve, Ma took the news very badly, as she reproached herself for not having been more thoughtful in the past to her eldest daughter Kate She sat and recalled her days as a young widow in Southend, but she still did not write to Kate and left this to Eve. What could Eve write? She had grown apart from her sister so long ago. She so wished that Algie was home to deal with the matter. She just did not know how they were to tell him of the passing of two people so dear to him. Eve commenced the letter so many times; she had always left the letter writing to her Ma, but both these deaths coming together had really taken the stuffing out of her Ma. In desperation she finally decided to leave it to Eve to convey the sad news to Algie.

Eve sat with paper in front of her wondering how she was to tell her brother the news of the two deaths, but tell him she must, and the sooner done the better!

*

A winter's day in the trenches; a lull in the fighting; the soldiers were cold and miserable. To take their minds off the memories of the past carnage, Algie and his comrades were playing cards, hesitating now and again to rub and stretch their limbs. Suddenly, a voice was heard "poste, poste, come and get it." There was a rush and scramble all hoping for a letter from dear old blighty, as they all welcomed letters from home. "Corporal Smythe, uhm, do I espie a young girl's handwriting?" and the young soldier hid the letter behind his back.

"Give it 'ere and let's 'ave less of yer cheek." Algie said as he made a grab for the letter. Eventually he managed to get it and was surprised not to recognise the handwriting. He tore it open quickly, glanced to see who had written it. Eve? Why would she be writing? Wonders never cease! Then he hesitated before reading it, thinking to himself, I hope Ma's not been taken ill? As at last he read the news from home. Whether it was from the stress of the past months or the shock of what he read, he started to sob, and he cried as he had not done since a child. The other fellows stood by aghast. He shoved the letter into his best mate's hand, who in turn read it, and, patting his friend's shoulder, endeavoured to show some form of comfort; these card-playing pals then made a discreet exit, so leaving their companion to overcome his grief. They had all been through it themselves in some form during these last three years. Men that had gone to the front as young boys had soon become, in many ways, men old for their years.

After composing himself, Algie reached for his writing paper and pencil. His pencil was now becoming a stub, and he must remember to fill in a chit for a replacement. He first wrote to his Ma and Eve. He said he was glad that his last letter to Gran was full of good cheer. Now the letter to his sister, Kate! What could a fellow say to a young Mum left on her own with two kids to bring up?

So the war went on, and as Algie and his pals experienced, or heard, of the loss of more of their mates, so they fought with more ferocity. After the memories of their Christmas spent together with their enemy they were to often feel guilty at this unnecessary slaughter of young men. The winter of 1918 slowly went by and the summer saw both the Australians and Americans doing well. Towards the end of August, Algie and what was left of his platoon, marched into a small town on the Somme capturing German troops the whole way. All told they gathered 5000 prisoners. They were kept busy making a camp for these prisoners, and Algie found his surroundings, for a change quite to his liking. A pleasant river ran through the town. Yes, thought Algie, 'this is a bit better'. There being no signs, indicating their whereabouts, Algie began to enquire from the prisoners as to where they were. He thought they were pulling his leg, or their English was poor and he had misunderstood, when they said 'Albert'. But, yes, he ascertained that this town was indeed called Albert. Well I never did thought this young Albert, perhaps at last, this is a good omen.

Algie and his mates were to stay in Albert, looking after the prisoners, until the war ended in the November. He was to find out quite a bit about his surroundings. Albert, before the war, had been known for its paper and linen industry, and the river passing through was the Ancre. Algie became quite attached to the area and considered it a strange coincidence that he should celebrate the Armistice in a town bearing his name. Yes, thought Algie, life held many surprises.

BOOK 2

CHAPTER 12

TO WALK THE STREETS

The news that the Kaiser had abdicated and the Armistice had been signed was received by Algie and his mates with jubilation. Algie was not in the habit of drinking heavily but he certainly had his fill on that day. He learnt that he was to stay in Albert until all prisoners had been released or moved elsewhere. This, now the war was over, he did not mind. He needed time, as did the rest of the men, to readjust. Also time to think of what lay ahead and what he was to do with his future.

As the weeks went by all the men had forty-eight hours leave. Algie and his mates decided to take the chance to see Paris, and they certainly saw this city by night and day. They left their barracks early one morning, having persuaded transport to loan them a vehicle. On the way they passed line upon line of refugees making their way home. Except for some elderly men, they were mainly women and children; a bedraggled slow weary party, already exhausted but jubilant that the war was over and they could return to their various towns and villages and back to the homes from which they had fled during the fighting.

On arriving in Paris Algie and his friends walked the streets, soaking up the atmosphere and seeing all the sights that they had only ever read about before. They had no difficulty finding a place to sleep that night; they were welcomed with open arms by the Parisians - had the English not fought with the French to save their country from devastation? But in no time at all the leave was over and it was time to return to Albert.

*

Algie was not to spend Christmas 1918 in England, but it was not to be too far into the New Year before he was to step foot on English soil again. As he came down the gangplank at Dover he vowed that never again would he sail away from these shores, but at that time little did he visualise the difficulties that lay ahead. Not surprisingly Algie was a changed man and he had no further interest in being a market trader. Sheltering in the trenches he had often thought about his future; his mind would wander back to those days when as a small lad he had hung over the walls of those posh houses up on Highgate Hill. He would day-dream of beautiful gardens and how he would lay them out. His day-dreams, under those terrible conditions, helped him to survive and as he stepped off that crowded troopship onto English soil once more, his thoughts returned to those beautiful gardens.

From Dover it was back to Salisbury Plain for a few more weeks, before being finally discharged. Yes it was as young men that these soldiers had last seen the plains of England, but now they were men far in advance of their years. Some were completely shattered, but Algie was one of the lucky ones, as his rough upbringing had stood him in good stead and he had survived far better than many others.

*

Back home the munition factory was closing and Eve was to leave her Mother's apron strings for the first time. She managed to get an introduction to one of the Government Offices in Whitehall, as a cleaner. This meant an early start, but she felt herself so fortunate in obtaining a job. The returning men were walking the streets looking for work, and she found it so sad to see the beggars sitting in Whitehall with their boards in front of them saying that they were injured at Ypres or on the Somme. She really wondered what this war had been about that our men should return to such poverty. This also worried Ma, as she did not know what Algie would do with himself.

A letter had arrived that morning from Algie to say that he was back in England and would be home in a few weeks. Ma's immediate reaction was that she should go to Mass that evening to give thanks for Algie's safe return. Later, as she walked down the street to church, she told herself that Algie would just have to go out and find a job and she would make sure he did just that.

*

Eventually the time came for Algie's return to Holloway Road. At first he was pleased that his sister Eve had found employment in Whitehall, but this was to prove frustrating and an embarrassment to him. After a few days at home with Ma, he started to walk the streets looking for work, some days he felt like giving up and staying in bed, but his Ma would have none of this. First thing in the morning she would shake him out of his stupor and remain standing there until he stepped out of bed. He would shout, "Go away Ma, how can a fellow get out of bed with his Ma standing there?"

His Ma was so determined that he should be out on the streets looking for work that she would have none of it. She stuck by his bed until he showed a leg, and then it would be "Out of 'ere young fellow and find a job." Then, after she had made sure that he had had a good breakfast, she would plant herself at the front door waiting to hand him his hat as he left, which inevitably he had to do just to satisfy his Ma. 'If only she knew how difficult it was! If only she knew!'

nevertheless off he would go, if it was only to walk to the Heath. Hampstead Heath was some distance, but it did not matter at least it got him away from his Ma and her bullying. It was whilst walking on the Heath one day that he got chatting to one of the keepers, who by chance mentioned that he was in need of an odd-job man. Algie quickly enquired for more details.

*

Life for Algie was to change. A jubilant Algie strode home that day, with an extra spring in his step. As he approached his home he lifted his hat to the neighbours at their doors; he often wondered if that was all they did all day stand at their doors and natter. My! my, thought these friends of his Ma's, our Algie is in high spirits tonight, glad someone is happy. Our lads fought for peace, but they haven't come home to much. On hearing his news, they shouted after him, "Good for you Algie, and the best of British luck to yer."

At long last Algie was in work. He enjoyed the outdoor life, and, although at first it was clearing up after others, and for the first couple of years he seemed to do nothing but sweep here and sweep there, especially in the Autumn when the leaves were forever falling, he took pride in his work, and was so thankful to be employed, not like those poor fellows still walking the streets, many with kids to feed. Eventually Algie was to receive promotion, and it was at this time that he decided to grow a moustache. It gave him more prestige and confidence and a different disposition. He definitely felt it gave him maturity and more authority when chasing the kids, to box their ears, when they were up to mischief. He was certainly not having them damage his Heath.

Yes, Algie enjoyed those years as one of the keepers of the Heath. He would leave home each morning at 7 o'clock to walk to work. His days of searching London for work had certainly given him a taste for walking. Come rain or snow Algie made it to the Heath and it was his pride to see his patch looking clean and tidy.

*

Eve was to progress from being a cleaner to a tea-lady. Ma was to often think how proud Gran Sparkes would be of her grand-daughter working in Whitehall. Of her other daughter, Kate, Ma had not heard from her since those black war days. She did often feel rather guilty about this and would say a quiet prayer for this missing daughter and family, after which she would feel quite satisfied that she had done her duty. When eventually Algie was able to take some holiday from work he made once more for Dorchester to visit his elder sister. He was not sure of the welcome he would receive, and, somehow, felt guilty that although single he had survived the horrors of war and returned, whereas his brother-in-law, a father of two small children, had not.

He did not tell his Ma where he was going, just that he was going away on leave - it was strange still calling a holiday leave, but he supposed that it was the memory of those short breaks in wartime meaning so much to a fellow from the trenches, that he would always think of a holiday as leave.

Ma was not very pleased at not being told more, and, in no uncertain terms she let Algie know it. "Where d'yer think yer gadding off to? Not after some girl, are yer?"

Algie smiled to himself and thought, if I was, I wouldn't tell you Ma. Memories of those pre-war romances came back. No, Ma, you would be the last to know, he thought, but did not say, as he kissed her goodbye. She shrugged him off in a huff, saying, "Behave yerself." Algie often wondered how old she thought he was. Behave yerself. He never did, what next thought Algie with a grin.

Kate was still in service near Dorchester. She had been fortunate in being recommended as a housekeeper to an old Captain. Knowing how her husband had been killed in the war, leaving her with two small ones, he was only too pleased to accommodate them all. Algie was certainly pleased to see his sister being cared for, but mind you she certainly earned her keep. The children were thrilled to see a real Uncle, and he was only too pleased for his late brother-in-law's sake to make a fuss of them. He was certainly shocked to find out that no one had informed his sister of the passing of their Gran, and even more shocked to learn that his Ma and Eve had not written, even though they must have read Gran Sparkes' letter telling of Cecil's death. Over the next few years he endeavoured to slip away to visit Kate at least once a year.

*

It was now coming up to ten years since those terrible days in the trenches. Some nights he was to still twist and turn and wake up in a hot sweat as he saw an enormous rat approaching him. It was a few moments before he realised it was only now a dream. He still considered himself lucky to be left only with such nightmares, as some of his mates were to remain in hospital for the rest of their lives suffering from shell-shock, from which they were never to recover.

Eve was now to see life from the other side of the desk, when she became an office worker, and now that there were two bringing home money, Ma was able to give up taking in washing, and, these days, just helped with the cleaning of the church.

It was very difficult in the Smythe family household, should you be feeling poorly, to take time off work. Ma just would not have it. 'No shirking in this 'ousehold,' she would say. This was going to prove a problem to Algie, as he now realised where his talents should be employed and intended applying for another job. He realised that he certainly had a knack for the designing on paper of flowerbeds, and wished to put these designs into practice, and he decided to keep his eyes open for work of this type. He would certainly have to be devious, where his Ma was concerned, when going for interviews. Algie had enjoyed his time spent on Hampstead Heath, but it was mainly heath land and there was not sufficient incentive for his main love.

Eventually, after a number of weeks, his luck was in, and he was to hear of a job tending the flowerbeds in Regents Park. He was fortunate that the interview was first thing in the morning. Ma looked at him suspiciously when he left home dressed in his Sunday best, but he was out of the house before she had a chance to question him, giving his moustache an extra twist in a defiant mood as he waved her goodbye. He walked to Kings Cross from where he got the circle line train to Regents Park. The interview went well. His ten years work spent on Hampstead Heath stood him in good stead, and after he had shown the designs he had drawn up of beautifully laid out flowerbeds, he was offered the job. It was certainly a proud Algie that returned to Hampstead Heath, later that morning, to give in his notice.

These flowerbeds were to be his pride and joy for many years and woe betide anyone who let their dog stray upon them. Yes, Algie loved his work, but something was missing in his life. He was now nearing his forties, and apart from those few romances in his younger days before the war when Ma interfered so rudely, he had not yet found the girl of his dreams. Time was running out and now that he had a decent job to support a family he must certainly be on the lookout!

Book 3

Marguerite and Bertie

1929-1934

BOOK 3

CHAPTER 13

SPRING IN THE AIR

Algie felt quite light hearted as he set off for work on a bright March morning in 1929. This was a time of year he enjoyed; a time of carrying out the plans made for his flower beds during those winter months. Yes, you could certainly smell spring in the air on this late March morning. He knew it was going to be a busy day, amongst other jobs there were the beds to be laid out with all those new plants delivered yesterday from the greenhouses.

On arriving at Regents Park Algie rolled up his shirt sleeves, collected his trolley, gave his moustache a twist, and thought, must make haste with the job in hand, and it was not long before he was putting his plan for the polyanthus bed into being. A back-aching job, but, if it turned out as well as his primrose bed that he had laid out yesterday, the sight alone would make it well worthwhile.

*

Back in Bedford Square, Marguerite Sinclair was that morning having an argument with her dear Mama, who had questioned the time taken up these days with walking out Snuff, her small spaniel. "Now do make it a short walk today Marguerite. Remember Sarah will be here tomorrow with little Janet and there is work to do," said a rather weary Mama.

"It will be done all in good time," snapped a slightly angry Marguerite. These demands from Mama made Marguerite all the more determined to take longer walks and spend more time away from home. Who did her Mama think she was talking to - a child? Really, thought Marguerite, I get so tired of her demanding ways.

Marguerite was still feeling slightly irritated at the embarrassing scene she had found herself in yesterday. She could still hear John Mullen asking her out and the awkward situation that had resulted. As she stepped out with Snuff on the lead, she went back in thought to the office and could hear her reply to his request – 'I am sorry John that is not possible, you see I have another friend whom I am courting.' Today she was thinking, how could she have said such a thing? How could she tell such a lie?

On leaving Bedford Square Marguerite turned into Tottenham Court Road. On the spur of the moment she found herself hailing a bus. Soon the conductor was by her, saying "Tickets please." "Oh! Park Crescent, please." That was certainly a sudden decision, thought Marguerite, settling back in her seat for the short journey. Whatever was she doing going to Regents Park on this busy day when she had so much to do at home? Oh well, she thought, it's too late now. She felt quite tired already from climbing those awkward stairs with Snuff in her arms. She really hated the way they were on the outside of the bus, so dangerous.

Marguerite had hardly got her breath back when the park was in sight and it was already time for another struggle down those dreaded stairs. She would most definitely walk home. She wondered why it was necessary, if you had a dog, even a small dog, to go up on top deck. She held on tight and gently edged her way down, stopping, whilst the bus came to a halt, before alighting. Once on firm ground Snuff was pulling on the lead ready to be off. He knew he would be let off that tiresome lead soon for a good run.

"Come on Snuff here's St. Andrew's gate, in we go. When we have passed the gardens you may have a run." Marguerite chatted away to her small King Charles spaniel, who was pulling more than ever. She was soon turning into the gate, by this time having to hold on to the lead even tighter. "Not yet, you'll have those keepers after you, not yet!" She had hardly said this when she was brought to a halt by the figure tending the flower bed. She hesitated. Of whom did he remind her? She stood still, deep in thought, and rather rudely staring at the face of this man.

"Looking at something, Ma'am?" asked Algie, standing up.

"I beg your pardon. I was far away," announced a somewhat embarrassed Marguerite.

"Lost in thought, eh," asked a smiling Algie.

"Why yes," replied Marguerite, who could feel herself blushing.

"Nice day!" asked a bemused Algie.

"Why yes." Marguerite could not help but stare at this gardener, he certainly reminded her of someone.

"Oh well, must get on." Algie replied, getting back down to the work in hand.

Marguerite walked slowly on, leaving the gardens behind her and she was soon able to let Snuff off the lead. She sat on a nearby seat, whilst he had a good run, still puzzling as of whom that gardener reminded her. She was so lost in thought that she forgot to keep an eye on Snuff. After a while she came to from her day-dreaming; it suddenly dawned on her why the face was so familiar. Why yes, of course, her dear Papa. That is who he is like! Papa! It is that waxen moustache that does it. Yes he was so like Papa, also that face in the portrait on the stairs at home, her Grandfather, whom she had never known. How strange, what an uncanny likeness. Marguerite stood up, feeling satisfied that she had solved the problem. Oh dear, where is Snuff? How silly of me, I was so far away in my dreams I never gave him a thought. "Snuff, Snuff," she called, but he was nowhere to be seen. "Snuff, Snuff," she called again, but he did not reappear. She hurriedly retraced her steps back to the gardens. Approaching the still bending figure of Algie, she said. "Oh, excuse me again. Have you by any chance seen my little dog pass by? I seem to have lost him."

Well blow me, thought Algie, if it isn't her again. Raising himself, he said, "Beg pardon, Ma'am?"

"Please have you seen my small dog?" repeated a worried Marguerite.

"No sorry, he ain't come this way Ma'am. I can't say I want him to, not near my flower beds," announced Algie.

Blow your flower beds thought a frustrated Marguerite. Blow your beds, where is my little dog? "Oh dear, what am I to do?" Marguerite said in desperation. By this time she was getting really worried, but she did not seem to be getting much help from this fellow. She turned to walk away, still calling out to Snuff.

On hearing Marguerite's call of despair Algie began to feel quite sorry for this dear lady. "'Old on, Ma'am. I'll go back to the 'ut and see if my mate has 'ad 'im 'anded in," announced Algie cleaning his hands down his trousers.

"Oh thank you so much, that is so kind of you," answered a grateful Marguerite.

Taking his time, off strolled Algie. It took a few moments to get into a stride after having bent down for so long. Oh well, he thought, a break won't hurt.

Marguerite got more and more agitated, especially when she looked at her watch and saw the time. What would her Mama be thinking now! The gardener seemed to be gone a long time and she longed to sit down. Looking around her she saw a seat by the primrose bed. Sitting there she became so intrigued by the pattern formed by the plants that momentarily she forgot her worries. Suddenly there was a yap, yap, and there stood the gardener beside her with a very excited Snuff.

"Sorry to make you jump, Ma'am. I took a short cut across the grass behind you. Is this 'im? Someone 'anded 'im in whilst I was talking to me mate." Algie was pleased to see the relief on her face. A tubby one at that, he thought. The dog leapt up at his mistress, licking her with excitement.

"Oh, thank you, thank you, sir. How can I thank you enough." Marguerite was trying to get her hand away from the excitable dog to shake this bemused gardener's hand.

Algie smiled to himself at the 'sir' added to the end of the thank you. He was not often called 'sir'. It took him back to school days. Yes, sir, no sir, and if you didn't use the correct title to the schoolmaster, it was a box round the ears, and it didn't half hurt. Yes respect had to be shown in those days, and this lady was respecting him for helping her. Oh well, interesting, and not such a young lady either. Yes, certainly interesting. He would look out for her again. The next moment Algie found himself asking, "Do you walk your dog 'ere often, Ma'am?"

"It depends on the weather and the time I have available," answered Marguerite hesitating. "I am sorry, I don't know your name."

"Bert, ma'am. Bertie Smythe." Algie heard himself saying. Bert, what made him say that. He had never been called Bert or Bertie ever. It had been Algie for as long as he could remember.

Marguerite, going to her handbag, was soon handing Bert a gold sovereign. "Well thank you again Bert, thank you. I will look out for you the next time I bring Snuff for a walk in the park. I only hope she behaves herself then, thank you."

Algie shook hands with this lady and found himself saying, "See you again, Ma'am, see you again." He watched as she hurried away, and thought to himself: Yes, see you again. It had certainly been an interesting morning, and as she disappeared into the distance, he thought to himself, she is certainly a buxom wench, just look at those buttocks. Yes! A well-bred young woman! Interesting!

*

It was to be a number of days before Marguerite was once more to make the journey to Regent's Park, coincidently it was to be just before another visit of her sister Sarah. This time she did not bother to get a bus, but walked all the way. She soon regretted this decision, and, as she approached the gates, she really did feel exhausted. She made for the seat by the still beautiful primroses, and, telling Snuff to sit down and behave himself this time, and he could not be let off the lead, whatever would that Bertie say? She made herself comfortable. She really did appreciate the quietness around her after the busy streets of London. She thought she really must make the effort more often to come to these beautiful surroundings. She began to relax as she breathed in deeply as the perfume of the flowers reached her.

Algie was at this time collecting some more plants from the greenhouse. Having finally loaded enough plants to keep him going until lunchtime, he once more made his way back to the flowerbeds, but he was suddenly aware of a dog barking. Oh no, thought Algie, not another blessed dog by my flowerbeds. His attention was suddenly drawn to the small dog sitting by his mistress. Snuff had recognised the approaching gardener and was by now getting quite excited, and, to Marguerite's embarrassment, tugging on his lead to get away.

"Quiet! Snuff." Marguerite patted her impatient dog. "Yes, I can see it's your gardener friend, but quiet now, don't embarrass us so. Quiet! Snuff!"

Algie approached them, thinking to himself that this was his lucky day, was he not due for his lunch break soon? He approached his friends, trying not to look too eager. He patted the dog and at the same time noticed that his mistress was looking somewhat exhausted. "You look fair whacked, Ma'am," exclaimed a concerned Algie.

"Well yes, Bertie, I am somewhat. The park is some distance from home. I suppose it would have been more sensible of me to have caught a bus," announced Marguerite, who found herself blushing and getting hotter still.

Algie found himself saying, "M'lunch break is in a couple of shakes. What yer say about joining me for a cuppa!" Algie, he thought, what's come over you? It must be spring in the air. He went on to say, "A good cup of char will revive yer."

Marguerite hesitated, and then thought, why not, it would only be for a short while, as this gardener chap would have to be back at work, and wasn't he so like dear Papa in looks? Yes, she thought why not, what harm could come of having a cup of tea with a park keeper? Before she knew what she was saying she gave him his answer, "Well that is very kind. I should like that very much. Thank you."

Algie could not believe his luck. Wiping his hands down his trousers, he then shook Marguerite's hand quite avidly, saying at the same time, "My pleasure, Ma'am. I will just finish the job in 'and. You rest yer weary feet. It won't take two shakes for me to plant these 'ere plants." Algie strode away with a new eagerness to complete another partly planted-out flowerbed.

Marguerite sat intrigued at the rapidity with which this gardener planted and transformed the flowerbed. He worked with such precision and certainly must have had a plan and layout in his mind. She would watch with renewed interest at the growth of these plants. It seemed no time at all before the job was finished and Bertie was saying, "Two shakes and I'll be with yer. Just got to take this 'ere trolley back to the 'ut, otherwise the guvnor will be after me. Will 'ave a tidy up and will be back in a jiffy." As an afterthought he called back to Marguerite, "I should give the nipper a run whilst yer wait, can't have 'im causing 'avoc at old Joes.", having said that he hurried off.

"Oh yes, yes Bertie" called back a puzzled Marguerite, as she thought, who was old Joe? She walked further into the park, where it was safe to let Snuff off the lead, telling herself she must really keep a close watch on him this time. She had to call her small dog back time and time again; as if she had not watched him closely he would have been off looking for his gardener friend.

There was no need for Marguerite to watch for the return of Bertie, for Snuff saw him long before she did and bounded over the grass to meet him. He scampered away from Marguerite so quickly he nearly knocked some children over in his eagerness to reach Bertie. They soon made their way to the nearest tea shop, which, of course, Marguerite immediately realised was Joe Lyons. She had never stepped foot inside one of these ordinary tea shops before, only ever having frequented the Corner Houses. Oh well, she thought, there is always a first time for everything. She definitely found the cup of tea most welcome, and the nippy certainly had a sweet smile, but, oh dear, thought Marguerite, I wish Bertie would not dip his biscuit into his tea like that, it was a little off-putting to say the least. What would dear Mama think! Oh bother, Mama, thought Marguerite, did it really matter what she thought, wasn't she now thirty-three-years-old? Who cared what Mama thought, wasn't she old enough to choose her own friends? Suddenly she realised that Bertie was saying something.

"Penny for yer thoughts. Bert Smythe at yer service. To whose company do I owe this pleasure?" asked an enquiring Bertie.

"Oh, I'm so sorry, Bertie," and then hesitating Marguerite replied with a smile, "I am Marguerite Sinclair."

"Marguerite? uhm! I likes that. Marguerite, just like me flowers. Yes I approve of that 'ere name. Goes down well that does," nodded a bemused Algie. And so the ice was broken and a pleasant lunch hour was spent. Conversation certainly seemed to flow easily, and Marguerite found she had not laughed and chattered so much since Papa's sudden death. Soon it was time to leave the tea shop and make for the bus. Marguerite had soon forgotten about her decision to walk home. Bertie helped her on to the bus, and whilst she climbed the stairs he stood with one foot on board, much to the exasperation of the conductor, who was shouting, "Urry up there. Get on or awf mate. Make up yer mind." This did not worry Algie at all. He shouted up the stairs, much to Marguerite's embarrassment, "Are yer sitting comfortably, me luv? Ta, ta, for now!"

As the bus disappeared into the distance, Algie thought to himself how he had enjoyed that break from the usual routine. Perhaps his new friend, Marguerite, would take another walk with her small dog. He most certainly would keep an eye open for them.

A bemused Algie returned to his flowerbeds and liked the picture of the new Algie that formed in his mind - or was it to be Bertie from now on? A Bertie dressed in his best bib and tucker walking out a fine lady like Marguerite. Yes, he liked the thought of the new image. Uhm! thought Algie, quite a warm cuddly lady. Oh well time will tell, but it was definitely a happy Algie that got down to his gardening on that spring afternoon in 1929.

*

As soon as Marguerite was on the bus she regretted her decision to ride, as, in no time at all she had reached her destination and it was time once more to descend those terrible stairs. Gripping Snuff under one arm she slowly and carefully descended. The wind had now got up making her feel even less secure. She could not help but notice that the conductor chap gave her an amused look as she eased herself off the bus. She blushed as she thought of Bertie shouting up the stairs to her. In her younger days she would have been so embarrassed at the incident, but now she shrugged her shoulders and thought who cares what other people think, who cares? Her steps quickened and she felt quite exhilarated from her unexpected encounter. As she neared home she dared Snuff to make a noise. She hoped her Mama would be resting.

Marguerite made her way down the area steps, remembering that the last time she had done so was on her return from Germany those many years ago. What a lot had happened since then, thought Marguerite. Cook was puzzled to see the sudden appearance of Marguerite. Marguerite apologised for being so late in giving a hand for tomorrow's visitors and promised to be down immediately she had freshened herself up. Cook was by this time feeling quite flustered, her age was beginning to tell, and really she thought the family did not give much help these days, she certainly missed young Sarah, who was always so good in the kitchen. How lovely it will be to see this young mother tomorrow, thought a weary Cook. At Marguerite's apology, Cook looked up and was somewhat surprised to see the flushed young woman standing before her.

"My dear, are you alright? You look a little hot!" enquired an anxious Cook.

"Oh, it is only the wind that has battered me rather," quickly answered Marguerite. Before Cook could say anything further Marguerite was out of the kitchen door and wending her way quietly upstairs, Snuff having remained behind in the kitchen quenching his thirst.

Later, on meeting up with Mama, Marguerite received a cold reception and was told in no uncertain terms that these long outings with Snuff had got to stop. Marguerite turned a deaf ear.

*

Marguerite usually looked forward to her sister Sarah's visit, especially now small Janet came as well, but this particular time it was to prove to be a rather frustrating day. Marguerite was to realise how time-consuming a small child could be. Try as she did she could not get a moment alone with her sister, and she had so much to tell her. In the end she gave up trying and amused herself playing with two-year-old Janet.

Sarah enjoyed her day spent at Bedford Square. It was so good to be back in familiar surroundings and to see Marguerite so enjoying small Janet, but did she detect something different about her sister. On her last visit she noticed that her sister was somewhat diffident and she seemed to be hesitant when they had a moment together, as if she perhaps resented Janet's presence? Was she perhaps a little jealous of her small niece, thought Sarah? I must speak to Robert. We must have Marguerite over to Wimbledon more often. It must be trying when you are in your thirties to still be at Mama's beck and call. Yes that is what she would do, thought Sarah, speak to Robert and see what she could arrange.

*

Over the next few weeks Mama and Cook were to get little help from Marguerite. She was always missing when required. Emily puzzled over this and went down to the kitchen to ask her loyal Cook's opinion. "Cook, do you find, these last few weeks, that Marguerite is acting a little strange?" asked a concerned Mama.

"Well, I have been rather puzzled, if not a little concerned, at how flustered she seems," replied Cook, being careful not to get dear Marguerite into yet more trouble.

"I must have a word with her. She is out far too much," announced a slightly indignant Mama. She was certainly not going to learn much from Cook, in whom Mama had hoped her daughter would have confided. Oh well, she thought, time will tell.

With practice Marguerite was becoming quite adept at making the stairs of the bus. She was now taking this means of transport both ways, as it gave her much more time with Bertie. If Marguerite timed it just right she could lunch with him most days. The nippy in Joe Lyons was becoming quite interested in this courting couple. She smiled to herself as she watched them laughing and lunching together. It was good to see an older couple enjoying each other's company. Looking at them the amused nippy thought they were certainly a mixed pair. It was certainly the rough with the smooth, thought the amused nippy.

Although Marguerite found Bertie in many ways quite rough and ready, in some things she found him to be a real gentleman and very considerate, and his looks brought back such happy memories!

Today Bertie was awaiting a decision from Marguerite. He had made a proposition to her and today he hoped he would get his answer.

BOOK 3

CHAPTER 14

THE DECISION

At night instead of sleeping Marguerite was to twist and turn, a decision had to be made.

Bertie wished to take Marguerite on a day's excursion to Bognor. How was she to escape dear Mama's clutches for a whole day? It suddenly dawned on her! Why yes! Why had she not thought of it before? She would spend a few days with her sister at Wimbledon, by this means Mama would not know of her absence from London. She immediately wrote to Sarah asking for an invitation, but in no way enlightening her sister as to her reason for wishing to stay.

The decision having been made, Marguerite set off on this summer's day to meet Bertie for lunch, eager to tell him of her plans. These days she did not always take Snuff; if she did not have him with her she would meet her Bertie at the café. Whilst waiting for Bertie she would sit talking to the nippy until Bertie arrived, the nippy and her were now on Christian name terms. Marguerite learnt that Nancy came from a large family living in Camden Town and she was not that many years younger than herself.

These days Algie finished his work sharp at 1 o'clock always eager to see his Marguerite. Today he was anxious to know her decision, as he could not wait to have a whole day with his new love.

Marguerite greeted Bertie with a smile and was soon telling him of her plans. He said he would book their seats immediately he finished work that evening. He would see if the charabanc would stop at Wimbledon to pick up Marguerite, he was quite sure that this could be arranged. The thought of a whole day together seemed to bring them even closer and as they sat in the cafe gazing into each other's eyes a flame seemed to be lit.

A puzzled Sarah was to receive Marguerite's letter. Although Marguerite spent quite a bit of time visiting her sister at Wimbledon, she had never before requested an invitation. Sarah was certainly puzzled and was longing to meet up with her sister once more. She immediately wrote back telling Marguerite that she was awaiting her visit with eagerness.

Somehow or other Marguerite had to find a reason to tell Mama why she wished to stay with Sarah. On mentioning it to her Mama fortunately she did not ask for a reason as it seemed quite natural for the two sisters to wish to spend some time together.

The days went by and Marguerite's short August holiday was to arrive. She set off in the cab somewhat excited at the thought of the time to be spent with her sister and small niece, but she looked forward more than ever to the anticipated wonderful day to be spent at the coast with Bertie.

*

Sarah and her husband Robert lived in a tree-lined suburban avenue. Their detached house had been built since the war. They had a substantial enclosed garden in which small Janet spent many hours. It was Sarah and Robert's wish to have a brother or sister as a companion for their daughter, they hoped this time it would be a boy, but they had to be patient as nothing seemed to be forthcoming.

As the cab pulled up in the drive Sarah was at the door to greet her sister. She was longing to know the reason for this unexpected arranged visit. She could not wait to learn more from Marguerite. Being a Sunday Robert was at home and hovered in the background clutching an excited small daughter's hand.

"Come in, Marguerite. Come in." Sarah gave her sister a warm hug. "Robert will settle with the cabbie," and turning to her small daughter, she said, "Yes Janet, you may leave go of your Papa's hand. She has been so excited and has been watching out of the window for the cab to turn into the drive. We were frightened that when she heard it she would run out under the wheels, so Robert has had to keep a tight hold of her." Janet needed no second invitation and flung herself at her Auntie Marguerite full of kisses and cuddles. This was going to be fun as it was not often that they had visitors to stay.

Marguerite envied her sister and her beautiful home. Perhaps there was the chance she may have something equally beautiful one day, who knows? It certainly seemed a possibility now. She blushed at the thought.

Janet was soon sent off with Robert to visit his parents, who lived nearby. Sarah needed time with her sister to talk without any interruptions of a small daughter.

Immediately they had left the room Sarah turned to her sister. "Now tell me Marguerite, why this sudden request to stay? I am longing to know. I believe you must have something up your sleeve." Looking at her sister's high colour she thought she most certainly had something to tell.

"Are you ready for some surprises," asked a bemused Marguerite.

"Tell me more, oh sister mine, tell me more," answered an impatient Sarah.

"Well! I have a gentleman friend," announced Marguerite, at the same time thinking to herself - did her dear Bertie come under the category of a gentleman? She doubted it, but on the other hand he wasn't a young boy.

Sarah hugged her sister with glee. "Oh Marguerite, I am so pleased for you." The sisters laughed together at their excitement.

"But Marguerite you still haven't told me why this sudden visit. I am sure it was not just to tell me you have a boyfriend?" enquired Sarah.

Marguerite went on to tell her sister of the planned Wednesday excursion to Bognor.

*

Marguerite and Sarah spent two happy days together, and then at 7.30 am on a bright, summer's day Marguerite stood at the end of The Ridgeway awaiting the charabanc. By the time it arrived Marguerite was in quite a fluster, thinking that perhaps it had gone another way, the driver forgetting that he had a passenger to pick up in Wimbledon, and so had left her behind. How could she think of such a thing with her dear Bertie already on the charabanc. Eventually it appeared, with a honk of the horn announcing its arrival. Down the steps sprung Algie.

The driver reacting with surprise said "My you are a keen young man," and turning to Marguerite he said, "I should watch him Ma'am. Don't let him rush you off y'er feet." Giving Algie a knowing nudge.

Algie was soon showing Marguerite into her seat and squeezed in beside her. Did it matter that his Marguerite took up most of the room. The warmth of her body squashed in beside him immediately sent a shudder down his spine and through his limbs. He clutched her hand with longing and gave her a welcoming peck on the cheek.

"Oh what bliss, me luv. A whole wonderful day ahead of us," giving her yet another peck on the cheek, much to the amusement of the kiddie leaning over the back of the seat.

Never before had Marguerite spent such a long journey sitting so close to someone of the opposite sex and she could not but be aware of the magic feeling between them. She wondered what her Bertie was thinking. She only knew that she longed to be on their own and away from this crowded charabanc.

A short stop was made for refreshments at Horsham, but they were soon on their way again. To Marguerite, used to the wide London streets, the main road now seemed to become rather narrow and the leafy trees seemed to reach each other in the centre. The scenery was really magic and took her back to her journeying through Germany. Eventually they were chugging up a steep hill over the South Downs and the driver was telling them that they were passing Chanctonbury Ring and so would soon be arriving at Bognor, just in time for lunch. Lunch, Marguerite thought, the mere mention made her feel hungry. Sarah had packed them a small hamper of food and Bertie had sensibly remembered to bring a rug to sit on. Marguerite was feeling quite ready for these goodies and could not wait to find a quiet spot.

By the time the charabanc arrived at Bognor it seemed to chug, like a tired beast, into an already crowded charabanc park. Everyone crowded off, the children pushing and shoving with their buckets and spades eager for the beach and making quite a din as they rushed off shouting - "Where's the beach? Where's the beach?" Algie and Marguerite let them get well away and when they were all out of sight they stopped and their lips met in a tender kiss at the thought of the whole afternoon and evening ahead of them. They strolled through a small park to reach the sea front. Algie was quite critical of the flowerbeds, but Marguerite thought them quite colourful. On arriving at the pier they strolled along the promenade past some elegant houses and hotels. They then sat on the beach to eat their lunch.

Having spent the whole morning in the charabanc and now their energy restored by the food, they decided to make for the coolness of the fields and retraced their way back to the pier, to the east of which they had noticed on their arrival some pretty countryside. They strolled hand-in-hand that magic feeling felt on the journey down still being very much with them. The smell of the sea giving them renewed vitality. Algie helped his Marguerite over a stile and they made for the shelter of some trees, away from the heat of the midday sun. They found a quiet sheltered spot and shaking the sand from their rug laid it down on the ground. Algie quickly drew his Marguerite down and into his arms. He kissed her as she had never been kissed before. This was the first opportunity that he had ever had to show his feelings for his new love. His other kisses had been snatched at opportune moments in crowded places and merely pecks, but this was different. They clung together. Did he detect urgency between them, a great drawing of ecstasy? Yes, this was different!

Eventually Marguerite drew away. She had never experienced anything like these passionate kisses before and she was quite out of breath. "Oh Bertie, what is this? This feeling between us?" gasped an excited Marguerite.

Taking her hand once more, Bettie said "My darling don't withhold it, let our love shine. Let us enjoy it," and so they kissed again with a great desire for each other.

Marguerite withdrew once more. She felt she must take control of her emotions, enough was enough. Things must not get out of hand and their relationship spoilt. They sat cuddled up to each other, planning how they could meet somewhere other than Joe Lyons, somewhere a little more private now that their true feeling was mutual between them.

With the heat of the day and their closeness they suddenly realised that they were thirsty, not only for each other, but for a good cup of tea. They reluctantly left their secluded place and made for the small town and a cosy tea place. Sitting over their cream tea they had eyes only for each other.

Sadly all good things come to an end and it was time once more to make for the charabanc. Some of the children were now quite tearful and sticky with tiredness. The sand from the beach got into their eyes as they rubbed them. Yes, after an enjoyable day, it was quite a noisy charabanc ride on this return journey, what with the attempted singing of some of the adults and the grizzling of the children, but nevertheless Marguerite was feeling quite tired and her head soon dropped onto Bertie's shoulder and she dozed with contentment.

Suddenly Marguerite was awoken by Bertie whispering in her ear. "I luv you, Marguerite! I luv yer so!" Marguerite squeezed his hand in acknowledgement. She felt this was all she could do in this crowded noisy charabanc.

In no time at all Bertie was gathering her things together and helped her down the steps. They had reached Wimbledon and as he once more gave her a farewell peck on the cheek she said, "Me too, dear Bertie, me too."

Marguerite waited and waved as the charabanc took her dear Bertie away from her back to London town. She found herself already longing for their time together at their new secret meeting place.

*

That night Marguerite could not get to sleep she could here Bertie saying, I love you Marguerite. I love you so. She had never in her life thought she would ever hear such words. Since her unfortunate experiences during the war she never thought she would be happy in a man's arms, but all was forgotten in the ecstasy of the moment. Yes, at last all was forgotten. She could live again. She fell asleep thinking dear, dear Bertie, nothing must take you away from me, nothing.

Marguerite was staying with Sarah until the Saturday, when Robert would drive her home giving Mama a chance to see her younger daughter and grandchild again.

During the next two days Sarah questioned her sister many times on this new-found love. Yes! her sister was most certainly in love for the first time. What is he like? When are we to meet him? Is he tall? Is he short? and so the questions went on and on. All Marguerite would say is - he is just like our dear Papa. Yes just like Papa, thought Marguerite - well in looks, but perhaps that was where the likeness ended, but when you are in love you overlook any faults.

Marguerite dared her sister to mention the friendship to Mama. She wished to have no interference from anyone in the matter. Nothing was to happen to spoil this relationship, no nothing.

*

Algie left the charabanc at The Angel and in the cool of the evening soon stepped out. He smiled to himself, as he strode down to Caledonian Road, at how much quicker he was walking as against the stroll along the promenade and through the fields of Bognor Regis. What a perfect day it had been.

Ma greeted him with, "Enjoyed yerself with yer mates, Algie?"

"Yes thanks, Ma," replied a smiling Algie. Little do you know, thought Algie, and that is how it's going to remain this time. Algie was determined that nothing was going to interfere with this relationship.

Later Algie laid in bed thinking of his buxom Marguerite and of her in his arms getting himself more and more excited. To calm down he gave himself a talking to - now young lad take it carefully. Young lad, he thought, you are thirty-seven-years-old! Yes time was running out and it is time you settled down old chap. The more he thought about it the better he liked it, and the excitement overtook him again. Now the next time you meet your love, take it carefully, Algie. You must not frighten her away. Remember Algie she is a lady and what a chance, but tread carefully, Algie. With these thoughts he fell into a deep and satisfied sleep.

Algie and Marguerite had not been in the habit of meeting on a Sunday, but their arrangements and their longing to be alone together was to alter this. They had arranged to meet at Jack Straw's Castle, on the edge of Hampstead Heath. They had planned this carefully, to avoid suspicion. Marguerite would have her Sunday lunch as usual with her Mama before leaving, and so they were not to meet until 3.15 pm.

Mama was full of questions about Marguerite's stay with Sarah; lunch took rather longer than usual. Fortunately Snuff took it into his own hands, he was in a hurry for a walk and nuzzled the dining room door open; rushed up to his mistress and let out a yap and would not rest until Marguerite wiped her mouth and folded her napkin. "Alright Snuff, I am coming for your walkies," with that she kissed her Mama goodbye, and thought to herself at long last, thank you Snuff. That blessed dog, thought Mama, he does not give me a moment's peace with my daughter these days, always wanting to be walked.

Marguerite was soon ready and waited until she was in Tottenham Court Road before hailing a cab. "Jack Straw's Castle, Hampstead, please," ordered a now excited Marguerite. She was longing to see her Bertie once more. It seemed quite a way, but being a Sunday afternoon there was not much in the way of traffic and reasonable progress was made. She spotted Bertie before he saw her cab approaching, and, my, oh my, doesn't he look smart, thought Marguerite, in his Sunday best? Yes she liked that Sunday smartness of her dear Bertie. She alighted from the cab and approached him, to her own surprise, rather shyly. He pecked her cheek and took her hand and they strolled away, first to the small pond where they admired the ducks, and Algie liked the reflection in the water of himself holding the hand of his lady friend. Yes the reflection suited him. They then strolled onto the heath reminiscing on their day at Bognor. Once more they found a quiet spot and Algie took his Marguerite into his arms, whispering his love for her and how since Wednesday he had missed her. Snuff, who did not think much of this short walk, had to be quietened so as to not draw attention to his mistress and her lover. After a while, and for the little dog's sake, they walked on, but stopped every now and then to kiss and murmur sweet-nothings to each other.

During the rest of the summer and early autumn the afternoon on the heath was their Sunday routine, but, so as not to cause suspicion at home, their meetings in the week were to be only on two days, so they savoured their Sunday afternoons together.

*

Marguerite's 34th birthday was fast approaching. Algie wished to make this a special birthday, one she would never forget. Although he wished to make this a surprise for her, he suggested that she should once more invite herself to Wimbledon. This was to be a special Saturday night and he did not want anything to spoil it. This time the cab was to take her to Charing Cross Station. He had booked a table in the nearby Corner House. They enjoyed their meal, which had cost quite a bit, with wine and all, from Algie's small earnings. They sat gazing into each other's eyes and suddenly Algie lent across the candlelit table and pressed a small box into Marguerite s hands, saying, "Happy birthday me precious, happy birthday me luv." She gasped and opened the box, and there inside was the most beautiful ring. Bertie took it out of the box and placed it on Marguerite's finger. If he could have reached across the table far enough he would have kissed her there and then, but there was a time and place for everything. No words were spoken, the two lovers just gazed into each other's eyes and the room became empty to them. They had eyes only for each other that evening.

From the Corner House they went to Leicester Square, and sat as young lovers in the back row of the cinema, but Marguerite and Bertie were not to see much of the film that evening. On leaving the cinema Bertie hailed a cab and stepped in after Marguerite. "The Ridgeway, Wimbledon, please mate," requested Bertie, at the same time thinking to himself - your mad lad, you've a long walk back, as you won't have a penny in your pocket. But love that evening took away all sensible thinking.

"But Bertie, you cannot come all the way to Wimbledon," questioned a laughing Marguerite, but he quietened her with a long loving kiss.

Finally he broke away, saying, "I would come to the end of the world with you me dearest," kissing her once more. "Relax, enjoy yerself," commanded this ardent fiance.

"Oh Bertie, I love you so." answered Marguerite, cuddling up to him.

As the cab wended its way through the London streets, Marguerite began to worry as to whether she should invite him into her sister's home, but she did not want to ruin a perfect evening. How would her sister and brother-in-law take to this rough-and-ready Bertie of hers? No she would not have him meet her family yet, she did not want to spoil a perfect relationship, and unbeknown to her sister and brother-in-law, Marguerite and her fiance took their farewells in the seclusion of the summerhouse, it was too chilly to hang around in the street. Bertie quite understood that he could not be invited in at such a late hour, but the summerhouse was far better. When they could keep out of each others arms, they talked for the first time of their future together. Bertie said he would keep his eyes open for some rooms for them, at the same time adding, "Darling, yer do realise we will not be able t'afford a property of our own?"

Marguerite assured him she quite understood and that she did not mind as long she was with him. Being in love, a small matter like that did not concern her, she only wished to be with her Bertie, wherever that might be.

How long and what time it was when they finally broke away from each other and Bertie said goodbye she did not know or care. She crept in-doors to be confronted by a very worried Sarah, but the time of night, or shall we say early morning, was soon forgotten when she saw Marguerite's beautiful ring. To Sarah this looked a cheap piece of jewellery, but on no account would she tell her sister of its cheapness. To her excited sister Marguerite it was a treasure of gold.

*

As the winter weather set in the Sunday afternoon walks on the distant Hampstead Heath had to stop. The lovers had to be satisfied with lunch at their cafe. Nancy was to admire the ring, which Marguerite had to be careful not to wear at home, and Nancy was so pleased and envious of this devoted couple, so much in love.

It was to be March before their walks could be resumed, and in the spring of 1930 Marguerite and Bertie once more enjoyed their strolls together and the opportunity of planning their future together. It was on one such Sunday that Bertie was to take Marguerite into his arms and tell her of his findings.

*

Easter was just approaching and Algie was trying to work out how he could get the holiday weekend away with Marguerite. He was in the kitchen munching away at eggs and bacon, and taking his time this Sunday morning, when Ma returned from Mass.

"Still at breakfast, yer lazy brute?" shouted Ma, as she came into the room. "By the way, Algie, did I tells yer that that young couple upstairs are leaving us?" asked Ma. "Can't say I'm sorry, they never had much to say, and she took up all the washing line with 'er washing," announced Ma, pouring herself out a cup of tea.

"Nowt, first I've 'eard of it," announced a by-now most interested Algie.

"Yeh, going out of town to one of those new places somewhere." Ma informed her Algie.

"Really Ma?" said Algie, wiping his mouth on his handkerchief. "Really Ma! interesting." Algie couldn't care where they were going, but this was really most interesting. Two rooms to let here on his own doorstep, most interesting Algie thought as he left the table and went into his bedroom.

BOOK 3

CHAPTER 15

TWO ROOMS TO LET

Whether it was a Sunday or not, Algie did not care, he hurriedly made his excuses to Ma and left the house in Holloway Road to see the landlord of this property, the only home he could remember. Yes this matter must be settled before he met Marguerite that very afternoon.

Later that morning an extremely chuffed Algie left the landlord's house with a hearty goodbye and a thank you mate. Algie had just got the first option on the two rooms above Ma's basement flat. He chuckled when he thought what a surprise his dear Marguerite would have when he told her he had at last found them their two rooms.

Algie was early arriving that Sunday at their meeting place on the edge of Hampstead Heath. As the cab drew up at the kerb he waved to Marguerite with an extra eagerness. He was at the door before the cabbie could get round to open it.

"Come Marguerite, come my luv," urged an excited Algie.

"Why Bertie, why are you so excited?" questioned a puzzled Marguerite.

"Just yer wait, till yer 'ears my news. Just yer wait my luv. You'll be so 'appy. As 'appy as can be," said Algie dropping his h's more than ever.

"Bertie, not so fast, not so fast,' laughed Marguerite, who was having to run to keep up with him, with his great urgency to get to the heath.

As they hurried along he said, "My dearest, I can't wait to take yer in me arms and tell yer me news." By now he was literally pulling Marguerite along behind him. Eventually they arrived at their favourite hideaway. Algie immediately pulled his Marguerite into his arms with such urgency that for a moment it had her quite worried. What was Bertie up to.

"Oh Marguerite, it won't be long now before you will be mine," exclaimed a still excited Algie.

"Oh Bertie, my love, do not keep me in suspense, tell me more," pleaded Marguerite.

So Algie told his Marguerite of the two rooms to let that he had found, but being very careful not to divulge where these two rooms were situated.

They clung to each other in their glade as they had never clung before, they were so happy. Oh how Algie longed for this buxom woman, but he remembered once more that she was a lady, and a fine lady at that, and he must still tread carefully until he had got her to the altar. He was fair panting with the need for her, but withheld his longing. They both agreed it was best for both of them to walk and talk.

*

Marguerite was adamant that her Mama should in no way hear of her marriage plans. She did not tell Bertie, but she knew that Mama would not approve of her choice, but it was her choice and her choice alone and nothing was going to come between them. She was determined to marry Bertie come what may. It was decided that gradually she would move her belongings to Wimbledon. She once more wrote an urgent letter to Sarah.

My dearest sister Sarah,
   Must see you urgently. Await invitation. Great news. Longing to tell you all.
       Your ever loving sister,
         Marguerite

As Marguerite wrote this letter, she suddenly realised that there was not a lot to tell, as she herself did not know where the rooms were or the slightest detail. In her excitement she had not asked.

This time Sarah had no need to wonder why her sister should need an invitation to stay. This surely meant that a wedding was in hand. She was nevertheless somewhat surprised when Marguerite stepped out of the cab and commenced to unload so many things. What was she doing?

All Marguerite would say was, "Please carry these into the house, Sarah. Don't ask questions now. I will tell you all once we have unloaded," exclaimed a by now rather tired Marguerite. It had been so difficult to load her belongings into the cab without being seen. She only hoped Cook had not been watching. No don't panic, she told herself, she surely could not see from the basement window what was going on at the kerb.

After everything was in the house, Sarah asked, "Marguerite, do tell me, why bring all these things? I am simply longing to know what you are up to."

Marguerite then enlightened her sister as to the plans that Bertie and she had made. She told her of the two rooms to let. "But please do not ask me about these rooms, because any more I do not know," stated an excited Marguerite.

"I expect they are super, and in a splendid house. Just you wait and see," announced an excited Sarah. "Oh I am so pleased for you both."

As to them being as super as Sarah believed, Marguerite, knowing her Bertie, was not so sure. She went on to tell her sister how Bertie was getting a special licence and that they were to be married at Whitsuntide.

Sarah could not withhold her excitement, but was she hearing correctly, what was her sister saying? "Now listen to what I have to say Sarah. Don't be too upset. Bertie and I do not want to have one of these Society weddings and all the trimmings that go with it. We are not a young couple and we are just going to slip away and get wed, and that will be that," announced a now serious Marguerite.

"Oh yes," agreed Sarah. "Just a quiet wedding, with the two families gathered at the church and then a quiet reception at a small hotel," announced Sarah, giving her sister a hug, and before Marguerite could interrupt, "And, perhaps little Janet as bridesmaid," Sarah tentatively suggested. She could see it all in her mind, how simply exciting.

"Sarah, do be quiet," said Marguerite holding up her hand. "Say no more. No two families, just the bride and groom and two witnesses at a Registry Office," announced Marguerite.

Sarah could not believe what she was hearing. She was not to attend her darling sister's wedding and her small Janet was not to be bridesmaid. How could Marguerite be so inconsiderate? She must meet this so-called fiancé and have it out with him. She was determined that her sister was to have the finest wedding in town. She went on to ask, "But Marguerite what will our dear Mama say?" Sarah was now feeling quite annoyed at her sister arriving so and telling her of all the arrangements made.

"That is the point, dear Mama is not to know," announced Marguerite.

Was Sarah hearing correctly, dear Mama not to be told? Really Marguerite this was going too far! So that was the reason for all these belongings arriving with her sister, what a darned cheek. Marguerite and Sarah were not in the habit of quarrelling, but during the next few days quarrel they did. They argued and argued about the wedding plans time and time again, until Robert was fed up with hearing about this wedding. Eventually Sarah had to succumb to Marguerite's persuasion, and, although bitterly disappointed, agreed to go along with her sister's plans. She helped to arrange yet another visit to bring along yet more of Marguerite's belongings.

After Marguerite returned home Sarah and Robert were to lie in bed and talk until the early hours as to what kind of fellow this Bertie could be to want to whisk his Marguerite away like this, and without even Mama knowing.

"Well." said Robert, taking his Sarah into his arms, "If they are as happy in their marriage as the two of us, Society wedding or not, who are we to complain." Sarah had to agree with her husband.

*

The next few weeks simply flew by. Marguerite agreed to Sarah's suggestion that they should go together to the West End to buy the wedding outfit. She felt that this was the least she could do, to give her sister that pleasure. Sarah would have had her sister dressed in a beautiful wedding gown, but Marguerite was adamant that an oatmeal coloured lawn suit was all that was needed. She would buy, on the day a fresh orchid to wear as a buttonhole.

Marguerite had agreed with Bertie that they should ask Nancy, their nippy friend, to be her witness.   She spent an enjoyable afternoon with Nancy choosing her an outfit in a pretty green, which went well with her auburn hair.   Bertie was to have, as his best man, his work mate from the days when he worked on the Heath.   He would forever be thankful to him for finding him a job in those days after the war, and this would be his way of finally saying "thank you mate".   The choice of these two as their witnesses seemed so right.

On enquiring about the two rooms, Bertie thought it best if Marguerite saw the rooms when he had got them in order, as he had quite a bit of decorating to do. He wanted only the best for his beloved and it had to be a surprise.   Of course, although disappointed, Marguerite succumbed to his wishes.

Arrangements were made once more for Marguerite to stay at Wimbledon for a few days before the wedding.   She was to leave the bare essentials in her room in Bedford Square, so as not to raise any suspicion.

The day before finally leaving the only home she had ever known, she spent quite a time down in the kitchen talking to Cook.   She felt quite sad, knowing the deceit she was to play.   Dear Cook had been with the family so long.   She certainly felt really guilty when she sat for her last meal with her dear Mama, whom she realised in all her protectiveness had only wanted the best for her delicate daughter.   How her Mama was going to take this sudden disappearance she dare not think.

When the cab drew up at the door Marguerite kissed her Mama goodbye, and much to Marguerite's distress, Mama said, "Now don't make it too long this time Marguerite. I feel so lonely without you."   Marguerite did not answer but as the cab drew away she felt tears dropping down her cheek.   To do this to her dear Mama was indeed harder than she had ever imagined!   She cuddled up to Snuff and said, "At least I'll have you to remind me of the old days," giving him an extra hug.   He was to stay with her sister until she was settled and then she would collect him.

There was one very difficult task that Marguerite had to do, soon after arriving at her sister's home she had to write some letters.   These two letters were to be sent by Sarah on the day of Marguerite's wedding.   One was to be sent to dear Mama and one to her elder sister Rachel.   This task she dreaded.

Sarah and little Janet greeted Marguerite with warm kisses, especially when Sarah saw her sister's tear-stained face.   Sarah herself would have been happier if she had met Bertie, and also if Marguerite had seen where she was to live.   It all seemed a very strange way of going about things, just going off like this to get married.   Yes, very strange, thought Sarah, nevertheless she had agreed to post the letters for Marguerite, that was the least she could do in this difficult situation.

Sarah had spent quite a bit of money on her sister's wedding present.   She was longing to present these fine articles, bought at Harrods, but would await Robert's return from work.   She suggested that without more ado Marguerite should write those two difficult letters and then the deed would be done.   Marguerite supposed her sister was right, if a matter needed to be done it was best done

quickly.   She sat down at Robert's desk and at about the third attempt finally
finished Mama's letter.

My dearest Mama,
  *I am writing to tell you that today, Saturday, 7th June 1930, I became the wife of my dearest
Bertie. We have been walking out for some time and it was our dearest wish to marry.*
  *We slipped away together. We did not wish for any fuss and wanted nothing to come between
us to spoil our relationship.*
  When we have settled in our small flat I will be in touch.
                              Your ever loving daughter,
                                   Marguerite

  Marguerite read it time and time again, and as she sealed the envelope tears
once more poured down her face.   She did not wish to be a hard-hearted
daughter, but realised the difficulties she would have had to face if she had done it
any other way.
  The letter to her sister Rachel was much easier to write, as since becoming an
adult she had grown away from this sister, having always been much closer to
Sarah.

My dearest Rachel and Edward,
  *Today, Saturday, 7th June 1930, I married my dear Bertie quietly at a private ceremony. I
am sorry not to have invited you all, but it was our wish to slip away together without any fuss.*
  Please take care of our dearest Mama for me.
                              Your ever loving sister,
                                   Marguerite

  Well that was that. She took the two envelopes and placed them in her sister's
hand saying, "Bless you Sarah.   I am sorry to burden you with the task of posting
these and having to deal with the outcome."   She hugged her sister, at the same
time saying, "I shall never be able to thank you enough, dear sister."   Sarah wiped
the tears from her sister's eyes, she realised what a difficult task this must have
been for Marguerite.   All was soon forgotten as small Janet was longing to give her
Auntie her present, Sarah broke away saying, "Well that is a good job done; now
come into the nursery, Janet has something for you."   Janet was by this time
jumping up and down with excitement, a parcel clutched in her small hands, she
pushed it towards Marguerite.   On opening Marguerite found the parcel
contained two pairs of beautifully embroidered pillow slips, edged in lace, and with
the words 'His" and 'Hers' embroidered in white .   Marguerite hugged her small
niece with delight.   Of course, not having a Society wedding, she would miss out
on all the fine gifts.   That evening Sarah and Robert gave her their gift - two pairs
of Irish linen sheets and enough beautiful soft blankets for Marguerite and Bertie's
double bed.   Bed, thought Marguerite, have we got one?   She had no idea what
furniture they had, oh dear!

*

Back in Holloway Road time was going far too quickly for Algie. It was not an easy task getting away from his Ma and into the rooms above. Not wanting to collect the keys from his Ma he had suggested to the landlord that he should retain them and each time they were needed he would just pop and get them - easier said than done! No, he did not intend letting his Ma know who the new tenants were to be until nearer the time. Every spare moment he slipped out, fetched the keys, and went up the front steps and into his future abode. A table and four chairs had been left behind by the previous tenants, a good start to the furnishings, thought Algie, but my, didn't the whole place need a coat of paint? This place was not fit for a lady yet, but it would be in good time. Yes he would make it fit for a Queen.

Algie decorated as best he could. He was not in the habit of doing any decorating, but when finished he stood back and was really proud of his achievement. He certainly hoped his dear Marguerite would appreciate the hardwork that had gone into it, he was fair whacked. The most important thing now was to get a bed. A good substantial bed, wasn't his beloved a buxom woman? Yes it must certainly be a comfortable bed. He stood there picturing himself cuddling his Marguerite in a huge four-poster. He laughed to himself at his thoughts, locked up the doors and went out into the street determined to search for this necessity.

It was the next day when Algie was on the way to get the wedding ring that he realised he was passing a second-hand furniture store, or shall we say a junk shop. He worked his way between the assortments of junk and found an assistant and asked whether there was a double bed for sale.

"Yeh, mate, I've got just the thing for yer. Bless me cotton socks one came in ere this morning. Aint it yer lucky day, mate." said the young cockney lad as he cleared his way through the wares. He at last found the bargain he was looking for and cleared a space for Algie to see more closely. "What say yer?" he asked. After some bartering Algie agreed that this was indeed what he was looking for and agreed to purchase this, with a double mattress thrown in, for a tenner. There was only one difficulty. He would have to transport it himself. He dared the cockney lad to sell it and went away to find some means of transport.

He remembered his pals down in the market, the pals from his pre-war days. He was sure they would help him. He was quite right. When they heard that dear old Algie was getting married a friend soon managed to find him an old barrow to borrow. He was certainly thankful it was summer as he pushed his bed home. What would he have done if it had been raining? What a struggle it was to get it up the front steps and into the house without drawing attention to anyone downstairs. He supposed, just in case Ma had become suspicious, he had best tell her he was moving out. Yes he would tell her that evening.

On returning the barrow to the market, Algie was to find that in his absence his mates had had a whip round and had gathered together various useful items as a wedding present. Algie thanked them and promised to bring the Mrs down to meet them one day. As he left with the gifts in his arms he thought to himself, that is hardly likely. No he did not think he would take a lady down there, no certainly not.

And so the time was to come when Algie was to broach the subject of leaving home. His opportunity arose when Ma remarked over dinner, "Yer looking fair whacked, Algie. What 'ave yer been up to?"

"Well, its like this, Ma. I've been 'ere moving furniture," announced Algie.

"Moving furniture? Who for? Yer fool of a man. Want to do yerself an injury?" asked Ma.

"For meself, Ma." Algie went on to say.

"Yerself, Algie? What for?" asked a puzzled Ma.

"Well yer see it's like this, Ma." This was difficult thought Algie.

"Well spit it out me lad, spit it out. What yer up to?" asked an impatient Ma, who was by now really wondering what her son was up to, and why he was having such difficulty in telling her. He had been acting mysteriously recently she thought. Had she not only said so the other day to young Eve?

"Well you see Ma, it's like this, I am moving upstairs into the vacant two rooms," announced Algie with relief that he had at last got it off his chest.

"Y'er what me lad? Y'er do no such thing me lad. Y'er not moving out of 'ere. No y'er not!" Ma was simply furious that her Algie would think of doing such a thing. "Do y'er 'ear me? Y'er not going to live up there." Whatever would she do without his money coming in? Whatever would she do, thought Ma? Turning to Eve she said, "Eve, just yer tell yer brother, he is not living up there." Eve was aghast at what her brother was saying, would he leave her alone with Ma? Ma could be difficult enough to cope with without being left alone with her.

"What do you mean, Algie. Going upstairs?" asked Eve.

"Just what I says. I've taken those two rooms and I shall be moving up the apples and pears next week," announced a determined Algie. "Stop calling me yer lad, Ma. I 'ave yer know I am nearing forty now, if you've 'praps forgotten and I will do whatever I pleases, so there Ma - take that and eat it." With that Algie went out of the room slamming the door behind him.

"Go after 'im Eve. Talk sense into 'im," pleaded Ma, wringing her hands with fury. But no matter how much Ma and his sister complained then and during the rest of the week, Algie would not listen.

Saturday came and Algie moved his things out and up the stairs. Later dressed up in his best bib and tucker, a carnation in his buttonhole, he took a last look around his new home and left for the Registry Office.

*

On Friday night Marguerite retired early to bed. The next morning her sister woke her with breakfast on a tray. She sat on the bed and taking Marguerite's hand in hers said, "Oh Marguerite, I wish you all the best. If you are as happy in marriage as Robert and I you have nothing to worry about." Being slightly worried for her sister, with this unknown Bertie, she then added, "Marguerite, when he takes you tonight, just relax and enjoy it. It will be the most wonderful night of your life.

Believe me, Maggie." With that she kissed her sister fondly and left her to enjoy her breakfast, adding as she went out of the door, "I will run your bath for you when you are ready. Allow yourself plenty of time, my dear."

Marguerite smiled her thanks and wished she could pluck up courage to ask her sister more about that side of married life, she felt so ignorant on such matters and knew so very little. She enjoyed her breakfast in the luxury of this lovely home, and after her bath dressed into her wedding outfit. She remembered she had to allow herself enough time to get her orchid. She was endeavouring to adjust her hat when there was a knock at the door and in rushed small Janet with something hidden behind her back. She was followed by Sarah carrying a beautiful bouquet of flowers, made up of every yellow flower possible surrounded by orange blossom and even a small sprig of myrtle. Sarah had even thought of a buttonhole for Nancy. What was this that Janet was now pressing into her hand? "A lovely horseshoe, thank you dear Janet, thank you Sarah." She hugged them both. Realising that Robert was standing in the background she thanked him too. And to make the party complete there was her Snuff decked out with a lovely white ribbon. She hugged him and promised to return for him soon. "God Bless you all. I only hope that I am as happy as you," said Marguerite as she dabbed at her eyes with her lace handkerchief.

The cab arrived and Marguerite hugged them all once more and thanked them all for sharing in her happiness. Sarah remembered the wedding presents and these were piled into the cab just in time with Marguerite's suitcase. "Holborn Registry Office, please." And so Marguerite was at last on her way to be married to her dear Bertie.

BOOK 3

CHAPTER 16

A NEW LIFE

Algie arrived in Holborn in good time and was relieved to see his best-man, Sid Eames, already there. They shook hands heartedly and decided that they just had time to wet their whistles before going into the Registry Office.

Making for the nearest pub, Sid bought them both a drink and lifting his glass to his old pal said, "The best of British luck to y'er Algie - oh, I mean, Bertie." laughed Sid. Algie had already put his pal wise to his new name.

"Thank you, mate. She aint arf a swell girl, my Marguerite. Yes a swell girl. I just can't wait to be wed." Having said that they drank up and Algie handed Sid the ring and they made their way to the ceremony. They went straight into the Registry Office to make sure they were out of sight before the bride arrived. "Unlucky to see yer bride before yer wed." said Algie.

*

What a long way it seemed to Marguerite from Wimbledon to Holborn. Her bouquet smelt simply gorgeous. She now felt she was in a dream; she also felt quite lonely in this cab on her own, dressed as a bride; she felt that this was all happening to someone else and not herself.

As the cab pulled up, Nancy, looking so different in her green outfit and her hair just so, was there to meet her. They placed the suitcase and presents in the hallway, fixed the orchid on to Nancy's lapel, and in just a few moments the Registrar appeared to say the bridegroom was waiting ready for his bride. Through the double doors Marguerite could just about make out Algie standing waiting with his best man. Marguerite suddenly remembered she had not arranged for any music to be played. No music on her special day! How could she have forgotten such an important thing! A wedding without music is like a day without sunshine she had always thought, but in her haste she had forgotten to arrange this important item. Oh well, she thought, too late now, and so in silence Marguerite, followed by Nancy, walked slowly into the room to be joined in matrimony to her dear Bertie. She smiled shyly at him standing in front of the Registrar looking so smart. She recalled saying, "I Marguerite take thee Albert...." why, of course, thought Marguerite her Bertie was Albert, "to be my wedded husband.....with my body I thee honour..." Yes a buxom one at that, thought Bertie. "...to obey..." Yes, thought Marguerite, I will obey you dear Bertie. And then suddenly it was all over and the Registrar was announcing them husband and wife. Turning to them he said to Algie, "You may kiss the bride." This Algie did quite shyly, and then the Registrar was congratulating them as, "Mr & Mrs Smythe," and that was it, the wedding ceremony was all over and they came out into busy Holborn as man and wife.

Marguerite had booked a table for four at the Strand Palace Hotel. Nancy took charge of the suitcase and wedding presents as the bride and groom were driven away to the Strand to their small reception, and then she hastily hailed a cab for herself and Sid. They were to remember for a long time that meal, taken in such splendid surroundings. After having opened their wedding presents, they suddenly realised that they had sat over the meal for quite some time and it was now 7 o'clock and the waitresses were endeavouring to clear the tables for the evening guests. The wedding party gathered their things together and made their way outside. A taxi was hailed and Nancy and Sid waved the newly weds goodbye as they sped away to their home together.

Bertie just about carried his bride over the threshold, he could not get Marguerite in quick enough before Ma could spot them. The cabbie waited for him to return to unload the luggage, and the presents they had opened over tea were quickly taken in. Nancy had given them, very appropriately, a tea service and Sid's present was a clock. Bertie handled the tea service with great care.

Marguerite glanced around her. It was certainly very fresh and clean. She walked into the kitchen. At least they had a table and four chairs. What about the bedroom. She opened the other door. So her dear Bertie had managed to obtain a bed. How lovely her sheets and blankets from Harrods would look tonight.

Her new husband followed in behind her with the bedding. "Well me better 'alf, I thinks an early night is called for. What says you me luv." asked a winking Bertie.

"Oh, Bertie, not yet. Give us a chance." said Marguerite giving him a kindly push away from her, and moving to look out of the window. "We will unpack my things first and then I will take a bath," announced Marguerite.

"Take a bath?" asked Bertie. "You'll be lucky me luv. Yer can 'ave a wash down at the kitchen sink," announced an amused Bertie.

"Why?" asked a surprised Marguerite. She then hesitantly asked, "Is there no bathroom?"

"No, my luv, there's no bath 'ere" answered Bertie, joining Marguerite at the window. "Yer see those chimneys over there," pointing out of the window at a building just showing over the top of other buildings. "That's yer bathhouse me luv from now on."

Marguerite could not believe what she was hearing, a bathhouse with other people, oh, no thank you, she would make do with the kitchen sink. Well, at least, tonight she would.   She thought longingly of that luxurious bath taken that morning back at her sisters.

They soon helped each other make the bed with the beautiful Irish linen sheets and soft blankets.   My, thought Algie, I bet this bed has never seen the likes before.

Algie had filled the kitchen cupboards with the food that he thought they would initially require.   He hoped his Ma would not miss the items taken from her cupboards.   Whilst Marguerite arranged her flowers in a jam jar, which fortunately she had found under the sink - she must remember to buy a vase or two after the Bank Holiday - Algie made them a cup of cocoa, which they sat down at their very own table and enjoyed.

After a while Algie once more suggested it was time for bed.   As it was now about 9.30 pm and it had seemed a very long day to Marguerite she agreed that yes it was indeed time for bed.   Algie discreetly disappeared into the bedroom whilst Marguerite had a wash-down, saying, as he went out, "By the way luv, the lav is on the landing halfway down the lower stairs.   Make sure yer lock the door, the 'ole 'ouse uses the lav." Oh no, thought Marguerite, where had she come?

She washed herself down as best she could and carefully unfolded her new nightgown, which was edged in beautiful lace.   She eased herself into it and eventually plucked up courage to enter the bedroom.   She could not help but smile when she saw Bertie in his old striped flannelette pyjamas.   In his haste to get the two rooms ready for his bride it had not occurred to him to buy some new ones for his wedding night.

Algie turned as his bride came into the room, he could hardly contain himself as he saw this beautiful buxom woman enter, looking as fresh as a virgin should.

"Come me love," he said, as he enfolded her in his arms.   Whilst he had waited for his bride he had opened up the bed ready for this moment.   They sank on to it. It creaked and Algie prayed that it would not give out.   His hands travelled all over his virgin bride getting to know every inch of her.   As he pummelled her bosoms, as if they were a football to be played with, she cried out "Oh Bertie." He took this to be words of affection, not realising the discomfort he was causing her.   As he went on fondling her breasts, she thought what is this tingling feeling, what is this sensation below and she sank into the bed further as he excited her even more.   She cried out with pain, and not without horror, as they truly became man and wife and she was a virgin no more.

Was this what Sarah had meant when she said that when Bertie took her she should relax and enjoy it.   She wished she had been forewarned, she felt bruised all over and the memories of the attempt that had been made in her youth came flooding back. She fought to shut them out of her mind.   She suddenly realised that Bertie was sound asleep. How dare he just shut her out like that after having taken her so. How dare he! She already felt unclean and in need of a bath. Marguerite eventually fell asleep reliving the day's events and wondering what was to follow. She had certainly had some rude awakenings.

Little did she realise more was to come, as being a Bank Holiday, there was no need for Bertie to rush up for work and he could not leave his bride alone. Each time Marguerite attempted to get out of bed he clung on to her with hunger and lust. Oh no not again she thought, why didn't you warn me Sarah? At last she pleaded with Bertie, "I love you dear Bertie, but enough is enough. Do please give me a chance."

"Just once more me luv. Come to hubby once more." Bertie was determined to take her yet again. What had he waited all these years for, and so his bride relented.

*

The Bank Holiday was finally over and Marguerite was able to surface from her honeymoon home. Like a dutiful wife she waved her husband goodbye as he set off for work. She took a look around her new home and made a shopping list of the necessities required. Fortunately her dear Papa had left his financial affairs well organized and on his death Marguerite received a monthly allowance, so money was not to concern her. She set off to survey her surroundings. She found a nearby departmental store and chose some curtains, a couple of rugs, amongst other things. She arrived back home feeling pleased with herself and more relaxed. Whilst waiting the delivery of the items she could not carry she busied herself changing the flower water and displaying her wedding flowers properly in their new vases, she had only placed them in water in haste on her wedding night and had not had the opportunity before this to display them as she had been used to. Yes she would always fill her home with flowers, their fragrance was so exotic. She sat and day-dreamed of how she would make this first home of hers the best in the street.

The day seemed to pass quickly and she suddenly realised that Bertie was letting himself in the front door. He was more than pleased at the transformation of the rooms. The rugs alone made the rooms seem more furnished.

Suddenly there was a shouting from below, "Algie, Algie, would yer like some grub?" Algie endeavoured to ignore his Ma. What next he thought.

On a repeat of the shouting, Marguerite frowned and asked, "My goodness that woman's got a voice on her. I wonder who she is shouting for?"

Bertie said he had no idea. Ma called again. Bertie endeavoured to entice his bride into the bedroom, at least that had a lock on the door should his Ma appear up the stairs. He could at least lock the door and take his bride once more.

Marguerite was having none of this, "No my dearest. You just wait for your desserts for tonight. You have had your honeymoon," announced a decisive Marguerite.

"Did yer not promise only last Saturday to obey yer hubby?" enquired a persuasive Bertie, at the same time keeping an eye on the kitchen door and sincerely hoping that his Ma would stay down below. He did not wish to make any introductions yet. He did not wish his new life to be spoilt. He pleaded with his bride once more, but Marguerite pushed him away from her and commenced to prepare the meal.

Later that evening, after the frustration of washing herself down at the kitchen sink with a now braver Bertie fussing around her, and before getting into the marital bed she glanced out of the window, prior to pulling the curtains. She looked over to the chimney pots and enquired from Bertie just what the bathhouse was like, and as to how many went in at a time. Bertie laughed so much at his wife's ignorance on such matters.

"How many go in at a time. Why half a dozen," he teased. "No! my luv. Just you," and then putting his arm around her he squeezed her affectionately and added, "Or perhaps with a little persuasion hubby could join yer."

"Get away with you Bertie," pushing Bertie from her.

"No, just you me luv, on yer own, of course. They don't 'ave any anky panky there." Algie thought perhaps he had teased enough.

"Do you mean to say there are lots of baths in separate rooms," enquired a puzzled Marguerite.

"That's just what I mean." Bertie went on to explain how you queued up, towel under arm, and were issued with a piece of green soap and then went in had your bath, and, if you were lucky a good soak, or, if you were not so lucky and the queue was long the attendant hammered on the door and shouted "Time gentleman, please." Turning to his wife he asked if that satisfied her and promised to take her with him when he next went. "Now cum along luv, beddy time. Come to yer desperate hubby, come," endeavouring, but not succeeding, to carry her to bed. Marguerite struggled free and reluctantly got in beside him, thinking to herself that she still did not fancy that bathhouse. No she thought she would get a cab each week and soak in the luxury of her sister's bathroom. Yes that is what she would do she would look forward to her weekly visits. The very next morning she wrote to Sarah saying that she would be visiting on Friday.

*

Back in Bedford Square the postman arrived and whilst taking breakfast Emily Sinclair opened her post. A Wimbledon postmark, perhaps it was a letter from Marguerite to say she was returning home. About time too thought Emily, these visits were getting too frequent. With her paper knife she slit open the envelope. Slowly she read the letter in front of her and could not believe what she read. Marguerite married! Marguerite married! She pulled the bell rope hard. Since the departure of Amy this bell was never used, and consequently it gave Cook a start when it rang in the lobby below stairs. Whatever can be the matter, thought Cook, her mistress must be ill? She rushed up to her mistress' bedroom as fast as she could and without stopping to knock rushed in.

"What is it, Ma'am? Are you alright Ma'am? You rang?" asked a concerned Cook.

Emily pushed the letter into Cook's hand and sank further down into the bed. Cook could not believe what she read. Marguerite married! "Oh! Ma'am. How could she do this to you. How could she?" and then as an afterthought, "I will get you some brandy."

Whilst Cook fetched the brandy, Emily lay trying to think why her middle daughter should do such a thing. She wondered, was she expecting and consequently had to marry in haste? She soon dismissed this idea from her head and decided that a Sinclair would have more sense than get into such a predicament, but then, on the other hand, had she enlightened any of her daughters as to what went on in marriage? No she certainly had not! She had thought this unnecessary. Did her Mother enlighten her on the subject? Certainly not! Such things were not mentioned in the Victorian era. By the time the brandy arrived, she had dismissed the whole idea from her head as other means of retribution came into her mind.

The brandy certainly revived Emily and without more ado, and with determination, she got dressed and ordered Cook to call a cab to the door immediately. Yes Emily knew what she should do!

*

Friday came and as soon as Bertie had gone to work and the breakfast things were washed Marguerite went out and hailed a cab. "The Ridgeway, Wimbledon, please." Marguerite was feeling really excited at the thought of seeing her sister again. It seemed a long ride but she sat back and enjoyed what she hoped would be the first of many such rides. Sarah eagerly greeted her, and Snuff was ecstatic at seeing his mistress. Marguerite was hardly in the house before Sarah was questioning her. She wanted answers to all sorts of questions, but all she got from her sister was "Yes fine, just fine." Did Sarah detect a trace of disappointment?

Before she could question any further, Marguerite asked for a hot bath. "Please Sarah, let me just lie in a bath. No more questions, please," and so reluctantly Sarah let her sister depart to the bathroom - where she was to stay the rest of the morning. Strange, thought Sarah! Very strange! Oh! Marguerite thought, lying here is just luxury, absolute luxury! Sarah thought her sister was never going to reappear. Why was she taking so long? It was as if she had used her bath as an excuse to get away.

Eventually the two sisters had their lunch, and the day together went by so quickly that it seemed no time at all before Marguerite was leaving again; leaving her sister with many unanswered questions.

*

The newly weds enjoyed their weekend. Like their courting days they went walking on Hampstead Heath. Walking on the heath reminded Marguerite that she must ask Bertie when she was to bring Snuff home. It was about time she had him with her. It was not fair to her sister having him all this time, and so this particular Sunday she broached the subject with Bertie, and this was when she was to receive a bitter disappointment.

"Me luv," said Bertie. He hesitated; he really did not know how he was to tell his bride that no dogs were allowed. He stopped walking, and taking both her hands in his, and looking her straight in the eyes he said, "I am afraid the landlord stipulated no dogs!"

"No dogs? Oh Bertie why didn't you tell me before, we could have looked for somewhere else?" She was shattered and said with mounting anger." It is too bad of you. You knew I had a small pet dog, and only a small dog at that!" She let go of his hands and walked ahead, deep in thought. She could not be parted for ever from her little dog. Wasn't it her dear Papa's last gift to her? Bertie stepped out beside her and their walk continued in silence. This was their first quarrel ever, and why did it have to be this very first weekend when everything had gone so well? Marguerite did not know how she was going to forgive Bertie for being so deceitful.

The following week Marguerite hardly spoke to Bertie and most certainly would have nothing to do with him in bed. In desperation on the Sunday evening she decided she had to ask Bertie where she should hang her washing the next morning. The washing had certainly accumulated and it must be done. "Bertie, I must spend tomorrow morning washing. Where should I hang it to dry?" asked Marguerite in quite a cold manner.

Bertie was rather taken aback at this question. He quickly answered, trying to pamper his wife, "Oh just you leave it to me, me luv. I'll hang it out in the garden when I gets in from work."

"A lot of good that will be. It won't dry then," answered an impatient Marguerite. Really, she thought, does he think I'm helpless. Trust a man to think like that. Oh well, she thought, I will find my own way down in the morning.

The next morning Algie went off to work thinking no more about the washing and relieved to see at least his wife waving at the window. He hoped that this stupid quarrel was over and done with.

Marguerite set to. There was certainly quite a bit of washing to get through and she was not used to this task, having always sent her washing to the laundry. It was at last finished and now to hang it out. With a bucket full of washing in each hand she made for the stairs and with difficulty edged her way down. On reaching the lower hallway she found it quite dark, except for a crack of daylight through what appeared to be a door at the far end. She made for this, finding the hallway very narrow for her plump figure. On opening the door she was certainly surprised at the extent of the back-yard. She realised she had not seen it all from her kitchen window. She supposed she could use the pegs in the bag on the line, and so commenced to hang out the washing. This task she found even more exhausting than doing the washing. It certainly played up her heart reaching above her head. Perhaps she should have left it to Bertie. She was thinking this when suddenly a voice called out.

"That's right luv, use me pegs!" shouted that woman from somewhere.

Marguerite stopped what she was doing. Wasn't that the same voice that called Algie for his meal each evening. Marguerite turned to see where the voice was coming from, and there sticking her head out of what Marguerite presumed was a kitchen window was a woman with curling rags still in her hair. "Oh, I'm sorry. I should have asked." Marguerite said shyly.

My, my, thought Mary Smythe, we have a lady here. She must be visiting her Aunt at the top of the house. Trust a lady like this to need to do some washing whilst she's visiting.

"Is yer Aunt feeling better today, me luv?" asked an inquisitive Mary.

"My Aunt?" questioned Marguerite. She didn't know what this woman meant, but as she didn't wish to get involved, she answered, "Yes thank you," and went on hanging out the washing.

Mary, realising she was not to learn much, slammed down the window and got on with the job in hand.

By the time Marguerite climbed upstairs with the empty buckets she felt quite breathless and had to resort to one of her heart pills. She realised that this was the first one she had taken since her wedding - well she thought married life must be suiting my heart; perhaps the pummelling she had suffered had done some good after all. Nevertheless, she would leave it to Bertie to get the washing in when he got in from work.

On arriving home that evening he enquired from Marguerite, "Well 'ave you had a good day me luv?", at the same time out of the window he caught sight of what he knew to be their washing hanging on the line; he turned with anger and demanded to know why she had hung it out.

"Why Bertie, of course I hung out the washing. It needs the fresh air." answered a puzzled Marguerite.

Bertie turned on her still angry. "I thought I told you to leave it for me to hang out." All sorts of things were going through his mind as to whom she could have met and what could have happened.

With raised voice Marguerite asked her husband. "Do you think I am incapable?" and with that they angrily turned from each other, once more there was a silence between them for the rest of the evening.

Algie waited until dark to get the washing in. Whilst endeavouring to do this, and making sure he left nothing in the garden, he thought to himself that on seeing Marguerite waving goodbye that morning he had gone to work with high hopes that their quarrel over the dog was over, but now look what had happened!

That night when Marguerite once more turned from him he demanded in frustration, "Do I 'ave to demand me rights as a 'usband, Marguerite?"

Marguerite heard what he said with horror and once more the grovelling drunken men of her youth appeared before her. She endeavoured to push the picture out of her mind and turned reluctantly to her husband before more ado succumbing to his wishes. He seemed more demanding than ever. Had he not been deprived from his rights this past week?

*

138

Mary Smythe was waiting with all eagerness for Eve to arrive home from her work in Whitehall. Eve was thankful that her working day was over. She found it quite tiring and then had to contend with her Ma all evening. She hoped this evening that she would get some peace and time to herself. As she let herself in her Ma pounced. "Just yer take a look me luv out of the window," she said, pulling her daughter over to the kitchen sink.

"Why! What at Ma? I've seen washing hanging on a line before!" What was so exciting about that, thought Eve?

"Yeh! But luv look again. 'Ave yer ever seen such a beauty of a nightgown? Fit for a Queen aint it? Look at it luv. Look at that there lace," Ma pointing at Marguerite's nightgown was really beside herself with excitement she had only ever seen such things in shop windows, never in her life on her very own line.

"Oh Ma, aint it grand," and then hesitating she asked, "Whose is it, Ma?"

"Cum and sit yerself down and I'll tell yer what I knows," said a secretive Ma. Mary went on to relate the conversation, held through the kitchen window that morning. "Now I tells yer what, Eve. Tomorrow evening you just keeps yer ear open for 'er to go to the lav and you go and meets 'er and yer finds out what's wrong with the old soul," suggested Ma.

"I thought you said she was young Ma?" questioned a by now weary Eve trying to have patience with her Ma. She supposed nothing much happened to excite Ma these days and something different was sure to get her going, she didn't arf go on over such silly things and come up with some right ridiculous ideas, thought Eve.

"I means what's wrong with 'er Aunt upstairs?" corrected Ma.

"Oh alright," said Eve, hoping her Ma would have forgotten the whole episode by the next evening.

*

Rachel had received her letter from Marguerite and could not believe what she was reading. She really must make one of those rare visits to Bedford Square and learn more from Mama. Fancy her sister Marguerite married. Just fancy that. She felt a little resentful at being left out of the celebrations, but then, on the other hand, she and Marguerite never had much in common, so it was hardly surprising.

So it was that within a few days Emily was to receive a visit from her eldest daughter. Immediately she appeared Emily realised that she must have heard the latest news, but Rachel was certainly very surprised when she learned that none of the family had been at the wedding and had not even met the fellow concerned. In fact she felt really sorry for Mama, but Emily would take no sympathy from anyone and all she would say was that Marguerite deserved all she got and that she had seen to the matter.

"Seen to what, dear Mama?" asked Rachel, but Mama was not forthcoming. Rachel contacted Sarah to find out what she knew, but she was unable to enlighten her. Rachel put the matter out of her mind thinking that only time would tell.

*

The next evening, immediately Eve arrived home, Ma sat listening for any movement on the stairs. She made Eve jump when she shouted, "Now Eve, some ones gone to the lav," hustling her daughter out of the door and up the stairs.

"Oh Ma do I have to," whispered an embarrassed Eve, but Ma just pushed her daughter on her way.

Eve soon returned to the kitchen. "It was only our Algie going to the lav." Eve laughingly announced to her Ma, and picking up a magazine relaxed once more.

Ma was determined to find out more. Later she once more sent her daughter scurrying up the stairs, and on coming out of the toilet Marguerite nearly bumped into the young woman waiting at the door. "Oh I'm so sorry, said an embarrassed and startled Marguerite.

"Good evening," said Eve rather shyly, thinking at the same time this is ridiculous, why does Ma have to be so nosy. "Staying here long," asked Eve, remembering her h's.

"Oh, I live here," announced Marguerite.

As he edged his way quietly to the top of the stairs to listen Algie thought, 'oh no, what next'.

"Oh, I thought my Ma said you were looking after your Aunt. So you have decided to stay with her after all?" asked an inquisitive Eve.

"My Aunt?" questioned Marguerite.

Algie listening from above began to get hot under the collar.

"Yes, the old dear on the top floor," answered Eve.

"Oh no. You are mistaken. I have just got married and have come to live on the landing above," announced Marguerite. Thinking about it she thought that maybe this could be a new friend, she seemed quite a pleasant girl, a little more ladylike than her Mother. She must get to know her better. On hearing the words 'married' Algie turned to make his getaway and nearly tripped. That's done it, he thought, now for trouble.

Eve was so taken back at what she had just heard and turned to rush back downstairs, but had the courtesy to say, "Oh, I see my best wishes." After saying that with a smile, she turned and went straight into the lav and shut the door, thinking what am I doing in here? Nevertheless, she stayed while she tried to take in what she had just heard. Good heavens! What would Ma say about this? Had she heard correctly? Yes she had definitely said she had just got married and lived on the next landing. Well wasn't her brother Algie on the next landing! My word what would Ma say, if Algie was really married? She contemplated for some time. She thought she heard Ma come out of the kitchen. Oh well she supposed she best go down and face the music, she had been long enough.

On returning to the kitchen, where Algie had started busying himself with the washing-up, Marguerite said, "Quite a pleasant young woman downstairs and different to her Mother." Algie did not answer. He thought the least said the better. He stubbed out his cigarette in the sink with intent. He rolled his own cigarettes and Marguerite was already finding this a distasteful habit.

"Don't do that Bertie. It makes such a mess." Marguerite pulled a face of disgust at the brown stained bits in the sink. She would have to clear all those up before going to bed. A job she found simply disgusting. "Put them down the toilet, please. There's a dear," she requested. Bettie looked with distain at his wife and thought, I hope she's not going to fuss over everything, but at the same time he was keeping a sharp ear for Ma. He was quite convinced that she would be bawling up the stairs at any moment.

When Eve arrived back down in the kitchen Ma quickly asked, "Well luv, what's she say? Is the old dear ill?"

"Well no Ma!" said Eve hesitating. "She doesn't live with the old dear." Looking at Ma and wondering what to say next. "She is just above, Ma."

"Just above? What yer mean luv, just above?" and then the penny dropped, and in a voice getting louder she said, "With our Algie. That's what you mean, aint it with our Algie?"

Eve could only shake her head in agreement and in a whisper said, "They are married."

"Married?" shouted Ma. "Married? Our Algie married? The artful dodger. More fool 'im."

Eve did not like the look on Ma's face. "Now careful, Ma. Don't take on so," said Eve, going up to Ma.

"Take on yer say. I'm not taking on. He can stew in his own juice, that 'e can. That's what 'e can do," said a defiant Ma. With that she flopped down in her chair from which she did not move for the rest of the evening. The frown on Ma's face worried Eve, as she wondered what was going through Ma's mind. She didn't envy her brother now that Ma knew. Suddenly Ma spoke. "Now we knows the reason for the posh nighty. Now we knows."

"Yes Ma. Now we knows, as you say." Eve sat there thinking of that beautiful nighty and quite envying her sister-in-law upstairs. It must be wonderful to be married, thought Eve.

Upstairs Algie could not believe that there was no shouting from below.

Later Marguerite said, "You are very much on edge this evening, Bertie. What's the matter?"

"Nothing me luv! Nothing! Let's go to bed." He felt that that room with the lock was the safest place.

*

Some days later Marguerite was conscious of someone calling her. Algie's Ma was half way up the stairs.

"Mrs Smythe, would yer mind clearing yer 'ubby's fag ends from down this ere lav. A disgusting 'abit I calls it, disgusting," having said that she retreated down the stairs again. That'll teach her, she thought. She can clear up after her Algie now. That'll teach them.

Marguerite stared at the retreating figure with disbelief. She wondered how she knew she was Mrs Smythe? That evening she told Bertie of how that woman downstairs had complained and asked him if he would remove the offending cigarette ends, but his reply came back fast and furious. "No luv, you made me put 'em down there you can get 'em out." He chuckled to himself at the same time thinking 'that'll teach her', but he puzzled as to what other tricks his Ma would get up to.

Marguerite was so taken back at what Bertie had said that she forgot completely to ask him as to how the woman knew their name. She knew by Bertie's tone that the job was hers to do. She put it off as long as she could but wondered as to what depths she had sunk?

*

The next Friday Marguerite took her usual trip to Wimbledon. Soon after arriving Sarah handed her a letter saying, "This arrived the other day addressed to you". Puzzled Marguerite looked at the envelope and at the City postmark; she slowly opened it. She was horrified at what she read; she went quite pale and sank into the nearest chair. Seeing how white her sister had become, and thinking that she was going to faint, she rushed to her sister asking, "What is it Marguerite? What ever is the matter?" Marguerite did not answer, but sat there with the letter in her hand, she just did not believe what she had just read.

BOOK 3

CHAPTER 17

REPERCUSSIONS

Marguerite sat there staring at the letter with disbelief, feeling completely shattered at what she had read. After a few moments, when she had composed herself, she handed the letter to Sarah. It was from John Mullen their late Papa's partner, it read:-

My dearest Marguerite,

It is with regret that I have to inform you that following your marriage your monthly allowance will be discontinued. This will take effect as from the end of this month, the 31st July 1930.

I am so sorry to have to inform you of your Mother's decision, as you know I have always had your wellbeing foremost in my thoughts.

Your humble servant,

John Mullen.

After reading the letter all Sarah could say to her sister was, "Oh no! How could our Mama do this to you?" At the same time thinking to herself she knew what Rachel would say - what do you expect, look how she has treated our dear Mama! Nevertheless, she felt so sorry for Marguerite of whom she was so fond. She tried to comfort her sister by saying, "Never mind, dear. I expect your dear Bertie will be able to support you, and will be only too pleased to do so. He must be earning quite a good wage as a landscape gardener."

Marguerite turned away from her sister thinking - little do you know. Perhaps she should never have said that her Bertie was a landscape gardener and been quite honest with Robert and Sarah from the beginning of the relationship and admitted that he was just a park-keeper, but the false impression had been made and there was no going back on it now. She sat there very quietly thinking about it and endeavouring to overcome the severe shock she had just received. She suddenly remembered, she had not mentioned to her sister the problem of Snuff, but perhaps this was as well, as she now had a good excuse not to have her beloved pet to live with her, as on Bertie's wages she would not be able to afford to feed a dog. She turned to her sister and said, "I'm afraid, Sarah, I will not now be able to take Snuff with me. I cannot possibly ask Bertie to feed Snuff as well as ourselves. Do you think Robert will mind if you keep him for me?"

How ridiculous thought Sarah not to be able to afford to feed a dog, but, nevertheless, what could Sarah say to her distressed sister. Giving her a fond hug she said, "Yes we will keep him for the time being, but I am quite sure Bertie will let you have him eventually. Cheer up, Marguerite, it will not be as bad as you think. You will survive my dearest." Survive! Thought Marguerite, you do not understand the situation.

*

It was a very sad and shaken Marguerite that returned home that Friday evening, and on showing the letter to Bertie he shrugged his shoulders and giving Marguerite a warm cuddle said, "Never mind, me luv, hubby will look after yer."

Yes, thought Marguerite, I am sure you will, but how far will your small earnings take us? By the time we have paid the rent and bought our food there will not be much left to keep me in the way that I have been used to. She then and there made up her mind that she must pay a visit to her late Papa's partner in the city. Yes she would fight her Mama's decision!

The very next day she did as planned and took a cab to the City. John Mullen was not at all surprised to see Marguerite. "Why Marguerite do come in." Taking her hands in his, which reminded her of that other occasion, he said, "May I take this opportunity of wishing you every happiness and success in your marriage." He said it with all sincerity, but at the same time wishing that it had been himself who was the lucky man. He had always regretted that he had not got far with the relationship with his late partner's daughter.

"Thank you, John." She wished he would let go of her hands. "You no doubt know why I am here?" Marguerite was determined to come quickly to the point of her visit. "I ask you John why should Mama take this legacy of my dear Papa from me?" asked a forthright Marguerite.

"I was quite prepared for your not unexpected visit, dear Marguerite, and so I have your Papa's last Will and Testament to hand." He went to his desk and picking up a document read out to Marguerite what her dear Papa had said….. Your dear Papa ends by saying - and I will quote – 'and upon her marriage this shall continue at my dear wife Emily's discretion'." Laying down the papers he looked at Marguerite's shocked face and said, "You see my dear Marguerite it is in your Mother's hands to do as she pleases."

Yes Marguerite thought I can quite see it was very easy for Mama to get her own back. She looked at John across the desk and beginning to feel very impatient, she asked, "Is this your final word on this matter, John?"

"I am afraid my answer has to be yes, my dearest Marguerite. I would have it to be otherwise but I have to abide by your dear Mama's instructions. It is out of my hands to go against her wishes. I am sure you realise this, my dear?" asked John as kindly as he could.

Yes Marguerite realised this only too well and she knew there was no point in arguing over the matter. Without more ado, and taking a last look at her dear Papa's portrait, and thinking - yes Bertie is very much like you in looks but she now realised, only too well, how different the two men were. She glanced around the office that she had known for so many years and which held so many memories. She reluctantly turned to go vowing never to set foot in this City office again. John hurried to open the door for her and offered to hail a cab.

"No thank you, John." Marguerite could not wait to take leave of this past admirer. She hurried down the steps and stood by the kerb waiting for a cab. John watched her out of the window. His heart went out to her as she stood there looking such a forlorn figure. He only wished he could have done more. He supposed it would be the last he would ever see of his late partner's middle daughter. He turned back to his desk; he could not bear to look at her any longer, sat down at his desk, buried his head in his hands, and thought I have now definitely lost her for ever. Until Emily had appeared in the office the other day he had always held some hope that he would stand a chance with Marguerite but he now knew that all was lost. Oh well! Thought he, they say every man has one love in his life and that was mine.

*

Bettie had agreed to pay all the bills, but this did not leave Marguerite much out of his small earnings for housekeeping, let alone cab rides to her sisters or for shopping in the West End. She felt really miserable at the thought of how things were to be.

It was not many weeks after her visit to the city that Marguerite woke one morning feeling quite groggy. She turned over and went back to sleep. On waking later she found, for the first time, that Bertie had already left for work. She wondered why she felt so tired and went into the kitchen to make a pot of tea. Bertie had evidently cooked himself some bacon and eggs, the mere smell of them made Marguerite feel sick. She really felt so poorly and returned to her bed. This was to be the beginning of some weeks of real misery.

The following Friday morning she slowly made her way outside, wondering how she was to stomach a long journey in a cab. Thankfully one soon drew up and it was not until she was well on the way to Wimbledon that she realised she had no money to pay the fare. Her heart started to beat rapidly and she became hotter and hotter as she worried as to what she should do. This did not help her feeling of nausea. A really distressed and ill Marguerite arrived at her sister's. Of course, in no time at all, Sarah had settled the fare and made Marguerite a cup of tea. Marguerite put it to her lips and rushed from the room. Sarah comforted her sister and asked her if she realised what was wrong.

"No!" said Marguerite thoughtfully, and then she suddenly realised what her sister was implying. "Oh no, Sarah, it can't be. We cannot afford a baby." She started to sob and to tell Sarah of her money worries. It was there and then agreed, much to Marguerite's relief, that Sarah would pay her cab fares each Friday, so enabling her to keep up her visits. Sarah would also arrange for Marguerite to see a gynaecologist that very next week. "But Sarah, we cannot afford a private consultation. Bertie pays into the Hospital Saturday Fund. I will go on the panel!" announced Marguerite, but her sister would not hear of it.

"No Marguerite. I am so thrilled for you and you must have the best attention. It would have been Papa's wish." said Sarah. Marguerite did not argue, but she thought to herself - I am glad you are thrilled, Sarah, I am not so sure I am. Eventually, after a relaxed bath and as the day wore on, she began to feel much better. She agreed with her sister that it would be better to not say anything to Bertie until the next week when it was confirmed.

By the time Bertie returned from work in the evenings Marguerite felt quite well and at the weekend she was able to conceal her distressful state, so it was a surprise to him when a week later, after the Consultant had confirmed that indeed Marguerite was expecting, she broke the news to him. Unlike Marguerite, Bertie was not a one to worry too much about money matters, and he took his wife in his arms and tried to reassure her of his pleasure at the news, he was so thrilled. He just could not believe that he was to become a father. He was certainly far more excited than his wife. As she lay in his arms he tried to reassure her.

"But Bertie, we cannot afford a baby!" she said, with tears pouring down her face. She was worried, amongst other things, as to how her heart would stand up to the extra weight. Also she wondered for how long she was going to feel so unwell in the mornings.

He endeavoured to comfort her by saying, "Me Ma was a widow and brought up five of us, so if she could do it so can we!" At the mention of his Ma it did occur to her that she had never met Bertie's Ma or his sisters. He had told her of Thomas in Australia and of how Kate, down in Dorchester, had lost her husband during the war, but where was his Ma and younger sister? She must ask him some time, but not now.

*

Downstairs Ma Smythe, whose hearing was quite good, heard this young woman above being so ill each morning and knew immediately what was wrong. She thought now was the time to approach her son. She would enjoy being a Grandmother!

After dark one evening Algie was collecting the washing for his wife when Ma cornered him. "Don't think I 'aven't 'eard you taking in the washing, me son. Trying to 'ide from yer Mother are yer, and so yer might. I 'ave also 'eard that lass of yours being ill at 'er kitchen sink, and I'm not daft. I knows whats wrong with 'er!" announced Ma. "Put 'er in the family way 'ave yer?" she asked.

"What yer say?" asked Algie, still trying to evade the issue that he was married.

"'Er upstairs, 'aving a kid?" asked his Ma.

Algie looked at his Ma and said, "She is me wife, yer know!"

"I knows alright. I knows she's yer wife. All the more fool you," answered Ma. This comment took Algie back years to when he took his first girl home.

Yes, he thought, I did right in not telling her before I had got hitched. He shrugged his shoulders and made for the stairs.

*

Because of Marguerite's past medical history the Consultant wished her to attend his clinic each week. Yet more expense, thought Marguerite. Like her sisters she was booked into Queen Charlotte's hospital for the birth. Bertie was really delighted when the baby quickened and he was able to cuddle up to his Marguerite and feel the movement of this unborn child of his. It made him feel years younger.

Autumn came and went and Marguerite shivered in their two rooms and wondered what she had done leaving her nice warm home in Bedford Square, but it was certainly too late now to turn the tables.

Sarah suggested that Marguerite and Bertie should spend Christmas with them. She could not wait to meet this brother-in-law. Marguerite soon made the excuse that owing to her impending confinement she would rather stay at home. This was quite an understatement on her part. How she would love to spend Christmas at Wimbledon, but she did not think Bertie would enjoy it, and that first Christmas of her married life was spent wrapped in a rug listening to the revelry of the passers-by in the street below.

The baby was due at the beginning of March. By the time January came Marguerite had to write to Sarah to say that her Friday visits would have to stop. She was now so large and her old kidney trouble had flared up and her legs were swollen to an uncomfortable size. Come February, Marguerite was admitted to hospital to await the birth. Marguerite's one fear was that Bertie would visit her at the same time as Sarah, but by strange coincidence this did not happen.

On the 5th March 1931 little Dorothy Smythe was born, a small sickly infant. Marguerite was not allowed to touch her, she was so delicate. Bertie had been allowed a peep, and was concerned to see such a fragile looking baby. Just like a china doll, he thought. The next day he had grave news to break to his wife. Little Dorothy had barely lived for twenty-four hours.

*

The death of Algie's child was a shock to his Ma, who remembered the loss of her daughter Connie. She endeavoured to make up any differences her and Algie might have had over his marriage, by looking after him whilst his wife was away. She also made up her mind that she would introduce herself to Marguerite, as Algie called her, on her return from hospital.

Algie supposed he had best write to his sister-in-law. Although he had never met Sarah and her husband he thought it might be a good idea for Marguerite to stay at Wimbledon for a while on leaving hospital. He did not wish to part from his wife for long, but realised that this was in her best interest and the comforts there would make it better for her to convalesce.   He was not without concern for her wellbeing.

Algie knew only too well that his spoken word was poor and he hated writing letters, but he knew this letter had to be written.   Sarah was distraught to hear the news, even more so as she was at this time expecting her second child, but at least from her brother-in-law's letter he did not seem such a thoughtless chap as she had been led to believe.   She wrote back to him saying that Marguerite would be welcome at Wimbledon for a few weeks and she looked forward to their arrival. Now at last, she thought, I shall meet this brother-in-law, but Sarah was to be disappointed.   Some days later, on the 20th March to be precise, a cab drew up and out stepped Marguerite.   What a sad figure she depicted standing on the drive all on her own.   Sarah told small Janet, who was excited to see her Aunt, to go back to the nursery, and trying to hide her own state of pregnancy as best she could she approached her sister. "Where is Bertie? Why isn't he with you?" asked a concerned Sarah.

"He is at work, Sarah.   It would not do for him to take time off. It is a busy time for him."   With that said she burst into tears, and her sister putting an arm around her led her into the house.

*

It was to be well into May before Marguerite was sufficiently over her great disappointment and able to return to the Holloway Road.   Bertie had written regularly, but to Sarah and Robert's surprise did not appear at Wimbledon.   Algie did not wish at this stage of their marriage to introduce himself to her family.   He fully appreciated the difference in their status.

Knowing that their first wedding anniversary was fast approaching, Marguerite decided she must make a determined effort to return to her rightful home.   She would surprise Bertie and be there on the next Friday evening when he returned from work, and so it was with regret that she took her leave of Sarah.   How she envied her with her small daughter and the prospect of yet another child.

Marguerite had difficulty in carrying her belongings from the cab and up the steps to her home.   Her legs were still very swollen, which made it difficult for her to walk.   As she opened the door she was surprised to see the woman from downstairs hoovering the hallway.   Equally Mary Smythe was surprised to see the sudden return of her daughter-in-law.

"Oh! me dear.   Just cleaning for Algie, yer know.   Must keep the place up to scratch thought I," said a somewhat excited Mary having realised what name she had used!

"Cleaning for Algie?" asked Marguerite.

"Yes, me son, Algie!" answered Ma Smythe.

"But I don't understand! Algie?" questioned a puzzled Marguerite.

"What yer call 'im then, when 'es at home?" asked Ma, but before Marguerite could reply she took her arm and led her to a chair, saying, "Sit down me luv. I'll make yer a nice cuppa.   Sorry about the babe.   These things 'appen to some of us.

Lost me own little girl, I did, but then she was eight years old, a real poppet she was," and then Mary Smyth went on to give her daughter-in-law her life's history. Marguerite sat listening in a daze at this woman, whom she now realised was her mother-in-law.

When Marguerite sighed at the thoughts going through her head, Mary said, "Oh well me luv, must leave you in peace to rest yer weary 'ead. Ta, ta fer now, me luv, be seeing yer." With that Marguerite's mother-in-law was gone, and Marguerite laid her head back in the chair and thought - that woman, that woman who did all that shouting for Algie was Bertie's mother. She could not believe it! Just you wait Bertie, just you wait!

Book 4

Richard

1934-52

BOOK 4

CHAPTER 18

A SECOND CHANCE

Algi let himself into his home; a home that felt lonely to him without his wife, especially at this time when he was endeavouring to come to terms with the loss of his baby daughter. Was that someone in the kitchen? I wish Ma would stay in her own place, thought Algie.

"Hello, Algie!" Marguerite called out.

"Marguerite! Marguerite!' Algie rushed up to his wife and then hesitated. What had she said - hello Algie? He stopped in his tracks. "Marguerite it's really great to see yer."

"Yes! Algie. I was hoping to see my Bertie!" said a sarcastic Marguerite.

"I'll explain me dearest. Yes I'll explain." said Algie', rather hurriedly.

"I have found two rooms to let, says he. We can wed, says Bertie!" Marguerite said the Bertie with great clarity.

"Come luv. It's great to see yer. Come and sit yerself down. Hubby will tell you all." Algie thought he'd try a bit of cajoling.

"Albert, I have a great mind to turn round and go back to my sisters, where I feel I belong!" said an indignant Marguerite.

"No luv, don't say that luv. Don't take on so. I 'ad best intentions," said a contrite Algie.

Marguerite sat down, she had a feeling this was going to be a long session of excuses from Bertie. He was still endeavouring to explain himself when it was time for bed. He cuddled up to his wife, so pleased to have her home once more, but she was having none of it. "No Bertie, not tonight. Remember I have just lost a baby and I come home to such a greeting. No Bertie definitely not tonight!" Marguerite could be determined when she so wished.

Algie turned over knowing he had to tread carefully, but it will not be for long he said to himself. Wasn't it every husband's right? He had waited years to find the right woman and he was not having his Ma take her away from him. Yes he would have to do some more explaining tomorrow - surely Marguerite would understand.

It took a few tomorrows before Marguerite condescended to forgive Bertie. She eventually said that he would always be Bertie to her, whether his Ma was below stairs or not.   One thing she made quite clear she was not prepared to go through having another baby yet - no not for a long time!

*

The months went by and their relationship returned to more or less normal. Time began to heal the loss of their first child. Mary Smythe kept herself to herself and gave up shouting up the stairs.   Marguerite began to get to know her sister-in-law Eve better and on some Sundays had her up for tea, which pleased Bertie.

Now Marguerite had found out the whereabouts of Bertie's mother and younger sister she showed an interest in visiting Kate, and so it was that that summer they managed to scrape enough money together to visit Dorchester.   It was some years since Algie had seen his sister.   The last time she was still housekeeping for a retired Captain, so he sent a letter to that last-known address. Fortunately, although the Captain had passed-on some years previous, Kate had been retained as housekeeper to the new owner, a somewhat younger man. The outcome of this was that they became more to each other than employer and housekeeper and after some months, her children now having grown up and left home, she married this quite affluent fellow.   On receiving her brother's letter she was somewhat apprehensive as to what her husband would think of this down-to-earth brother, his first contact with her relatives, other than her children.   She need not have worried, she found her sister-in-law, Marguerite, a likeable woman and they all enjoyed their week together.   Marguerite could not help but smile at how the reverse had happened to Bertie's sister. There she was coping with Bertie and his Cockney ways and Kate had learnt to live above her station. Yes, it was certainly a strangely mixed world!

The following year they could not possibly afford another holiday, but did manage to relive their first day out together by going on an excursion to Bognor and Worthing. A day they thoroughly enjoyed.

At Christmas 1933, Marguerite and Bertie entertained both Ma and Eve to dinner.   Bertie showed his appreciation that night the only way he could. As they lay in each others arms they were the closest they had been for a long time.

It was just before their fourth wedding anniversary that one night Marguerite turned to Bertie and said, "Bertie hold your hand here." Taking his hand in hers she placed it on her stomach, and asked, "Do you feel anything?"

He suddenly sat up in bed with excitement and said, "Why yes, me luv, there is a movement," and then, realising what he had felt, he said once more, "A movement, me luv. Do you really think?   Could it be?" questioned Bertie.

"Well," said a thoughtful Marguerite, "I have felt fine, no sickness but come to think about it I haven't seen my usual," and hesitating, slightly embarrassed she added, "Only a little these past few months."

"Few months?" questioned Bertie. "That's it," said he with determination. "Off to that 'ere 'ospital for you tomorrow me lass."

Much to Marguerite's surprise, on her visit to the hospital the next day, she found she was indeed possibly five months pregnant, as the baby had already quickened. How different to last time, when she was so poorly for weeks on end, she thought. How much better!

*

Sarah was so pleased for her sister. Her second child, Frederick, named after dear Papa, had been born in the July following the loss of Marguerite's baby daughter. He was now a thriving small boy soon to celebrate his third birthday. Eight-year-old Janet adored her small brother. Marguerite once more enjoyed her weekly visits to Wimbledon. Her sister, brother-in-law and children were certainly her saving grace.

Marguerite's second pregnancy went very well, but, as the months went by it was felt by both Bertie and herself that she should spend from Monday to Friday at her sisters. This she enjoyed and she found she was much more relaxed and she was able to rest her legs, which once more were rather swollen.

September came, but no expected baby, but as her dates were so uncertain no one worried. The month of October came in foggy. On the Monday the fog appeared to have lifted somewhat so Marguerite set off as usual for Wimbledon, but she decided that this must be her final visit until after the baby was born.

*

The return journey on the Friday seemed tedious, the fog was settling down once more and the cab ride seemed extra bumpy. Whether it was this or not, but that night pain was to rack Marguerite's body and she clawed hold of Bertie, sound asleep beside her. She shook him hard, saying "Bertie, Bertie, do wake up please, the babies on the way!" She clawed on to him once more as the next contraction came. She had never experienced such pain before. Last time, of course, she was in hospital and they possibly gave her an injection to see her through. "Bertie, Bertie," she clung to him calling him again.

Bertie eventually woke up and when he realised what was happening he sprung out of bed. Whilst pulling on his trousers he shouted down the stairs for Eve to come and look after Marguerite whilst he went out to phone for an ambulance. He was soon back saying that there was a pea-soup of a fog, the likes of which he had never seen before. He just did not know how the ambulance would get through and how they would reach hospital in time. Eve started to boil up as much water as she could in case of need.

At long last the ambulance arrived and Marguerite was helped into it. Handing Algie a torch, the ambulance driver said, "You'll have to walk in front, mate, and my attendant will walk at the side. You can't see a darned thing in this fog it is so thick."

155

Marguerite lying down in the back of the ambulance started to count the seconds between each contraction. As they slowly moved through the London streets she prayed that they would reach the hospital in time. They seemed to be moving at a snail's pace and she was by now thinking - I shall have to push. I shall have to push! Suddenly the vehicle came to a stop and there seemed to be people rushing everywhere. They gently lifted her out of the vehicle. As they rushed through the door she screamed and the fellow, with a stethoscope round his neck, running along beside her, was saying, "A small dark head is appearing. Do get a move on."

BOOK 4

CHAPTER 19

DECISIONS

Marguerite & Bettie's second child was born in the corridor of that London hospital, before even reaching the delivery room, but how lucky it was that they had even reached the hospital.

Algie was running along having difficulty in keeping up with the trolley bearing his wife who was being pushed along quickly by the hospital staff; in fact no one had asked him who he was or seemed at all concerned at him following. Before they got as far as any room, as such, Algie was to learn that he was the father of a son. Yes, a son Richard, a name that had already been decided. A son was born, a son that had a good pair of lungs on him and who certainly let rip as they rushed down the corridor.

On arriving in the delivery room Marguerite just could not believe that it was all over. As pain once more racked her body she glanced down at this dark haired baby that had been placed in her arms. The nurse moved quickly to take the baby whilst Marguerite finished the job in hand. It was then, and only then, that Marguerite felt the utter exhaustion and the chest pains returned. She did not remember the rest of that night nor the following day, but woke up feeling weak and exhausted. She immediately asked for the whereabouts of her baby. He was quickly brought to her and she was enthralled by this dark-haired small child.

After a few days Marguerite felt recovered enough to start worrying as to where this precious baby would sleep in their meagre home. If Sarah visited before she left the hospital she must ask her if she had a cradle that they could borrow for the baby. She wrote to her telling her of the birth and asking her to visit. She gave this letter to Bertie to post. It was as he left the hospital that he studied the envelope and then stuffed it into his pocket, thinking, oh no, you are coming straight home this time my love. No taking my son off to Wimbledon. Home is the place for you, and so the letter remained in his pocket and was not posted. He did not stop to think that Sarah would not know of the arrival of her nephew.

The Doctor was not keen for Marguerite to feed her baby. They felt this would exhaust her too much, but she was adamant. The joy and closeness of those moments of the baby held to her breast was something she was to remember always.

Arriving at the hospital one evening Algie was surprised to be met by the Consultant. "Mr Smythe, I believe. Please, may I have a word," Algie followed this fellow into a nearby room. Fearful of what he was to be told. "Mr. Smythe, your wife will soon be leaving our care, and I just wanted to tell you that there must be no more babies." He went on to say, "As you must well know, your wife has a heart condition. To have more children would endanger her life!"

This was the first knowledge that Algie had of his wife's heart condition. Marguerite had felt that there was no need to burden him with what she felt was an unnecessary worry. She had learnt to live with this all her life. Algie was indeed shocked to hear this news, but did not let on to the Doctor that this was the first indication that he had had of his wife's condition. He went on to ask, "Doctor do yer mean I have to abstain from you knows what? I means Doctor this is asking a bit much of a fellow?"

The Doctor smiled at this cockney chap's ignorance and went on to explain that there were ways and means of hopefully not having a baby and went on to explain the caution he should take. He warned him that if he did not follow his instructions and his wife fell for another child her life would be in danger. It was, therefore, a nervous Algie that took his wife and baby home to the Holloway Road. He had decided that he would not let on to Marguerite that he knew of her heart condition. He felt that if she had wanted him to know, she would have told him.

Ma Smythe and Eve had found some blue and white flowers and had made the bedroom look as pleasant as possible. Algie had prepared a drawer as a cradle for his son. As Marguerite laid Richard into this she could not help but shed a tear at the thought of her small son sleeping in a drawer - what would her dear Mama think if she could see her grandson.

Marguerite was puzzled why she had not heard from Sarah; so soon after returning from hospital, and after Bertie had gone off to work one morning, she prepared Richard and set off to visit her sister. Sarah was both surprised and delighted to see Marguerite with her small son. Marguerite could not believe that Sarah had not received her letter, but at the same time she did not think that Bertie would have forgotten to post it. All was soon forgiven at the lack of communication and the two sisters spent a happy day together. Sarah was concerned that her delicate sister had not received the care of a Maternity nurse. After her confinements she really appreciated the help that she had received, but there was Marguerite coping all on her own! She hoped she would not over do it. She lectured her sister as to the care she should take. Marguerite smiled and thought little do you know the circumstances I live under! She was certainly glad of all the baby clothes that Sarah showered on her and even more so for the precious cradle with the blue drapes still on it from when it was used for small Frederick Percival.

On arriving home from work that day, Algie was really annoyed to think that Marguerite had made the journey to Wimbledon, but was astonished at his son's beautiful cradle. He denied that he had forgotten to post the letter and was thankful that he had destroyed it.

A few days after Marguerite's visit, Sarah called on her Mama to tell her the news of another grandson. She was to find her Mama in decline and going downhill very quickly, and it was not to be many weeks before Emily Sinclair was to pass away and join her dear Frederick. Marguerite was determined that she would go to the funeral even though her Mama had shown a hard side to her and left her penniless.

Although Marguerite had got used to the shock of finding out that the family downstairs were her in-laws, she was adamant that they were not going to interfere with the bringing up of her son. She had not much in common and was sure the less Richard saw of them the better. She did not wish him to learn his Grandmother's way of speaking. It was going to be a task in itself to train him to speak properly with Bertie's example.

It was, therefore, with baby in arms that Marguerite set off for her Mama's funeral. She sat at the back of the church, she hoped unseen, and at the graveyard she stood well back in the shelter of some trees, but John Mullen had spotted Marguerite in the church and looked at her sorrowfully standing all alone away from the rest of the family. At the grave he longed to go over to her and bring her nearer, and after the ceremony was over he made his way to talk to her but she quickly disappeared before he could reach her.

*

Richard was still only a toddler when the King died and his son abdicated in favour of his younger brother Bertie. Marguerite felt some sympathy as she listened to the wireless to the King's abdication speech as to how he had decided to stand by his beloved. Had she not had to make a similar decision in order to follow her love in a different way of life? Now Bertie, his namesake, was to be their new King. Whilst Richard played at her feet, she sat pondering and thinking back to that coronation day when dear Papa took the whole family to the splendid pageantry. She smiled as she thought of Bertie and his escapade of selling union jacks on that day - how different their two childhoods had been.

Once Richard got passed the toddler stage and was firm enough on his feet to help himself on and off the bus, Marguerite took him to Regents Park to watch his Daddy at work and to play with his ball; well away from flowerbeds of course. As she sat watching her small son she recalled those visits from Bedford Square with Snuff on lead. She thought how Richard would enjoy a small dog to play with in the park but it was not to be and Snuff was now well settled with the family in Wimbledon. He was now beginning to get old and slower no longer boisterous like that day when he ran off. Marguerite smiled to herself with the memory. How her life had changed since then!

Although Marguerite endeavoured to keep Richard apart from his Grandmother, he, nevertheless, loved to ride his small car, passed on by his cousins, up and down the garden. She used to cringe as she heard her Mother-in-law chatting away to the small boy, "Ain't you got a lovely car? Dicky boy" or "Come and see what yer old Grans got for yer, Dicky." Marguerite time and time again asked Bertie's Mother not to call their son Dicky. His name was Richard! All that Ma Smythe would say was "What's the matter with Dick, that's what the children are called 'ere abouts and that's what I'm calling 'im." She went on to think to herself, - Richard, she had never heard such a posh name. They had always been Dick in the Holloway Road and Dick he would be, so there!

Marguerite also had to still come to terms with the idea that people in this area went to the public baths for their weekly bath. She smiled at the thought of how naïve she had been when she first came to the Holloway Road. Although she could never bring herself to go, when Richard was four years old she had to agree that he was too old to use the tin bath brought in from the backyard, and so most Friday evenings would see small Richard going off, towel under arm, hand in hand, with his Father for this weekly ritual. First of all he was nervous of the bright green tiling and the echo they caused, but he soon got used to it and enjoyed the time spent chatting whilst queuing with his Daddy.

Whilst they had gone, Marguerite sat and daydreamt of the time when Mary fell taking the hot water to the nursery. She must ask, Sarah, about Mary and her family. Marguerite looked out of the window at her surroundings thinking to herself as to how her life had changed. She supposed she was contented with this new life, but on the other hand she wished for a better life for that small son taking his weekly bath.

*

The years were to pass with the worry of a war hanging over everyone's head. Algie assured Marguerite that this time he would not have to go and fight as – 'hadn't he done his stint in the last war'. She was not so sure, and the thought of being left alone with Richard in the two rooms worried her, especially when workman came and commenced building a shelter in the garden. It made the threat of war seem so imminent. Richard playing in the garden enjoyed the company, and with his small wheelbarrow filled with earth he thought he was a great help to the workmen.

Gas masks were given out. Richard was rather disappointed that he could not have one of those Micky Mouse ones, but his Mother explained to him that they were only for babies, and wasn't he a big boy now ready for school. To encourage Richard to wear his, they all sat for a very short while some evenings with them on. Richard thought how funny they all looked, but he hated wearing the smelly thing. He liked the small box that they were packed away in and used to carry it around the house pretending that there was a war.

It was hoped that four year old Richard would commence school in the Autumn term. The thought of parting with her son horrified Marguerite. She found his chatter so amusing and was so worried that he would learn bad ways and that his speech would deteriorate. Also she had taught him to keep himself clean and tidy, and the thought of how he would come home from that school round the corner worried her. But thankfully for Marguerite school for Richard was to be delayed!

As war was declared Marguerite and Bertie listened to the wireless and they talked long into the night. They knew full well that the children in the area were being prepared for evacuation. Should Richard be evacuated? Of course Bertie said he could take his wife and child down to his sister Kate in Dorchester, but no, Marguerite did not think that would be wise. Kate had already brought up her family and was enjoying some peace now! Algie assured his wife that he could look after himself, and hadn't he his Ma and sister downstairs? This Marguerite knew only too well! Nevertheless, she had to agree that Bertie would be looked after well.

Finally a decision was reached. Marguerite would go to the office, set up for arranging evacuation, the next day. As Richard was not yet five-years-old there was the possibility that Marguerite would be able to go with him. Yes, now was certainly the time to go and arrange something, as no-one could forecast what dangers were to be met if they stayed in London. She was frightened that she would leave it too late; she could not bear the thought of Richard being sent away from her on his own.

The next morning it was soon confirmed that Marguerite would be allowed to accompany her four-year-old son. Their names were taken. They were given a list of the essential things that they were to take with them. They were handed some labels and told that not only were their cases to bear these labels but they were both to have one attached to their coats. They were both given a full medical. Marguerite worried as to whether she would pass hers, but nothing to her detriment was said. They were told to go home and wait. When further arrangements had been made they would be informed.

The whole Smythe household felt very unsettled as they waited for news of the evacuation. Ma Smythe and her daughter knew only too well how they would miss small Richard, and Ma had to admit that she had grown quite attached to her daughter-in-law.

It was to be a bright September morning in 1939 that Algie took his wife and small son to Kings Cross to join up with hundreds of small labelled children, some of the younger ones clutching their Mother's hand; others being led in long crocodile lines to the trains getting up steam at the platforms. Yes, they were all off to an unknown destination. Algie clung to his wife with affection and ruffled his son's hair as a token of his love for this son who he knew only too well he was going to miss. Tears streamed down Marguerite's face as she waved from the train window. What dangers was she leaving her Bertie behind too? How long were they to be away? All these questions rushed through her mind as the train drew out of that London station on that September morning. It was only now that she realised only too well how she would miss Bertie and the life they had made together.

BOOK 4

CHAPTER 20

THE EVACUEES

Richard sat wondering why his Mummy had cried as she waved goodbye to Daddy, but he was soon to forget that small episode as the excitement of the rare treat of riding on a train took over. He looked at the other children in the compartment and at others passing by in the corridor; he thought he had never seen so many children before.

Whilst Richard was occupied, Marguerite could not help but think back to that other train ride before the Great War; another journey to the unknown. She remembered how nervous and uncertain she had felt, and yet, at the same time excited. Yes, she thought, it is rather the same today, we are going into the unknown and yet there is a certain amount of excitement about. The children were pointing out things to each other out of the window. You could tell this was the first train ride for many. Her mind went back to that farm on the edge of the mountain range in Germany. She thought once more of that young German couple and wondered if Hans Peter had survived that other war and whether he and Christa had had any family, she supposed she would never know!

Moments later Marguerite came out of her day-dreaming and she had just pointed out the seed factory to Richard, where she told him his Daddy's seeds came from for those beautiful flowers in the park, when they drew slowly into a station. All signs had been removed, to confuse the Germans if they should invade, and there was no other indication to say where they were, but Marguerite knew only too well from the Sutton Seed factory and others that they were pulling into Reading station. We have not gone far yet she thought! They seemed to stand in the station for some time and then an announcement was made asking all passengers to alight. Now what's up thought Marguerite gathering their belongings together.

To the billeting officers waiting on Reading station, the evacuees getting off this train seemed to be a very mixed bag. Some ragged urchins with barely what you call shoes on their feet, others in Sunday best and some in smart school uniform. Then there was the other group, standing separately – small bewildered children clasping their Mother's skirts. Marguerite realised that she was one of the few with only one child.

Richard was to remember this day as a day when for the first time he was to come in contact with so many people. He was fascinated by the way the children had to form into long queues, two by two, with their teachers standing alongside.

They stood for what seemed a long time and watched with excitement as the train was shunted out of the station. As the queues started to move Marguerite realised that this must be the end of their train journey, as there appeared to be charabancs waiting on the station approach and she could see children being loaded on to them. It seemed a long time to Richard before they were finally to get on to one of these charabancs, but it was only a very short journey to a hall before they got off again. They had to go through yet another medical. Marguerite had a lot of explaining to do to Richard as to why they kept having a comb put through their hair; not having experienced this before she found this a little embarrassing.

After more waiting around, the parties of schoolchildren were dealt with first and the hall started to empty, leaving behind a handful of Mothers and children. At long last back into a charabanc again and off through the streets of Reading and out into the country, passing through villages, all quite different to each other. Richard thought he had never been for such a long ride. This was even better than going on a London bus.

Eventually they turned through a large entrance; Marguerite could still see the fittings for the beautiful iron gates and railings, which she imagined had been removed to be melted down for the war effort. They drove along an avenue of trees, which seemed to go on for quite some time, finally drawing up at the magnificent doorway of a mansion, the likes of which the children on this charabanc had not seen before.

The Lord and Lady of the Manor were at the door to meet this contingent of unknown entity. They were certainly fearsome of what they were to face. The billeting officer had arrived quite unexpected some weeks before, asking the number of rooms in the mansion, and no word had been heard of since that time until the previous day. The billeting officer had again visited, with a file of papers in his hands, to inform them that they had been allocated a dozen or more children, accompanied by their Mothers, and that they would remain with them for the duration of the war, which it was hoped would not last for many months. To their great shock they were told that these families would be arriving the next day.

The staff had been busy moving furniture and making suitable accommodation for this unexpected intrusion into the lives of Lord and Lady Somerfield. Not knowing how many individual families there would be, final arrangements were still to be made.

As Lord and Lady Somerfield stood in the porch of their mansion watching as the charabanc drew up there seemed to them to be more than a dozen wide-eyed children staring at them. The whole of London seemed to have arrived.

*

Soon this motley crowd were gathered in the great hall, the Mothers even wider-eyed than their offspring. Marguerite thought she had never seen such a magnificent place since visiting the chateaux in Germany. She was by now feeling quite heartened and happy at the situation she found herself in. Richard had been struck quite dumb at what he saw, as had many of the other children. A most beautiful oak staircase wound up to a galleried landing. Each door, to these London evacuees, seemed to be edged in gold.

The Mothers were told to take a seat. They looked at the beautiful carved tall back chairs and hardly dare sit on them. The children were told to sit on the floor; in no time at all, much to the consternation of their Mothers, they were sliding around on their bottoms on this highly polished hall floor. Richard had only to be told once to sit still and behave like a little gentleman. He looked up at his Mummy and whispered to her that he wished to go to the toilet. Marguerite was not sure whether to raise her hand or to discreetly take him to find this necessity. She told him to stay where he was and asked a maid standing nearby if the children could find the cloakroom. The maid went and spoke to Lady Somerfield, who soon introduced Maud, the youngest of her staff, and told the children to follow her in an orderly fashion to the toilet. More than one mother looked askance at this request. Marguerite, realising the confusion, whispered to a nearby mother, who stood up and in a really loud cockney voice announced, "Go along kids. I expect yer all need the lav by now?" At this an orderly queue was formed. Richard was loath to join the other children without his Mother, but she soon persuaded him to file out with them.

The billeting officer took this opportunity to speak to the Mothers. "May I introduce you to Lord and Lady Somerfield, who have kindly opened up their home to you people from London? Lady Somerfield tells me that some of you will be housed in the servants' quarters below stairs and the remainder will be, for the present, housed on the first floor." She gave the mothers a few moments to take this in, and then she went on to ask the mothers of more than two children to go and stand by the side passage. This they soon did and gradually the children returned and went and stood by their mothers. This left just Marguerite and three other woman with seven children between them. On realising that they were to be the lucky ones and to be housed in the main building, they smiled shyly at each other. By now Marguerite was seeing in her mind luxurious bathrooms and possibly four poster beds. Yes, thought Marguerite, this must be my lucky day.

*

As the remaining mothers had already surmised, Lady Somerfield informed them that they were to be housed in the main part of the house and were to carry themselves at all times with decorum, as there would often be guests around. They were to keep their children in check at all times. Marguerite smiled to herself when she heard one Mother turn to another and say, "What's she on about? T'aint my station of life this 'ere place!" With a shrug of the shoulders Em answered, "No Bet, t'aint mine either, bit too posh for the likes of me!"

They were soon shown to their rooms by Lady Somerfield herself. They were first shown the bathroom they were to share and were told that a large walk-in linen cupboard was to be turned into a small kitchen for them. Richard was astounded at the size of the bedroom. They were told that to begin with they were to take their meals with the other families down in the servants' quarters.

Marguerite realised she had little in common with the other mothers but she was determined to get along with them as best she could. The children were soon charging up and down the oak panelled landing. Richard stood at the door of the bedroom watching them, shyly taking it all in. Not having started school he had never been taught how to play with so many children.

Soon there was a clapping of hands and the Nanny of the house was telling them, in no uncertain terms, that that was not how they were to behave and they were to be quiet and go into their rooms. She thought to herself she would have to take a roll-call of these children and get some discipline into them. She had not yet dared venture down below stairs. If this was an example of what she was to face, she was already fearsome of what her own small charges would pick up from this mixed bag of children. The mere thought of bad language was of concern to her.

*

Down in the kitchen, Cook and her staff had been told to prepare tea for this multitude that had arrived. Her Ladyship apologised for this intrusion, but pointed out that for once this was out of her hands. This state of affairs that they found themselves in was not her wish, but it was what the country as a whole had been told to do. Never in her walk of life had it been known before, never, but evacuees they had been sent and they would all have to cope with the situation as best as they could. She went on to say that, "Just for today they were to have their tea served in the main hall all together."

Cook could not believe what she was hearing, but was only too thankful that she had made a substantial number of cakes that morning. They would certainly be needed. By the time the sandwiches had been cut and the tea placed in the hall Cook was really quite beyond herself with the worries of what was to come.

Whilst the mothers drank their tea the children gulped down milk, the creaminess of which they had never experienced before. When Cook realised the amount of milk that was being drunk, she made up her mind, there and then, that the mothers would have to be taught how to squeeze the lemons and oranges to make their own drinks; otherwise they would certainly need a cow on the doorstep.

The sandwiches and cakes soon disappeared, and whilst the mothers returned to their rooms to unpack, Nanny gathered all the children around her. She divided them into groups with an elder child in charge. Of the seven who were to stay in the main part of the house, she put twelve-year-old Edith in charge. She was told it would be her responsibility to see that there was no more charging up and down the landing and the oak panelling was not to be touched with sticky fingers. Quite a responsibility for a young cockney!

That night a house full of evacuees tucked down in soft beds, the comfort of which to the majority had never been known before. Marguerite lay down in the large comfortable double bed, and even though small Richard seemed to kick all night long, for the first time for many years she was quite content.

*

Life soon settled down to a routine. The older children went off to the village school and returned home some evenings looking the worst for wear, having been embroiled in fights with the local children. The local children resented the intrusion of these London evacuees into their idyllic country life and did not enjoy sharing their desks; they resented it even more if they had to give up their desks to these strangers. Yes, there were many fights, but after a few weeks the kindly headmaster had them under control, and some of the village children were quite envious of the evacuees living up at the Manor.

For Richard the first taste of school was nearly identical to his Mother's schooling. With five other small evacuees he was taught in the schoolroom of the manor with young Douglas and Barbara; the small son and daughter of the house. The two elder children were away at boarding school. Richard settled down well and enjoyed the company of this small group. Miss Thompson, the governess, found him quiet but attentive and eager to learn; he was certainly quite a different child to her other new charges.

Life was certainly quite different for these London mothers. Below stairs it was quite cramped and many an argument ensued with Cook and her staff, who did not appreciate having to share their kitchen with so many women. Inevitably friction was caused and gradually the numbers reduced as the families returned home.

Over the weeks Marguerite became quite close to the other three mothers, Em, Bet and Ruby, who shared the bathroom and small converted kitchen. They went out together to collect blackberries, and much to passing farmers amusement sang all the old London songs whilst they gathered them. Many a comment was made on Marguerite's beautiful voice.

The children were disappointed to learn that owing to the war they were not able to have their usual bonfire night, but Lord and Lady Somerfield organised a party instead. That same evening some of the soldiers from a nearby barracks were invited to join with the mothers for a sing-song around the piano. Lady Somerfield was a keen pianist and had had the piano moved into the main hall. It was quite like old times for Marguerite gathered round the piano singing the old tunes. She sung with gusto, really enjoying herself

The children, supposedly asleep on the first floor, crept out of their beds. Edith was a thoughtful child and went and collected Richard. As they peered through the banisters of the gallery unnoticed she warned them to keep very quiet. They were so fascinated at the grown-ups enjoying themselves that not a murmur was heard from these bright-eyed youngsters. The party went on quite late and eventually the children got tired of watching and listening to their elders and returned to their beds and were soon fast asleep.

That evening Marguerite realised what little social life she had had since her marriage and how she had missed these occasions. She enjoyed talking to the officers accompanying their men. They complimented her on her fine voice and on leaving said that they hoped that whilst they were in the area there would be many more such evenings.

A few days later as Marguerite and Richard were leaving for a walk they were stopped in the hallway by Lady Somerfield. "Mrs Smythe, the other night I could not help but hear what a beautiful singing voice you have, my dear. Captain Armstrong said on leaving that he hoped that they would have the pleasure of hearing you sing on your own sometime."

Marguerite was a little taken by surprise, but nevertheless had the courtesy to thank her Ladyship, who went on to ask, "You have had your voice trained, my dear?"

"Why yes, when I was a young girl, ma'am," answered Marguerite.

"Mrs Smythe, may I suggest that with such a lovely voice you should keep up your singing. In fact, next week I intend to have Captain Armstrong and a friend to dinner. It would give my husband and me great pleasure if you would consent to sing to us after dinner," said her Ladyship.

Marguerite hesitated to reply her mind going back to that occasion many years ago when she was requested to sing to after-dinner guests. She stood for some minutes not knowing what answer to give. She had no music with her and it was many years since she had sung at such an occasion, but she suddenly found herself saying, "It would be a pleasure, ma'am".

Lady Somerfield seemed pleased at her answer and went on to add: "Wear one of your crisp white blouses that I have seen you in. I am sure Nanny will lend you a dark skirt to wear with it."

"Thank you, your ladyship. I will certainly ask her," replied Marguerite, relieved to think that that was a problem solved.

As she turned to take her leave, her ladyship said, "There is a good selection of music in the piano stool. Take a look sometime, and I will accompany you should you wish to practice." Once more Marguerite repeated her thanks.

Richard stood by quietly taking in the conversation; his Mummy was to sing, perhaps he could go and listen. On their walk he chatted away to her questioning her about her singing, and on their return they went and sorted through the music. The piano had been returned to the drawing room and Richard sat on the warm carpet looking around him at all the splendid ornaments and pictures. The choice of music was vast and in no time at all Marguerites had picked out a selection from which her Ladyship could choose.

*

Marguerite had written to Bertie each day posting it once a week, but she did not mention her singing. She told Richard that this was to be their secret. For some reason, only known to Marguerite, she did not wish to share this return to the past with Bertie.

Small Richard was to be even more surprised when he heard his mother practising. He sat on the floor once more with his legs crossed, as Miss Thompson had shown him, entranced both by his Mummy's voice and the playing of the piano. Lady Somerfield was to think what a delightful child and so well bought up. Marguerite's voice echoed up to the first floor, and afterwards the other mothers were to question Marguerite as to where she learnt to sing so well, but she was not that forthcoming as she did not wish to brag.

Nanny was only too willing to lend Marguerite a black skirt and also gave her a piece of black velvet ribbon, which fixed by a brooch at the neck made all the difference to the white blouse with starched collar.

Richard was somewhat put out when the Saturday evening arrived and he was put to bed even earlier than usual. He had not realised that he was to be satisfied with the rehearsals and that this particular Saturday evening was not for small boys. The other children were also disappointed when they found that the piano was not to be moved from the drawing room. No peeping through banisters this time!

At 7 o'clock sharp Lady Somerfield sent her own personal maid to collect Marguerite. She entered the lounge feeling very shy and was even more nervous when she found that after cocktails she was to be escorted into dinner by Captain Armstrong. It had not occurred to her that he had no wife to accompany him. Over the meal he was very attentive and informed Marguerite that he was really looking forward to hearing her sing again, especially as this time she would be singing solo. The meal over, whilst the men retired for their port, the ladies drank their coffee and Marguerite prepared her music. Still feeling a little nervous she was to soon commence her singing. As she sang, in her mind she went back many years and she relaxed, and the guests were enraptured by her beautiful voice. When her appearance was over they called for an encore, and to Marguerite's own surprise she started to sing a selection of Italian folk songs, this time unaccompanied. Lord and Lady Somerfield sat in wonder as this London evacuee entertained them. When she had finally finished she was invited to sit with the guests, but she declined, and much to Captain Armstrong's disappointment returned to Richard, who was by now fast asleep.

The next day Lady Somerfield called on Marguerite personally to give her thanks and to ask whether she would be willing a give a repeat performance on Boxing Day; a request that Marguerite was only too willing to accept. Later that afternoon there was another knock on the door and a beautiful bouquet of flowers was handed to Marguerite. Attached was a note saying – 'with many thanks for a marvellous evening, from an admirer'. She knew only too well who had sent these flowers. She was thankful that her small son was yet unable to read, but nevertheless she discreetly tore up the card, blushing as she did so, just in case he decided to give it to Edith to read.

In no time at all November seemed to be over and preparations commenced at the Manor for Christmas, a Christmas that was to be so different for these London families. Marguerite began to practice her singing each day. Richard had soon got tired of listening to his Mother and was only too glad to join with the other children in preparing and making the decorations.

Lord Somerfield had approached the Air Raid Warden's post to ask whether permission could be given for carol singing. He was told that providing all torches were half-shielded, as was the authority's rule these early war days, and as long as they did not shine them up in the air, they saw no reason why this year the carol singing should not proceed as usual. Why not? They said, who could forecast what was to come? So it was that the evening before Christmas Eve the excited families from the Manor went out carol singing, finishing the evening at the Vicarage. A group of very tired but happy children returned to bed that night.

A beautiful Christmas tree had been placed in the main hall, and on Christmas Eve morning Richard helped to decorate this magnificent tree, whilst Marguerite wrapped up some presents. She felt guilty at not joining Bertie for Christmas but the authorities were not happy at the evacuees returning in their masses to London – owing to the phoney war these children were streaming back to the metropolis. Marguerite was far too happy in her surroundings to contemplate returning.

Richard was really an excited child as he returned to join his Mother for lunch this Christmas Eve. He could not wait for bedtime to come and for Father Christmas to arrive.

*

Back in the Holloway Road, Algie felt very lonely in his two rooms without his wife and son. Of course Ma tried to make it like old times, but she was an old lady now and things were not the same. The letters arriving from Marguerite he read to his Ma, who in turn said, "I think it's about time that young Maggie returned with that nipper of yours. Her rightful place is 'ere in what should be her rightful 'ome." As much as he tried to explain to his Ma, she would say, "Whoever 'eared of a wife going off and leaving 'err 'ubby to cope." He tried to stick up for Marguerite and to repeat numerous times that because of the war all the Mothers and children had left London for the country. His Ma replied "There t'aint no war 'ere!"

Marguerite's latest letter was full of the preparations for Christmas, and how young Richard was still being taught by the Governess in the schoolroom and getting on well with his lessons and with the other children.

"See, learning to live above 'is station, that's what he's doing. Yer 'ave trouble there when that wife and kid returns, you mark by words, son!" remarked his Ma, when listening to his latest letter.

Algie looked at his Ma in despair. At the back of his mind he knew that there was some truth in what she said. How would his young son cope with the other kids at school after such an introduction to education? His Ma went on to ask, "Going to get 'em back for Christmas, Algie?"

It had occurred to Algie that as things were so quiet, and the threat of bombing had not materialised, that it might be time to fetch his wife and son home. Yes, he thought, he must write and suggest that they return.

Algie was not keen on letter writing; he could write poetry but found it difficult to put his thoughts into words in a letter, and so the letter did not get written.

Algie did not have to work on Christmas Eve, in fact with the war and the cutbacks he was getting worried as to how long he would have a job in the park. He had heard that the laying out of the flowerbeds would stop for the duration of the war.

It was all on the spur of the moment that he rose early on Christmas Eve 1939, and without saying a word to his Ma or sister Eve, made for Paddington station. Algie had definitely made up his mind that he wanted his wife and small son home for Christmas. He was lucky on arriving at the station to find that there was a train leaving for Reading at 9 o'clock. It was now 8.30 am, just time for a cuppa, thought Algie. He pushed his way amongst the service men that crowded the railway buffet and had been lucky enough to get a pass for Christmas, and soon sat down with a welcome cup of tea.

The thirty minutes went by quickly and it was soon time to make for the train; it was not often that Algie travelled by train and although he had to stand in the corridor he enjoyed his journey to Reading. He was not certain how he was to travel the seven miles to the village and so to the Manor. It took him some time to find the bus station, but eventually he turned a corner and there were the country buses. He made his way to the enquiry kiosk and was pleased to be told that there was a bus which would take him to within a mile of his destination. It was not leaving until one o'clock and so he had time to wander around the town and to have a snack to eat in Joe Lyons. He felt as though he was on holiday and excited at the thought of seeing Marguerite and his small son again. Yes, he had certainly missed them and it would be good to have them home once more. He thought how unnecessary it had been for them to have left London in the first place, but who was to know!

The bus came on time and chugged along the country lanes. Algie was really enjoying the ride when the conductor suddenly called out that it was Algie's stop. On stepping off the bus Algie stood for a while not knowing which way to turn. Was that an ARP chap standing on the corner? Algie smiled to himself as he thought that was the first sign he had seen in this remote place that there was a war on. He hurried up to the warden and asked, "Please mate, could yer tell me which way I turn for the Manor?"

The fellow smiled as he said, "Quite a walk my man, about a mile along the road here," pointing at the country lane winding along in the distance.

"Thanks a lot mate." Algie raised his cap.

"Come to visit the evacuees?" the fellow asked, and before Algie could answer went on to say, "My word we had some troubles with them at first, but they've settled down well now. Entertained us with their carol singing last night," announced this local chap with a smile at the thought.

"They've settled well then? Well, just the same I've come to get me missus and nipper 'ome. T'aint no war in London," with that Algie raised his cap once more and went on his way.

My, thought this local chap, I wonder which ones you have come after. You certainly seem determined. Hope they are as pleased to see you!

Algie stepped out breathing in the good country air. Even though a cold wind swept across the open fields he was soon warm with the good exercise. After leaving the lane and turning into the drive Algie thought this went on for ever and ever. What a place to be stuck in, thought Algie. I should think they will all be glad to be back in the city from this isolation. On arriving at the mansion he stood and looked at this magnificent house and pondered at the thought of his wife and son living in such splendour. He approached the heavy oak door and raised the knocker, soon a maid answered.

"I've come for me Missus and young nipper. Smythe is the name," announced Algie.

The maid looked at this cockney chap, who said he was Marguerite's husband, and had difficulty in hiding her surprise. She had some doubts at what she was doing but she supposed she had better show him into the hall, if that was who he said he was. "Would you mind stepping in and waiting in the hall, sir," asked the maid. "I will fetch Mrs Smythe." She ran up the stairs smiling and thinking, 'well I never did'.

"A gentleman to see me?" questioned Marguerite. Perhaps it was another bouquet of flowers, she wistfully thought. The maid just smiled in answer thinking, 'somehow I don't think you will be very pleased to see this bloke – Christmas time and all!

Telling Richard to remain where he was, Marguerite made her way down to the hall. She could not believe her eyes when she saw who was standing there; all she could mumble in her surprise was, "Why Bertie, it's you? Why are you here?" Thinking at the same time how glad she was that she had torn up the card attached to the flowers. It would never do for him to see she had an admirer.

"I would think you are pleased to be rescued from this back and beyond place."

"But Bertie we have been made most welcome here," she quickly replied before anyone could hear his comments. Thinking most welcome, little do you know!

BOOK 4

CHAPTER 21

REAL WAR

Algie was a little surprised at Marguerite's greeting. This was not what he expected. "Yer don't seem so keen to see me!" exclaimed her cockney husband.

"I thought you would have at least written to say you were coming. It is Christmas Day tomorrow! I do not know whether I can ask if you can stay at such a time!" answered Marguerite, slightly annoyed at the interruption to her new life; at the same time remembering that she was to entertain the guests on Boxing Day.

"I knows that, that is why I'm 'ere, to take you both 'ome for Christmas, where you belong. There ain't no war on in London!" stated Algie.

At this announcement all Marguerite could say was, "Oh Bertie, my love!"

Upstairs in the bedroom, with the excitement of Christmas, the inquisitiveness of the small boy got the better of him; he crept out to peer through the banisters, Who should he see down below in the hall but his Daddy – another Christmas surprise he thought. He rushed down the stairs as fast as his small legs would carry him, shouting, "Daddy, Daddy, have you come for Christmas?" He rushed up to his Daddy and flung himself into his arms.

"Well!" said Algie, "at least someone is pleased to see me!" releasing his son's small hands from his neck.

"You had better come up to our room, Bertie." Marguerite said, and as an afterthought added, "It's good to see you."

Over a cup of tea she endeavoured to point out to Bertie that Christmas Eve was the wrong time to move a small child from one environment to another, but even though Richard tried to point out that Father Christmas would not know where he was, Algie was adamant that they were to return home to Holloway Road immediately. He thought to himself, he did not wish to face his Ma if he did not return with his wife and child.

On realising that Bertie was not going to let them remain at the Manor for Christmas, Marguerite eventually gave up the argument and reluctantly began to pack their things, whilst Richard once more asked his Daddy how Father Christmas would know where to find him. Algie hugged his small son, who had grown so much taller in the time that he had been away, and assured him that he would get a message through, putting the matter right straight away. This seemed to satisfy this five-year-old child.

Marguerite was conscious of the fact that she would be letting her Ladyship down, not being available to sing on Boxing Day. She left Richard with his Father whilst she went to explain her predicament. Lady Somerfield had already heard from her maid that Mrs Smythe's husband had arrived. She took Marguerite's hands in hers and said, "I quite understand, my dear. Your place is with your husband!"

Marguerite thanked her Ladyship for being so understanding, but could not keep back the tears.

Lady Somerfield had become quite fond of this London mother and went on to say, "Marguerite, promise me you will keep up your singing and please write and let us know how you are coping with life."

Marguerite assured her Ladyship that she would indeed write and from now on would definitely, when at all possible, practice her singing. She went on to say, "Thank you for taking us into your home and for encouraging me with my singing. I shall never forget the time spent with you. Thank you." Once more she could feel tears welling up in her eyes.

"Come now, Marguerite, I will get Fenton to drive you to the station. Cheer up! It is Christmas, you know!" Lady Somerfield reminded Marguerite. She went on to say, "Now I will wait in the hall to meet your husband and say goodbye. We shall all miss you and that dear little son of yours!"

Marguerite returned upstairs thinking – Christmas! But little does her ladyship realise what a different Christmas it will be in just two rooms above mother-in-law.

Marguerite knocked on each door in turn to say goodbye to the other mothers. They gathered with their children on the gallery landing to wave goodbye. The children shouted to Richard, "see y'er Dickie Bird, 'appy Christmas." Marguerite shuddered, at the mention of Dickie Bird, and wondered how her small son would cope back in the Holloway Road and especially when he commenced at the school round the corner.

Nanny had joined her employees in the hall and pressed into young Richard's hands some paper-chains for him to make-up when he got home. She felt so sorry for this small lad being carted off at such a time. How very inconsiderate of Mr. Smythe. Miss Thompson had gone away for the Christmas holidays and would certainly miss her small charge when she returned. She had only said to Nanny, before she went away, how well he was doing.

After Marguerite had introduced Bertie to Lord and Lady Somerfield they stood with their youngest two children, Douglas and Barbara, at the door of the Manor House to wave goodbye. The children politely shook hands, saying, "Goodbye Mrs Smythe. Goodbye Richard, and a happy Christmas to you both." Marguerite once more thought – a happy Christmas – a Christmas so different to what she had expected on rising that morning.

*

Richard enjoyed the ride to the station. He chattered away to his Father pointing out various places of interest, as they passed through the now familiar village, in which, only the previous evening, they had been singing carols.

On the train Marguerite could not help but think how good it was to see Father and son enjoying the train ride together. Yes, she thought, perhaps I belong to both worlds – the rich and the poor – a decision that would soon change when she got back to the two rented rooms. Richard immediately wanted to know where were the Christmas tree and decorations, and how would Father Christmas reach him here? He was still chatting nineteen to the dozen and in his excitement asking so many questions that a number of times Marguerite was to hold her breath when Richard remembered just in time the secret of Mummy's singing.

On meeting up once more with Ma Smythe and Eve, all her mother-in-law could say, after giving Marguerite and Richard a fond hug, was "about time you came back too, there aint no war 'ere!" Marguerite sighed to herself as she thought, yes but this is quite a different life!

A tired, excited small child was soon put to bed with the promise that Daddy would endeavour to find a Christmas tree in the morning and that he would help Richard to make his paper-chains, whilst Mummy cooked the dinner. What dinner? She reminded her husband that he would also have to go out and find some Christmas fare. Algie felt the change left from his rail fare in his pocket and thought what with?

That night, tucking up with his wife, he whispered, "It's good to 'ave yer 'ome again. I promise you you'll be alright 'ere." Marguerite giving into her husband thought – dear Bertie, I certainly hope so!

The next morning Algie took Richard with him when he went visiting friends, to explain his predicament and begging for a spare chicken and whatever they could spare. Later they returned home bearing gifts and plenty of food. Whilst his Mother helped Ma down below to prepare a reasonable Christmas lunch, Richard, encouraged by his Dad made paper-chains and decorated the small Christmas tree they had found thrown on a rubbish heap. None of it looked as grand as at the Manor, but it certainly looked quite festive, thought Marguerite, as she inspected their endeavours.

After all the company that they had got used to, Marguerite and Richard found it a quiet lonely day, but looking at the joy on Algie's face, Marguerite supposed she had done the right thing in returning with her husband. That evening she sat day-dreaming of the past few months and a smile came to her face. Algie looked at her and asked, "happy me luv?"

What could she say on this Christmas day? "Yes, Bertie my love, I'm happy!"

*

As promised Marguerite wrote to Lord and Lady Somerfield thanking them for their hospitality and with encouragement Richard put a small note with it. In the New Year she received a letter back, saying the guests missed her singing and Captain Armstrong had suggested that she should go along to the Marylebone

Halls, where entertainment was being organised for the troops passing through London. She was to mention his name.

Fortunately Richard had remembered to keep their small secret of his Mother's singing ability. Marguerite wondered as to how she was going to find a way of going to the Halls? She suddenly remembered Bertie saying how his Gran Sparkes had spent her evenings cleaning offices in the City. Of course, that is what she could say she was doing! She did not wish to deceive Bertie, but somehow she did not think that he would agree to her singing, although they needed the money.

Algie, knowing that his job in the park was coming to an end, was only too thankful when Marguerite offered to take a cleaning job. Good for her, he thought, evidently she had not picked up any highbrow ideas at that Manor after all.

Leaving Bertie to baby sit Marguerite called at the Marylebone Halls and was able to make the necessary arrangements to sing to the troops at least three times a week. She returned home feeling pleased with herself and looking forward to this new venture.

The first evening soon arrived and Marguerite set off for the Halls and found the dressing room allocated to her. To her surprise she found arranged in a vase a most beautiful display of flowers, bearing a card, saying – 'I wait your singing this evening with anticipation – from your ever loving admirer, Captain Armstrong.' Oh no! had she after all been wise to accept this offer to entertain.

That first evening Marguerite did not feel that she had given of her best. She was nervous and felt that she lacked practice, but Captain Armstrong was to think otherwise. At the end of the evening he appeared in her room and going up to her and lifting her hand, in a gentlemanly fashion, kissed it and said "that was superb, Marguerite. I shall look forward to many such evenings." He stayed chatting rather longer than she felt was necessary. He would have liked to have escorted Marguerite home, but she declined his offer.

Marguerite's evenings now being organised she had to work out a daily routine. Owing to most of the children having left the area the schools had been closed, but with the so-called phoney-war continuing so many had returned to London that there was talk of opening them up again some time soon. On enquiring it would appear that this was not to be until the new school year began in September, that would mean Richard would be coming up to six-years-old. Marguerite decided to carry on the good work that Miss Thompson at the Manor had commenced and to teach him what she could at home. He had learnt his alphabet and how to write his name. Marguerite, for her singing purposes, had to become familiar with languages once more, so she endeavoured to introduce her small son to French. A foreign language before he had even commenced school! Unlike his Mother he did not enjoy these lessons and was not very co-operative, but he did enjoy hearing stories of the past and loved his first History lessons with his Mother.

Having some earnings now of her own, Marguerite was able to once more take a taxi each week to her sister, Sara Richard really enjoyed these visits, which enabled him to play with his cousins. Robert and Sara had not yet taken their family away from Wimbledon, but should there be bombing they had the cellar reinforced as a shelter. Marguerite explained to her sister what she was doing with her evenings and took the opportunity on these weekly visits to practice. She was quite sure that the response of the audience showed that the practices were really worthwhile. Marguerite also had needlework to do on these visits and was glad of Sarah's expert help with this task. She was lucky in receiving parcels of clothes from Lady Somerfield, who knew only too well that Marguerite could alter and put these beautiful dresses to good use. Marguerite liked to look presentable for the troops passing through London on their way to the front. It took her back to the days in Bedford Square, during the First World War, when she sang to the troops before they left for the trenches, but her singing now was to vast numbers of troops and not just round a drawing room piano.

On one of the visits to her sisters she left Richard under her care and went off to meet Captain Armstrong. He was to be drafted overseas and she felt that the least she could do, in all kindness, was to give a day to him. A day she was not to regret. Captain Armstrong was a charming host. That day he took her to places that she had not visited for many a year. That evening when he returned her to Wimbledon she felt flushed with excitement and realised she was treading on dangerous ground. She would have liked to have introduced him to her sister, but with Richard probably standing in the background felt this would be unwise. She could not burden such a small child with yet another secret.

*

It was to be only a few weeks into the new year of 1940 that, as forecast, Algie's job as park-keeper was to finish. He was at a loss to know, in these early days of the war, what work to do next. He was certainly too old to be accepted in the Forces.

One day Algie happened to pass by the Air-raid Precaution Centre when he spotted a notice asking for men and women to take the opportunity to learn to drive and to train as ambulance drivers. He went in, and after an interview, was accepted. He was not sure how he would cope with this new task; he was also not at all sure that he wished to be an ambulance driver, but, nevertheless, he would at least learn to drive.

Algie persevered with his driving lessons and to his surprise he eventually obtained his licence. Marguerite was really quite proud of her Bertie. Before arrangements could be made for him to put his driving to good use as an ambulance driver he saw another advertisement, this time for bus drivers, as many had gone to the war. The London Passenger Transport Board were urgently in need of qualified drivers to fill the vacancies. Now Algie thought that this is what he really would enjoy doing! He applied, and having just been well taught he was accepted. So it was in the spring of 1940 Algie Smythe became a bus driver.

Knowing that his Father was now driving buses, Richard took a great interest in the ones going passed the house and would wave from the window to each one passing by, just in case it was his Daddy driving. Sometimes Algie would take him on a bus to Gamages in High Holborn, to see the large departmental store, especially the toy department. It was hard to tell who enjoyed it more, father or son! Algie stood enthralled, whilst Richard on tip-toe was mesmerised by the small trains travelling around the room.

It was not long after Algie commenced his new job, and Marguerite had got into a regular routine of going to the Halls, that it was once more feared that bombing was to commence in London. In late May and early June families once more started to stream out of London for the countryside again, but this time, with Richard due to commence school and Marguerite with her new contacts, it was decided to sit it out in London.

*

About that time Marguerite was to receive sad news. In early June she returned to her dressing room after a very successful evening's performance, to find waiting for her a fellow in light blue, which she knew was the uniform of the men, injured in battle, who were returning home on sick leave from Dunkirk. The fellow hesitated, as he controlled his emotions, before telling her his reason for calling. He had been Captain Armstrong's batman and had brought a letter for her to read. At the look on this fellow's face she knew that this was going to be bad news. With her hands shaking she opened the letter and read –

My dearest Marguerite,

If my valued batman should survive the horrors of this war and reach home after my demise, he will endeavour to deliver this to you himself. I shall have died fighting for my country, but with you and your beautiful voice forever in my thoughts.

I have loved you Marguerite from the first time we met! This I hope and believe you knew!

Your affectionate and late admirer,

David Armstrong.

With tears in her eyes, Marguerite slowly folded the letter and without thinking tucked it into her dress close to her heart, as if grabbing on to that last close encounter. In a broken voice she thanked the batman for bringing the sad news to her and went on to ask how Captain Armstrong had died. This young man went on to tell her how they had just reached a boat but the Captain hesitated and helped one of his injured men in first. It was at that brief moment that a piece of shrapnel hit him and he went under. The batman said that if the Captain had not stopped to assist the injured man he already would have been in the boat!

For a number of weeks after Marguerite had received this news Algie was to wonder why his wife was looking so forlorn. He hoped that after coping with their small son all day her cleaning job was not becoming too much for her. He questioned her, but she denied that she was finding this a burden, and said she enjoyed getting away in the evenings.

*

In late August 1940, as forecast, just as Richard was looking forward to starting school, the bombardment of London started in earnest and Marguerite was to dread her journey to the Halls and hated to leave her small son behind in the Anderson shelter that Richard had enjoyed watching the workmen build before the war. This shelter proved to be very damp, and in fact when it eventually flooded was impossible to use. With the continuous raids some people took to sleeping down in the underground. They would be seen each evening as dusk approached making their way with their bedding tucked under their arm for the nearest entrance. Algie did not wish his family to seek this protection. For some reason he was not convinced that they were in any immediate danger.

Most evenings, just after Richard had dropped off to sleep, the air raid siren sounded and at Marguerite's insistence Algie rushed and grabbed Richard from his now warm bed. It seemed to be a nightly routine to be woken suddenly and, sometimes with bombs already screaming down, clutched in his Father's strong arms they would wait in the doorway of the house for a lull from the falling shrapnel. So many guns had been placed in the parks around London that the shrapnel from them was pouring down like rain. Algie knew how dangerous this could be, as he had felt the full force of it hitting his bus. He would stand waiting for the safest moment to rush his small son to the communal street shelter, where neighbours would already be gathered.

On the evenings that Marguerite was home, and whilst waiting in the porch watching the shrapnel falling, Marguerite could see David Armstrong in the water up to his waist lifting an injured man into a boat. She would shut her eyes endeavouring to rid herself of this sight, and then watch as Bertie rushed to the shelter with small Richard. On seeing them disappear in she would send up a prayer of thanks and when she felt it was safe would rush to the shelter herself.

Richard was always to remember the smell of that shelter, quite different to the smell of his gas mask. It was a smell of bricks and mortar, as if the inner walls had never had a chance to dry before the outer walls were built; and a smell that you get when people are packed in close together. Just inside the door was a cubicle which contained a make-shift toilet. Some people were not so particular – or it could be that they were too frightened to isolate themselves in the cubicle – the two fire buckets one containing water and the other sand would be used by some instead of the toilet. Perhaps they would approach the toilet cubicle only to take fright as the whistle and explosion of yet another bomb landed.

Algie managed to arrange his duties so that he was home on the evenings that Marguerite worked. The evenings that Algie was in the shelter he kept the occupants amused by his ghost stories and the many tales he would have to tell. Richard looked at his Daddy in amazement as the stories unfolded. As the bombs screamed down so Algie chattered away endeavouring to keep up the morale of this band of cockneys. On the evenings that he was working late he insisted that his family should retire to the shelter immediately darkness set in, or even earlier should there be a raid, as Marguerite found it impossible to carry her now quite heavy son. These were different evenings. Richard wished that his Mother would sing as she did then they were evacuated, but on whispering this suggestion to her she was quite adamant that she would not, and cuddled her small son on her lap and when he was eventually asleep gently placed him in the bunk that had been allocated to him.

When the bombing became worse, the three evenings that Marguerite supposedly went to do her cleaning a forces car was sent to fetch her. The neighbours, making their way to the shelter thought that Marguerite was cleaning military offices. On the first evening that this car arrived Algie was puzzled and meant to tackle his wife on her return, but when on arriving in the shelter the suggestion of where she was cleaning was put to him he was so convinced that this was a fact that he did not question his wife further. It so happened that Marguerite had already decided that that was what her answer would be, but knowing Bertie's inquisitive nature she was rather surprised when he never enquired about the car. Little did Algie know of the narrow escapes she had in the short distance to her evening's work, or the risk she was taking singing to a hall full of service personnel.

Much to Richard's disappointment the commencement of school was once more delayed. Marguerite was so thankful that she had the ability to teach him herself, but since returning from being evacuated he missed the company of the other children and had really been looking forward to school.

BOOK 4

CHAPTER 22

A DOUBLE TRAGEDY

After the fall of France and with the fear of invasion Sarah felt that it was time for all the family to meet up and for her small nephew Richard to meet his Aunt and Uncle at Harrow. So a very excited Richard left Holloway Road with his mummy for a day out in Harrow. His cousins from Wimbledon were there and he met another cousin called William, looking very smart in his Air Force uniform. He was the only son of Richard's Aunt Rachel, his Mother's elder sister, and Uncle Edward Tremaine. He was to remember being told that his cousin flew aeroplanes. He recalled arms outstretched going round the drawing room with his other cousins pretending to be aeroplanes. They were told to sit down and to stop making such a noise and to behave. Yes he remembered he had to be grown up at that party. He never saw that cousin again, as he was one of the first pilots to lose his life in the Battle of Britain. Rachel and Edward Tremaine were never to quite recover from the loss of their only son.

Marguerite regretted not having seen more of her eldest nephew and took his death, on the top of losing the Captain, very badly. Her health showed signs of deteriorating and she had to resort once more to her heart tablets, especially after receiving yet another shock.

*

It was just after breakfast when there was a knock at the front door and Mary Smythe, as she was prone to do when anyone came to the door, slowly climbed the stairs and opened the heavy front door, and there stood a couple of policemen. The taller one greeted the old lady, "Morning to you. Can you please inform me whether a Marguerite Sinclair lives here?"

"Marguerite, Marguerite. Yes we 'ave a Marguerite in the house but not that t'other name you mention," answered a very puzzled Mary.

At the mention of her maiden name Marguerite, followed by an inquisitive young son, went to see who it was at the door. "Good morning, can I help you? I am Marguerite, Marguerite Sinclair was my maiden name." Marguerite was becoming rather concerned as to why the police were asking for her.

"May we come in? We have a matter to discuss with you, please?" requested these two policemen. Mary Smythe was still hovering in the background and feeling very puzzled at this visit. The policeman could not but note this elderly lady and her inquisitiveness, and hastily suggested that perhaps after all it would be better if Marguerite accompanied them to the local police station.

Telling Richard to stay with his Granny, and checking that there was indeed a police car parked outside, she collected her coat and followed them down the steps, still very puzzled as to what they should want and why an interview at the police station? Had Bertie's bus met with an accident? As she was swiftly driven through the streets all manner of things were going through her mind as to what they should want with her.

The two young men showed Marguerite into the interview room; a rather stark forbidding room with just a table and four chairs and very poor lighting on this rather dull day. The same policeman who had so far done all the talking and giving a slight cough asked "Mrs uhm!"

"Smythe is my married name," answered a still puzzled Marguerite.

"Mrs Smythe, are we to believe that you know Germany well?" the policeman asked.

"Yes, I travelled through Germany at the beginning of the First World War in my attempt to reach the safety of England," replied Marguerite.

The same policeman went on to ask, "Does the name Fritz mean anything to you, Mrs Smythe?"

At the name of Fritz, Marguerite froze her mind going back to that terrible experience so many years ago and that horrible encounter with Fritz. "Yes, I met a middle-aged man called Fritz Smidt soon after leaving Heidelburg in 1914," answered a now rather nervous Marguerite.

The two policemen, both having noted Marguerite's startled manner at the mention of the name Fritz, consulted with each other, and after a while replied, "No, Mrs Smythe, that definitely cannot be the Fritz we are referring to. This name on our records gives Fritz's surname as Werner." Endeavouring to make this middle-aged, somewhat plump woman relax, they cleverly changed their manner of interrogation. The other policeman, who had not at that stage had much to say, took over. "Marguerite, tell us about your journey through Germany all those years ago."

Marguerite, by now feeling more relaxed with this friendlier attitude, began to relate and relive those far off days and experiences of arriving in Heidelburg and her studies, and told of her endeavours to reach England on the outbreak of war in the late summer and autumn of 1914. As her story progressed a picture formed in the minds of these interviewers.

"Tell us, Marguerite, the surname of that young farmer and his wife?" asked the policeman.

Marguerite could not believe that she had been so foolish in not asking the surname of Christa and Hans Peter. "I am so sorry, but you will never believe that in my stress of endeavouring to live as Congettina Spirotti I never found out this young couples German surname. I have often regretted it, as I have been unable to contact them since.

"Marguerite, can you take your mind back and tell us whether this newly young married woman was expecting a baby?" asked her interviewer.

Marguerite thought back, but could not point to anything that gave her a reason to believe that Christa was expecting. She answered quite confidently, "I cannot recall thinking that Christa was in that condition, sir. Having spent a number of hours with her I am sure I would have known."

Once more the two policemen consulted with each other and then the same interviewer turned to Marguerite and said, "I think you have been able to prove to us that you are the person we are looking for, and enough is enough, and we will come to the point of our reason for bringing you here this morning." He went on to confirm with Marguerite that she was indeed in her maiden days Marguerite Sinclair who had travelled widely through Germany and had confirmed without question that she had met Hans Peter and Christa Werner. He went on to tell Marguerite that in June 1915 Christa gave birth to a baby son, who, in the absence of her husband, called him Fritz, and that before Hans Peter could return to Germany to see this much wanted son he was killed whilst fighting on the Somme. This news was a shock to Marguerite, and how she wished she had contacted Christa between the wars and met up with her again and been introduced to her small son.

The policeman went on to inform Marguerite that the previous month one of our spitfires had shot down a Messerschmitt, as it came across the English Channel and over the English coast. He went on to tell Marguerite that on searching the doomed plane the home guard found the body of the pilot; in his breast pocket they found a letter addressed to Marguerite. He handed this to her to read:

To whom this may concern,

Should my son, Fritz Werner, aged at the time of writing this letter 24 years, be killed whilst on enemy territory, please see that this reaches a Marguerite Sinclair (alias Congettina Spirotti), a London Solicitor's daughter, and please tell her that I gave birth to Fritz exactly eight months after we parted. Just after my small son's first birthday Hans Peter was killed fighting on the Somme, having never met his baby son.

As she read this tears welled up in Marguerite's eyes as she once more thought of how she had never met up with Christa and her precious son between the wars. She immediately thought of the death of her nephew, William, in similar circumstances; immediately came to her mind the saying – 'an eye for an eye and a tooth for a tooth', but how cruel life could be and what a waste of two young men's lives. Suddenly her chest pains became quite intolerable and she apologised to the two policemen as she reached for her handbag containing her heart pills; she quickly swallowed a tablet. She was to ever wonder how Christa found out her true name and that her dear father was indeed a London solicitor.

BOOK 4

CHAPTER 23

NEAR MISSES

The two policemen felt sorry to have given this woman such a shock, which she appeared to have taken badly. They gently helped her out to the car, and on dropping her home the door was quickly opened by a concerned Mary, "take care of your daughter-in-law Ma-am, she has had rather a shock

Marguerite hoped that the police were satisfied with their interrogation and that would be the end of the questioning. She decided there and then that immediately this terrible war was over she would endeavour to contact Christa.

On entering the kitchen to her surprise there sat Algie looking slightly annoyed at his Mother fetching him from work, thus cutting down the well earned money he would be bringing home on Friday. Marguerite was thankful that young Richard was still downstairs with his granny as she realised she had some explaining to do to Algie.

*

Richard had often talked of his visits to Gamages to see the toys and his cousins had pestered their Mother to take them too, and so as there was a lull in the raids, the very next day Marguerite had arranged to meet her sister and small children at the restaurant of Thomas Wallis, another departmental store in High Holborn; this arrangement she was very thankful to be able to keep to stop any unnecessary questioning from Richard, as to why the police had come.

They all sat at a very large table, covered in a spotless white starched tablecloth. Whilst a quartet played soft music, Richard and his cousins enjoyed finely cut sandwiches and cream cakes. It might not have been real cream but the fairy cakes were certainly very tasty. Whilst Marguerite and Sarah chatted away the children became more and more excited about their visit to the toy department, and finally the two older women had to give in to the children and take them across the road. Richard felt quite grown up as he led the way. This certainly was a memorable day; just to watch the children's faces was a delight.

It was to be only three days later that the Thomas Wallis store received a direct hit and many were to lose their lives. Richard was really still too young to appreciate the narrow escape they had had, but Marguerite could see the customers partaking of their tea, in what seemed such a peaceful atmosphere; many times the faces of the quartet appeared to her, and both Sarah and Marguerite would never forget this very sad episode in their lives.

Marguerite's nerves really became bad, and some nights when they dashed for the shelter she felt she could scream – why had they not stayed in the country in that fine manor house? She was even more unnerved when one morning on coming out of the shelter she stood with Richard and felt the heat of the flames reaching them from the bombing around St Paul's, which was only just over a mile away. The whole sky seemed to be blackened by the smoke with a red glow every now and then breaking through.

Realising how bad his wife's nerves had become, Algie suggested that perhaps it would be a good idea to have an evening out together and suggested going to see one of the films being offered at the local cinema. At this suggestion Marguerite was not too keen at going into such a crowded place – strange as she was entertaining in such a similar place three times a week, but then she was kept busy and her mind occupied.

Algie endeavoured to reassure her, saying, "my love, there are seven cinemas in reach of our 'ome, I am sure that the 'un is not going to chose the one we are in to drop his bomb on!" Marguerite relented and really enjoyed her evening, but it was to be only the next week that that cinema also received a direct hit and everyone inside perished. Marguerite shuddered at the thought of her Richard being left an orphan.

Richard was to remember forever the screams of the bombs landing and the continuous barrage of the guns. The dust seemed to get into everything. Each morning they surfaced from their shelter, and were amazed to see their home still standing and to think that they had survived yet another night. As the weeks went by more and more houses were destroyed and the streets around them flattened. Their main road was left as if they were on an island, and they wondered at their miraculous escape.

Richard's Grandmother was responsible for collecting the rent from the other tenants in the house and also from another house owned by the landlord. Auntie Eve now took the responsibility of collecting the rent from this other house. Richard occasionally went with her, but sat uncomfortably in the front room of the house, which had a smell of it's own; front rooms, known as the best room were hardly used in those days. Whilst his Aunt chatted to the tenants Richard sat quietly and even at that young age had an uncomfortable feeling, perhaps a premonition, that all was not right. It was to be only a few days after a visit with his Aunt that the house was destroyed by a bomb and all the occupants killed. As young as he was when Richard heard about this he wondered at the strange feeling he had noticed when sitting in that home.

When driving his London bus Algie could not always hear the siren above the noise of the engine, but his conductor would give a signal on the bell to let him know. He would immediately take his bus to the nearest shelter entrance where his passengers would alight and make a dart down the steps of the shelter. Often it would be an underground station entrance, but not until all his passengers had left would Algie abandon his bus, and many a time he would only just make the shelter. On occasions his bus would be hit by falling masonry and shrapnel, and on returning to it after the raid it would not be driveable. Some evenings on arriving at his home shelter he would wonder at his many narrow escapes of the day, and yet he would remain calm and resilient. He decided that his training and experiences in the first world war had stood him in good stead, but he was to worry that he had done the right thing in bringing his wife and young son home on that Christmas Eve of 1939 to face these dangerous days; why had he listened to the opinion of his Ma, he thought he had learnt his lesson many years before, but evidently not!

*

Although Marguerite's health was deteriorating she was determined to keep up her singing to the troops – she felt this to be her war effort.

At last in May 1941 the raids in London were to cease for a while and the evacuees once more started to trickle back to their homes. In September the school was re-opened, and so at nearly seven-years-old the day had arrived for Richard to at last start school. He was certainly quite ready for this venture. Having been so much with his Mother he had no cockney accent, and to the teachers of this London school seemed quite a different child to his companions.

Each morning Richard would set off with his Mother, his gas mask in a small box around his neck. In the bottom of this box would be another small box containing his iron rations, consisting of a small bar of chocolate, Ovaltine tablets and Rowntrees gums, and sometimes, as a special treat, some lemonade powder, chocolate powder or sherbet. This small box of iron rations was just in case there was an emergency and he was not able to be collected from school and had to remain in the air raid shelter for a number of hours; otherwise on no account were the children allowed to touch these small boxes. They were placed under the gas mask in safe keeping, hopefully to be forgotten by these small charges.

At first Richard encountered a hard time. He was teased at being so different, but when the other children found out that he had been an evacuee and had tales to tell like themselves he soon made friends. The first few days seemed to be taken up with learning to disappear under the desk when the whistle sounded and not to reappear until the teacher sounded two blasts. The new children thought this quite a game and preferable to joining a long orderly queue to the shelter. It was considered too dangerous for the children to play outside, especially as no hand bells were allowed to be used for calling them in. One thing that Richard hated was sitting for what seemed a long time with his gas mask on. The rubbery smell made him feel sick, but he dared not take it off, and the more he felt sick the hotter he got and the smell got worse, but the threat of the Germans dropping gas was still very much in mind and the practice with gas masks had to be carried out.

Thanks to his Mother, Richard was well advanced in his lessons and the three months spent in the classroom at the Manor had got him used to learning in a group. When the school bell went at the end of the day he was eager to find his mother waiting outside; as young as he was he understood the dangers, under which they were living, and there was always the fear that his parents could have been involved in a raid. The walk to and from school each day reminded him of how lucky they were to have survived so far. He chattered all the way home. One day on passing under the air raid siren it went off and they nearly jumped out of their skins. Marguerite felt that she was going to have a heart attack with the fright and clasped her breast. Richard was really quite concerned for his mother, and immediately on arriving home made her a cup of tea; he was very proud at just having learnt to do this.

The routine of life went on, but it was sad to see the people living in the bombed devastated buildings; some had been re-housed in new prefabricated homes, small colonies of which were to be found round and about, but there were too many homeless for all to be housed, and some refused to leave what remained of their homes, hoping for compensation when the war was over. They seemed to think if they left their property they would lose it. The Smythe family were so grateful in these terrible days to have their home in one piece.

Richard made good progress in his first year at school and soon left the infant class and moved upstairs to the juniors. He enjoyed doing what he called proper sums and had a good memory for the multiplication tables. He was not quite so good with his spelling.

The war years slipped by and the numbers increased in the Junior School, people got tired of being away and somehow found places to live in the area. The memories of the raids being so much in Marguerite's mind and her evenings being taken up with singing, she did not encourage Richard to join any out of school activities, and so his life very much evolved around school and home, until Germany endeavoured to have the upper hand.

The time had come when Marguerite no longer had to meet her son from school. It was now 1944 and he was nine-years-old. It was a bright May Day, and Richard was walking home from school with a group of friends, when suddenly there was this awful rattling noise, that seemed to cause the shuddering of the ground. One of the boys glanced up at the sky and there coming towards them was this flying object with a flame coming from its tail. It appeared to be coming straight towards them. The boys shouted a warning to each other and flung themselves on the ground.

BOOK 4

CHAPTER 24

A NEW HOUSE

Marguerite was working at her kitchen sink when she heard the rattling noise which seemed to shake the house. Her immediate thought was an earthquake in the midst of this war, but then she saw it. A flying monster, with flame from its tail, getting lower and lower, and then the ground shook as it landed. She knew by the kitchen clock that Richard would be on his way home from school, and as she realised with horror of where it could have landed a most terrible pain went through her chest and down her arm. Somehow or other she managed to reach the bedroom and so take one of her heart pills. She lay down on the bed her thoughts running wild.

*

One by one the boys lifted their heads, not daring to get up from where they had flung themselves. They were all smothered in dust, but otherwise unharmed. Not like some of their other friends also on their way home from school; a number were to lose their lives that day. A warden appeared, and after ascertaining that the young lads were not injured in any way, except for shock, gathered them together, reassuring them. He took them to a nearby ARP post and gave each one a well sugared mug of tea to help still the shock. After a while he escorted them, one by one, to their homes.

Marguerite was roused by a hammering on the door. She slowly made her way along the hall, hardly daring to open the front door, as she was fearful of what she was to hear, but there stood young Richard, covered in dust from head to toe, but otherwise unscathed. Bursting into tears he flung himself into his Mother's arms. Marguerite hugged him to her and the warden said, "Let him cry." He went on to explain what had happened. "I should make him another cup of tea, me love – 'elp steady the nerves. And take one yerself, yer certainly looks as if yer need it!" suggested this kindly warden.

Although a number of these doodlebugs were intercepted by barrage balloons placed across the North Downs, a great many still reached London and the devastation was terrible.

Realising what a narrow escape their small son had had, and that it was inevitable the school would once more be closed Algie and Marguerite decided that it was time for Richard to leave London for the safety of the country. That evening when the car arrived to take Marguerite to work she sent it away again, her place was definitely with her small shocked nine-year-old.

The next morning Marguerite went along to Islington Town Hall to arrange for Richard's evacuation. Whilst there she tentatively enquired whether by any chance she could be evacuated as well. She was asked if she would be willing to be in charge of a group of children. She realised that this was possibly the only way she could accompany Richard and so agreed. She left the building with the inevitable forms and list of clothes that were to be taken. She was told to present herself with her son for a medical the next day. Her immediate thoughts again were – 'what if I should fail?'

Algie was not at all sure that he wished his wife to accompany Richard. He felt that this was fussing over his son too much and that he was quite old enough now to go unaccompanied, but Marguerite was adamant. In her mind she felt that with her nerves once more shattered she could not stand up in that vast hall and sing to the troops; at least going away she would have her mind occupied. She would have liked to have contacted Lady Somerfield, but she knew that the Manor was now a hospital for the wounded being returned from the front and there would be no room for evacuees.

*

Within a week a host of children and some adults with labels once more pinned to their clothing gathered at the school. Algie had escorted them that far but had to leave them there and go to work. Before making for the station, Marguerite was given her small band of boys, mainly friends of Richards, including the lads who had suffered the shock of the first doodlebug to land off the Holloway Road. In small numbers they were gradually taken to Kings Cross Station. Richard was really quite excited at the prospect of perhaps another Manor house. His Mother endeavoured to warn him that this time being evacuated could be quite different!

Marguerite settled her brood into the compartment and was soon telling them, "No! You are not to start eating your food yet! We do not know how long we shall be on this train!" Being boys they were already longing to tuck into their parcels of food. At last the engine got up steam and to a great cheer, by the many children on board, they started to chug out of the station.

Marguerite was feeling really tired from the exhaustion of the past few weeks and soon fell into a deep sleep. She dreamt she was a young girl once more travelling through Germany and a doodlebug was chasing her. She was suddenly awoken by the boys shouting excitedly, "Look Ma Smythe, look." She woke and followed their gaze out of the window, and there in the distance in flames was a plane limping home from its mission. They all stared in horror as in a ball of fire it crashed to the ground.

"What do we do, Mum?" asked Richard.

"There is nothing we can do son from a moving train that would help." She looked back as they sped away from the sight and sadly announced to these young lads, "I am afraid it would be too late anyhow!" At the same time she was thinking to herself, 'was she to ever get away from the death of casualties in the war?'

For the next hour it was a quite subdued group that journeyed to their unknown destination. When lunchtime came the food they had consumed seemed to give them more energy and their incessant chatter during the long afternoon soon gave Marguerite a headache. The journey seemed to go on for hours and it was tea-time before very tired and by now dishevelled and sticky Londoners arrived at a station somewhere in the north; it was, in fact, Manchester.

Marguerite and her band of boys were taken by coach to the outskirts of Manchester to a new housing estate, partially finished when war broke out. The houses had now been hurriedly completed and made habitable for these evacuees.

Although Marguerite had six nine-year-old boys in her care the house seemed quite large after her two rooms. The kitchen was quite modern, with a grey boiler, with small round lid on top through which to shovel the coal, and a tool, that she found difficult at first to use, to open up the front for letting some heat out into the room. This small boiler heated the water, what luxury, thought Marguerite. Some of the boys had been living in the remains of their bombed homes and so were really thrilled at what they saw. There were three bedrooms. The smaller one she allocated to two of the boys who were brothers. Much to Richard's disgust he was to share a bedroom with this Mother, and the other three boys had the other room.

The billeting people soon arrived with stretcher beds, supplied by the WRVS, and rough army blankets and flannelette sheets, which were to prove rather hot in the midsummer weather. Now they knew the exact number they soon returned with pillows. The first meal was taken sitting on the front room floor. The children had each brought an enamel mug, plate and assortment of cutlery with them. The excitement of the day soon caught up with these children, and Marguerite was to wish that they would soon tire as she endeavoured to break up a pillow fight before the feathers from the new pillows went flying.

Marguerite was not used to disciplining a group of children and after only two days felt shattered, but a routine did eventually materialise. She would take them for long walks, which helped to improve her own health. They would walk along the Manchester Ship Canal and stand on the towpath and watch as the turntable road bridge went round to let a ship through. Once the boys started to fidget she moved them on, as she was fearsome that one might push the other into the canal. She was thankful that they were not living too near the canal, she would not have had a moment's peace of mind.

It was not to be too long before it was the new school year and the children were settled into the local school. Of course, there were the inevitable fights between the 'blessed 'vacees' and the local children, but gradually everything settled down. Marguerite was thankful for Richard that he had the support at school of the other perhaps tougher children with whom he was now sharing his home. The children started to bring work home to do in the evenings, as they had just over a year to prepare for that inevitable scholarship.

During the day peace reigned, in this little bit of England, and Marguerite was able to rest a little, but she missed singing to the troops. With the children out of the way she commenced to practice her vocal chords and she was soon to be glad she had taken the opportunity to do so. The boys came home one Friday asking if they could go to Saturday morning pictures. The local cinema gave a special session mid-morning for children. The next day Marguerite took them all along and took the opportunity to do her shopping whilst they were all occupied. Whilst waiting for them to come out she stood reading the notices, amongst them was one announcing that Saturday afternoons were given over to entertaining service personnel. She enquired and offered her services, which, of course, on hearing of her previous experiences was welcomed and great interest was shown.

The boys really enjoyed their Saturdays. Pictures in the morning, a snack in the cinema restaurant whilst Ma Smythe, as they called her, practiced her performance on stage, and back into the pictures to be entertained the whole afternoon. They were permitted to sit quietly in the side seats and listen to the troops being entertained. They were really proud of Ma when she appeared and were astounded at her beautiful voice. Marguerite felt rather guilty that they should spend their whole day in the cinema, but at least they were occupied and not getting into mischief.

Preparations were to soon begin for Christmas 1944. The ENSA group organising the Saturday afternoon entertainment suggested that the lads should be involved in the Christmas show, so it was that Marguerite organised them into a group, playing various instruments – one with a comb between paper, another with saucepan lids as cymbals. She found that one of her lads could sing well, and with a little training he crooned to the noise the others made with their makeshift instruments. Richard was on the drums, a set had been lent to them. They practised well and it was arranged that they should be in the Christmas performance on the Saturday before Christmas. Marguerite was quite surprised at her ability to get this band of children organised.

*

Back in London it was not long after Marguerite had left with the boys that Algie was after all thankful that his wife was away from London. No sooner had the doodlebugs ceased than a new dreadful bomb arrived, silently and unexpectedly from the skies. The V2 flying bomb gave no warning as it hit London. The first the people on the ground knew about this vicious new bomb was when it had landed, causing yet more fatal casualties and devastation.

Algie felt the responsibility of his bus passengers very much on his shoulders, as now the siren would more often or not go off too late for people in the streets to take cover. For the first time in this war he felt the strain. On the spur of the moment he arranged to take some holiday, and very early on the Saturday morning before Christmas he took a fast train to Manchester. He arrived at the house, just after lunch, to find no one at home. He knocked on a neighbour's door and was told that Mrs Smythe spent her Saturdays at the local picture house with her brood. He asked for directions and made his way there, thinking to himself why do they want to spend a whole day watching pictures? After some cockney persuasion and banter the usherette showed him to a seat. He realised that this was an entertainment for the troops that he had walked in on. He feared that he had come to the wrong cinema, but before he could leave again the next item was announced. He could not believe his ears or eyes when Marguerite stepped out onto the stage. He sat spellbound as his wife's beautiful voice reached him. After her first number the audience cheered and clapped and he felt like standing up and shouting out – 'that's my wife up there', he felt so proud of Marguerite entertaining the troops.

When the interval arrived and the lights went up the excited boys got up from their seats on the side of the cinema and made for the entrance. Richard could not believe his eyes when he spotted his Father sitting at the back of the auditorium. He was in too much of a hurry to keep up with the other boys to stop, but called out to his Father, "Hi, Dad! We are not coming home with you this time!" Having said that he disappeared with the others, leaving Algie thinking, no hugs this time for his old Dad, and my hasn't he grown up!

BOOK 4

CHAPTER 25

TO WAVE GOODBYE

Algie sat there at the back of the stalls day-dreaming wondering where his son had disappeared to and why he was in such a hurry. He was glad that he had taken two week's holiday. He would need to get to know this son of his all over again, he could tell by his tone of voice that he had grown up considerably in these last few months.

The lights dimmed once more and the inevitable notice came up on the screen – 'should the siren go would the audience please leave the auditorium in an orderly fashion and make for the nearest air-raid shelter'; this was followed by adverts, the latest news reel, and a short film and then the entertainment began once more. Algie wondered if Marguerite would sing again. The compere once more appeared to the cheering of the service personnel filling this cinema on this Saturday afternoon before Christmas and announced as a special treat they were now to be entertained by a young group called 'the Covacs'. A great cheer went up as the six ten-year-old lads appeared carrying various unusual instruments. Algie realised that the young boy carrying the drums was his own son, Richard. "Well I never did!" Algie muttered to himself. "I have certainly arrived in Manchester just in time!" These boys got a warm welcome from the men apart from their own sons that Christmas. Algie was highly amused at the antics these lads got up to and the sound they achieved from those various instruments. The taller lad had certainly been taught to croon well. Algie wondered who had taught his son to play the drums. Marguerite had found this out of her reach and one of the many talented men of the Ensa group had coped with this task. It was a very excited group of boys that took their bow that afternoon, and left the stage to a tremendous acclamation. Algie once more stood up from his seat and shouted encore as loud as he could. The lads returned to a great cheer and repeated their performance. The afternoon ended with Marguerite and the other singers leading the audience in the singing of carols. Algie thought that he had not enjoyed himself so much for many many months.

After it was all over, Richard rushed to find his mother in her dressing room. "Mum, guess whose here?" he asked his Mother excitedly.

"Well, no one we know, Richard! We don't know anyone in Manchester," announced his puzzled Mother.

"Just guess, Mum. Go on, have a guess." pressed an excited Richard.

Realising that it was coming up to Christmas, Marguerite asked, "Oh no! Not your Father?"

"Yes! Dad!" answered Richard, and seeing his Mother's worried expression went on to add, "Don't worry. I've already told him that we are not going home," announced a smiling Richard.

Algie pushed his way out of the picture house, he had one aim in mind to find somewhere to buy flowers for his wife. His luck was in, there on the corner stood a flower-seller. There was not much to choose from, but any flowers were better than none. He would have liked to have bought the boys some sweets, but he did not have his sweet coupons with him, so that was out of the question. He raced back to the cinema, clutching the flowers, wondering if his son had yet told his Mother of his arrival. He soon met the boys in the foyer.

"Hello Dad. I wondered where you had gone," said Richard, and went on to add, "I've told Mum, that you are here."

"Good for yer, son; well what about giving your Dad a hug," asked Algie, but Richard was not going to do that in front of the other boys, and so shook hands with his Father, in quite a grown-up manner.

Marguerite soon appeared, wondering what she was going to hear from this husband of hers. She was not going home, not with the lads to look after. On seeing his wife approaching, Algie immediately went to her gave her a hug and handed her the flowers, saying, "Me luv, I was right proud of you this afternoon. Real proud, I was."

"Thank you. Bertie. Where did you get the flowers?" but before Algie could answer, she remembered to add, "It is good to see you, Bertie."

"What about us, Dad?" questioned Richard.

"You were smashin, lads, real great." And turning to the tall lad that had done the crooning, Algie said, "you've got a good voice there me lad, a good voice."

"Thanks, mate," and then, realising what he had said, smiled apologetically and added, "thank you sir."

Richard then introduced the boys to his father, and Algie went on to point out that he would have liked to have bought them a small reward for their achievements that afternoon, but because of the sudden unknown surprise he had been unable to think of anything on the spur of the moment, but he would make it up to them over Christmas.

Walking back to the house, Algie announced that he had taken two week's holiday and did not have to return to London until the New Year. Marguerite was relieved to hear this and pleased to think that there would be no argument this time about her and Richard returning to London, and what a great help he would be with the boys over this busy period. By the time they reached home they had learnt all about the terrible V2, which they had only seen on film at the cinema and in the newspaper photographs. They felt relieved to think that this fearful object had not reached them in the north.

Richard was only too glad to move in with his three pals, leaving the bedroom for his parents. Algie was impressed by the way Marguerite had made the home so comfortable. She quickly pointed out that she had received a great deal of help from the billeting people. Also, Sarah, on hearing that her sister had a house to furnish, had sent many things. Algie looked around him and decided, there and then, that after the war he must find a house for his wife and son.

Marguerite had more money for housekeeping this Christmas than she had had for many a year; she was, of course, paid for looking after the evacuees. Also the troops had raised quite a considerable amount of money in appreciation of the lads' entertainment, and a representative from ENSA arrived that week with a very large hamper of goodies. Christmas 1944 was to be the happiest one that Marguerite had spent in her married life. There were not many presents to go round but the fun of being together, as such a large family, made the festive occasion seem more special. Richard encouraged his Father to tell his ghost stories, as they sat round the tree, with candles alight to give a special effect, on that Christmas night.

That New Year the boys were allowed to stay up to celebrate what hopefully would be the year that the war ended. Algie assured them, even if in his heart he was not at all certain, that he thought peace was in sight.

The time eventually came for Algie to return to London. All five boys went with Ma Smythe and Richard to see him off at the station. As the train moved slowly out he waved from the window, thinking how he would have loved a large family. It had certainly been a great holiday - the best yet, even though there was a war on.

*

Before long the winter of 1945 was to pass and it was hoped that peace would soon reign. The boys settled down at school and the two that were due for their eleventh birthdays before September sat for the inevitable scholarship. March came and the bulbs in the garden began to show their heads, some even bursting into flower early. Marguerite enjoyed the month of April spent in her small house.

Whilst with them at Christmas, Algie had managed to obtain a wireless set. He explained to Marguerite that she would have to get the batteries re-charged occasionally, this she had recently forgotten to do and on this early May morning she could not get any reaction from the set so it was with surprise that she heard the news, as the boys burst in from school. They all tried to shout at the same time that they had no school tomorrow as peace was to be announced. She soon sent one of the boys off to the garage with the wireless batteries, as she said it was one thing that they must have working properly on this special occasion. The next day they listened intently as Churchill announced the end of hostilities, and then later the King spoke to the nation. A King, who had overcome his speech impediment so well, spoke to his beloved country at last at peace, except for the war with Japan, which it was hoped would be over soon.

The children went out looking for flags to buy to hang over the front door. Marguerite met with all the nearby neighbours to arrange a street party for the following Saturday. A party that was enjoyed by all, a party that went on to the early hours, the children's tea party followed by dancing in the street.

After all this excitement some of the evacuees began to worry. Not all had homes to return to; families had been split and many homes were just a pile of rubble. Marguerite assured her boys that she would not abandon them until all had been returned to their Mother, Father or a near relative. She received a telegram from Bertie 'Coming to get you both, post haste'. She sent a telegram back -'Hold on! Boys must be sent home first.

Marguerite need not have worried, as once peace was announced things moved quickly and relatives seemed to appear overnight to collect their offspring. Marguerite and Richard stood at the gate sadly waving goodbye to the boys as they left one by one, and then they turned and hand in hand went back into the house to clear up, before returning to London themselves, by train a few days later.

*

It was to be many years before London was to recover from the devastation of these war years. The bombed sites were gradually grassing over and the wild flowers were to grow. Some families were re-housed in the new prefabricated houses, which became quite cosy, but others remained in the hanging buildings, making the most of what was left of their homes, including some of whom she called 'her boys'. Looking at these nearby families, Marguerite realised that she must be thankful for her two rooms, but the war years had taken their toll. She had been too busy to take proper care of herself, but now a great tiredness set in.

It was not to be until September 1945 that Richard once more continued his schooling. It was to be a busy year ahead with the scholarship to be sat in January. He was just to miss a place at grammar school, and in September 1946 each morning he was to set off for a central school in Clerkenwell. It was now to be his turn to wave to his mother as the bus passed his home. By October he had settled well at school and was enjoying the new subjects. Suddenly life was to change and there was to be no one to wave to anymore. It was the day after his twelfth birthday that he returned home from school to emptiness. Where was his Mother? He called, but no reply! His now very aged Grandmother shouted from the bottom of the stairs.

"Yer Ma has been taken ill me luv," announced his grandmother with emotion in her voice.

"When Gran? Where is she?" asked a by now tearful Richard.

"She must 'ave suddenly turned from the window after waving to you this morning, picked up the post and was reading a letter, just like my own Ma did many years ago, and just collapsed in a 'eap," answered his Gran tearfully. "Your Dad found 'er when 'e finished his shift and came 'ome to dinner." This had all been too much for the old lady; she turned and made for her kitchen and collapsed into her chair exhausted.

Richard rushed down to his Gran and endeavoured to comfort her, at the same time trying to take in what he had just heard. After a while his Gran recovered her composure and went on to say, "Yer Aunt Eve has arrived 'ome early so that she can take you to the 'ospital. She's gone to get yer some fish and chips, me luv."

"Thanks, Gran," but he didn't think he felt very hungry. With concern Richard asked, "Isn't Mother coming home tonight?"

"No me lad, she's somewhat poorly!" sighed his Grandmother. Sitting there that afternoon she had been thinking as to how her young grandson would cope if his Mother should not recover. They had been that close, she thought. Whatever will he do! "You just pop up those apple and pairs and change out of that new school uniform of yours. Yer Aunt won't want yer spilling yer fish and chips down 'em, will she now? You go and change, there's a good lad," requested his Gran.

Richard did as he was told and slowly climbed the stairs; already noticing the quietness of the two rooms without his Mother. He was used to telling her of the happenings of the day, and she was such a good listener. He supposed his Dad was interested, but he always seemed to be telling a tale himself and did not really take in what was being said to him.

Aunt Eve soon arrived with the fish and chips, but even the smell put Richard off, but he dutifully sat down and picked at it and ate what he could. Neither his Gran or Aunt forced him to eat, they felt so sorry for this young lad and what they feared he would have to face.

On the way to the bus, Richard stopped and bought his Mother a bunch of flowers, which took him back to that memorable occasion when his father presented his mother with those flowers in Manchester after she had sung so well. He was not used to hospitals and it seemed to him to be a rather dismal old building, with a strong smell of disinfectant hanging about it. He was shocked on approaching his Mother's bed to see a very solemn Father sitting holding his Mother's hand. She appeared to this child to be asleep, but was in fact still unconscious. Richard dutifully kissed her, but there was no response and his mother showed no signs of recognition. He sat down beside his Father, and it seemed an endless time that they sat there not saying a word.

After about an hour Algie finally spoke. 'Eve, take the child 'ome. I shall stay the night."

"I will stay with you Dad, if you like." Richard said quickly.

"Thanks me lad, but this aint a place for a child. Off yer go with yer Aunt, there's a good lad." With tears in his eyes Algie gave his son a fond hug.

Richard bent once more and kissed his Mother and left the dimly lit ward. At the door he turned and waved, just as he had done that morning from the bus, just in case his Mother was seeing him.

BOOK 4

CHAPTER 26

MEMORIES

There was no school for Richard the next day, as his Mother passed away that night without regaining consciousness. Richard felt that he was in a bad dream. The two rooms seemed so empty and his Father was a shattered man, sitting in his chair listless.

Richard sat looking at his Dad and daydreaming of the memories of the happy times spent with his Mother. He was a five-year-old child peeping through the banisters at the Manor. He could see his Mother standing by the piano, dressed in a black skirt and beautifully starched white blouse. She looked quite elegant that night. He smiled to himself as he heard her singing. The faces of the men around looked with admiration at this woman as her beautiful voice filled the room. Yes, that is how he would remember his dear Mother!

Sitting in the chair, Algie was far away, back digging the flowerbeds when he was conscious of this buxom woman staring at him. He smiled to himself as he remembered saying – 'call me Bertie', He was back on Hampstead Heath telling his beloved that he had found two rooms to let. Was she ever happy in those two rooms? Somehow he doubted it. He was down at Bognor, when he first took her in his arms. Algie was so pleased that he had spent two weeks in Manchester the Christmas before the end of the war. A Christmas spent in a small house with a large family around her. Yes, a happy time! He could see his Marguerite on that stage singing. He wondered at his wife's beautiful voice. He had meant to ask her about this, but it was too late now. "Bertie"! He said the name to himself quite softly. "Bertie"! His son glanced worriedly at his Dad murmuring to himself. Algie smiled sadly at his son, as the thought went through his head – 'Bertie was now dead and gone too'! He would be Algie only from now on; and so the endless day went on, Father and son just sitting with their memories and occasionally looking at each other. The day when a dear wife and mother had died.

Richard did not understand all the arrangements that had to be made when a person died, but the next day he dutifully went with his Father on the various calls that had to be made. His Father tried to explain to this young lad how a death had to be registered, but young Richard found it difficult to concentrate on what his

Father was telling him, The shock had been so great that he felt that he was following his Father around in a daze.

*

Richard and his Father had always enjoyed walking on Hampstead Heath. Even as a baby in the pram Algie would take his son on the Heath. They would hardly be out of sight of the Holloway Road when Algie would take out of his pocket a dummy such a thing was abhorrent to Marguerite. Algie would wipe the dummy first down his trousers, just in case any tobacco had got stuck on it, and then shove it in his small son's mouth. If Marguerite could have seen she would have been horrified at all the germs going into this small son's mouth, but Richard seemed to come to no harm. With these memories going through his mind and the business arrangements all having been attended to Algie suggested to Richard that they should go for a walk on the heath.

That November day they seemed to walk for miles making for Parliament Hill, and stood sadly looking at the views of a still devastated London. As they stood there, suddenly Algie turned to his young son and said, "Well me lad, it is you and me together now!"

"Yes, Dad. I'll look after you Dad!" said a tearful Richard.

"Yer a good lad," said Algie. "Never thought I'd 'ave the likes of you. Yeh! Yer a good lad," repeated Algie, with a break in his voice, as he ruffled his son's hair.

After this conversation Father and son went on walking silently with their own thoughts going through their minds. As they made their way off the heath, Algie once more told his son of how he had been a Keeper on this heath. A tale young Richard had heard many times. They glanced in the gardens of the houses on Highgate Hill. Algie smiled to himself as he thought back to those days when as a young kid he had day-dreamt of having a garden such as these. He had certainly not come far; he hoped his son would do better.

*

The days slowly went by. There was a delay in the funeral taking place as a post-mortem had to be held, because Marguerite had only been in hospital such a short time. During the days that elapsed Algie was to worry as to whether his young son should attend his Mother's funeral. He also did not know how he was going to tell Marguerite's sisters of her passing. Algie worried over this and then suddenly thought why not send Richard to tell them? So it was that that particular evening, over the supper table, Algie said to his son, "Richard, there's somethin' I'd likes yer to do for yer old Dad. Somethin' I can't do as I've never met them."

"Never met who, Dad?" asked Richard.

"Yer Aunts, Rachel and Sarah and their families," answered his Father.

Richard would have liked to know why his Dad had not met his Aunts, but before he had a chance to ask, his Father went on, "I want yer to go over to

Wimbledon, me lad, and tell them about yer Ma's passing." Richard shook his head sadly, as his Father went on to say, "do yer think you can do that for yer old Dad?" This matter had really been worrying him. Why he had not met his in-laws he did not know, but he could never bring himself to do so, realising that they were of a different station of life to himself. It was not a pleasant task to ask a young lad to do, but he did not feel he could cope with it himself.

"Why yes, Dad, I will go. That is if I can go by taxi. I would not be sure of my way by underground," said Richard.

"Well, what says you, son, if yer go tomorrow. The sooner the better, ay lad," suggested Algie.

"Okay. Dad, I'll go tomorrow. Aunt Sarah's going to take it badly, Dad. Mother and her were very close," said Richard, seeing in his mind his Mother fondly chatting to her sister

"Yeh, I knows me lad, and I'm right sorry to give you the task of telling 'er," said Algie, feeling rather guilty.

They continued their meal in silence. Richard sat pondering as to how he was to tell his Aunt about his Mother.

*

The next morning Algie hailed a taxi for Richard; before seeing him into it he handed Richard a letter which he pointed out to his son was very important and should immediately be handed to his Aunt. He waved to his young son as he so bravely went off on his mission. His Father had said he was to tell his Aunt that his Mother had not suffered at the end and had gone peacefully.

In the taxi this young boy wondered as to where his Mother would be now. She had not been a very religious woman, and the thought now worried him. Perhaps he should start to go to Mass with his Grandmother. At least he could help the old lady down the road. Yes, that is what he would do, thought Richard.

As he approached Wimbledon he felt very confused and did not know how he was going to tell his Aunt the sad news. As the taxi drew up, his cousins, realising it was Richard arriving, rushed to the door, pushing each other to get there first. "Hi, Rick! Great to see you," they chorused. Richard just smiled sadly in reply.

Sarah hovering in the background was puzzled to see her young nephew all alone. As he turned to come into the porch she surmised, by his face, that something was very wrong. "Auntie, please may we talk?" he said, as he slowly came through the front door

"Yes, of course, Richard. Whatever is the matter?" Turning to her daughter and son, she said. "Go along you two leave us alone for a while. You can see Richard later." They took one look at their Mother's concerned face, went to plead to stay but changed their minds, and went slowly back to their toys in the playroom.

As they turned into the drawing room Richard burst into tears, and reverting to his childish name for his Mother, said, "Mummy is dead!" They were the only words for a time that he could get out.

Sarah went white with shock and could not believe what she was hearing. Marguerite dead! She took her nephew into her arms, as any Mother would, and endeavoured to comfort him. The pent up emotions of those last few days were at last relieved and he cried and cried as he had never cried before. As he grew older he was to wonder his Father's reasons for sending him to Wimbledon. Was it to the comfort of his Aunt's arms? Sarah did not ask any questions, she would just wait until this young boy was ready to talk. He handed her the letter that his Father had given him, and she left him for a moment to read it on her own, and then went to find the youngsters to tell them the sad news.

Richard spent the day at Wimbledon sitting in the comfort of this warm home, occasionally picking up a book but not reading more than a paragraph at a time. His concentration had completely gone. His cousins did not try to distract him, but on their Mother's advice left him to himself.

Sarah sat with her own memories. She was a small child lying in bed watching her sister getting dressed. She was standing at the window of the Bedford Square house with Nanny, watching, perhaps with some jealousy, as Marguerite went off in a cab with Mama and Papa. She remembered the terrible worry when Marguerite was missing during the first world war, and the memory of this was brought back to her on once more reading the letter that Richard had brought with him.

*

Sarah knew that since the end of the war her sister had been endeavouring to trace Christa Werner through the British Red Cross. Marguerite had hoped that having also lost a nephew this German mother would understand and be helped in her loss.

As Marguerite turned from the window on that misty November morning she went to the door and picked up the day's post, always hopeful that there would be a letter forwarded by the Red Cross. This morning she felt that her luck was in as she strolled back to the window to get more light to reassure herself that there was indeed a letter with the stamp of the Red Cross on the envelope, she opened it and read, in a translation Marguerite presumed had been carried out by the Red Cross:

My dear Marguerite, or should I say Congettina,
Yes, my loss has indeed been very great and I feel desperately sad that the two wars with your country have treated me so badly.
I cannot, therefore, find it in my heart to correspond or meet up with you after all this time, but I trust that time will heal and that eventually we will meet.

Christa

Having read the letter Marguerite suddenly slumped to the floor.

Sarah was to always think that Christa got her own back in the death of her sister, but how cruel wars can be, even after the fighting is over.

*

Sarah continued with her day-dreaming and could see Marguerite leaving for her wedding to Bertie; a man that even now they had never met. She pondered in her mind as to whether her sister had been happy in her marriage. Sarah could see her sister's face when she returned home that day from her tour of London with that Captain Armstrong. She wondered as to what would have happened to that relationship should he have survived the war. She shook herself out of her day-dreaming, thinking that she must contact her sister Rachel immediately.

When Uncle Robert, on being summoned returned early from work, he just patted his nephew's shoulder in sympathy – there was no need for words.

That evening Richard's Aunt and Uncle drove him back to Holloway Road, but dropped him at the door of his home still not to meet their brother-in-law. They felt that today, after all those years, was not the time or place for introductions. Before Richard left the car, Sarah placed her arm around his shoulder and quietly said, "You know, Richard, there is always a welcome at Wimbledon for you, son." As she said, son, an idea came to mind, but this would have to remain as a thought for a while.

*

Richard arrived home that evening to find that in his absence his Mother's funeral had taken place. Algie had decided not to let his son participate in such a sad event, and when he had waved goodbye that morning he knew only too well what was to take place later that day. Richard was to never see his Mother's grave. He said to his Father he wished to remember her as he knew her, not beneath a patch in the ground. He had no wish to remember her in that form. This decision Algie appreciated.

After the warmth of his Aunt and Uncle's home the two rooms seemed very cold and dismal, with an inevitable sadness about them. Algie suggested that his son should return to school the next day, where the staff had been shocked and sad for this lad who had lost his mother in his first term at senior school and for it to happen to an only child the day after his twelfth birthday.

Richard became very attached to the school environment. He worked well at his lessons, as he knew that would have been his Mother's wish. He hated his French lessons, and got turned out of the singing class, because the teacher said his singing voice was too flat – he thought how disappointed his Mother would have been that he could not sing. He got great satisfaction from English and History and was able to give extra time to these lessons. At home he enjoyed planning his own newspaper, but this was to remain a hobby at which he was to spend many happy hours. He did not interest himself in joining any outside school activities, but, as planned in his mind in that taxi on his way to Wimbledon, he commenced each Sunday to escort his Grandmother to Mass. He felt closer there to his Mother than any visit to a graveyard. Richard had difficulty in understanding the Irish priests, but became interested watching the serving boys. He eventually became a server, leaving home before school some mornings to assist at early morning Mass.

About once a month Richard stayed for the weekend at Wimbledon and really enjoyed the company of his cousins. One particular weekend his Aunt and Uncle put a proposition to him. They said that would like to adopt him and to bring him up with his cousins as a son of their own. Of course, the decision was to rest with Richard himself and also his Father. He was not to hurry with an answer and he had a whole month to consider this proposition before visiting them again. A month in which to decide as to whether he should leave his father; that is if his father agreed to these suggested plans. Richard realised that this would mean he would lead a totally different life. This was going to be a difficult decision for a lad so young.

Richard lay awake at night pondering over this decision. Every night a picture came into his mind of his Father and himself walking on Hampstead Heath. They were standing on Parliament Hill looking at the devastation of London and he could hear his Father saying, 'Well my lad, it is you and I together now' and his reply 'Yes Dad, I'll look after you Dad.' So many nights this picture came into his mind and he knew what his decision had to be. After what his Father had said, how could he desert him? Yes, Richard was quite definite in his mind that he would stay with his Father and look after him at all times. In fact, now that he had made up his mind, he would not even discuss it with his Father. The next time he went to visit his Aunt and Uncle he would tell them of his decision.

Sarah was, of course, disappointed at her young nephew's decision, but quite understood and said she hoped that young Richard would continue his monthly visits.

*

Richard and his Father continued to enjoy their walks together and Richard decided that he had made the right decision in staying with his Dad. Looking at his Grandmother he could see that she was now looking a very old lady and when his Aunt was not available he would do small errands for her.

Richard was now a lad tall for his age. Not a boy to have many friends, but those he did have were very close to him. David, his particular friend, would come home from school with him and they would play monopoly or some other board game. At the weekends these games would go on for hours.

Suddenly life was once more to change for Richard. He continued to spend a weekend each month at Wimbledon. He felt that this gave his Father a break, but his Father seemed to spend more and more evenings and weekends away from home, and the walks on the heath with his son became less frequent.

About eighteen months after his Mother's death, Richard returned home one Sunday evening to find a woman installed in the two rooms. With his arm fondly around her, his Father introduced her to Richard, saying, "Son, this is Elsie." Richard could not take in what his Father said next, he could not believe what his Father was saying, he just stared at this woman in disbelief. All Richard could hear, those few months ago, was his Father saying, 'It is just you and me together now son'.

BOOK 4

CHAPTER 27

ANOTHER WOMAN

"Did you 'ear what I said Richard. This is Elsie, yer new Ma," said his Father.

Oh no, thought Richard, you are quite wrong Dad, I have only one Mother, whether she is here or not! But, as he had been brought up to do, he manly shook hands with this woman standing in front of him. At the same time thinking to himself, I must get Dad on his own and find out more about this interloper.

"I am going down to see my Gran," announced Richard, making a quick get away, slamming the door as he went. With that he was down the stairs like a shot. "Gran, who is this woman upstairs called Elsie? What is she doing here?" questioned Richard, startling his Gran who had been asleep in her chair.

"Fool of a man, that there Pa of yers. He's gone and taken another wife. He's married that woman up there," announced his Gran in a shaky voice.

"Married her? Why?" asked Richard.

"Says 'e loves 'er, me lad. That's why!" said his Gran, who went on to say, "Can't see what 'e sees in 'er after yer Ma, who was a fine lass, but 'spose we'll 'ave to accept 'er," said his now weary Grandmother.

"He says she's my new Mother, Gran. I don't want a new Mother," announced an indignant Richard, in a very definite tone of voice.

His Gran eased herself from her chair, and putting an arm round her young grandson, said, "I don't 'spose yer do me lad, but yer Dad needs company. You'll understand when yer older, me lad," said this old lady.

But that was just the point Richard didn't understand his Father's change of mind and wanted an explanation now, and he went on to say, "But Gran, Father said we were to look after each other," announced a bewildered Richard. "How can we go for our walks on the heath with that woman hanging on to him?" asked Richard.

His Gran could not give this lad an answer and just shrugged her shoulders and eased herself once more into her chair.

After some time, Richard reluctantly returned upstairs to the bedroom. His Father had recently screened off a corner of the room to give this growing lad more privacy. He looked at the double bed and felt sick at the thought of his

Father in it with that woman. He had just become enlightened, by talking to his pals at school, as to what marriage meant, and he shrugged his shoulders with disgust.

Later a voice called out. "Time for bed me lad. Come and get yer cocoa if yer want it," shouted this supposedly new mother. Richard took no notice and that night went straight to bed without his usual warm drink. He lay in bed too confused to even cry. Later he tried to shut a deaf ear to that woman on the other side of the screen with his Father.

The next morning both had gone to work before Richard was up. He was used to his Father having left the house early. He remembered he meant to ask his Dad if he was going to the school on the next Wednesday evening to see his work, but, thought Richard, why bother to ask he had never been to the school yet and was not likely to do so now. His Mother had been very interested and never missed. His Father had always asked about his school work, but had been quick to point out that that place was not for him to visit, he would leave it to mother.

That Monday morning on the bus to school Richard was very quiet. He was thinking of how that was the second time things had happened whilst he was away for the weekend; the first his Mother's funeral and now this. He was far away in thought, and it was not until his pals said, "Come along, Ricky. Are yer coming to school today or not?" Richard suddenly realised they had in fact arrived at their bus stop and the conductor was shouting. "Get a move on you lads. Come along now get a move on." Richard quickly clambered off with his pals, but he walked along with them in silence.

"What's the matter Ricky?" they asked in turn, but young Richard shrugged his shoulders and walked along, or should it be said shuffled along on this particular morning, which was very unlike him. As a rule he was a very upright lad.

That day his teachers noticed that they had a very sullen Richard Smythe in front of them. In the staff room they were to comment how very unlike Smythe to look so withdrawn. He was usually so attentative to his lessons, it was so unlike him.

After the initial shock of meeting this new Mother, Richard spent more time shut in the bedroom doing his homework, and it was noted that he hung on late at school and was in no hurry to go home. His teachers were pleased with his work, but, nevertheless, were worried at his outward appearance. He seemed recently to be slouching and to be no longer caring about his appearance. They reported this matter to the attendance officer, who promised to call at the lad's home, which in time he did, but try as he did he was unable to get an answer to his knocking at the front door, and as this lad attended school regularly there was nothing he could do.

Algie was not too pleased with his son's sullen attitude, and one day he walked into the bedroom and said, "Dickie, me lad!" This name annoyed Richard, he made allowances for his Gran using it, but not his Father. "Dickie yer not trying to like yer new Ma? Yer better make an effort or there will be no trip to yer Aunt's next weekend me lad," announced Algie.

Richard looked at his Father with disdain and answered, "I am not going this weekend Dad. They are away, so there!"

Algie was surprised by his son's attitude, and with exasperation said, "Don't yer cheek me, son. Yer get a box round yer ears. There's always a first time for everything, lad." With that Algie turned, went out and slammed the bedroom door, thinking to himself, that his son was getting a bit too big for his boots. I must take him in hand, but it was to be Elsie who did just that.

Elsie had had enough of Algie's sullen son. Algie had not told her that she was to be surrounded by his family. It was bad enough having a Ma and sister-in-law downstairs, but she had not been enlightened before she signed the marriage certificate that she was to take on a young son as well, who would also share the privacy of their bedroom. A lad who was only just reaching his adolescent years with all the difficulties that went with them. If his Pa wouldn't take him in hand she would! And, thought Elsie, she would start this very minute.

Elsie had thought that she and Algie would at least have this weekend to themselves, but Algie had just told her that Dickie was not going away after all. Oh, thought she, wasn't he? Well he would get out of that bed and do something useful for a change. Algie had just gone out to get the morning paper, so she took the opportunity to take matters into her own hands and hammered on the bedroom door. "Show a leg lad, do. There's work to do when you've had yer breakfast," announced this recently so called new mother. Richard heard what she said, but just turned over and got further down under the bedclothes in his screened corner. A few moments later the bedroom door was violently flung open, and by now an irate Elsie appeared. Flinging the bedclothes back from Richard, which in turn knocked the screen over, she got him by the legs and dragged him from the bed, knocking his head hard on the floor. She continued to drag him into the kitchen where she left him like a dog under the kitchen table. He lay there in complete shock, stunned from the sudden awakening and from the blow to the head.

Algie returned with his paper just as Richard sat up rubbing his head. "What yer doing down there, lad?" asked his Father. Richard did not answer. Algie turned to his wife questioningly, but she just shrugged her shoulders and got on with the washing-up. Richard roused himself and sat sullenly at the table. When he did not touch his breakfast, Elsie removed it and placed a pile of pea-shucks in front of him, saying, "P'raps you can empty those 'ere peas and do somethin' useful for a change." Richard looked at these green things and just did not know where to start. "Helpless creature," said an impatient Elsie, whilst showing him what to do with the peas. "Did yer Ma not teach yer anythin?" she asked with sarcasm in her voice.

At the mention of his mother tears started to drop into the freshly shucked peas. Being conscious of his tears Richard suddenly got up and went out of the front door, slamming it behind him. That morning he seemed to walk for miles, cutting along streets that were not familiar to him. He noticed that people were still living amongst their belongings in the open bomb damaged buildings. Thinking of these poor destitute Londoners he eventually plucked up courage to return home. That weekend was only a foretaste of what was to come.

*

Unbeknown to Algie his new wife had spent time on and off in a hospital for mental disorders. She would be quite normal for weeks on end, but then suddenly her whole disposition would change.

Richard did not understand what was wrong with his new mother, he only knew that she was a very strange woman. During the week he was able to keep away from her, as after his meal he had homework to do and so went to the relative safety of the bedroom, but it was the weekends that were to be dreaded. He longed for the monthly visits to Wimbledon. In the taxi on his way he was often to wonder at his decision – yes life would have been so different if he had accepted his Aunt and Uncle's offer to adopt him, but, thought Richard, the decision had been taken and I must abide by it. There is no turning back now!

Sarah and Robert worried at the change in their nephew, but question as they did they were not to learn much from him. They knew that his father had taken another wife but that was all. Richard was a lad who would chat to them if he so desired, but if not, it was impossible to get a word out of him.

It was now coming up to the school holidays. Richard was looking forward to the days spent playing monopoly with this friend David. School holidays were great, as there was no need to hurry to get up; in fact sometimes David would arrive and hammer on the front door and a tussled sleepy head would eventually come and open it.

School finally finished for the term and the usual arrangements were made, and Richard promised to be up and dressed for once, but before David could arrive an incident was to happen that was to have drastic repercussions on Richard's life.

Elsie had been to the Doctor and been put on the panel. She had not been feeling too well of late, and so to Richard's horror she had not on this particular morning gone to work. The first that Richard knew that she was still in the house was when he was suddenly awoken by a figure bending over him. It was Elsie with a hot iron just grabbed from the range. Somehow or other he managed to struggle and evade the hot object in her hand and leapt out of bed, the screen once more went flying and Elsie landed on top of it. Without stopping to collect his clothes Richard rushed downstairs to the relative safety of his Grandmother's flat.

"She's mad, she's mad!" shouted a terrified Richard, shaking with fear.

"Whose mad, me lad?" asked the surprised old lady. Whatever was the matter now, she thought, but all her grandson would say was – 'she's mad, she's mad!' They were the only words that the severely shocked Richard spoke for weeks. He sat huddled up in a chair shaking with fright. His grandmother wrapped a rug around him to keep him warm. The old lady just did not know what to do, as all that day she watched the lad sitting shaking with fright. She was quite unable to climb the stairs to find Elsie, so he would have to stay in the chair until Eve arrived home. She endeavoured to tempt him with warm drinks and snacks, but he did not want to know.

David arrived and hammered on the door as usual, but after a while he gave up waiting for his sleepy friend to answer and went away inevitably disappointed.

To old Granny Smythe this seemed to be the longest day of her life. When Eve eventually arrived home from work she found her Ma greatly distressed after her long day agonizing over her grandson. Eve in turn tried to talk to her nephew but without success.

Immediately Eve heard her brother's key in the front door she called to him to come straight down the stairs. Thinking his Ma to be ill he hurried down. He was astounded to see young Richard still in his pyjamas, and wrapped in one of his Ma's rugs, cowering in the chair with his body shaking all over. The picture of his small sister Connie immediately came to mind, and he rushed up to Richard feeling his forehead for a temperature, but Richard immediately turned away from the touch of his Father's hand. Algie looking at his Ma and sister standing by asked, "What's the matter? Is the lad ill or somethin?"

"You tell us, Algie," answered his sister in a somewhat offhanded manner.

"Yer the one to find out from 'er upstairs," his Ma said crossly.

Turning to Richard, Algie asked, "What is it lad, what is it?" but no answer came from his young son.

Algie rushed upstairs to Elsie, but on questioning her she was nonplussed. She remembered feeling odd on awakening that morning, but she wasn't telling her husband that. The least he knew about her mental condition the better. If the lad didn't want to come back upstairs it was alright with her. Anyhow his rightful place was with his grandma, she told her husband, he wasn't' hers to look after. She also said, "Whilst we are on the subject, I want to move away from 'ere into a proper council 'ouse." Algie endeavoured to pacify her and said he would look into the matter in time, but at this moment he was concerned for his son downstairs.

The next few days went by. It was as if Richard was tied to the chair. He would only leave it to go to the toilet, and it was the outside toilet he would use, no way was he going even half-way up those stairs. He would still not get dressed. Algie took time off work, but could not get any reaction from his young son, and so in desperation called the Doctor.

The Doctor said the lad had suffered a severe shock. Had something happened at school? Perhaps he was being bullied! The family listened to the Doctor's suggestions, but did not enlighten him as to whom they thought had frightened this young lad. The Doctor prescribed some pills for his young patient and left him in the care of his father and grandmother, quite puzzled by the young patient. He knew only too well that something had seriously gone wrong with this young lad's life to make him so withdrawn.

Whilst his Ma had her afternoon rest, Algie tried to talk to his son. He told him about the idea of a council house. He talked of the small garden at the house in Manchester, and suggested that they might have one similar, but taking one look at his son's face he could see that the lad was not taking too kindly to that idea. He gave up trying to talk to his son.

The Doctor had been adamant that at the end of the school holidays Richard was not to be forced back to school. It was Eve who had to visit the school and explain the situation. The teachers were sorry to hear of this young lad's sudden illness, and they informed his Aunt that recently they had been most concerned about his welfare. They told Eve that they had heard from one of Richard's friends who had been evacuated with Richard and his mother on how devoted mother and son were and that he had not taken too kindly to a replacement mother; they hoped sincerely that time would heal.

Eve brought school work home for Richard to do. It was having this school work to do that gradually encouraged Richard out of the chair. His Aunt moved in with her mother so enabling Richard to have her small bedroom, and this was a great encouragement to him, but it was noticed that whenever he was in there he locked the door. Gradually he began to talk to his Grandmother and Aunt, but no mention was made of what had happened on that first day of the school holidays. He still had nothing to say to his Father.

Algie eventually succumbed to his wife's pleadings and went to the council offices and put his name down for a house on one of the new estates being built on the outskirts of London. In a matter of time these houses were completed and he broke the news to the family downstairs that he would be leaving the two rooms above.

Richard broke the silence to his father, by saying quietly, "I am not coming with you Dad."

"Why not, son?" asked his Father, but that is all Richard would say, and he just turned his head away and no explanation came from this lad to enlighten his father of the reasons for his decision. To any questions he would simply reply in the negative.

So it was that just before Christmas 1947 Algie left the home, where he had spent many years, and went with his second wife, Elsie, to a new council house. He was very loath to leave his young son behind, but realised that in his present state of mind it was the best thing to do.

Immediately Richard knew that his Father and Elsie had gone he agreed to return to school. At first he was very nervous of leaving the house, looking behind him all the time, just in case that horrible mad woman should pounce on him. He walked along pensively as if keeping within himself. On shaking hands with the headmaster it was noted that this young lad's hand was all of a shake. What a sad state of affairs, thought this Head, a lad that used to walk so tall to be so withdrawn and shaky. Yes it was so sad, especially as the war was not so far behind them and the Smythe family had indeed been lucky to escape any damage to their home and had come through those years unscathed; now this should happen to this likeable lad. Yes, to lose a mother was indeed a terrible thing for an only child to face.

On meeting up with his pals again, it was not to be long before Richard commenced to recover, but when his father came to see his old Mother Richard would lock himself in his room.

His Aunt Sarah had written asking why his visits had ceased, and it was Aunt Eve who eventually persuaded Richard to once more visit Wimbledon. Sarah and Robert were shattered at the change in Richard, but on asking him what had happened the only answer they got was – "no there is nothing the matter." They did learn, however, that Father had left the Holloway Road and gone away with his second wife. They puzzled as to why Richard had not gone with them, but were to learn nothing further from this young lad.

*

It was about three months after Algie and his wife had left the Holloway Road, and before arrangements could be made to re-let the two rooms upstairs, that Richard arrived home from school one day to be told by his Grandmother that his Father had returned.

"But why?" asked Richard with concern, but before his Grandmother could answer, he went on to ask nervously, "Where is Elsie, Gran?"

All his Gran would say was, "Yer Pa will tell you soon enough."

Richard immediately went to his room, locking the door behind him. He could not get down to his home work, he was that worried as to whom was upstairs.

Algie was mulling over in his mind as to how he could approach his son, and as to how he could tell him what had happened. He now knew himself what his son had had to face on waking that morning. He looked around the two rooms and his mind went back to his first wedding day when he had brought his bride Marguerite home for the first time. Yes, thought Algie, I have let you and your son down badly. He sat down at the kitchen table, the same table that Marguerite and he had sat at drinking their cocoa that first evening many years ago. As old as he was he sat at that table and cried like a small child. Yes, he certainly knew what his young son had gone through.

Later Algie composed himself and commenced to clear away any signs of that second wife. It was his dear hope that his young son would come back to live with him now that that nightmare and shocking episode of his life was over. When he felt that the two rooms showed no signs of that woman and the horror that this must hold for Richard he went downstairs.

Richard shook as he heard the footsteps coming down the stairs. His Father called out to him. "It's alright son, she aint 'ere. You can come out of that room of yours. Yer quite safe, she aint 'ere." Richard unlocked the door and slowly came out of the room; he immediately noticed that his Father was looking rather dejected. He longed to ask him what had happened and why he had come back so suddenly, but he said nothing.

Algie went up to his thirteen-year-old son, whom he loved dearly, and patting him on the shoulder, said, "It's all over now my son. She ain't coming 'ome 'ere no more. She's mad son, right mad."

BOOK 4

CHAPTER 28

TO SHAKE HANDS

Algie was once more to ask, "Did yer 'ear what I said, son? She ain't coming 'ome 'ere no more. I"ve had 'er certified."

Richard looked at his Father and did not really know what he was talking about, but he understood well enough that that dreaded woman was not coming home again.

Algie went on to say, "I don't know what 'appened to you that morning son, but she went for me with a carving knife." He went on to tell his son of how he had found out that Elsie had a medical history and she had no right in marrying him, as she was already betrothed many years ago to someone else, so that made his marriage invalid.

Richard did not understand what all this entailed, but what he understood only too well was that his Father was returning home to him. He still did not enlighten his Father as to what had happened on that Monday morning, now some months ago. He had shut it away at the back of his child's mind and had not spoken about it to anyone and had somehow told himself that that event had never happened. It was as if it had been a bad dream and had all happened to someone else. All he understood at this moment was that the relationship between him and his father was to return to more or less normal.

Later that evening he followed his Father up the stairs, but before settling in he had one request, "Please Dad, do you think Aunt Eve would mind me keeping her room as my own. I shall be really happy if I can sleep down there," said Richard. "Otherwise, Dad, we can return to normal."

Algie patted his son's head and said, "I am quite sure Aunt Eve won't mind you still 'aving 'er room." and he went on to ask his son, "What say yer, me lad, if next weekend we go for a walk on that there 'eath."

"That would be great Dad." With that said Father and son shook hands and were friends once more.

*

Life slowly returned to normal. Richard gathered a few new friends around him and gradually went further a field. He got on well at school and chose to study commerce subjects in preference to the sciences. His only disappointment was that history was not included in that course. In his final year he became house captain. The headmaster knew that this lad had been through some sort of trauma, but did not question him further, but what he did notice was that he was returning to more or less his normal self, except for the still slight tremble of his hands. He hoped that by making him house captain it would give him more confidence, and he knew that the lad would have plenty of patience with the younger children and would prove to be a good ambassador for the school.

One day whilst out walking on the heath, Algie turned to Richard and asked, "Son, yer leave school at the end of this year. What yer going to do with yerself lad? How yer going to earn yer living?"

Richard took a time answering his Father, but then said, "I don't really know Dad, I enjoy working out my own newspapers, but I think I will keep that as a hobby."

"As yer wish me lad, I expect we could some'ow find someone to speak for yer, if you had yer 'art set on Fleet Street, but as yer say lad, may be best to keep it as an 'obby. Good to 'ave somethin' to do after a day at work," said his Father.

They walked on for a while without talking, both deep in their own thoughts. Eventually before reaching the busy main road, Richard turned to his Father and suddenly said, "Dad, I think I would like to go into Law."

Good heavens, thought Algie, my son wants to be a copper. He turned and with surprise enquired of his son, "D'yer mean the police, son?"

"No Dad. I think I would like to work in a solicitor's office," announced Richard, and then added: "I mean in a solicitor's office to start with."

"What d'yer mean to start with, lad?" enquired his Father.

"Well, Dad. When we went up to the Law Courts with the school, we walked through the Temple and I saw all those brass plates on the doors. My pals and I stopped and read some of them, and it started me thinking along those lines." Richard started to laugh as he announced this to his Father.

"Don't laugh at yerself, lad. I say good for you. I believe yer Ma's father was a Solicitor or somethin'. Yer must take after 'im," said Algie.

After this conversation they made their way home. That evening Richard was in his room finishing off his homework when his Father knocked on his bedroom door. "Just come to say goodnight, and I think that's a great idea of yours thinking of going into law. I should speak to yer Head about it son. He'll be able to tell yer how to go about it, lad. It's certainly a good idea on your part son. If you make it lad, I shall be right proud of you."

"Thanks Dad. I'll speak to the Head tomorrow," said Richard. "I'll let you know what he says. Goodnight Dad."

"Good night, son. See yer tomorrow evening." That having been said Algie made his way upstairs feeling happy with the relationship between himself and his son. He smiled as the picture came in to his mind of this young lad as a city gent.

At the next opportunity Richard spoke to his headmaster. Interesting thought Mr Sargent, looking at this young lad standing the other side of the desk. "Well you are certainly on the right course, Smythe, commerce subjects. Pity you had to give up history, but then on the other hand you could always study that subject, amongst others, at evening class. Yes, Smythe, I think you are making a wise choice." He was pleased that this lad was thinking about his future. He must certainly do the best for him. He had not had much of a childhood, what with the war and everything else. In many ways this boy had grown up too soon. As he walked to the door and shook hands with this tall young prefect he said, "Leave it with me, Smythe. I will make some enquiries on your behalf."

"Thank you, sir. Thank you very much," said Richard, feeling quite pleased with himself, as he turned to walk down the corridor to join his friends for the mid-morning break.

*

Before anything further could be decided on this matter, Richard was to go through yet another drama. His Grandmother was to die. He knew she was an old lady, but since his Mother's passing he had become quite close to her. He enjoyed escorting her to church each Sunday. He knew that some Sundays she was really not well enough to attend but she was adamant that nothing would make her miss going to Mass. He was quite sure that sometimes from his position, as a server, he could see his dear Gran nodding off. Yes, he would miss his Granny Smythe.

This was to be the first funeral that Richard was to attend. To cheer him up his Father suggested that he should be measured for his first suit, a charcoal grey one. It was made up in record time, as Algie still had friends amongst the Jewish tailors down in the East End.

At the funeral, glancing at his son so smartly dressed, Algie thought, 'Yes Marguerite, you would be right proud of your son.' It was strange, thought Algie, of the relationship that had built up between his Ma and son. Very strange, when he thought back to the day when he first brought Marguerite home to Holloway Road and his Ma shouted up the stairs, 'Algie', and Marguerite asked Bertie, 'Who is Algie?' Yes, very strange, thought this old lady's grieving son. Some months passed and Richard began to accept his Grandmother's death and endeavoured to befriend his Aunt in her grief.

*

On arriving at school one morning Richard was called to the Head's office. Handing him an envelope Mr Sargent said, "I have been able to arrange an interview for you on Monday, Richard, at a solicitor's office in the City. Take this opportunity Smythe. They are a good firm with contacts in the Inner Temple."

All Richard could say, in his excitement, was "Thank you, sir. Thank you very much." A solicitor's office in the City, thought Richard, with contacts in the Inner Temple. He could not believe his luck, but first he had to get through his first interview.

"Have you a suit to wear, Smythe?" asked his Headmaster.

"Yes, sir. I had a suit made for my Grandmother's funeral," answered a relieved Richard.

"Good lad. You will look your best then." Shaking his pupil's hand, he went on to say. "May I wish you the best of luck Smythe. And I mean it lad, you deserve it."

"Thank you, sir. Thank you." Richard returned with a smile on his face to join his pals in the classroom. As far as he knew he was the first of his contemporaries to have such an interview and he felt really proud of himself.

The weekend seemed to drag as he waited for Monday to arrive. His Father was right proud as he watched his son leave home for the interview. It appeared to Richard to go well, and that evening he said to his Father that he was quite hopeful of getting the position there as a Junior Clerk.

"Don't be too sure, me lad!" His Father still remembered the numerous interviews that he attended after the First World War. "It's yer first interview, remember," said his Father who hoped sincerely that his son would be successful.

"Yes, Dad. I know," said Richard.

Before the week was out Richard arrived home from school to find a letter waiting for him. He looked at the envelope addressed to, 'R. Smythe Esq.' and with the name of the solicitors printed on it. He opened it, his hands shaking this time with excitement and anticipation. He stood in the hall reading the letter over and over again and he then turned and rushed out of the house.

BOOK 4

CHAPTER 29

OUT INTO THE WORLD

Richard could not wait for his Father to arrive home from work. Rushing out of the front door he stood on the steps and read the letter once more:

Dear Mr Smythe,

Appertaining to your interview of Monday last, we are pleased to offer you the position of Junior Clerk, to commence at a salary of two pounds per week. You will work from 8.30am until 5.30pm. After a probationary period of three months you will be required to join a Pension Scheme, approved by the practice. On termination of your employment you will be required to give one month's notice.

If these terms are favourable to you, you are requested to commence your duties as from the 3rd September 1951.

Please confirm that you accept this position.

Yours truly,

R. George (Chief Articled Clerk)

Clutching the letter in his hand, Richard rushed out into the street and jumped on the first bus that came and went to find his Father, hopefully having a break in the bus garage. On arriving he appeared around the door of the driver's snug. One of the men called out. "Are yer after yer old man, son?"

"Yes please. Is he in at the moment?" asked a still excited Richard.

"He should be coming in any moment now at bay three." Then looking at his watch, he said, "Yeh, he should be in at any minute," answered the driver smiling, at the same time thinking to himself, 'a pleasant lad Smythe's son, but where had he learnt to speak so well? He went on to think 'a good looking lad, but wants feeding up a bit'.

Richard went over and joined the queue at bay three, and soon he spied his Father at the wheel of a bus turning into the garage. It soon pulled up alongside and Richard raced round to greet him, as he stepped down from the cab.

"I got it Dad. I got it!" said Richard, waving the envelope at his Father.

Algie pretended to be ignorant on the matter of a letter, but at the same time knowing full well what his son was talking about. "Got what, me lad and what yer doing 'ere?" asked his Father.

"I got the job Dad," said Richard, shoving the letter into his Father's hands.

"Wait a shake. Let's get somewhere safer. We don't want to get mowed down by one of these 'ere buses. Come on lad follow me," said Algie leading his son over to the safety of the buildings. Algie then read the letter and shaking his young son's hand heartedly, said, "Good on yer lad. Good for you and the best of British luck to yer. You deserve it lad. About time somethin' came right for you me son. Yeh! about time."

Richard glanced at his Father, who was standing there with tears in his eyes, so pleased for the lad and quite overcome with the announcement of the news, but even more pleased to think that his lad had come all the way to the garage to tell him.

"Thanks Dad. I couldn't wait until you came home," said Richard.

"Will yer stop and have a cuppa with yer old Dad, son?" asked Algie.

"No thanks, Dad. I will make my way home now." Taking the letter from his Father, Richard said, "See you later Dad."

Algie stood and watched his tall young son striding away, and with pride in his heart turned and went into the snug to tell his mates the news.

That evening, for the first time, Algie took his young son out for a celebration drink. "A special occasion me lad. A right special occasion this is. Yer Ma would be right proud of you," said Algie, and raising his glass said, "To you son and the very best of luck."

"Thanks Dad," said Richard feeling really grown up in the pub and pleased with himself.

*

Not only was Richard Smythe commencing work in that year of 1951, but London was celebrating the centenary of the Great Exhibition. The south bank of the Thames provided the site for the Festival of Britain.

Richard and his pals decided to celebrate the finishing of their school days by going to the other side of the Thames to this grand exhibition. A day they were to remember for a long time. The lads stepped out over Westminster Bridge and walked past the new Festival Hall built for the occasion; a building of modern character. On reading the advertisement board outside, Richard thought his Mother, with her interest in music, would have enjoyed the concerts to be held there. He was quiet for a while as he thought, when he was earning, how he could have taken her to one of the many performances. As they approached the Festival site they could see the Skylon, standing tall, and the oval Dome of Discovery. Yes, a happy and memorable day was spent. This group of lads from Holloway and other parts of Islington, stepping out on adult life, found the exhibition of great interest.

The day spent at the Festival of Britain gave Richard an appetite for more and he spent many a happy day during that August, prior to commencing work, visiting the museums of London. Before returning home one day he strolled through the Temple Gardens and so into the Inner Temple. He looked up at the buildings and dreamt of himself in one of these sedate looking offices. In his mind he could see a gold plate, bearing his name in bold letters. Richard smiled to himself at his day-dream.

Another memorable occasion was the visit with his Father to the Battersea Festival Gardens and Fun Fair. His Dad was not too keen on the noise and excitement of the Fun Fair, but the beautiful laid out gardens were of great interest to Algie, taking him back to the earlier days laying out the flowerbeds in Regents Park. Richard would have liked to have tried out the many amusements. Some days later, and before commencing work, he returned with his pals to enjoy these various amusements never seen in London before.

*

Monday, 3rd September 1951 eventually arrived. Dressed smartly in his charcoal grey suit, Richard presented himself sharp at 8.30 am at the offices of these Solicitors' in the City of London. John Mullen, now an elderly gentleman, very rarely visited the City office and had more or less retired from the practice, leaving the business in charge of his very capable staff.

The first few weeks were a little tedious to Richard, who had been used to studying hard. All he seemed to do all day was make tea, run errands and put away heavy files, but his greatest pleasure was when he was sent to take a file to the Inner Temple. The first time he entered the door of one of these Chambers he felt so proud and had the strange feeling of having been there before.

As Christmas approached, mention was made of the impending visit of Mr John Mullen. Richard was told that this elderly gentleman always put in an appearance before Christmas to present his staff with Christmas wishes and a bonus. Richard was intrigued to meet this unknown boss, who bore the name of this City solicitors, and one cold day in mid-December, Richard arrived back from lunch to find a short stocky elderly man standing in the office looking out of the window. John Mullen was lost in thought, hearing Frederick Sinclair asking him to go down and buy a paper from the newsvendor on the corner. He was so far away in his thoughts that he did not hear the new lad, on his return from lunch, coming in the door.

Mr George gave a slight cough, in an endeavour to draw Mr Mullen's attention to this lad's entrance, and said, "Mr Mullen, sir."

At being spoken to John Mullen came out of his trance and turned to see in front of him a tall dark-haired young lad, standing nervously just inside the door. "Mr Mullen, this is our new junior clerk, Richard Smythe."

John Mullen shook the new lad's hand and thought, 'Smythe, where have I heard that name before?' He said nothing on this occasion, and Richard busied himself to the tasks in hand. The old man later took tea with his staff, and after wishing them a Happy Christmas and presenting them with their bonuses, turned to leave the office, but not before he took another discreet look at the new office junior. Richard felt really nervous with the Senior Partner staring at him, and was thankful that Mr Mullen did not appear at the office very often.

*

February 1952 saw the sudden passing away of King George V1. Sitting in his chair, in his small house in Norbury, with a rug around his legs and endeavouring to keep warm, John Mullen heard the news as it was announced on his radio set. He sat there thinking back to when the late King's great grandmother died. He remembered the happy occasion of the coronation of King Edward VII, when Frederick Sinclair brought his family back to the office to tea and the unveiling of his portrait. He could see that portrait of his late partner now, in the office above mantelpiece. That fine face with dark moustache.

Sitting there in his home on that February morning, it suddenly came to John Mullen as to whom that new office boy had reminded him. 'Could it be?' thought John Mullen. 'Now what was Marguerite's married name? Curse this memory of mine,' thought John Mullen. He sat there endeavouring to gather his thoughts together, and then after a while reached for the phone, dialled the office number and asked to speak to Mr George.

On being told it was Mr Mullen on the phone, Mr George hurriedly picked up his extension. "Good morning, sir. Are you well, sir?" he asked, being surprised at receiving a call from his boss.

"As well as can be expected these days," answered John Mullen on the other end of the phone. "Mr George, what did you say that new lad in the office was called?" he asked his articled clerk.

"Why, Richard Smythe, sir." answered Mr George.

"Smythe! Smythe!" repeated the old gentleman at the other end of the phone, and he then went on to ask, "Mr George have we a file for a Mrs Marguerite Smythe?"

"Hold on a moment, sir. I will have a look at the client's index cards," said a puzzled Mr George. He duly looked up the name on the cards and returned to the phone. "Why yes, sir. We have a file under the name of Marguerite Smythe, sir."

"Thank you, Mr George." And much to the surprise of Mr George, the elderly Mr Mullen went on to announce, "I am getting a taxi and coming over this afternoon," and before Mr George could reply or ask any questions the phone was put down.

*

That February afternoon, just as Richard was making tea in the poky corner of the office, he could see through the dingy office window a taxi drawing up, and much to Richard's surprise stepping out of it was Mr Mullen. Richard opened the office door to him and was surprised when the old gentleman immediately requested tea to be served to him in the small ante-room, which served as an interviewing room. He also requested Richard to join him there. Richard completely taken by surprise nervously went and prepared the tray of tea and joined the elderly boss, who immediately asked, "You are enjoying your job my lad?"

"Why, yes thank you, sir," replied Richard.

"We must get to know each other better," went on to announce John Mullen.

Good heavens, thought Richard, what am I to talk about to this funny little man? He was by now feeling too nervous to even think of drinking his tea.

John Mullen's hand shook as he put his tea to his lips, he was feeling quite excited as he thought back to the days long past. "Where do you live, young man?" asked Mr Mullen.

"I live with my Father, sir. In Holloway Road, sir," answered Richard.

The mention of the Holloway Road immediately rang a bell to the old gentleman. "And what about your Mother?" asked John Mullen.

Sadly sir, she died when I was eleven-years-old," answered Richard.

John Mullen was silent for a while as he thought of the possible demise of his beloved Marguerite. He looked intently at the young lad sitting in front of him. He felt sure he could see a likeness to his late partner, Frederick Sinclair. Richard could feel himself getting quite hot under the collar as the old man continued to stare at him.

"Tell me lad. What was your Mother's maiden name?" asked John Mullen.

"I am sorry, sir. I really don't know, sir." Richard was puzzled as to why this old gentleman should ask such a thing.

"What was her Christian name? You know that, of course?" suggested the old man.

Richard relieved that he could at least answer one question put to him, smiled and said, "Marguerite, sir," and was surprised at the reaction to his reply. The old man's face immediately lit up.

"And did this Marguerite, your Mother, have two sisters?" asked John Mullen.

"Why, yes sir, my Aunt Sarah was the younger," and then Richard hesitated. Only having met the other aunt once, before his cousin went away to the war, he could not remember what she was called. He sat there trying to think of her name, but before he could reply the old gentleman in front of him said it for him.

"Was it Rachel, my lad?" asked John Mullen.

"Why yes, sir, that was the name, sir!" Richard was now indeed very surprised that the old gentleman knew so much about his Mother's family.

Well I never did, thought John Mullen, this must be dear Marguerite's son, what a strange coincidence. He eased himself up from his chair, and as he left the room he said to Richard, "Just you wait there. I will be back in a very short while."

Richard sat there puzzled at all this mystery. What was going on? He could hear some furniture being moved, and then John Mullen returned followed by Mr Atkins, another clerk, carrying a large picture frame. "Just you look at this portrait, young Richard. I have every reason to believe that this is your late Grandfather. Mr Atkins held up the portrait showing a tall dark-haired Victorian gentleman. Richard stared at the portrait and could not help but think that the moustache was just like his Father's. Indeed certainly the face looking at him very much resembled his Father.

"Well lad, what do you say, do you think this is your Grandfather?" asked the excited old man.

"Well sir, I hardly know what to say. The portrait is indeed like my own father," announced Richard.

"Yes, your Mother told me on her last visit to this office, when she stood for the last time in front of her dear Papa's portrait, that he so resembled her husband. Mind you this was many years ago, before you were born my lad." The old boy seemed so excited by the turn of events and went on to tell Richard. "I had the portrait taken down, covered and put behind the bookcase when I stopped coming into the office. My partner, your Grandfather, would not have forgiven me if in my absence it had become damaged." Mr Mullen then went on to say, "Well, I never did, it is a small world." Hesitating for a moment, he then went on to ask Richard to bring in his birth certificate. He said he would like to look at this when he next came to the office.

John Mullen, now feeling rather tired from the excitement and events of the day, sent Richard out to stop a taxi, and after giving strict orders that the portrait should be re-hung above the old fireplace, bade everyone farewell.

Not much work was done in that Solicitors office for the rest of the day. The staff sat talking of the amazing turn of events. Fancy their office junior being their late partner's grandson. The Secretary smiled as she said, "Poor old chap, Mr Mullen does so like to reminisce and talk about the good old days. I bet this has made his day, the past catching up with him like this."

*

That evening Richard could not wait for his Father to return from work. He was tempted to tell his Aunt Eve about his Grandfather, but felt this would be unfair to his Dad. Immediately his Father's key was in the door he was waiting. "Guess where I am working, Dad?" he asked his Father.

"In the City, aren't you m'lad?" And then hesitating for a moment, when the thought suddenly came to him that this lad of his might have left his job without telling him, he said, "Now lad what 'ave yer been and gone and done?"

"Gone and done? I haven't done anything, Dad! You know Dad when we first talked of me going into a solicitor's office, you said my Mother's father was a solicitor," reminded Richard.

"Yes! m'lad. That's right" said his Father.

"Well guess where I'm working, Dad?" asked an excited Richard.

Algie looked at his excited son and asked, "Yer never working at yer Grandad's office, me lad?

"Yes! I am Dad, at that very office." Richard then went on to tell his Father of the happenings of the day, and as the tale unfolded Algie could not believe his son's luck. He already could see his son taking over the whole practice. Algie went to bed that night a happy man, but his son downstairs in his bedroom lay in bed longing to know more about his Mother's family. He made up his mind that he would not wait for his monthly visit to Aunt Sarah, but would go this very next weekend. She was the one who would possibly be able to tell him more about his Grandparents. Yes, he longed to know more about his Mother's background.

Before going to work the next morning, Richard found that his Father had already left out his birth certificate for him to take to the office. On arriving at work he found that the portrait had once more been hung in its rightful place. Richard stood under it studying every feature, and at that moment so wished that his Mother was still alive.

*

Before that visit to Aunt Sarah could take place, the office received another phone call from John Mullen, who had been sent Richard's birth certificate. To the surprise of the Secretary he left a message to say that young Richard should meet the old gentleman at his St James's Club that next Saturday at 12 noon.

'What now?' Thought Richard, as he made his way on that Saturday morning through St James's Park. He was usually interested in his surroundings, but this morning he was too intent on getting the meeting ahead over as quickly as possible. He did not even notice the shooting of the early crocuses around him or the noise of the early cygnets chasing along behind their mother on the lake. His Father had made him go out and buy a new shirt and tie. The stiffness of this new collar was already rubbing his neck and making him even more nervous. He had never been inside a London Club before, and when he saw the commissionaire standing outside he was even more nervous.

The Commissionaire looked at this young embarrassed lad arriving and asked him, "Can I help you, sir?"

"Yes, please, sir," said Richard. "I have come to meet Mr John Mullen." Having said that the Commissionaire directed Richard to where the elderly gentleman would be sitting. Richard following the instructions went through some heavy oak doors into the largest lounge that he had ever seen. Looking around him he spotted John Mullen smoking his pipe and sitting in a huge leather chair.

On seeing the arrival of young Richard, John Mullen laid his pipe in the enormous green ash tray and struggled to his feet. Richard duly shook the old boy's hand, and John Mullen asked him what he would care to drink. Algie had endeavoured to advise his son on what to drink, and so Richard said, "Just a soda water, please sir".

Mr Mullen beckoned to a waiter to bring the young lad a soda water with, shall we say, a dash of whisky? At the mention of whisky, Richard thought, 'Good heavens I have never tasted any spirits before, but he supposed there was a first time for everything'.

Once they were settled back in their seats Richard's elderly companion said, "Now where shall we begin Richard? Perhaps I should tell you a little about myself. I was taken on by your Grandfather, Frederick Sinclair, as an articled clerk at the turn of the century."

My, thought Richard, trying to tot up the years and at the same time looking at this elderly gentleman in front of him, you are, as I thought, well in to your seventies.

John Mullen continued by saying, "Your Grandfather had gone into practice as a solicitor in the City to satisfy his own Father, who was a Barrister of the Inner Temple." Richard could not believe what he was being told. "I know, your Grandfather always felt that he had let his Father down by not being called to the Bar".

Richard sat there thinking to himself, and then had to repeat to the elderly gentleman what he had just been told. "Sir, you are telling me that my Great Grandfather was a Barrister of the Inner Temple?" asked Richard in surprise.

"Yes, my young man, the late William Sinclair, your Great Grandfather, was indeed called to the Bar in the mid-nineteenth century. His gold plate bore his name for many years." John Mullen informed his young protégé.

Now, Richard thought, I know why I enjoy walking through those grounds and studying the gold plates and why I get that strange feeling on entering those offices in the Inner Temple. Now I have the answer – my great grandfather was there for many years. It is my history. He could not believe what he had just heard. Wouldn't his Father be surprised?

John Mullen went on to say, "I have so much to tell and ask you. Your dear Mother used to come to the office quite often with her Father. I suppose she must have been about four-years-old when I first met her." The old gentleman was quiet for a moment with his own thoughts of those days many years ago. He then continued, "I can see her now as a six-year-old., It was the day in 1902 of Edward VII's coronation when the whole family came back to the office to partake of tea and to see their Papa's portrait for the first time."

Mr Mullen was quiet once more with his thoughts, so Richard took the opportunity to take a sip of his drink. He was glad it was only a sip as the whisky bit his throat. The old gentleman then suddenly started talking again, and to Richard's embarrassment went on to say, "It was when your dear Mama was in her twenties that I fell in love with her." John Mullen having said that fell into another silent spell.

Richard could hardly wait to hear more., what was this elderly gentleman saying; he had been in love with his Mother?

Old Mr Mullen went on to say, "Yes, I loved her dearly, but she did not reciprocate my affection for her." At this point he sighed with the memories of Marguerite before his eyes. "I know that her dear Papa wished that there would be a match between us, but when she was in her thirties, and her dear Papa died, I tried again, but I had left it too late. She had already fallen in love with another."

"Who with, sir?" asked a by now inquisitive Richard. It was really intriguing hearing of his Mother's love life.

"Richard, your dear Father had come into her life and she had eyes for no one else, and, in fact, ran away to get married. Her Mama was so shocked to learn of her marriage and to hear where she had gone to live that she cut her off without a penny. In fact on her marriage to your father her Mama had nothing to do with her daughter Marguerite for the rest of her life."

Young Richard listened intently to all the information he was being told; he now knew why his Father had had no contact with his Mother's family. He had often wondered, but his Mother would never talk about it.

"Your Grandfather, her dear Papa, of whom she was so fond, had passed away a few years before." announced John Mullen sadly nodding his head with the thoughts of those days. Then changing the subject he went on to ask. ""Tell me Richard do you remember your Mother having a small dog? Or was that before your time? I cannot remember his name, but it was her dear Papa's last birthday present to her."

Richard looked puzzled at this question. He could never remember having a dog at home, but thinking about it his Aunt Sarah had had a small dog, but before Richard or his cousins had been born, but, of course, it had died some years ago. Richard found himself telling John Mullen all about Snuff. "We have never had a dog, sir, but my Aunt Sarah has told me about her small dog that she had been very fond of. Snuff was the name.

"That's him, Snuff," replied an excited Mr Mullen. He then went on to tell Richard of how when Marguerite had been a small child his Grandfather enjoyed his pinch of snuff, and how his Mother had remembered this and named the small dog accordingly.

After the story of the small dog, John Mullen ordered some delicious sandwiches, and they both sat back enjoying these with their second drink. Richard was not too sure that he liked the taste of the whisky, but at least it gave him confidence.

Suddenly Mr Mullen started chatting again. "Yes, I loved Marguerite dearly for all those years, and now I have found a way of proving my affection for her. Richard, I have visited your Aunt Sarah at Wimbledon and caught up with all the news of your dear Mother's family, and of how your poor Aunt Rachel lost her only son during the war; and Sarah assures me that her own son, Frederick, is not interested in going into Law." At this point he hesitated, and looking straight at Richard he suddenly announced, "Richard, I propose on you reaching twenty-one years of age to make you a partner in your Grandfather's practice."

Richard could not believe what he had just heard, and said, "I beg your pardon, sir. Would you please repeat what you have just told me?"

Much to Richard's embarrassment the old gentleman stood up, and, as if announcing it to the whole room, said "Richard Smythe I intend to take you into partnership and to rename your Grandfather's practice, Sinclair, Mullen & Smythe. I have your Aunt Sarah's approval." With that the elderly John Mullen wearily sat down.

All Richard could do was to repeat, "Sinclair, Mullen & Smythe!" and at the same time to wonder how much influence his Aunt Sarah had had in this decision.

"Yes, Richard, one day, when hopefully you have your very own gold plate in the Inner Temple, the business of Sinclair, Mullen & Smythe will be your very own and you will be a wealthy man".

This young lad, who had only commenced work in the City the previous year, could not believe what had just been said and sat there repeating to himself – 'a wealthy man – a wealthy man.' Was he hearing correctly?